RANDLE IN SPRINGTIME

Also by Geoffrey Cotterell

Then a Soldier
This is the Way

RANDLE
IN
SPRINGTIME

Geoffrey Cotterell

EYRE & SPOTTISWOODE
LONDON

This book, first published in 1949, is produced in full conformity with the Authorized Economy Standards and is printed in Great Britain for Eyre & Spottiswoode (Publishers) Ltd., 15 Bedford Street, Strand, London, W.C.2 by The Chapel River Press, Andover, Hants.

11.48

For
ANTHONY

PART I

HOWARD RANDLE, Lieutenant, Royal Artillery, was as pleased to be sent to Hamburg as his battery commander was delighted to see the back of him. "The trouble with that kind of chap is he's only thinking of his demob," the latter said to the Colonel. "His group's going out pretty soon. What I want is a fresh green little subaltern who can bring a bit of keenness into training. Randle was absolutely finished, a complete wash-out. What's the use of passing these people to us for a couple of months? The chaps never get to know them and now we're at last getting a young intake, it doesn't seem reasonable to me that the subalterns they send us——"

"You know, Bertie, it makes me feel frightfully ashamed, but I can't think what the fellow looked like."

"But that's exactly the thing about Randle. One wasn't conscious of him at all! Why units like this should be treated as a sort of dumping ground for throw-outs, I don't know. Even if you have decent officers, it's still hard enough to cope."

Howard didn't care. He was on the right hand front seat of a jeep, speeding along the seventy kilometres to the nearest troop train stop. He took off his cap, put up the collar of his greatcoat and whistled gaily to himself, enjoying the breeze on his face, enjoying above all the last sight of the bare rolling country which had nearly driven him crazy for nine weeks. The driver beside him was envious.

"Don't want a driver there, do you?"

"I'll see if there's room on my personal staff."

"I'm cheesed off with this dump all right."

"What's your group?"

"Fifty-six."

Howard laughed. The sound was unexpectedly loud and infectious. He enjoyed other people's misfortunes and made no bones about it. At the same time his own made him sullen and unapproachable. He had had no friends in the battery

3

and the men did not like him. His over-familiarity with them was not to be trusted.

"You'll be out by Christmas—next year."

"You're nearly through yourself, aren't you?"

"Nearly." He spoke with curtness. You could treat people too easily. "What's this place called?"

"Don't know, sir."

The jeep hurried through a village of farm buildings and a few cottages, dowdy with lack of paint and activity. A young man with long fair hair and no legs watched it from a doorway without interest. Some small children scattered out of the way.

"No traffic sense. Think they'd never seen a car sometimes, wouldn't you?"

"Bloody awful, aren't they?" Howard nodded. He was good humoured again.

They were on a long, straight, cobbled road. The usual notice flashed by: IT IS A SERIOUS OFFENCE FOR W.D. VEHICLES TO CARRY CIVILIANS. Howard took out a cigarette case from his greatcoat pocket, put a cigarette in his mouth, then leaned forward to use his lighter, sheltered from the wind.

The jeep slowed down to cross a Bailey bridge. Some workmen were busy demolishing the last traces of the old concrete structure, which had been blown up. They were middle aged or old, wearing their little black peak caps. One of them beckoned the jeep on.

"Nice of him," the driver said.

"Generous. We put up his bridge and he lets us go over it."

"Got a sauce, haven't they?" the driver laughed, as they bumped on to the road again and he speeded up.

Howard, pausing in his satisfaction at his posting, found time to envy him his air of vibrant health; the glowing skin, close cropped hair, the smile of enjoyment. Well, the driver was not more than twenty. He had probably looked much the same himself, but ten years of beer and as little exercise as possible made a difference. The thought worried him a little.

However, there was no denying the posting. After six years

4

the army was over as far as he was concerned. He said, " It's such a gloomy damned countryside, isn't it? You wonder what the hell people did even in peacetime——"

"I expect they parided the chickens and made 'em goosestep."

The brown fields that lay on either side of the road stretched away for miles until they met the hazy blue of hills. "I suppose it's miserable at home as well," Howard thought. His own life, apart from the army, had been spent in an atmosphere of City traffic, cinemas, piers, tennis courts. It was another reason why he was so glad to be going to Hamburg. Even the English countryside was not so dull as this. It had signs of activity, hoardings, lorry pull-ups, road houses; if they had looked desolate in the war they represented something that had been there once: not this bleak nothingness. Yet his fellow officers had seemed to enjoy themselves. The locality was well-known for its bird life. They went for long tramps looking out for rare specimens and talked about them afterwards in the mess, interminably, while Howard, sitting alone, stared at his glass of beer and looked almost as bored as he felt.

"Well, I should have been in the nuthouse if they'd kept me here much longer."

"Nice and comfy, too, sir."

Ahead of them a lorry was grinding slowly along. A crowd of faces stared out from the back of it. Dressed in the usual variety of semi-uniform, fur coats and dusty rags, they were of every age and the same age, every experience and the same experience. They were defeated, poor, hungry, depressed, pale and helpless. They stared without embarrassment as if they felt that they had reached the bottom of misfortune and there was nothing left worth covering. Howard sat up as the jeep came close, conscious that in front of Germans one ought not to slouch. He tried to stare back at them with composure. They sat, crouched or stood without moving, like a collection of waxworks, and it seemed unnatural when one of them spoke to the woman next to him. What lay behind their expressionless eyes was impossible to know. Sticks of useless

5

old-fashioned furniture could be seen at the front of the lorry, forming a grotesque frame to their faces. Howard felt himself colouring and looked away. Meanwhile the driver had begun to hoot, for the lorry was in the middle of the road and it was impossible to pass.

"I bet the bastard can hear all right."

"He may not be able to. The lorry's making the hell of a din. God knows what stuff they use for petrol."

"He's got no right to hug the middle, anyway." He put his finger on the hooter button and kept it there, deafeningly.

The lorry continued without altering its course. The driver was moving the jeep from side to side of the road, looking for an opening, and keeping the hooter going all the time. Howard looked everywhere but at the faces, which were, however, gazing down at the jeep without bitterness or amusement. He glared at them for a second defiantly. But they were not ignoring him, on the Dutch resistance model, staring through him as if he were not there. These people were behaving as if they had no emotions at all, as if the jeep's angry hooter, the red-faced lieutenant and the swearing young driver were all in the nature of things. Still the lorry went on, and in the jeep Howard felt himself perspiring, while the driver became more and more angry. It was not only inconvenient to stay behind the lorry, it was also a matter of prestige. Howard tried to look as if he was quite content and interested in its wheels in an objective way, as if he were studying a German make. They were not going at more than fifteen miles an hour and the lorry seemed likely at any moment to collapse into dusty fragments. The driver spat, "It's a bloody good joke for them, isn't it? I bet those rotten bastards in the back are enjoying it. If they had any guts, they'd show it."

"They look a miserable bunch." The jeep plunged into a six-inch hole filled with water, and a splash of mud caught Howard on the cheek. "Blast!" he exclaimed, furious. The whole damned lot must be laughing behind their faces. He began to hate them. "At least it's a comfort that they are miserable," he said. "We have the last laugh. When you think what these swine have done——"

"I'd put the whole lot in Belsen and tell 'em to stew there, sir, I would."

"That's what they want, a taste of their own medicine. I suppose this lot have come from the East. God knows why we let them come back."

"The Russians have got the right idea."

"It's a pity we can't kill the lot."

"Whoa! Here we go!"

The lorry swerved into the side to make way for an oncoming staff car. The driver waited for it to flash by, varnished, beflagged, red tabs in the back in sheltered comfort, and then he flung the jeep forward and round the lorry, tearing down the road. Howard caught a glimpse of the offender, a stolid middle-aged man wearing the long peaked old army forage cap. He appeared not to notice the jeep, but to be concentrating hard on his steering wheel. The ordeal was over and Howard felt lightness of heart again; he told himself that he had not really been embarrassed or uncomfortable at all. He chuckled.

"My God. I wouldn't be in their shoes, would you?"

"I've half a mind to run him in," the driver still smouldered.

"They looked in pretty terrible condition. Of course, if it were the other way round, I suppose we should be foot-slogging it to Siberia, let alone getting lifts to get home."

"Oho, they'd have had it in for us all right! Not that you'd think so, the way they carry on to you. Make you want to cry sometimes, don't they? They never did nothing! Oh, no!"

"I've never really spoken to them much," Howard confessed, with a glance at the speedometer. A notice had just warned: Watch Your Speed. "Mind yourself, there are some redcaps in that jeep."

"I seen 'em," the driver grinned, slowing down to below forty miles an hour, as another jeep, containing three Military Policemen, approached and passed them. "Mind you, some of them are all right. Hans and Fritzy we got working in the

7

garage, they're two decent blokes, you know. Good workers, they are, too. Tell 'em what you want and they do it. Then, take my frat I go with, what harm did she ever do? Pleased to have been on the winning side, mind you, but never was a Nazi and never heard of no concentration camps—though there was one half a mile away—still she never could have done much, could she?"

"Oh, some of them aren't so bad, I suppose."

"Anyway, give me home sweet home, that's what I say."

"What are you going to do when you get there?"

"Go in with my brother. He's got a garage. Great North road. Smashin' business it is."

"Well, you're settled then."

Howard was also settled. In civilian life he had been a clerk in the Oxenbridge Assurance Company, earning five pounds a week at the time of his call-up. Though he longed to be demobilised, he tried not to think about his future. On his last leave he had been to see Mr. Waters, his departmental manager, and the sight of the office, and the bus and the teashop queues outside, had depressed him immeasurably.

"It's hard to say how things will be," said Mr. Waters. "There will be a lot for men who have been in the Forces to learn, with all the fresh legislation—quite apart from what they've forgotten. But I don't think you have any need to worry, Randle. The General Manager was saying only this morning that we'd be getting a flood of demobilised men soon and that he was looking forward to seeing them back. Of course, you mustn't expect the carpet to be laid down, you know." He changed the undesirable subject. "Anyway, I hope the office will be looking more respectable when you come back."

"What was it, a V.1?" Howard tried to speak calmly and hide the loathing he felt for the thin, middle-aged man with his horn-rimmed spectacles and air of complacency.

"Just round the corner. Luckily it was a Saturday afternoon or we might have had a severe shaking. Mr. Goodge's ceiling

8

came right down. We lost I don't know how many windows and there was plaster all over the place."

"Mr. Waters, what will the pay situation be?"

"Three hundred," Mr. Waters said. "That's fifty pounds per annum increase on your nineteen thirty-nine salary. So you see the company is being very generous."

"But the cost of living's twice as high——"

"For all of us, Randle, don't forget that."

Howard was speechless. Only when he was in the street again, almost pushed out, could he think of something suitable. He met Mary in the Strand Palace and gave her an account of the interview that sounded optimistic. That had been rather silly, perhaps, but she knew him only as an officer. She hadn't seen him in the uniform of an insurance clerk. Anyway he was not at all sure that he had convinced her. "I expect we'll manage, Howard," had been her non-committal reaction.

It was no disillusionment, of course. Everyone had prophesied impudent treatment, wherever he had been in the army, officers and men alike. Howard threw away the stump of his cigarette and lit another. On their right they were passing an UNRRA D.P. Camp, desolate and almost empty. He looked at it curiously and for a moment his own annoyances seemed small. The camp receded into the bleakness of the whole landscape, with its printed signs on the road, its cosy lights in the office hut, its delousing centre, its ghosts. Howard forgot it at once. They bumped over another Bailey bridge.

He worked himself into a state of indignation and bitterness. In God's name what was he fit for now? He had forgotten everything he had ever known and he had never known much. Moreover the capacity to learn was beyond him. The six years had been too long. Four of them as a lieutenant—that itself wasn't much of a recommendation. People who had dodged the column altogether were sure to have the impertinence to look critically at his record. It was a matter of pride to Howard that he hadn't been the sort of bastard that got promotion. Anyway, if he had gone to the office as a brigadier with three D.S.O.s, Mr. Waters' attitude would

9

have been precisely the same. The thought gave him some satisfaction.

"Hauzendorf," the driver said. "Four kilometres. There's a smashing 'YM' there, sir."

They passed a huge red brick barracks. It looked new and efficient. The front gardens were neatly kept, with their surrounding stones whitewashed. Painted and varnished notices advertised the regiment in occupation. The sentry at the gate was smart, his trousers like knife edges and his webbing scrubbed white. Howard considered it all a delightful sight. It signified what he was leaving behind.

"Plenty of bull there," he commented. It was the kind of joviality for which he was suspected. The driver sniffed, but did not reply.

Hauzendorf was one of the small towns which had avoided damage. The sugar beet factory by the station was its only considerable industry, and it had not been bombed. In the main street the Military Police Information Centre was spic and span. The officers' shop with its models, dressed as generals, and shirts and caps and ties looked at first sight like an ordinary prosperous business. The Garrison Theatre, which had been the town cinema, was showing 'Meet Me in St. Louis.' There was a queue of soldiers outside. The last of the spring afternoon sunshine picked out the quaint tops of the buildings and made it all seem very attractive. The Germans themselves walked along as if they had suddenly found a little enjoyment again. There were more of them on the pavements than there had ever been before the war. All the unbombed towns had trebled their populations, and the local inhabitants said it was better to have been bombed.

"This lot look pretty good on their thousand calories."

"Too true. Here's the 'YM,' sir."

"I could do with a cup of tea. D'you think these things will be all right?"

"Safe as a house. Redcaps only a hundred yards away."

"Will it be all right for me to go in?"

"There's an officers' partition."

The Hauzendorf Y.M.C.A. canteen was dark, as the windows had been boarded up, and was lit by electric light all day. This, together with the smell of the well-scrubbed floors and the wet feel of the tables, gave it a lethargic atmosphere. A radio blared out the British Forces Network programme, its volume never varied. Three German girls chattered to each other behind the counter. Except for a table occupied by two sergeants the big room was empty.

"I'll sit here," Howard said. At the far end there were half a dozen tables segregated by a notice hanging from the ceiling: Officers Only. Since the place was deserted there was no point in going to it. The driver went to the counter and bought two cups of tea and two cakes from the large assortment that were on show. Howard watched him talking gaily to one of the girls. When he came back with the tea and cakes, he had also a carton of boxes of matches. The driver was enthusiastic.

"Look, sir, if you go up, she'll give you one, too."

"But I don't want them."

"Don't want them? Got to look after yourself, you know, sir."

"Well, I'll get them if you like; you can have a double stock."

"That's talking!" said the driver. "It'll keep me for a month."

Howard went over and asked for his supply. The girl was a plump, pretty blonde. "Pleace!" she beamed, handing over the matches and his change from a ten mark note.

The driver had gone out to the jeep for a moment. He returned with some paper and came over to the counter to ask the girl to pack him a dozen cakes. She was willing to do this as well and the parcel was carefully tied up.

"Quite a shopping day you're having," Howard said. "Are you worried you might feel hungry on the way back?"

"It's for my frat, not for me," the driver grinned.

"Oh, I see."

They went out to the jeep again. Four small boys were waiting by it. Howard glanced at his baggage, but nothing had been disturbed.

"Have you cigarette for my farder?"

"Go on!" the driver said. "Skidaddle! Scram!"

The boys retreated a few yards and stood, watching, as they climbed in and drove off. Howard was silent. He felt slightly guilty about the way he had helped the driver with his black marketing. His late battery commander had been very strict about that sort of thing. He had told Howard at his first interview:

"Randle, there's one thing I'll mention and have done with. In this unit we do not deal on the black market and in particular any officer found associating with it in any way is for the high jump toute suite. Not that I'm suggesting you would, of course."

But there had been no need for anxiety. Howard had always obeyed the rules. He flattered himself that he had principles and that he lived up to them.

The road was again bounded by dreary farmland. They passed two city-dressed, middle-aged men wheeling an old cart in which a woman and a child were sitting. Within a quarter of an hour dusk had fallen. The driver did not lessen the jeep's speed, but he appeared to be looking more cautiously ahead.

"Never like being out like this. I heard a bloke got his head chopped off on the old wire only the other week. This is just the light you can't see it. In the dark it's all right."

"Are you trying to scare me?" Howard asked. "Because you've succeeded. Just you keep your eyes skinned. Not that I believe that old wives' tale."

"All the same it's good country for hiding in."

"Take me back to dear old Essex," Howard groaned. "At least they have no werewolves there. I'll have a fag to soothe my nerves. How are we off for time?"

"We'll be at the station by eight. Then you'll have a good half hour."

"A good five hours more likely."

"Last time I was there it was two days. It was in the flood time last year. They packed us off to the R.H.U. It was terrible, sir. That place never ought to be allowed."

"Don't be so encouraging."

The driver trod hard on the brake and the jeep skidded to the left of the road. Howard clutched at his seat and remembered that although he had a revolver he had no ammunition. The driver swore and jumped out. He went to the middle of the road and pulled over a piece of wood covered with spikes like the end of a large rake.

"Birthday present. Wouldn't have helped the tyres, would it, sir?"

"It would have knocked us into the ditch. My God! Lucky you saw it."

"I'd like to get the bastard who put it there. He was probably watching."

"Do you think——" Howard glanced up and down the empty road. There was no sign of movement. The few trees were too thinly spaced to conceal anyone. A military notice said: 'Careful. Slippery road when wet.' Near it, in German: 'Glatteis.' "Oh, hell, no, I expect it's off a plough or something."

The driver shrugged his shoulders. He seemed a little disappointed.

"Maybe."

The driver slung the article to the side of the road. Howard sat in the jeep, wishing that they would drive on quickly. He did not feel at all calm.

However, after they had gone a kilometre, his confidence began to return.

"You know I'm not sure you weren't right, perhaps it was there on purpose, you never know."

"I'm damn sure it was, sir."

"Pity in a way there wasn't a Kraut hanging round. A good incident would relieve the monotony."

"There'll be plenty of incidents before long," the driver said happily, accelerating. "This country won't stay quiet."

"It's bloody cold." Howard shivered, pulling his coat lapels in upon his chest and envying the youth and regular P.T. which enabled his companion to be warm enough in battle dress. A mile farther on their headlights shone on a large white arrow, on which was printed: 'Reichsautobahn.' They turned up a circular road, once brilliant with smooth white concrete, now shabby and pock marked, and came on to the main road, its two parallel ribbons stretching into the distance in both directions.

"Watch I don't go to sleep, sir."

"Like a hawk."

However he began to doze. He woke up suddenly half an hour later to find that they had arrived at a petrol point, where a young private, wearing a glamorous beret with a green tassel, filled their tank and then scribbled on the jeep's workticket without uttering a word.

"Talkative," the driver said, as they left.

Howard chuckled. "You'd think they'd be glad to see a white man in a place like that."

"I expect he's got some frat in at the back."

"Very highly sexed all you boys seem to be."

"Well, sir, you can get anything you like for a bar of chocolate. It's silly not to take advantage, isn't it? I mean all there is else to do is stay in and read or something."

"I suppose life seems different to you battle veterans," Howard said. "Sometimes I'm sorry I spent my war in a training regiment instead of the brothels of the middle east. Christ, I had a dull time." He felt amused at the thought of how shocked his battery commander would have been, had he overheard them. To judge by the conversation of the officers in the mess the men's only interest was the football team.

The autobahn went on as straight as an oil pipeline. Here and there a sign pointing to the right indicated an unseen town a few kilometres away that they were passing on one side or the other. If the place was on their left the side road circled and went over a bridge or descended and went under the autobahn, so that it was never crossed. Occasionally some lights twinkled from a farmhouse, sullen and hopeless. It was said that the people who lived in them were the only

14

Nazis left; they were not hungry enough to be apathetic and they were filled with the complaints of the refugees who sheltered there, unwanted but unavoidable. Looking at them made Howard feel homesick for England with its cinema queues, dog tracks and dance halls. He held on to his seat as the jeep skidded to turn into the left hand track of the autobahn; the right was being used as a dump of scout cars and bren carriers, which would apparently rot there for ever, as dead as old newspapers. The road itself had little of its heyday gloss. The join in the cement in the middle had split, leaving a jagged channel three or four inches wide which would have shocked the Fuehrer.

"Tell me," Howard asked. "How much d'you think you'll make in your garage?"

"Well, my brother's making ten quid a week, and he says it's going to expand by the time I come out of this lot, so I reckon I'll be all right."

Howard was silent, furious. He did not doubt that the driver would also get his ten pounds a week or that the garage would expand. He was always meeting people who were successful, who had opportunities and luck thrust upon them. It was quite to be expected that this boy would be earning more than he. The divine unfairness of things could no longer surprise Howard, but it enraged him daily.

"Next turning. Almost there now, sir."

They left the autobahn a little farther on and drove along a narrow tree-lined road which was decorated with a variety of painted notices. The Town Major, R.E.M.E., the R.H.Q. of an infantry regiment and a petrol point all advertised themselves gaily. There were several warning notices, 'There is NO Transit Accommodation in This Town,' 'Speed Limit 25 M.P.H.', 'Do Not Overtake.' 'Town Centre' with a large arrow pointing upwards, which meant straight on, was repeated so often that it had a cumulative effect; as if the town centre was something exciting not to be missed.

It had been a busy town of four hundred thousand people before it was bombed. Six buildings out of ten were destroyed, and it was as unpleasant a sight as existed in Germany. The outskirts through which they passed were untouched. The rows of neat red brick workers cottages, with their fairy tale high roofs, looked cheerful and homely. A tramway began and almost at once they were in the town itself. After two or three streets that were standing but depressed and untidy, the jeep came to the main bombed area. It was not too easy to drive in the twilight, for piles of debris on either side forced a crooked progress and what was left of the road was full of potholes. Neither of them commented on the hundreds of burnt out buildings or the sudden expanse of devastation that met them when, obeying the direction arrows, they turned down a street where some block-busters had fallen. For hundreds of yards there was only a mess of powdered stone, cement and brick, and here and there a jagged piece of wall, standing like a decayed tooth stump in a putrid mouth. The jeep bumped and splashed its way through.

"Well, I'm in good time," Howard said, puffing. "Are you sure this is the way to the station?"

"Certain, sir. I was here last week."

"Will you be going straight back? It's a damn long run for you."

"Not likely. I'll go in the N.A.A.F.I. here for a bit. You won't forget to see if they want a driver in Hamburg, sir, will you?"

"I'll see what can be done," Howard assured him.

"Here we are, sir. Paddington ahead."

"Bloody good show, old boy."

At the end of the devastation there was a square, on two sides of which there were undamaged buildings and on the third the shell of the railway station. The jeep pulled up in front of it. As if by a conjuror's trick, for the square and all the surrounding streets had been silent and empty, there seemed to be thousands of people in the station. It was the same scene that there had been in the main street of Hauzendorf, but it was exaggerated a hundred times. The pavement in front of the entrance was filled with ragged children, who immediately approached the jeep. The driver, however, shouted at them in a friendly way, "Shove off, see?" and they kept clear, watching Howard carefully. He was just about to throw away the stub of a cigarette. Almost before it reached the ground a child had covered it with his foot and bent down greedily to pick it up.

"Damn nuisance these kids," Howard said. "If you like to hump in the baggage I'll stay here on guard. Otherwise you'll find yourselves without any tyres."

"I'll go and get a truck."

The driver jumped out and strode away. A path opened before him in the crowd. As soon as he had disappeared the children looked at Howard again. One of them came close and stood beside the jeep.

"Have you dog-ent for my farder?"

"Oh, go away."

The little boy took no notice. He was small, barely higher than the jeep, and wore short trousers, a jersey and a pixie-like cap, probably from some kind of German fatigue dress. He had close cropped fair hair, spoiled by ringworm. He was dirty not with mud, except on his bare feet, but with being unwashed. "He must be bloody well crawling," Howard thought. He tried to eye him severely or at least with firmness, but the boy's expression had an impudent charm which made it difficult.

"For farder, for my farder."

"You ought to be in bed. Go away, can't you, blast you?"

"For my farder."

Howard hated him, didn't believe him and felt uncomfortable. He was not callous. "God, at home they've no bloody idea of this," he thought. Just as they hadn't of the ruins. He glanced beyond the boy, hoping to see the driver. There was no sign of him. The crowd was as thick as ever. He pulled out a cigarette and hiding it beneath the palm of his hand passed it across. He was rewarded by a smile of delight. The mouth was in a filthy state, too. A small greasy hand seized his for a second and the child's voice spat happily into his ear, "Tenk you, tenk you!"

17

"Go on, shove off, didn't I tell you?" the driver was back, grinning all over his cherubic face. "Got you a porter, sir. Here 'e comes."

"Good work." Howard hoped his weakness had not been observed.

"If you don't beat it," the driver went on cheerfully, for the boy was still smiling at Howard, "I'll give you a four-penny one on your backside, see?"

The boy ran away.

"I was nearly giving him one myself," Howard said.

A middle-aged German came up, wheeling a truck, and when he had halted it by the jeep saluted him.

"I've told him what train you're on, sir." His English seemed to be quite understandable to Germans who hardly knew a word of the language. He added to the porter, "You know what to do, don't you?"

"Jawohl," the man nodded.

"I told him you'd give him a couple of cigarettes, sir."

"Right ho."

"So when we've unloaded, sir, if you don't mind, I'll leave you. There's an officers' canteen on the right when you get inside, next to the R.T.O.'s office. And here's my name and number, sir, if you should remember about me, and my category. I got wounded in Belgium, sir, so I'm not much good to the unit."

Howard took the slip of paper. When all his baggage was on the truck, the driver smiled and saluted.

"Good journey, sir. Cheerio."

"Cheerio, old boy."

He turned and followed the truck through the crowd. Ahead he caught a glimpse of the three main platforms, which were on a lower level than the street. The right hand one, reserved for Allied Forces, was almost empty. The others were packed tight with Germans, from one side to the other. Expressionless, dressed in the usual mix-up of out-of-place smartness and utility, carrying bundles and bulging suitcases, they stood waiting patiently for a train. There was an air of immobility about them as if they were in a still photograph. In the entrance hall and round the barriers, where Howard was relieved to see two military policemen, the Germans moved about purposefully. A few of them seemed to be showing off their strength as they walked to and fro, weighed down with baggage, their shoulders set well back and their step over springy. Howard tried to stride in a military way, hoping that he looked every inch an officer. His fingers crunched up the slip of paper the driver had given him and he dropped it without thinking. He followed the truck towards the R.T.O.'s office, where the clerk told him that so far as was known the Hamburg train was running three to four hours late.

"I should leave your bags here, sir. You can wait in the canteen."

"That's what they call organisation, I suppose."

He watched the German with the baggage truck unload, gave him his two cigarettes and went towards the canteen. A train had arrived at one of the far platforms. It was already overcrowded and the waiting mass swarmed upon it. Howard stood still for a moment, watching people climb on to the buffers between the carriages.

"Anyway they've got their damn train," he thought.

He went into the canteen.

PART II

CHAPTER 1

I

HAMBURG in its first peace-time spring was still a great city. Over a million people lived there, mostly in homes of one or two rooms. Not so spectacularly destroyed as Cologne, whose centre was like a smashed toy town, there were nevertheless areas where you could drive in a motor car for fifteen minutes and not see a standing building, but only acres of dust and rubble. However, the skyline round the two lakes, the inner and outer Alster, looked much the same as before the war. It was still possible to look across the water from the Lombard Bridge and see the Rathaus and Nikolaikirche towers beyond the roofs of the Jungfernstieg, the once elegant shopping centre. All the buildings looked unpainted and poor, except for the Vierjahreszeiten Hotel, which was a British mess, and Shell House, where the town major had his office. The bridge was always busy with troops, Germans, displaced persons, Control Commission officials wearing khaki or blue uniforms with green and yellow badges—the egg and spinach, the troops said—and the stream of Military Government cars, beetle-like Volkswagens and the large Mercedes and Horches which had once belonged to gauleiters and industrialists, and were now for the use of high British officers, or junior British officers who knew their way around.

Howard arrived the following evening, red-eyed and weary. The journey had been slow, with hours spent in sidings while the special duty trains and important cargoes went through—the leave train could always wait—and with draughts and wind pouring through the glassless windows of his carriage. His temper was not improved when he found the R.T.O.'s office ignorant of the telephone number of Sociology Division, the unit to which he had been posted. "There's probably an amendment which hasn't reached us yet, sir," the clerk said; it was no comfort. But Howard was told that the Division's office was only a quarter of an hour's walk away and, leaving his bags behind, he set out. He crossed the Lombard Bridge, lost his way three times in the next twenty minutes, and finally, perspiring and enraged, was led to the office by a German policeman. A large Mercedes Benz was standing outside. Howard looked at it angrily. His pleasure at being posted to the Control Commission had disappeared; and his feet were hurting.

A girl with a fur coat and a heavy smell of scent came out as he went in, and he felt a little better. The building was deserted and he went up the stairway to the first floor. He knocked hopefully at the first door he came to, on which was a notice: 'Major H. Cardington.' From this moment things were different. A hearty voice told him to come in. He pushed the door open and saw a man with a dark moustache and a friendly, though vacant look. Aware of the importance of the first salute, Howard braced himself, stood to attention—for the last time in his military career—and brought his hand up smartly.

"Good evening, sir!"

"My dear chap," the major answered, quite overcome. "Good evening."

Howard explained that he had been posted to the Sociology Division.

"Oh, my God," the major said, and that was all he did say for several minutes, until he collected himself and went on, "Well, my dear chap, we are delighted to see you. I am sort of in charge here just now as the director is away, perhaps he knows about you. Are you a friend of Johnson Trant's? Oh, well, anyway if you'd really like to join us, it'll be all right, of course. How lucky you came when you did. I had to come back to type out a curfew pass for a friend of mine. I expect you could do with some dinner, couldn't you? We've got a slum of a mess, but the only thing is we're on our own. Though I don't see the place much myself."

A few minutes later Howard was beside him in the Mercedes Benz. It was the largest and most comfortable motor car he had ever sat in. He began to feel complacent again.

The Kasselallee, in which the mess was situated, was one of the formerly pretentious and now bedraggled streets close to the larger of the two Alster lakes. Some of the houses were used as billets by the Military Government and these looked as clean and opulent as in the old days, the rest were shabby and overcrowded. In front of number 82 was a sign: "Sociology Div. Officers' Mess." It was a yellow brick house with astonishing Gothic windows. It had belonged to an S.S. lawyer and his wife.

The front door was opened by a white-coated German servant, who hurried down to the car to bring in Howard's bags, which they had picked up at the station on their way. Inside there were carpets, quietness, a cloakroom with a wash basin to the right, a door opening into the mess to the left. Howard had a glimpse of a large table set for dinner and another white-coated servant waiting unobtrusively. The hall itself was large and rather gloomy.

"It's much pleasanter on the other side of the Alster," the major said. "There are a lot of very good billets there. On the other hand you're close to the Atlantic here, which is quite a point. Now have a wash, my dear chap, if you'd like to, and then come in and have a drink."

Howard found soap and a towel ready beside the basin and spent five minutes reviving himself. When he came out, tidier and fresher, the major was waiting for him.

"Ready, old boy? This way."

Howard followed him across the hall into a heavily furnished drawing room, which was now called the ante-room of the mess.

"Hullo, Hugo."

"Hullo, Mike, hullo, John," the major said. "This is Howard Randle. He's come to join us. No notification, of course. I expect he's really supposed to be on his way to China. Oh, sorry—this is Mike Hemsleigh, John Styles. Busch!"

Howard nodded to two Army captains who were in the room. They looked different, but had much in common.

Styles was fair and stocky, Hemsleigh thin, tall and dark. They both had a silk handkerchief protruding from one sleeve, five inches of medals, a private income and comfortable prospects, eight or nine months in a prison camp and personal experience of near starvation. They belonged to different regiments, but these were similar units, permitted traditional variations of dress and always engaged in the best battles. Styles stood in front of the mantelpiece and Hemsleigh lay on a sofa, at the head of which was a small gold-coloured lion.

The German waiter came in and the major asked, "Busch, has the mess anything to drink? I've sold all mine."

"Two more Schlichtes, Busch," Hemsleigh said. "Did I hear someone else coming in?"

"Miss Ford and Mr. Schroeder, sir."

"Only one Schlichte, Busch, I must push off," the major said. "Look after Randle, Mike, will you? Busch, Mr. Randle can have dinner, can't he? I'm not in, so there must be enough. Hullo, Elizabeth, hullo, Peter," he went on, as a young man and a girl in the uniform of Control Commission civilians came in. "This is Howard Randle. Look after him, will you? I've got to dash off to Magda's."

With this the major nodded to Howard, who was now sitting uncomfortably on a chair, as far away as possible, and left the room. Both the newcomers smiled at Howard, who stood up and then sat down again, trying to assess whether they should be friendly to him or not. They had been young refugees and for years they had worked to become more British than the British. Their accents and command of idiom were wonderful. Peter Schroeder's carefully correct slang, his old-school-tie voice, his immense moustache, almost straight from an Eighth Army cartoon, were part of an act of a very high order. He never faltered, he raised his eyebrows at exactly the right moments, and controlled his emotions. He had taken the stock upper-class English character of continental fiction and made himself into a replica. Elizabeth Ford, on the other hand, tried to fit the mood of whatever company she was in. She echoed other people's remarks brilliantly and those who met her for the first time came away feeling that she was a charming and intelligent girl. The impression dulled with closer acquaintance. She agreed with too many opinions.

They decided not to commit themselves with Howard and he sat in his chair, trying to look as inconspicuous as possible. On these social occasions he was always ill at ease.

"Have a drink?" Hemsleigh said.

"Not for me." Elizabeth shook her head. "We've just paid a short call at the Atlantic. Too horribly crowded for words."

"I'll have a glass of beah if I may, old chap," Peter Schroeder said.

"And a beer, Busch."

"Busy day at the office?" Styles asked. "We've been swanning."

"Loads of work," Elizabeth said. For Hemsleigh and Styles she used a languid, casual manner. "I suppose you heard Bonzo's news. His papers have come through at last."

"What papers?"

"Naturalisation." There was a slight, awkward pause, for she and Peter Schroeder were still technically Germans. It was a fact that was never out of their minds. Peter flopped into an easy chair, his legs stretched out wide apart, his hands in his pockets. Elizabeth went to an elaborate side table, on which were some three days old English newspapers. She looked at them carelessly.

Busch brought in the drinks, bowing over his tray to Howard and Peter Schroeder in turn. Hemsleigh signed the chit.

"Busch, any sign of Miss Hackster?"

"I zink she is on her way down, sir."

"Right, you slip our soup in like greased lightning, Busch." Hemsleigh stood up. "Excuse us, Randle, will you? Come on, John."

The two captains strolled towards the door and Miss Hackster came in. They stood aside for her.

"Good evening."

"Good evening." In her blue Control Commission uniform Miss Hackster could have been mistaken for a handsome police-woman. She was tall, well groomed, full chested and serious. She prided herself on her progressive outlook. Her smooth voice tingled with self esteem. "Good evening, Elizabeth."

"Oh, good evening, Sybil."

Styles and Hemsleigh disappeared. Miss Hackster smiled at Peter, who was one of her favourites. He stood up to offer her a cigarette. She accepted it and bent to receive his light. There was nothing she liked more than to be given a little attention.

"Thank you so much." She lowered herself with a sigh on to the sofa. "I'm quite exhausted. If one has ever known real sunshine, to be deprived of it for a whole day is more than depressing. And Pratt has been as irritating as possible about the files once again. Never did anyone keep a filing system like Pratt!"

"This is Mr. Randle, Sybil," Peter said. Howard stood up again. Miss Hackster had seen him as soon as she came into the room, but now she affected surprise. She was not very interested in Army lieutenants.

"Oh, how do you do? You have joined us?"

"Well, I think so——" Howard began, but she cut him short at once.

"Ah, here she is, the naughty girl!"

The woman who entered was small and nervous. She was Miss Hackster's great friend and shadow, and was trodden on by her unmercifully. Too weak and good-natured to try and protect herself, she was a year younger than Miss Hackster, who was forty, and she had once been married; both of these facts her friend could never quite forgive.

"Good evening, Mrs. Pratt," Peter said. He did not bother to offer her a cigarette as well, nor to introduce Howard, who sat down, forgotten.

"Oh, good evening, Mr. Schroeder."

"Don't speak to her!" Miss Hackster cried, with whimsical

severity. "No one is to speak to Pratt until she has found my file B.35!"

"Oh, Sybil!" Mrs. Pratt sat down beside her and sounded near to tears. "I swear I put it with the others in the green cupboard, I swear it. I told you I remembered seeing it because of the memo from Port Security Control."

"Don't fib. You know I can't stand a deliberate fib, Pratt."

Busch knocked and entered to announce that dinner was ready.

"We will wait a few moments, Busch," Miss Hackster said. It did not occur to her to ask anyone else. "The others will be here at any minute. I hate this habit of going in in ones and twos, don't you, Pratt?"

"Oh, I agree! I do, Sybil."

"Perhaps I have lived too long in a Latin climate." Miss Hackster had spent several years in Italy as the secretary of an Italian countess. "One is sometimes ashamed of one's own country's manners. Perhaps I am too exacting."

"Some Germans have very nice manners," Mrs. Pratt murmured, without thinking. She could have bitten her tongue off.

"I imagine you're thinking of Herr Scholle, Pratt. I do wish you wouldn't be quite so familiar with him. As a matter of fact I decided today to have his Fragebogen checked to make quite certain about him."

There was a silence. Mrs. Pratt sat holding her hands tight, a flush spreading over her small shining features.

"We called in at the Atlantic for a drink," Elizabeth said. She was always sorry for Mrs. Pratt, when she was being bullied. "It was frightfully crowded, wasn't it, Peter?"

"Oh, frightfully."

"I hear that Mr. Hamilton has been naturalised." Miss Hackster was aware that the subject had been changed, and made the most stinging remark she could think of.

"Yes, it's splendid for him, isn't it?" Elizabeth's voice was bright.

"He must be very pleased. Oh, good evening, Mr. Maxton-

Hill! I thought you wouldn't be very long. Pratt said she thought you were just clearing up. Did you get your call from Econ Div? They were chasing you all over the building."

Howard looked up from his gin at the newcomer, a small, plump man with rosy cheeks and a bald head. He sat down beside Mrs. Pratt.

"Yes, they got hold of me, Sybil. Their octopus tentacles reached and sucked me dry of my knowledge of the use of the screw washer by the inhabitants of the British Zone. They are now as wise as they were before." His voice was arch and vivacious. "Now if only they had wanted to know the current price of Steinhäger or Players No. 3, I would have been delighted to oblige! But screw washers—no."

"Definitely not screw washers," Elizabeth said, while Mrs. Pratt giggled admiringly and Miss Hackster smiled.

"And as I told them, the worst part of it all for me was that they expected me to know! Think of all the people, all the departments, all the sub-departments at the Esplanade Hotel," he continued, for he enjoyed being amusing to the ladies, "think of the whole of Esplanade 6, all the tortuous little channels of Military Government, and they have to choose Sociology Div to give them their answer about screw washers! As I told them, 'This division is not a sordid little fact-finding bureau. If you want to know something, ask a German! They know everything, after all.' It's so absurd to waste one's own time, isn't it?"

"Quite absurd!" Elizabeth said.

"And I was right in the middle of a most profitable deal in silk stockings."

"Oh, Mr. Maxton-Hill, you're thoroughly wicked!" Mrs. Pratt cried.

"He is a bad influence and I won't listen to any more."

"And I had reserved a pair for you, Sybil! No longer!" He glanced in the direction of Howard. "Whom have I the honour——?"

"That is Mr. Randle," Miss Hackster said, as if she were pointing out a piece of furniture.

"How do you do?"

Howard nodded back to him. He was beginning to feel a little dazed. The atmosphere in the ante-room had softened. Miss Hackster always said that she had a special bond with Mr. Maxton-Hill because like herself he had lived abroad for years. Now there was another knock at the door and this time Busch was accompanied by the English batman, Hammond, who wore a white jacket instead of his battledress blouse and an expression of contempt for everyone in the room. Ignoring Miss Hackster, Hammond addressed Mr. Maxton-Hill.

"Excuse me, sir, but it's all ready and the cook says the soufflé'll spoil, if you don't go in."

"Thank you, Hammond. Well, Sybil, what is your desire? Shall we adjourn to the soufflé?"

"I don't think we should wait any more for the others."

"We shall eat forthwith, Hammond."

"Right, thank you, sir. Not seen Mr. Morton, have you? D'you know if he's coming in to dinner?"

"The movements of Capt. Morton are, alas, a closed book to me, Hammond."

The batman made a sign with his thumb to Busch, who hurried away. Hammond was slim, dark and calm. He ruled the five German servants of the house with friendly but iron discipline, with something of the attitude of a leading gangster. If they played the game, he looked after them—in every way: cigarettes, food, coffee—but one slip and Hammond sacked them. He did this by giving the name to Hemsleigh or Styles, and the man or woman was sent for at once and told to report to the local Labour office. The departure was witnessed by Hammond, who had acquired all the skill of a customs official; he rarely lost supplies except on purpose. He lived as a friendly autocrat, taking care that his job was performed efficiently, and he had signed on for an extra year in the Army.

Miss Hackster smoothed her uniform and led a procession into the mess, the former dining-room of the S.S. occupant. She managed both to look stately and yet to hurry so that

31

there was no possibility of anyone preceding her. As a Technical Officer class two she was the senior woman of the Sociology Division and she tried to ensure that no one ever forgot it. She was followed by Elizabeth and Mrs. Pratt. Mr. Maxton-Hill, Peter and Howard were the rearguard. They passed out into the Gothic inner hall of the house. The mess, which led off it, was distinguished for three chandeliers which would have been quite suitable for a film of old Vienna, and for its quantity of large-scale mahogany furniture. Miss Hackster walked to the head of the table with an air of assurance that courtiers were bowing on either side. In fact the two already seated, Styles and Hemsleigh, did not look up. Miss Hackster was aware of this but the fixed smile did not leave her face. Busch stood behind her chair and she gave him a gracious little nod as she lifted her skirt and sat down. Two white-coated Germans came forward from the service hatch. Mrs. Pratt went meekly to her left, Elizabeth to her right. Mr. Maxton-Hill sat opposite Peter and Howard. Styles and Hemsleigh, who had now received their soup, made as much noise with it as possible, in order to irritate Miss Hackster. There was a gap of several chairs between the two parties.

Almost immediately, however, it was filled. Reminded by the soufflé, Miss Hackster had begun to describe the exquisite cooking at a house in Florence where she had dined, when she was interrupted by a burst of raucous laughter from the hall.

"There's Charlie," Styles said. "He sounds lit up."

"Doubtless he is celebrating some profitable deal," Mr. Maxton-Hill suggested.

The door opened and Charlie Morton came in. Miss Hackster stared at him. She hated vulgarity. He was twenty-eight and spoke with a slight cockney twang. His over brilliantined hair and half-inch side whiskers were accompanied by an untidy battledress, which seemed always on the point of losing pens, handkerchiefs and other stray articles that were half in and half out of his pockets.

"Hi, gang!" he cried, sitting down next to Styles. "What

an evening! Old Bonzo's outside, Kay's going to carry him in in a second—we began celebrating his naturalisation and he's absolutely stinking! It's wonderful—he's marvellous, the old wizard. Sybil, my sweet, you're looking adorable. Just too, too divine!"

Bonzo Hamilton was a middle-aged German Jew who wore horn-rimmed spectacles with very large frames and a battle-dress much too big for him. He had spent eighteen months in a concentration camp but seemed astonishingly free of its memory. Miss Hackster did not like him, out of jealousy, and had often been sarcastic about the English surname he had adopted, but she had been careful to be outwardly friendly; he was the closest associate of the division's chief, Mr. Johnson Trant, and especially now that his naturalisation was through he was very much on equal terms with her. He came in, beaming through his glasses, followed by Miss Blandison and Mr. Hopwood, who were both Control Commission civilians.

"Bonzo is going to have a Union Jack waistcoat made," Charlie continued, his mouth full of bread. "With neon lights switching on and off. Here, where's old Busch? Busch!"

"Yes, sir, please?"

"Any Bordeaux left? Two bottles wanted."

"Please," Busch said, acknowledging the order.

"Sybil," Charlie said, "you're beautiful tonight colon. Oh, my goodness, am I repeating myself ? What say to a nice trip to the Atlantic tonight? Warm us up for the frat."

"No more!" Hamilton chuckled. "No more, no more, my young frient! I cannot derink more!"

"Charlie's been dreadful, oh, he's been dreadful!" Miss Blandison cried. "I don't know whether I'm on my feet or my head!"

"Either way's the same to me, Kay, my love. You'll come along and like it. Modesty won't get you anywhere, Kay, not these days. You want to get some spunk in yourself! Go out and face life with a smile and a song! What say, Hoppy?"

"Don't you dare lead Hoppy astray any more," Miss

Blandison said, giving Mr. Hopwood a protective squeeze. "Hoppy, don't you take any notice of him!"

"Ee ah won't!" Mr. Hopwood said. He was a little, healthy, grey-haired man, who took things as he found them. He was too good natured to be rude to Miss Blandison, who treated enmity as a sign of frustrated love and lack of it as an open invitation. At thirty-one she had managed to convince herself that all men found her attractive. They did not. She was plain to look at, was rarely not suffering from a cold and had a passion for organising other people's affairs. At the moment she was itching to know who Howard was.

"All the same Bonzo is going to give a party, aren't you, Bonzo?" she went on. Neither Styles and Hemsleigh at one end nor Miss Hackster and Mrs. Pratt at the other were listening and she raised her voice. "Everyone pay attention! Bonzo is going to have a party!"

"Kay, do put a sock in it, you're overwhelming me," Charlie said. "Calm down, my girl, calm down!"

"Charlie, I think you're mean."

Hemsleigh and Styles were discussing ballet and Miss Hackster was asking Mrs. Pratt if she thought that anywhere there was a view one could consider comparable to that from the hotel at Stresa, overlooking Lake Maggiore.

"Damn good soup tonight," Peter said.

"No, Sybil, I don't think there is, truly I don't."

"I never know why people say the Vic-Wells dance. It's mime, pure mime."

"I wonder if we shall ever not have red cabbage," Mr. Maxton-Hill said, helping himself to a generous portion. "One feels that the spark of originality is missing below stairs."

"Nevertheless we have already eaten more calories at this meal than a German gets in a day," Miss Hackster said, as she stretched for the mustard. "Sometimes I feel ashamed of our rations, don't you, Pratt?"

"Oh, yes, I do."

"Sybil, did you hear that Fräulein Brosch fainted this afternoon?"

34

"I hope you sent her home, Kay."

"With my chocolate ration—I just had to, it seemed so mean to have it in my pocket just to nibble at, when she was weak with hunger."

"I noatice you doan't mention teaking mine to repleace it!"

"Oh, Hoppy, you mean beast!" Miss Blandison gave Mr. Hopwood a playful slap on his knees. "I did not, so there! Seriously I was ever so worried about Fräulein Brosch. She's such a nice old thing and she just doesn't know how to look after herself."

"She was too honest for too long," Mr. Maxton-Hill said. "That's the trouble with having been brought up before nineteen fourteen."

Hammond had come in and was having a whispered conversation with Charlie Morton, which was, however, easily audible to Howard. He listened, fascinated.

"Hey, Bonzo!" Charlie called out to Mr. Hamilton. "What's a Leica IIIA worth in coffee? There's a bloke at the door wants to sell."

"Lizzen, Charlie, I do not know today's price."

"Look here, Hammond, go see what he wants, see? If he won't suggest anything, I'm not ready to talk, see?"

"O.K." Hammond went away.

"Hey Busch, get the wine poured out quick," Charlie said, rubbing his hands. "This'll be quite an evening if I can get me a Leica. Mike, got any spare coffee?"

"The only coffee I have I drink," Hemsleigh replied. He and Styles left the black market alone and were very disapproving about it.

"Now, now, that's not friendly. How about you, Sybil?"

"You know my views," Miss Hackster replied.

"Did I mention you were looking beautiful tonight, Sybil?"

Mrs. Pratt giggled. Charlie blew her a kiss. He said, emotionally, "Pratt, my darling, I dreamt last night that we were on a desert island, me in a zoot suit and you in a sarong! Are you coming to my party tonight?"

35

"Oh, Charlie, thank you, but I don't think so, are we, Sybil?" She looked half fearfully at Miss Hackster for guidance. It was forthcoming.

"I hope I'm broadminded, but it just happens to be my opinion that these affairs bring discredit on us all."

"Hear, hear, I quite agree!" Miss Blandison cried. "I think you men are perfectly awful."

"All the more for us!" Charlie said, undismayed. "Twenty-five bottles of Steinhäger—that'll take some working through." Suddenly he noticed Howard. "Excuse me, you wouldn't have any coffee, would you?"

"No, I'm afraid not."

"This is Mr. Randle," Miss Hackster said. "Mr. Randle has joined us."

"A new member!" Charlie reached across the table and shook his hand. "Morton's the name and it's the only one worth remembering. Welcome."

"Did you have a good journey?" Miss Blandison asked. "I mean, have you come from somewhere?"

"From beyond Hauzendorf. I was twenty hours in the train."

"You mean you had to take the ordinary leave train?" Mr. Maxton-Hill gasped. "How ghastly for you! You must be nearly dead. Sybil, he must be nearly dead!"

"You poor man!" Miss Blandison smiled. "Still, I expect the meal will make you feel like a new man."

"You mean you'll feel like a new man," Charlie said.

"I just won't speak to you again, Charlie! Don't listen to him, Mr. Randle, he always pulls my leg like this. But, thank goodness, I never mind being teased!"

The arrival of Howard's sweet saved him from having to say anything more. He picked up a fork and bent down to eat, a little at sea. But there was no longer room for doubt. His luck had turned. At his old mess, he reflected, they must now be in the middle of the nightly stirrup pump fight. It was pleasant to think about it. And the sweet was delicious.

He ate greedily.

CHAPTER 2

"WELL, what do you think of it here?" Kay Blandison asked.

Twenty minutes had passed and they had now returned to the ante-room, which was fortunately large enough to accommodate several groups. Busch had served them all with tea. Miss Hackster, Mrs. Pratt and Mr. Maxton-Hill were on the sofa in front of the fire. Hemsleigh and Styles were together in a corner. Elizabeth, Peter and Mr. Hopwood sat on three upright chairs. Mr. Hamilton was in an easy chair by himself. Howard was sharing a small sofa that stood against the back wall, with Charlie Morton and Kay, who had patted the seat beside her and beckoned him across.

"What do I think of it?" he said. "So far it's wonderful."

"It's not too bad here really," Kay said, as though she considered that in fact it was. "What have you been doing? By the way, you don't mind my asking questions, do you? I mean, I always say it's the only way to break the ice. You looked so shy and reserved during dinner, I felt ever so sorry for you; it's never easy to go to a new place, is it?"

"You're doing well, Kay," Charlie said. "Don't forget I'm here rooting for you."

"Be quiet, Charlie. Now Mr. Randle, have you just come from Berlin?" She used her most winning smile. "Oh, no, how silly of me, I remember you saying Hauzendorf."

"I was in a battery, just an ordinary unit, doing training and so on."

"It sounds dreadful. But I expect you had a nice old castle or something to live in, didn't you? The army always does itself well, not like us on poor old Control Commission."

"It was bloody awful," Howard chuckled.

His experience as a member of the occupying force had not been luxurious. The billet had been a small modern house with little comfort. A German woman did the cooking, but

37

the result had been poor, mainly because she sold a quarter of the officers' rations every week; this had not been investigated as the battery commander had a horror of eating better than the men and was only satisfied when the officers ate worse. They had had no German servants. There was no furniture in the bedrooms and very little in the mess. The battery commander had disapproved of requisitioning more than was absolutely necessary. He said that you enjoyed soldiering all the more if you lived hard. There was, moreover, no officers' club within reasonable distance of their area. On one occasion when the battery commander was away, three of the brighter spirits, who did not include Howard, commandeered a jeep and drove all the way to Hamburg, had a party at the Atlantic Hotel and returned, towed by a fifteen hundred-weight lorry after they had skidded off the road, to find him unexpectedly back. There had been an atmosphere in the mess for days afterwards. Of course Howard, though guiltless, had received the brunt of his bad temper. A dozen petty criticisms; some gunner's hair too long, an inaccurate parade state—how marvellous it was to be away from it all. He did his best to describe it to his two listeners, delighted to be able to tell someone. They appeared never to have heard of such conditions. He exaggerated confidently about battle courses, sleeping in the wet, training the new young soldiers to fight D-Day in Normandy again and the incredible spit and polish, from which Howard himself was demonstrably a rebel.

"You poor thing!" said Kay Blandison, patting him on the knee.

"The question is will I be able to stay here. I don't know anything about sociology, and the major's never heard I was coming. It'll be just my luck to be put on the first train back."

"Don't worry about that! Hugo won't let you go once you've arrived. Why, there are all sorts of things you can do. Administrative assistant, liaison, German personnel, there's simply no end. Besides we don't come under Hamburg Mil. Gov., you see, we're an independent division, that's what makes it so nice."

Howard was comforted, although he was not enthusiastic about his left ear being bathed in her warm, moist breath. When Kay liked someone, she made no bones about showing it. Her forwardness shocked him. Moreover he did not find her at all attractive. He noted the clumsy way she had plucked her eyebrows where they had met naturally over her nose and the blotchy complexion which reflected an unhealthy blood stream.

"How long have you been in Germany?"

"Only two or three months."

"I hope you're not a big black marketeer."

"Never even sold a cigarette," Howard confessed. He felt rather ashamed about it, especially as Charlie Morton was looking at him in astonishment.

"I'm very glad to hear it!"

"Come off it, Kay," Charlie said. "Keep to the straight and honest now. You know quite well you sold a bottle of Schlichte last week just for one thing. A nice little profit of two thousand per cent."

"Well, what if I did?" Kay was furious. "I don't call a little thing like that being on the black market! After all, if Control Commission won't forward my pay, what am I to do? They make us do it. But you needn't think, Charlie Morton, that I like doing it, or would do it if I didn't have to! All I was saying to Mr. Randle was that it was refreshing to find someone whose hands are clean."

"Which reminds me," Charlie said. "Where's that blighter, Hammond? It's time that fellow made up his mind."

Miss Hackster's voice was raised, asking Busch for more tea.

"Who's the old girl?" Howard whispered.

Kay giggled. "Don't be so awful! Never let her hear you say that! It's Miss Hackster. She's our only woman T.O.II."

"What might that be?"

"Technical Officer class two—what a lot you've got to learn! Never mind, I'll have to teach you. Miss Hackster's a very cultured, intelligent woman."

39

"Says you."

"She is, Charlie!" Kay lowered her voice. "She's very progressive and left wing, Mr. Randle. Next to her is Mr. Maxton-Hill, we call him Maxie. He's sweet, but I suspect there's more to him than meets the eye. The other one's Mrs. Pratt, with the mousy hair, everyone calls her Pratt. She's terribly good natured and everyone adores her. She's a T.O.III like me. Then those two in the corner are Mike Hemsleigh, the one with the moustache, and John Styles. They're very nice really but a bit snooty if you know what I mean. I don't think you're like that, Mr. Randle, so it's quite safe to tell you. Oh! I hope he didn't hear."

Styles had got up and sauntered across to them. His expression bore all the embarrassment of an Englishman determined to be sociable.

"I say, Randle, your name rings a bell. Were you in the bag by any chance?"

"Bag?" He had no idea what was meant and showed it. Styles looked more embarrassed than before.

"Mike Hemsleigh and I thought perhaps you'd been in—in a prison camp with us."

"Oh!" Howard grinned. "Not likely!"

"The only bag he knows is something different, isn't it, Kay?" Charlie said.

"Oh, you!"

"Perhaps it was Normandy, then?"

"No, old boy," Howard said firmly. "I was never in a battle, thank God." He felt a little flattered that the other should think it possible. "It must be some other Randle you're thinking of." He went on with an affected accent, "One of the Shropshire Randles, perhaps. Actually we are the Mile End Road branch, don't you know." Kay gave him an appreciative giggle. Howard felt he was doing well.

"The bottom has arrived," said Styles, returning to his corner. "But Kay is at last perfectly matched."

Hammond, the batman, came in and made his way across to Charlie Morton. He bent down discreetly.

40

"He wants fifty-five pound of coffee, sir."

"Here's your black market," Kay said. "Fifty-five pounds indeed."

"Who does he think I am?" Charlie demanded. "The Home and Colonial? It's not reasonable." To Howard's astonishment he was making no attempt to lower his voice. "Hey, Bonzo, did you hear that?"

"I did!" Mr. Hamilton chuckled. He took off his glasses and calculated. He replaced them. "Thirteen thousand, seven fifty marks. Well, you must remember it's not three months ago."

"Shall I make him an offer?"

"You can try, sir," Hammond said. "But he looks a wily bird. Got a smashing overcoat on. Busch says he's one of the Reeperbahn boys, so it's stolen, of course."

"Isn't it disgusting?" Kay said to Howard.

"Hammond, me old china, I got to think. What are my assets, apart from my winning personality? Two half pounds of coffee to start with. It's pathetic."

"It's five hundred marks," Mr. Hamilton said.

"Thank you, Bonzo. Then two bottles of champagne at four-fifty each, isn't it?"

"Fourteen hundred so far." The batman had produced a pencil and paper and was noting it all down.

"Hammond, this is causing me pain. Five years pre-war on the road and here's a Kraut swindling me at the door. Who's occupying this country?"

"You'll have to think of some more, sir."

"Hundred cigarettes, that's four hundred at least. How much for whisky?"

"Four hundred."

"All right, that's two thousand two hundred. Go and see what he says to that, Hammond. Tell him there's not fifty-five pounds of coffee in Hamburg; he must be crazy. Tell him it's my final last word and if he agrees I'll throw in a signed photograph of me."

"I don't think it's enough," Hammond said.

"If there's any nonsense, my final, unalterable offer may include my camp kit and two blankets."

"Okay."

"I almost hope he doesn't take it," Charlie said. "If not we'll open the whisky and have a little drink in my room, to celebrate your arrival. Where are you sleeping, by the way?"

"I don't know. The major said he'd see to it after dinner, but he seems to have disappeared. My kit's out in the hall."

"He can have Bobby's room!"

"Next to yours, Kay? Well, I never, what a coincidence."

Howard sat between them, content to let anything happen. His only discomfort was the realisation that Miss Blandison reminded him strongly of Mary. It was not a physical resemblance, unless of movement or gesture, and besides he was not attracted. Perhaps it was merely the enthusiasm with which she had set about making him welcome.

"Let's go upstairs and get you settled in comfortably, Howard."

"Thanks," he said, and felt a little inward shiver. For there was the echo again. It was just in this way that Mary had begun to use his Christian name, with the same purposeful, maternal note in her voice.

They stood up and Charlie at once spread himself full length on the sofa, regarding them with a quizzical look.

"If she gets dangerous, there's a fire alarm on the landing," he said. "By the way, if you're not feeling too tired, I've got a party on tonight to which you're most cordially invited."

"Thanks, old boy," Howard said, turning in response to a sharp tug at his arm.

"Charlie, don't be mean!" Kay was angry once again. "Don't for goodness sake drag him into that. Besides, he must be exhausted. I won't have you interfering, so there."

"Don't carry on so, my dear! I never knew such a girl."

There was no escape. Howard was already half-way out of the room, tripping up over Elizabeth's chair as he went.

"Oh! Sorry."

"Couldn't matter less," she smiled.

"See you later, old man," said Peter Schroeder.

One of the waiters, to whom Kay spoke in German, carried his valise and suitcase upstairs to the second landing. They followed him. The stairway was dark, but wide and well carpeted.

"Must have been a big noise who owned this," Howard said.

"Goodness no. Just an S.S. Sturmbannfuehrer. He was a lawyer. In Neumünster now. I saw his wife when we took this house over." Kay wrinkled her face. "I didn't like the look of her."

"I don't suppose she liked the look of you," Howard grinned. "Circumstances alter faces."

"You're teasing me! But I don't mind." They had arrived. "Here we are. Danke schön, Huhn."

"Bitt' schön." The waiter passed them and went downstairs again.

"You don't mind my coming in, do you, Howard?" If he did, it was too late, for she was already in the middle of the room, looking round critically. "I'm just making sure no one's been helping themselves to any of the furniture. Of course it's very old fashioned."

"But solid," Howard said. "And warm. The central heating bites you, bless it." He walked across to the window and peered between the frilly lace curtains. "Is this the street?"

"No, it's the garden side. It's small and a mess. Do you like gardening?"

"No."

"You're like me. Lazy." She was sitting down on the velvet covered high backed armchair, feeling in the pockets of her uniform for a packet of cigarettes. "Smoke? Catch!"

He dropped it and bent down to pick it up. He was now beginning to feel irritated. No sooner was one in a really good billet than new problems arose. He struck a match for the cigarettes. As he bent towards her, she half closed her eyes and then opened them suddenly to stare into his. Howard had an idea. He hurried to his suitcase and began to open it.

43

"I must do this before anything else." He felt almost exultant, as he took out Mary's photograph. This would teach her.

"Oh, is that your wife?" Kay did not sound in the least dismayed. "Do let me see!"

"No, it's my fiancée."

"What's her name?" Kay was holding the photograph at arm's length, as if she were long sighted.

"Mary."

"She's quite pretty, isn't she?"

"Yes."

"Are you in love with her?"

"Of course."

"I don't believe you," Kay Blandison said, handing it back to him. "You men are all the same. You say you love us and kiss us and give us meaning glances and it's all a sham. Thank goodness I can see through you." Her expression softened. "All the same I'm sorry you're not married, Howard."

"Sorry?"

"I can give so much more to a man if he's married," she smiled. She was looking coquettish. "I bet you think I'm shocking and wicked! What sort of a girl can I be to come into a man's bedroom like this?"

The question had crossed his mind. He put the photograph of Mary on the small marble-topped table by his bed.

"Well, you tell me," he said with a grin. "What sort of a girl are you?"

"You're wrong about me, quite wrong, really you are!" The words came out in a torrent, startling him. She had stood up, breathing hard. Her cheeks, on which she used no powder, were pink.

"I'm sorry, Miss Blandison——"

"Kay, I thought I told you my name was Kay." In a second, it seemed, everything was all right. She had relaxed and was smiling. "I didn't think you were going to be stand-offish. But anyway you're tired and you'll want to write to

44

Mary; or I'd have let you take me down to the Atlantic. Do you like dancing? You'd be surprised how few men there are here who can dance."

"I'm one of the many that can't."

"I won't know that till I find out by experience!" she said whimsically. "But, Howard, all I've really come in for is to ask you please, please, please, not to go to Charlie Morton's party!"

"Oh?" He gave up. She was standing in front of him, humble and eager. "Well, I don't know that I'm particularly feeling like a party——"

"Oh, I knew you wouldn't, Howard, thank you very much!"

"Don't mention it." This settled it. She was crazy.

She began to talk quickly, staring at a spot on the carpet behind him, as if she were a child confessing to something naughty.

"I expect you think it's interfering of me to ask you, but it isn't really; you see all the men here go fratting and it simply isn't fair on us girls. They all do it except Peter Schroeder, they're mean, all of them, Maxie, Mike, John—and of course Charlie's the worst of the lot. I can't think what they see in these German women. Goodness knows I have no racial feeling or anything like that, but I do think that when English girls are here, the men might at least think of us."

"Well, so far I'm not guilty," Howard said.

She was delighted.

"Oh, Howard, I'm so glad you've come!" She was the flirt once more. She gave his arm a motherly squeeze. "Of course, it's not that I've been left all alone, sometimes I just don't know how I've kept going—why, I believe I could write a book about you men! Some of the parties—especially the Navy—but now I'm going to let you unpack in peace and write a letter to your Mary."

"Thanks."

"I might call in with something for you a little later." She was going. "Oh, the bathroom's the second door on the right.

45

The water's hot about twice a week. You can post your letter at the office."

"What time does work start?"

"Ninish. We're lucky there. Mil Gov have to be there at eight-thirty. Au revoir."

The door closed.

"Well!" said Howard. He looked round the room as if expecting her to reappear from some corner. But there were comforting sounds from the other side of the wall. His cigarette was half finished; he raised it to his lips and blew out the smoke slowly.

There was a knock at the door. She had returned.

"I said I'd call in with something but I happened to find it right away." She had come in with a bottle, which she placed on the table. It was Pernod. "I thought you'd have missed this month's ration, so you might as well have this; it wouldn't be fair for you to have nothing, would it?"

"Well, thanks!" He could no longer be surprised. Miss Blandison gave him a full, meaning look and left the room. Howard scratched his head and sighed.

Anyhow the room was warm and comfortable. The taste was foreign to him—Howard preferred the modern style—but it was all very solid. It had cost money. Round the walls were pictures of stags and hunting scenes, copies of engravings, all in heavy gilt frames; not the kind of thing he liked, but they were impressive. There was a wardrobe and a heavy dressing table with a tall frame for a mirror, from which the glass was unfortunately missing. They'd fetch a price in London, Howard thought. But so would the carpet, the cloth on the table, the curtains. They'd been comfortable here in their time; and this was only a spare bedroom! Six years in the bloody army because of these bastards; and they could still laugh at you, even if the husband was in an internment camp, and his wife had been thrown out of the house. There'd been plenty of years of luxury beforehand. The drawers of the dressing table were all empty. There was a book lying in the wardrobe. He picked it up and read: "Winthur—Gesammelte

46

Werke." It smelt of must. The pages were closely printed in the thick German Gothic letters. There was a faded ink inscription on the flyleaf: "Deine Dich liebende Leni." Howard threw the book down, and had to cough from the dust that came up.

He began to unpack, undoing the straps of his valise, which contained his camp bed, blankets, service dress and boots. The valise unrolled flat on the floor. Its contents looked strangely out of place in this civilian room, although on the bare boards of his previous billet they had seemed quite natural. He drew out the uniform, which conformed to his expectation by being creased all over; nevertheless he swore, as though surprised. He hung it in the wardrobe. The rest could stay on the floor. He turned to the suitcase and took out his pyjamas, which he threw on to the bed, his shirts and underclothes and washing kit. They'd better all go in drawers. The suitcase itself had been the drawer for some months now; it was a system that had saved trouble, but in this room it would hardly do. Oh, well; later. He yawned, stood up and then went over and lay on the bed. There was immediately another disillusion. Beneath the eiderdown he felt not the caress of a mattress but the sharp protest of an army palliasse, full of straw. He swore again. Might as well have the camp bed and be done with it. The batman, he reflected, had had a foxy look. Probably he had knocked off the mattress. In that case Howard was going to knock it back. They wouldn't make a monkey out of him.

He raised himself up on his elbows and found his cigarettes. Then, having lit up, he sank back again, more contentedly, and looked at the ceiling. It had an elaborate cornice with some kind of floral design, badly chipped in the corner directly above him. He smoked slowly, staring at the ruined plaster-work, ignoring the thought which was repeating itself in his mind: he ought to write to Mary. He closed his eyes. I'm damn tired, he thought, and he had almost dozed away when the ash fell from the cigarette end on to his lips. He jerked his head.

"I thought that was going to happen."

Charlie Morton had come into the room and was sitting on the table, regarding him. Howard rubbed his eyes, swinging his feet from the bed to the ground at the same time.

"Hullo."

"I came up to make sure you were safe from the clutching hand of Kay, bless her sweet little soul."

"Oh!" Howard chuckled. "She's gone for the moment. Who does she think she is—Cleopatra?"

"Now don't you say a word against my Kay. She's a nice typical English girl right down to her slip showing. Don't let her worry you. Be firm and she'll wear off."

"It's nice to know."

"I shouldn't have left you alone with her right away, old boy, but I was doing some business. Not doing it, as it turned out. A IIIA Leica, too. St, st. Oh, well, I saved my whisky. Have a drop?"

Howard saw that Charlie Morton had brought a bottle with him, together with two glasses.

"Thanks."

"Where are you from? Before the unit you were telling us about, I mean. Middle East?"

"England."

"My God, you must be glad to be here."

"That hadn't occurred to me, as a matter of fact." Howard accepted a quarter tumbler of whisky. "It seems very comfortable here, of course, but give me London, thank you very much."

"Home bird, eh?" Charlie said. "Very nice, too. I'm an Ealing man myself. But all in due time, it seems to me. You can't do business in London, I mean, can you?"

"How do you mean?"

"Business, old boy! Ye old schwarze—the black!" His companion winked at him. "Come off it, old son, you're a sly one and no mistake!"

"Oh," Howard said, "I see. The black market."

"Yes, yes, yes," Charlie murmured. "You make me feel awful, you do, really."

48

"Well——" Howard coloured. He felt rather foolish. He tried to make his admission as casual as possible. "The fact is, old boy, I haven't been operating."

"Go on!" Charlie seemed genuinely surprised. "Do you know—look, my dear chap, I hope I'm not offending you or anything—I took one look at you and I said to myself: there's a man with his eye on the ball. No offence?"

"Not at all," Howard said. "I'm flattered."

"I could have sworn it, but, there, I shoot my mouth off too much. I know my faults. You're sure there's no offence?" Charlie made a gesture as if he wished to shake hands on it, but he changed his mind. "I'm glad about that. Have another drink—go on, finish that up."

Howard obeyed, suffered the pain of heartburn for a second and then felt very well. He handed over his glass.

"You do a lot of business?" There was something deferential about the question.

"Not a lot, old boy." Charlie Morton poured out even more whisky than before. He seemed now to be rather intent on justifying himself. "I just keep my head above water. The way I look at it, if you want to change a pound every time you want forty marks, all right, go on and change it; but if you get the chance to make a bit or pick up something nice, well, go on and take it, I say. We won the war, didn't we? It irritates me the way you hear people go on about that sort of thing. If you ask me, it's our right to do these bastards here in the eye. Think what they'd have done to us! Don't you agree?"

"I do."

"I've got a job worth fifteen pounds a week to go back to. You know what that's worth in England today: nothing. But as it is I've had six months here without touching my army pay. It's just been piling up nicely for me. It's all very well for these pukka sahibs like Hemsleigh and Styles. They can afford to have principles. I can't: that's the difference. Do you blame me?"

"I don't."

"Good," Charlie Morton said, relieved. "I'm glad of that,

old man. Howard, isn't it? I raise my glass towards you; you're a white man. You'll come to my party, won't you? You like women? I have several nice lines to interest you. You can see I've been on the road, can't you? What's your racket?"

"Insurance."

"Christ. Oh, well, you've got to live, haven't you?"

"I play the piano in a brothel, evenings," Howard grinned. He was feeling pleased. It was delightful to find someone to whom he could talk freely, to say nothing of being invited to a party within a few hours of arriving in Hamburg. He was far too tired and the wise thing was to go to bed; however, he had decided to accept. He had been wasting his time too long. What was the point of going to bed early in order to wake up not feeling tired; who had the benefit of your freshness? Certainly not you. Besides, if the major he had met was his chief, it would hardly matter if he didn't arrive at the office at all the next day. Let them whistle for him. He sipped at his whisky again. Strength and dare-devilness crept smoothly into his being.

"Come on, now," Charlie said. "We ought to be going. Only one thing, see which bottle your drink comes out of. I've put two little pencil dots on the bottom right hand corner of the labels of the ones I've got. If there aren't any dots, you want to watch out. It might be all right, but you never know where they get it from. People are dying like flies. Three in Cologne the other day."

"Damn good idea." Howard felt he was showing some perspicacity of his own merely by nodding to the advice. Charlie Morton must be made aware that he was leading round a man who was well able to take care of himself. "It's the best way." Back at the battery the dartboard would be in full use and the major talking about wild birds. He'd like the whole lot to walk in and see him. This was the life. He said, "I feel like a party, old boy."

They stood up. Howard noted with satisfaction that the other was round shouldered and if anything in a worse physical condition than himself. At the battery they had all regarded

hard exercise as one of the pleasures instead of the most dis-
agreeable features of life; they were healthy young men who
jumped out of, rather than heaved themselves from armchairs.
Nor were there creases in Charlie Morton's battledress
trousers. The latter replaced the cork in his whisky bottle.
Howard laughed. There was no particular reason, but he felt
like it.

They went down the stairs, pausing on the first floor at
Charlie Morton's bedroom, which was so large and luxurious
that Howard's seemed an unfurnished attic in comparison.
"Don't forget I've had time to organise myself," Charlie said;
he still appeared to be justifying himself. "Got to look after
number one, you know." They left the whisky and the glasses.
Charlie stopped in front of a mirror to dab his face with after-
shaving lotion. "Makes me seductive, somehow—like some?"
They continued downstairs, but at the bottom their way was
barred by Miss Blandison.

"Gangway for a naval officer," Charlie said.

"I knew this would happen!" she cried. "I won't speak to
you, Charlie, not ever again! You always spoil everything.
As for you, Howard, it's mean of you, oh, I think it's the
meanest thing! I asked you not to, you know I did, and he's
talked you into it."

"My dear girl," Charlie began, "my dream, my ineffaceable
memory——"

"I hate you for this."

"I love you, full stop, I adore you——"

"Please don't go, Howard, please don't go!" She seized
Howard by the lapels of his battle dress blouse.

"Don't forget we're only going to see if we can get you some
stockings," Charlie said.

"You needn't think I believe that." However she loosened
her hold and stood aside. She said to Howard, "You're as bad
as any of them."

"Worse," he grinned.

She walked away abruptly through the open door of the
ante-room. Inside Peter Schrœder and Mr. Hopwood were

playing draughts and Sybil Hackster was talking to Mrs. Pratt. Her deep voice drifted out into the hall. "One's chief trouble is that not to share the religion prevents one from fully appreciating the glories and colour about one; but I have always found, Pratt, one can't compromise in that sphere, not, at least, with my background——"

"On we go," Charlie said. "This way to the races, pal. We'll get our titfers and be off. I've got my car outside, provided nobody's swiped it in the last half hour."

Howard followed him, delighted with himself.

CHAPTER 3

THE flat was on the top floor of an apartment house in an undistinguished street. Before the bombing it might have been the lodging of a small shopkeeper or a clerk; but now the fact that it had stood and remained self contained in its old shape made it valuable and sought after, a rare, luxurious home. The double front doors of the building had to be opened from within after prolonged ringing. Inside was a dark, cold hall with tiled steps and the iron cage of a lift that no longer worked. A staircase twisted round and round the shaft. On every landing were two entrance doors, each with a list of half a dozen names and dates of birth; these were typewritten on cardboard or paper, stuck on with paste; beneath them was the old name plate of the pre-war occupier, one name where there were now six. Although everything was swept and clean, there seemed to be invisible dust about, a musty smell, as if there had been no fresh air, no window opened, no disinfectant for years; the building was like the clothes of a prisoner. On the top floor only one of the two doors had been forced to the list. The other exhibited a single name, painted in small white letters: Schöffler. Charlie had pushed Howard through as if he were welcoming him to his own flat, bringing home someone from the office to meet the wife. The guide who had been downstairs to open the doors for them followed, grinning; he had the sort of face that was always grinning. He was a small man, neatly but exotically dressed in a blue ski-ing suit, a white shirt, a red tie and black patent shoes. "This is Herr Scholle, a real white man," Charlie had introduced them. Howard shook hands without enthusiasm: Herr Scholle did not seem very trustworthy to him. But he had no time for such critical judgements once they were inside the flat. A woman came towards them with heavily jewelled hands outstretched. "Waal, I sure am glad to see you at last, yes, sir!" She spoke old fashioned American with a German accent. Howard was amazed, not least by the red fingernails and expensive scent; he had unconsciously imagined that it was the British officers who were to provide the glamour for some grateful Fräuleins to enjoy; in the noisy scene before him this was not at all the case. Khaki battle-dress was slovenly beside the converted ski outfits and lounge suits with padded shoulders, the cream shirts and ties with large square knots. The women seemed all to be young, attractive and expensively gowned. Howard was very sensitive to social distinctions, it was one of his habits to announce proudly, "Well, of course, I'm one of the lower middle classes, old boy!" a statement whose possible truth he feared and resented; and immediately he was inside this crowded room, he felt that he was receiving patronising glances. There were handsome men with monocles and duelling scars and lively men wearing over large spectacles, comedians who talked with extravagant gestures at a tremendous rate; they might have been film extras doing a continental scene. The room would have been hot enough without any heating but a log fire burnt in the grate; in front of it there was a large settee fully occupied by girls whose backs were to the rest of the room. They wore variations of Russian military style, bunched up shoulders and cloak effects and almost all had the same pageboy hair style, allowing it to fall lazily across the forehead. Hemsleigh and Styles sat in armchairs at the side. They noted Howard coming in but made no sign of greeting. They, of course, he reflected bitterly, fitted in perfectly; although he was surprised to see them there at all. He heard Hemsleigh's voice raised: "But I assure you, my dear Ilse, I was personally starving————"

Howard moved about for an hour like a shy, sullen small boy at a children's party. He drank several glasses of German gin. No one was interested in him at all. Then why invite me? he wondered angrily. He was surprised to see Elizabeth Ford and Mr. Hamilton, to whom he had not spoken in the mess; they recognised him and smiled, but they were arguing with someone in German and Howard could only pass on, trying to look purposeful, and feeling a little drunk.

"Ve were talking of potatoes, which are not procurable in Hamburg. Do you know vy not?"

He was suddenly conscious that he was being asked a question. The man who asked it was one of the comic-looking Germans with large spectacles that had transparent frames. His hair, at which Howard could not help staring, was brushed straight back from his forehead, ending in a shaggy mess hanging over the back of his neck.

"Oh, sorry," Howard said. "My God, I don't know."

"You do not know?" The little man's eyebrows almost reached the top of his head. "You are a British officer, you are in charge, you take out potatoes, but vere? But vere?"

"Search me," said Howard. He was not quite sure whether to feel annoyed at the presumption of a German in taking him to task or guilty about what had been done with the potatoes. He adopted his rude, hearty manner. "I'm just a simple soldier, old boy. All I do with potatoes is eat them."

"You? So!" The little man turned to the auburn haired girl next to him. She was well but more simply dressed than the others and not so noticeable. "You hear zat? It iss exactly vot I have been saying to you!"

"Oh, that is not fair!" she laughed. She added to Howard,

54

"I absolute you—no, no, I absolve, yes? I absolve you completely from the charge."

The little man uttered a sharp grunt, stared up at the ceiling and then turned and seized Howard's hand.

"Neumann!" he said fiercely. Howard stared at him and the girl continued to laugh. She seemed to be enjoying herself.

"Er versteht nicht, er versteht nicht!" she giggled. "Please, sir, Dr. Neumann is but introducing himself."

"Oh!" said Howard, feeling mollified at her use of the word "sir"; it was high time he received a little respect. "Beg pardon. Er, my name is Randle."

"Neumann!" the other repeated, with a bow, like a jack-in-the-box.

"Randle!" Howard grinned.

"Mensch, Mensch!" the girl went on giggling. "Oh, but that is very, very funny, yes!"

"Excuse me," Dr. Neumann said, with another quick bow; and he hastened away to inform another group of his newly-found proof of the reason for the potato shortage. Someone filled Howard's glass, but not before he had casually made sure of the two dots on the label. The girl remained. She was also drinking.

"Nice drop of methylated," Howard said. "Goes down well except for the heartburn."

"No!" She shook her head, smiling. "I do not understand! Not so fast."

"Who was the little potato man?"

"Dr. Neumann? Very, very clever. He has all plans but no one listens. Do you know the story of the goldfish?"

"No."

"A Russian had this bowl of goldfish. So he tooks the fish out and eats them." She was beginning to shake with laughter again. Howard pretended to be amused. "Then an American has this bowl and he takes the fish out till they are dead and then puts them back into the water." Now, approaching the climax, she was almost hysterical. "And then—and then an

Englischmann has the bowl and he cries and says I will not be so cruel as the others and so he leaves the goldfish in the bowl, but he drains out all the water and the goldfish die just the same! Is it not very, very good?"

Howard laughed with her, a little puzzled.

"You are already long in Hamburg?"

"No, as a matter of fact I've only just come."

"Oh? Are you also with Sociology Div?"

"Yes," Howard said, wondering whether it was in order for a German to question him. However, he instantly dismissed the thought as absurd and added, "I've just come from the country, near Hauzendorf."

"So near the Russians," she said meaningly. "Soon you will be fighting. Is it so that you have had incidents there recently?"

"Don't you believe it."

"It is so. Everybody knows. Of course you must be discreet."

Howard was exasperated and, as the Schlichte had now softened his social inferiority feeling, he said, "Well, if you know so much, why ask?" But she had gone. A man with a very soft voice asked him if he had heard the goldfish story. When he replied that he had, the man asked why the English didn't do something to improve the German newspapers which were such a laughing stock. The man accepted a cigarette and said it was a pity the English were losing their popularity.

"I didn't know we had any to lose."

"Oh, certainly, when you liberated us, as we thought——"

"It's the first I've heard of it."

"I assure you we looked forward to your coming. Why else did so many of us come to Hamburg? But now we are disillusioned one hears it everywhere: the Russians are not so bad. It is terrible but I assure you that is the way people talk. Tell me one thing. Why cannot we have some of Denmark's surplus?"

"I'm blowed if I know, old boy."

56

Rather oddly this answer proved to be quite satisfactory. The man at once looked more friendly.

"It's a deliberate policy, of course," he smiled. "But why? What is the motive? It stands to reason that all policy has a motive."

Howard shrugged his shoulders. They touched glasses. The man said, "Goot luck!" and then went away. He stood alone, beginning to feel a little dizzy.

Two pencil dots, bottom right-hand corner: so long as he could see them, the drink was all right, old Charlie had guaranteed it; so long as he could remember them, he himself was all right. Pretty good reasoning, old boy, he decided. Where the hell was the woman he'd just been talking to? Oh, there she was. She was talking to the man by the gramophone. The records were all old, but nostalgic; bloody good. Louis Armstrong playing Stardust. Funny to be hearing it here, one of his favourites. Someone had spoken to him. He turned. A small face grey-white with powder, little lips made big with paint; revolting. Look out, old boy.

"You are not enjoying yourself?"

"Oh, yes, I am," he smiled. "In my own quiet way, don't you know."

"Dance with me."

Howard found her in his arms. She wore a tight cossack-like dress. She was extremely forceful. The dancing space was twelve feet square, an alcove off the main room of the flat; she seemed to regard it as a ballroom. It was difficult to hear the music. The babble of conversation was overpowering.

"My favourite tune," he said.

"It ees?" She was pleased. "How charmant."

"C'est absolutely smashant. Where did you learn English?"

"Oh!" she raised the pencilled lines which had taken the place of her eyebrows. "You are laughing at me, is it not? You most not. No!"

"Never mind, I can't speak a word of your language, except ich liebe Dich."

She went into a peal of laughter and then began to croon

57

huskily into his ear: "In der Nacht schläft der Mensch nicht gern alleine——"

Suddenly Charlie Morton was whispering to him, "Have a care, me ole cock-sparrow, that dish is marked poison, handle with sterilised tongs."

"Sharlie!" the girl cried, letting go of Howard and seizing the party's host. "You are saying naughty zings?"

"Strike a light, Sophie, let a bloke alone. Hey, Howard, well, what a pal——"

Howard had taken his chance, unscrupulously, and was now dancing with Charlie's partner. She was beautiful. He had noticed her as soon as he came into the room. She wore a long-sleeved white evening frock against which her skin was cool and attractive. Her fair hair was taken straight back behind her ears, but the effect was not severe. She wore simple pearl ear-rings. Her face, which was almost on a level with Howard's, was mature but fresh, unlined and expertly made up. He thought: "Classy bit of goods, by God."

"Poor Charlie," she smiled. "That was bad of you, very, very bad."

"You've got to take your chances."

"Oh! That is worse!" She had perfect teeth. "But that is a terrible girl, I think."

"That's what I thought."

"But she has just come to Hamburg. From Berlin."

"She's still a terrible girl."

"She is not of a very good social standing, but nowadays all are mixed."

"I knew we had something in common," Howard said. He was perversely fond of debunking himself in his officer and gentleman status; but it was always more from a desire to bring down other people a peg than from a sense of reality.

"Common, that is the word, yes." She had quite misunderstood. "You are a friend of Charlie's? Also in the Sociology Division?"

"I only arrived today."

"So. Then let us hope you will stay."

58

"Thank you," he said, amused. What a nerve they had, to talk patronisingly, to welcome, even to ask questions! Defeat had in no way destroyed their fantastic bumptiousness. Still, this was an attractive woman, no doubt about that. Easy and uncomplicated to dance with—or perhaps it was that he was dancing very well. Moreover she was friendly but self-contained; because for her part she was pleased with herself there was no need for him to be anything but natural. He was glad she had misunderstood. For something to say, he asked: "What time does this party stop?"

"But of course it does not stop," she said. "It goes on all night to beat the curfew. Unless we have a pass, we must be indoors by half-past ten."

"I forgot that."

"Besides it is so nice and warm here," she smiled. "Is it not? It would be silly to leave and go back to one's cold room."

"You mean you live in one room?"

"But of course," she said seriously. "That is all we are allowed. It is terrible. Did you not know?"

Her misfortunes were of no concern to him. He was on the point of answering, "My dear good woman, what do you think I live in at home—Buckingham Palace?" or "Of course I know and who's to blame but yourselves, may I ask?"; in fact a whole series of cutting replies were half formed in his brain; but in the end he said: "Well, how about this flat, for instance?"

"Frau Schöffler is really a Dane, so she puts herself as a D.P. Of course for a D.P. all is possible."

Howard felt exasperated. She had spoken with no bitterness or resentment, but merely as though she were stating the fact of an injustice to which she herself was indifferent.

"Of course," he said sarcastically, "they're very lucky. Such a nice time they've been having."

"It is true."

There was a pause, while they found another record for the gramophone. A tall German with a monocle came up, said,

"Excuse me" to Howard and then broke into his own language. He was telling her a joke, it seemed. Her laugh was as attractive and as sophisticated as everything else about her. She was altogether too self-assured. Howard began feeling resentful. It was all very well to be friendly with them, but they had no right to carry on as if nothing had happened, as if the Nazis hadn't existed or the war not been lost. They were taking no notice of him at all; they had forgotten him. He turned away sulkily.

"Well, did you enjoy your dance with the Gräfin?" It was a coy, masculine whisper.

"Oh, hullo," Howard said. He had been joined by a Control Commission official to whom he had been introduced an hour or so before. He was a smooth-faced, youngish man with a wisp of grey in his perfectly brushed hair.

"What a scene, isn't it? What wouldn't the *Daily Mirror* give to be here? Think of the headlines!"

"It's amazing."

"Come into a quiet corner, my dear, and have a real drink."

Howard was rather startled to find his right arm linked with the other's as they pushed their way to a small table against the wall. His companion bent down and picked up a bottle concealed beneath it.

"It's only Schlimovitch but I promised Charlie to bring some bottles. The others are circulating. Look, I've put this cross on the top left-hand corner of every label. Take my tip and don't touch anything else. I can guarantee it not to kill and one never knows at these parties."

"What did you call her?"

"Who? Oh, the Gräfin. Didn't you know? She's a von Schwollenburg. Dirtie Gertie, I call her. My dear, the stories one's heard about that woman——"

"I'm not surprised," Howard said. It was untrue; he was astonished. He realised also that he was not feeling well.

"Oh, now we want another glass. One second." He darted away and was back almost at once. "Yes," he continued, "an absolute menace and you may quote me! And now tell

60

me all about yourself. I must explain that I always seize upon a new face like this—one has to keep up to date in Hamburg nowadays. I saw Charlie bring you in. My name is Panting. Conrad to my friends. I am a rather decrepit, rapidly aging T.O.II."

"Listen, old boy, I can't drink all this, I'm pretty tight already——" Howard murmured.

"My dear, I am never anything else from six o'clock onwards every day. Although of course one does get to be quite immune, it's terrifying, really. And after all this is really a very sober party, isn't it? Very ordinary; some of the places one goes to—quite reminiscent of the old Berlin—when they go in for these things, they do it properly——" He stopped and clutched Howard's arm. "Do listen," he whispered, "there's the most fascinating little argument on my left. The girl in black is accusing the man of cheating her over the price of a loaf——"

His voice became dim and he was swinging from side to side, just as everything around started to turn blue in colour. Howard breathed deeply and closed his eyes. A sound like a cat's purring started up in his head. He was perspiring.

"Well!" said Panting. "That's the quietest and most methodical pass-out I've seen in many a long day. But it couldn't have been my Schlimovitch——" Wearing his most amused smile, he supported Howard, who had collapsed. "Entschuldigen Sie, gna'es Fräulein," he said to the girl in black. She made way for him to pass and he began to pull his burden into the hall of the flat. "A gentleman has had his baptism of fire water."

CHAPTER 4

"So you are feeling better now?"

The girl held a handkerchief which smelt of eau-de-Cologne in front of his nose. Howard had opened his eyes. He was feeling terrible but not so bad as before.

"You are better?"

He blinked uneasily, confused, and remembered what had happened. He had passed out. He had been talking to a Control Commission civilian; the heat and the gin had come over him; what a display in front of Germans; what an officer —and yet he hadn't been tight mentally at all. He could remember thinking quite logically as it happened, just as he was thinking logically now. They might send him back to the battery after this. What a bloody fool. He ruined everything that was given him. He became conscious of the girl and her voice. It was the one who had told him the goldfish story: there, if he could remember that, he couldn't be drunk.

"I'm all right, perfectly all right." He tried to sound peremptory. He shivered with a sudden feeling of cold, although the atmosphere was stuffy and warm.

"Take deep bretts."

He obeyed unwillingly but the eau-de-Cologne was soothing. Now he did begin to feel better. Oh, God! He was lying on the floor. He raised his head, which was painful to his neck, and then pulled himself up a little, resting on his elbows. Where the hell was he? The party was going on somewhere: he could hear voices and the gramophone. He saw hazily a gas oven, an empty range, a pile of fur coats on a table.

"It is the kitchen," the girl giggled. "They have brought you here."

"They!" said Panting, who stood by the door. "Really, Hilde, I do wish you'd give credit where it's due. Ich bin böse, wirklich böse. It was I alone that brought him, careless of the strain to my heart. We were just beginning to have a gossip and he sank abruptly away out of this world."

"I'm sorry," Howard said. "It was the heat, old boy. I wasn't tight. Sorry to be such a bloody nuisance."

"I am honoured to have served. For the moment I will leave you in Hilde's womanly and capable hands. I thought I'd just stay in case you died or did anything silly. Au 'voir."

He went back to the party. Howard sat up against the wall.

"How long have I been here?"

"Perhaps ten minutes."

"It was very kind of you to come and—and look after me."

"Oh, it is nothing."

She was silent and Howard was puzzled. All at once he seemed to have become very attractive to women. First Miss Blandison and now this girl who was moreover pretty. Presumably she had some kind of motive; help for its own sake he did not even consider. If it was sex she wanted, there were far better prospects at the party than himself; and they all looked well fed. He shifted a little to ease his heartburn. The girl put the handkerchief on his forehead. Extraordinary, he thought, how people had the idea that all German girls were dumpy Fräuleins. This one would have made a good pin-up Goldwyn starlet. He looked at the long auburn hair falling across her forehead, the slim legs with their sheer silk stockings, the face with its small, well made porcelain-like features, the eyes, brown and long lashed, which were now suddenly gazing unembarrassed into his.

"And now you are better?" she smiled.

"Tell me," Howard said. "Are you what we've been fighting against for six years?"

"Please?"

"Let it pass."

"Did you wonder why I came out to help you?"

"It kind of passed through my mind. I don't fool myself it was my boyish charm."

"Boyish charm, what is that?"

"My—my—oh, God—well, my good looks——"

"Oh, I see." She pressed the handkerchief a little harder

63

on his forehead and lowered her voice. "I must ask you if you would be so good as to take me home."

"Take you home?" He was half shocked. He chuckled. "You don't waste much time, do you?" She looked puzzled. He went on, "I don't want to be impolite, my dear, but you see this is my first night here and I've got to start work to-morrow. God alone knows how I'm going to as it is. Repeat the invitation some other night, and I'll be delighted." What a place, he thought, what a place; you better look after your little self, Howard, my boy. "But thanks very much for the medical treatment."

"I must get home and I have no curfew pass. If I am stopped they will send me to prison."

"Stay here, then." He wasn't going to fall for that. "They told me you all stay here the whole night until the curfew's over."

"But if you would go with me they would not stop me."

"Who wouldn't stop you?"

"The German police."

"The German police," he said doubtfully. "I bet they wouldn't stop you. Hell, they're on your side."

"No, no, the German police are much more against us. But you will not do it. I am sorry, I should not have asked you."

"But be reasonable, my dear girl——" Once again he was exasperated. The way people calmly put you in the wrong was amazing, positively amazing. And she was so passionate about it, her voice was almost trembling. Not only her voice. She seemed to be fighting to control herself, dry-washing her hands, working her teeth against her lips as if she was about to burst into tears. A ham performance, he thought, as he felt himself giving way; it had been easier to be firm with Miss Blandison. He said weakly: "Can't you get someone else?"

"No."

"Oh, God." He had an idea. "Look here, I must find Charlie—that is, Captain Morton."

He struggled to his feet and immediately felt ill again.

64

For a moment he thought that he was going to be sick, but he swallowed, breathed deeply and the feeling was gone. His eyes were aching, his stomach was uncomfortable; if he were to sit down again, he would pass right out. He felt clumsily for his cigarettes, and, finding them, offered one to the girl. She took it silently.

"Well, well, if it isn't the new man!"

Howard turned to the door.

"Oh, hullo. Thank God. I was just coming to find you."

"How well you're looking," Charlie Morton said. He came in. "What divine saucers under your eyes, my dear. So this is what happens when your uncle's not watching. Collar and tie undone, hair all askew, oh, Howard Randle, I never would have believed it of you. My chum Panting told me you'd passed away, I was coming with a wreath. He probably didn't understand."

"Look here, old boy, do me a favour and tell the lady I can't get her home, will you?"

"He works with you?" the girl asked Charlie.

"Hasn't he told you? Well, you snake, Howard. So you're one of those weak, silent men."

"I was overcome by the heat." Howard was re-fixing his collar and tie. "I've tried to explain that I've just arrived and don't know where I am in Hamburg yet. She says she'll get arrested."

The girl had picked up one of the fur coats and was putting it on. Charlie helped her.

"It was about your getting back that I wanted a word with you, old boy," he said. "I'm just a little bit involved in there and I was wondering if you could make your own way. It's only ten minutes walk. Eighty-two Kasselallee."

"But I can show him," the girl said. "It is on my way."

"Where are the others?" Howard asked, clutching at a straw.

"Gone, old boy, I'm afraid. They all went five minutes ago and you were out of sight, so to tell you the honest truth, I'd clean forgotten about you. But this dear sweet girl will show

65

you the way. You can ring the front door bell, there's a chap on duty all night."

"You're a fine friend in the grass."

"So you'll be quite all right," Charlie said in a tone of relief. He was clearly living in a world of his own. He slapped Howard on the shoulder and walked with concentrated steadiness to the door. "I felt responsible for you, you understand. Have another drink before you go, there's still plenty left. Help yourself, old boy."

"Oh, God," Howard said, when he had gone. "I suppose we may as well start. Are you sure you know where I'm to go?"

"Of course."

"I may feel better in the fresh air." His indignation faded and he chuckled. The girl was waiting impatiently; she wore a fur coat, a fur muff and a fur hat. It occurred to him that she was the most luxuriously dressed girl that he had ever accompanied anywhere. Portrait of a starving German, he thought. "Do I look respectable?"

"Please?"

"Okay," he said. She went out before him into the hall of the flat, where he found his greatcoat and cap. The party was going on in the living room. The gramophone played 'I Can't Give you Anything but Love,' the words sung in a rhythmic baritone by a German. Charlie Morton and the red-haired woman were dancing. Otherwise, except for Panting, the English had gone. More of the Germans were now sleeping. The air was thicker than ever. Howard's head was throbbing. He caught snatches of Panting's conversation with a German: "I would be most interested to come along, it's most kind of you, I'm quite absorbed in the German Youth problem——"

"Ought I to say good-bye?" Howard said.

"No, no, it is not necessary."

"All right, let's get going. You lead the way." When they reached the street he stopped for a moment on the pavement to take deep breaths of the cold air. "That's better," he said. "What was it you said your name was? Lauren Bacall?"

"Hilde Nahler." She slipped her arm in his and pushed him firmly along. "It is very polite of you to come with me. My flat is so very small and cold, but we will have some coffee? I have nothing else to offer, everything is so terrible for us."

"The people at the party didn't look very starving."

"Not yet. At present it is only the little people who really starve. We of high social standing can still perhaps manage a little, but for how long will it be? When will you help us? Another year and even we shall have nothing. The English aristocracy should help the German aristocracy. How else will the Communists be stopped?"

Howard did not reply. He went on breathing deeply, and holding his breath for three or four steps at a time, in an effort to clear his head. Her voice was low and very earnest. The foreign accent was what made it attractive. But what a capacity they had for talking nonsense; it was hardly believable. All the same it amused him to be walking along with a girl from the German aristocracy. Lucky she didn't know what a punk she was out with, he thought.

"Halt!"

"What the hell——" Howard began. The girl had tightened her hold on his arm. Suddenly he was conscious of two helmeted figures standing in a doorway. A torch flashed. Howard blinked; the light was painful.

One of the policemen stepped forward and saluted.

"I am sorry. Goot night."

"Good night to you," Howard said. He squeezed the girl's arm and they walked on. He felt like giggling. The sensation of power was delightful. So she had been right; it was amazing. It was something he had never known in his relations with Mary. In the sort of encounter one had at home with policemen, shop-girls or cinema attendants, it was he who had blustered, lost and looked silly and Mary who had retrieved whatever might be left, with a parting shot, perhaps; she had a talent for withering remarks, but they were usually made too late, so that their recipient was Howard. He asked: "Do you really mean they would have arrested you if I hadn't been with you?"

"Of course. My brother just spent fourteen days in the prison at Osnabrück."

"Good lord," Howard said. He was so buoyed up that he lost consciousness of his heartburn. "Did they treat him all right?"

"It was terrible."

"Isn't that in the British zone?"

"Of course."

This answer meant to Howard, who always loudly despised patriotism, that the brother must be talking nonsense. He was slightly irritated, but reflected that the girl herself could hardly be expected to know better.

"How much further is it?"

"A few minutes only. The next street on the right is Kasselallee where you are living. Thus you will easily return to it."

"Where's this brother of yours at the moment?"

"He has gone to Lüneburg. I think he will be back to-morrow."

"You're not married?"

"Yes. But I have heard nothing since eighteen months. He is perhaps dead, perhaps not."

"Oh—I'm sorry." No need to feel embarrassed, he decided; after all, he had probably been killed over London or while pouring flame on our boys, torpedoing a merchant ship: excellent. "He was in the army?"

"Of course." It seemed to be her favourite phrase, impatient and intolerant. "He was taken by the S.D. for being one of the men of twentieth July."

"He was an anti-Nazi?" It was quite true what everyone said, he reflected, with an inward grin: you never by any chance met a Nazi; they'd all hated it, every minute.

"Of course." There it was again, calm as custard; this time he nearly said it for her. She jerked him sideways to avoid a ruin of jagged rusty metal; it was a small DKW car

68

which had crashed months before and burnt itself out. There was some bomb damage in this street; only the outer walls of some of the houses were standing. It was more understandable to Howard than the acres of destruction through which the train had passed. You could imagine one resigned family without a roof or personal comfort and be glad or sorry for the witless squandering of its hard-earned stores; an obliterated area was as unreal as the figures in a national budget. Looking through the darkness at the ghostly, broken brickwork Howard felt a little complacency. "Bloody well teach them not to start anything again," he said to himself. And the Germans, who respected force above all, must naturally be impressed by the officers of a conquering army. This business of being able to take a girl past a policeman, merely by being oneself, was really quite logical and in order.

"Quite nice to get the air, isn't it? Bit cold though."

"It is terrible." She shivered. "And now here we go left and this is the street where I am living. It is quite beautiful in the daylight with the water and all the green leaf."

There was a canal on one side of the road and a closely packed row of differently styled villas on the other. In front of one of them half a dozen British army cars were parked. A sentry stood moodily in the gateway, oblivious of them, browned off and cold.

"Don't they ever stop you?" Howard asked.

"The soldiers? Oh, never. They are behaving quite well in that house."

They passed under a railway bridge and stopped a few yards farther on. Opposite Howard could see the roof of a small boat-house, some steps leading down to the water and above them the shape of a willow tree.

"So. We are here."

He followed her up the six white steps. There was the usual long list of names on the front door, but it was too dark for him to read it plainly. She opened the door with a key and he stepped inside, feeling that perhaps there had been something a little too matter of fact about the way she had released his arm. She switched on a dull hall light. He had time to note a stairway with a carpet, a sign of reasonable comfort, and the name in gothic letters on a door: Nahler. This one she opened and stood aside for Howard to enter.

He found himself in a warm, feminine sitting room, softly lit by a standard lamp in one corner. Its flowered silk lampshade was magnificent and caused a pink glow all round. Howard was immediately impressed by a cupboard filled with glassware and pottery and a profusion of tasselled cushions on the divan. There was a smell of burnt herbs in the room, as incongruous as the black kitchen stove whose funnel disappeared into the window curtain. Between this and the standard lamp there was a low, round table, surrounded by three easy chairs. Howard noticed with a shock a crescent of untidy fair hair crowning the back of the nearest one.

"Oh, wie schrecklich!" the girl said, and laughed softly as she had at the party. "He is already back."

"I'd better go." Howard was anxious. You never knew what the man might think.

"No, no! He must wake!"

Howard took a hesitant step forward and looked down on the cherubic, splendidly contented face of a man between thirty and forty years old. The girl switched on the main light of the room. The sleeper sighed happily. She hurried across and shook him.

"Otto, auf! Auf!"

"Oh—pfui—ach——" Otto murmured; and his head jerked up. He opened his eyes. "Was denn?"

"Wir haben einen Gast!"

"Ach, Kind!" He stirred himself a little more.

"I really ought to go," Howard insisted. Otto caught sight of him for the first time and suddenly became alive.

"Ein Engländer! Warum hast Du nicht gesagt——"

"Ja, ja, ein Engländer!" she laughed.

Otto sprang out of his chair, ran his fingers through his hair, wiped his hands down the side of his crumpled grey suit and beamed with delight.

70

"I'm sorry you had to wake up——" Howard began.

Otto seized his hand and shook it fervently.

"Good bye!" he exclaimed. "I am so pleased to make you welcome, sir! Please excuse that you found me so terribly asleep. My sister, Hilde, has always surprises for me!"

"Otto is very fond of meeting Englishmen," she said.

"That is so!" replied Otto, who had not yet let go of Howard's hand, and he began to sing discordantly, "John Brown's body lies amouldering in his grave, John Brown's body lies—isn't it, isn't it? Ha! Ha! But we have nothing to give you. That is terrible."

"I shall make some coffee."

"Ach, coffee!"

"Are you sure you can spare it?" asked Howard, who was most relieved by his warm reception.

"What we have we can spare," Otto said, releasing his hand. "What we have not we cannot—isn't it?" He pointed to a chair. "Please, sir. But first your coat—excuse me."

He helped the guest off with his greatcoat and carried it away to lay it on the divan, holding it lovingly as a boy with a new cricket bat. Next to the divan was another door, half open, through which the girl had gone. Howard could see the end of a bed but no more. He sat down and felt in his hip pocket for his cigarettes. There were only four left. Unfortunately the packet had been seen; he could hardly put it away.

"Two stars a lieutenant!" Otto returned. "I also was a lieutenant! Leutnant Hubinger, Leutnant Otto Hubinger; one can hardly believe it." He sighed, but was immediately cheerful again. His English was improving. "What folly that we should have been fighting each other—is it not? No, sir, no, thank you! I will not smoke, you have too few."

"Don't be silly, take one." Howard felt ashamed of his meanness. He liked the look of this fellow; there was an air of warmth and friendship about him. "Please do," he insisted, now gratified by his own generosity.

"Thank you, sir." Otto took it with the speed of a conjuror.

"Gold Flake? That is very fine." He leant across to take Howard's lighter and held it for him.

"Thank you."

"So!" Otto lit his own, returned the lighter and laughed, "Gold Flake, Plyers, Voodbines—I can remember we had a wonderful store of them in forty—left by the English! I think you had notting to smoke at home for a long, long time. Isn't it?"

"Oh, we got along," Howard said.

"Now I have to do what I can with this." He showed Howard a pouch half full of what looked like irregularly shaped tea leaves. "Our terrible Ersatz. Oh, well, it will all come right again in time!"

The girl had been coming and going from the second room. She had taken off her coat and hat and Howard glanced at her appreciatively; the walk had given a colour to her cheeks. He thought suddenly: "I wish to God Mary were like her." But there was no getting away from it, his fiancée was much more like Miss Blandison; this was the sort of girl you saw on the screen and were resigned to never seeing anywhere else. In spite of his favourable reaction to her brother, who was now happily blowing smoke rings, Howard wished the latter could disappear. He had a feeling that the girl would like it too.

The coffee was being heated on the stove, whose fire was still just glowing.

"Otto, tell Herr Rondle of your experience in the prison."

"Hilde, no!" Otto was shocked. "No, no, that he does no want to hear!"

"But he does not know of such things; it is right that you should tell him. It was so terrible, Herr Rondle, Otto must share a room with three others—four in the one room, all together. Disgraceful, no?"

"It was the dirt, you understand." Otto was apologetic, but once he had started he became earnest. "I am first arrested by a Schupo—a—a policeman, a most rough fellow, and forced to spend the night with poor criminal types who

72

are quite lousy, you understand, and then I am judged—by an obvious communist, who takes delight that I have been an officer—such people are of course in power everywhere—and I must spend a further fourteen days in this terrible place. All because I am on the street at fifteen minutes past eleven o'clock. Ridiculous!"

"Bad luck, old boy," Howard murmured.

"I was in a small dirty, cold room, full of small living things, with the toilette in the middle—oh, oh!" Otto made a disgusted face, as if he could hardly bear the memory. "One lousy blanket, some stroh and all the time the company of three lower class criminals. Such companions for me, a man of culture, a man of July 20th. And the guards—oh!"

"British?"

"No! No! Some English soldiers were there, yes, but they were good fellows—the sergeant major has given me an English paper to read—and when the German guard comes round, it is immediately taken away. Not allowed. Forbidden. Get up. Sit down. Attention. Oh!"

"It was the Germans who treated you badly?"

"Of course!" Otto exclaimed, as if he were repeating the obvious. "That is what I ask you—why do you allow it? Why do you permit such things to happen?"

"Men of such low class, Herr Rondle!" Hilde brought the coffee over and set it on the table.

"Well, you can't blame us for what Germans do!" Howard scored a point triumphantly.

"Alas," Otto sighed. "My country has many such people. So mean, so revengeful—but that is what comes of putting communists and little people in positions of authority—why do the English ignore our cultured classes? But it is wrong to ask you such questions. An officer is an officer. An order is an order. Have you perhaps heard the story of the bowl of goldfish?"

"I have."

"Amusing, no? Now tell me, why do you not use ships to bring coal up to Hamburg?"

"Always politics!" Hilde passed Howard his cup and their eyes met as he took it. He experienced a pleasant little feeling of excitement. Her glance was as steady and unashamed as it was provocative. What a dish, he thought. "I hope you will like the coffee, Herr Rondle, it cost much money on the black market."

"Ah, what is money?" Otto said. His good humour had returned. "But there is a story which will amuse you. One of the black soldiers in the American Zone rings at the door of a flat in München, a great enormous fellow, and the German lady opens. Before she can say nothing he is in her sitting-room and he puts packets of cigarettes and chocolates on the table. All without speaking. Then he points to it and says to her in his deep voice. 'Foor-ein-bisschen-Libbe,' he means, 'For a liddle love.' She, the poor lady, is quite, quite terrified, she goes away from him saying, 'No, no, no!' and he comes towards her. She is alone. She will be ravished. She weeps and prays to him to go. The black man stops, he is surprised, he cannot understand. 'Have mercy on me!' she exclaims. And the black man shrugs his great shoulders, turns to the table and gathers up all the cigarettes and chocolate but for one small bar. 'Onne Libbe,' he says, that is, 'Wizzout love.' And he goes."

Otto shook with laughter.

"What, no rape?" Howard grinned.

"Is it not a good story?"

"A very good story."

"These so terrible black men," the girl said. "I am not able to understand why they are there."

"In the American Zone it is all unbelievable," Otto said. He had a curious trick of not blinking his eyes, as if he were trying to be hypnotic. "When they are not black men, they are Jews. And what is worse, German Jews. Yet our German girls go with them all. It is awful!"

It seemed to Howard that it was the Germans whom Otto was complaining about more than the British or the Americans, but he did not say so. The coffee was unsweetened, but well made; he was feeling very comfortable. On the wall in front of him, behind Otto's head, was a large gilt-framed picture of a mountain waterfall under the sombre sky which Howard associated with old and expensive works of art; it fascinated him for a moment, uneasily. The scene was vast and bleak; fir trees were like small feathers beside huge rocks. What a place to be lost in, he thought.

"You see this red swelling on my cheekbone?" Otto said. "That is from a Jewish soldier questioning me. Pah!"

"What for?" Howard asked.

"For having been a member of the Party. Such people should not be allowed to wear a soldier's uniform. I can tell you it's a relief to be in the British Zone. The English and the Germans are of the same type."

"Perhaps," Howard said, and hoped that the word sounded subtle. He thought indignantly of the German concentration camps—a hit on the cheek wasn't much to get annoyed about, after them. Of course, to take a broad view, there might be something in what Otto was saying. And he was admitting straight out that he was a Party member; that at least was honest; you could respect a man who did that. He said: "Of course you can understand a Jew feeling that way——"

"Why?" Otto asked. "I worked and fought for my country, as you do now. The best Germans are not those who refused to do either, Herr Rondle. You are an English officer. You must know how I feel."

"Oh, of course," Howard said. He was like a customer whose sales resistance has just collapsed, convincing himself that he has really made a bargain. It was obvious that this was an extremely pleasant couple, the sort of people you saw from your bus, in London, driving in large and comfortable cars. The feeling that they treated him as on their own social level pushed nationality, war and politics aside. He tried to look as though at home he was the owner of a Lagonda. This quality of furniture, the air of elegance, the oil paintings, were all things to which he also was accustomed. What a pity, he thought then, that he had only two cigarettes left

75

he felt very much like smoking one, but it was impossible with three of them round the table. And clearly there would be three until he left. His ideas about the girl had been preposterous. This was no tart. He asked a question, apologetically, which had been troubling him for some time:

"What do you do for a job?"

Otto laughed. "That is indeed the great question. My business is in textiles but because I am a former Party member I can do nothing. And yet I am a man of July 20th. Ridiculous!"

"He travels all about to retain his former associates. It is terrible. I am not easy for him when he travels."

"Textiles cannot make battleships," Otto said, fixing Howard again with his good humoured but unrelenting gaze. "Yet the Russians steal my warehouse and stock at Leipzig, the Americans allow me to do notting at Stuttgart and the English give permission for me to do a little, but make sure there shall be no coal for me to begin. For the moment there is still some money. But then what?"

"I expect things will improve," Howard said, and reflected that if they did Otto would be an independent, apparently prosperous business man, while he, Howard, returned to the semi-poverty of working as an underling at the office; but then, if the Germans really got going again, he might become Otto's English agent. It was an idea.

"And I am a secretary with—with Dr. Neumann, whom you have met at the party."

"You work?" He was surprised.

"Of course."

"The potato man?"

"Yes!" she giggled. "That is right! He is a very, very clever man."

"And what does he do?"

"He is a publisher."

"Oh." Howard was not interested.

"You are not fond of art and culture?"

"Not a lot."

"I do not understand the English," she said. "That they are so inartistic and without culture, and yet are of the Teutonic type. We, too, like to ride and hunt, but we also know languages, we must learn Goethe and Schiller and Shakespeare; and in England it is enough, I think, to ride and hunt."

"Oh, I don't know," Howard said. All his life he had spoken of English people who hunted, fished or shot with angry sarcasm, but now that he found himself classed with them, he made no attempt to deny it. He felt instead rather pleased. When he glanced at his watch and saw that it was gone three, it was with reluctance that he decided he must go and get some sleep.

They tried to persuade him to stay; but Howard was on his feet. He was starting in a new job, he had after all only seen his new colleagues off duty; it might be very different at work, and there was no sense in taking risks. He could remember so many army instructors, friendly, free and easy over cocoa and buns, who had been devils a minute later when the course was on. He must get back. Otto shook hands with him enthusiastically.

"It has been a great pleasure, sir." A depreciatory gesture round the room. "I am only sorry we must be like this."

Only the girl came with him to the door.

"Now where the hell is it I've got to go?"

"It is so simple. Kasselallee eighty-two. First right second left. Five minutes only. It is not so dark now; soon the birds will be heard."

"Well, thank you for the coffee."

"Oh, that was nothing. If you wish to come again, you will always be welcome."

"Thank you. Next time I'll try and bring something."

"Please. That is not necessary."

She smiled and pressed his hand. Howard leant forward to kiss her and checked himself. She did not appear to be expecting it. Or had he left too soon? She was immensely desirable. He released her hand with an effort and said: "Well, good-bye."

"Good-bye."

He heard the door close behind him as he reached the pavement. Outwardly the house was dead. Howard walked along, wondering. By the time he reached his bedroom he was convinced that he could have her for the asking. As he cleaned his teeth he paused and winked at his reflection in the shaving mirror.

CHAPTER 5

HOWARD stirred uncomfortably. He was hot, his mouth and throat were dry; he pulled the bedclothes round him closely. To move was horrible, to get up unthinkable. But he must get up, this was his first day; or else—God knows he had had countless rockets for being late in his army career —you never knew, some two-faced bastard would call it a poor show and he'd be off back to the battery. All the same, another minute, another two minutes would make no difference. Howard shivered in a small defiant ecstasy and refused to be conscious.

"Your tea, sir," the quiet voice said again.

Howard felt indignant as he gave way. Life was relentless; the few moments of pleasure you managed to experience were always cut short; for him if not for other people. He turned again, still holding the bedclothes tight, and opened his eyes, which began to ache at once, together with a pain that throbbed in the middle of his forehead. A German servant stood there, holding a cup of tea. Howard grunted unhappily.

"What's the time?"

"Five minutes before eight."

"God, it's early."

78

"Please, sir?" The German was a middle-aged man with silvery hair. He wore a perpetual frightened look.

"What's your name, old boy?"

"Please?"

"What are you called?"

"Ah, so. Doring."

"Doring, eh? Doring. I've got a bloody headache, Doring."

"I will get you somethings for it," Doring said, without hesitation. He spoke with great sympathy. He had been a waiter in a Hamburg restaurant until the war, then an unwilling and useless soldier. This job was the best he had ever held in his life. He laid down the cup on the bedside table, next to the photograph of Howard's fiancée. Then he bowed and retreated towards the door, backwards at first as though Howard were royalty. The latter was still half asleep. He felt worse now than when he had at last crawled into the bed four hours before. He blinked fiercely and then stretched out a hand to pick up the cup.

The first sip did him good. Now he took in the room again and in spite of his hangover he was able to chuckle. It certainly was comfortable. Nice to have a manservant, too; better than an English batman. Howard sipped his tea again and remembered the party. He chuckled again.

"What a performance!" he thought. It was worth a headache. Really, he could still hardly believe it. Of course, he knew that sort of thing went on. There had been gossip in the mess, scandalised stories in the English newspapers. But Howard had become used to the idea of being a reader, a spectator, one of the queue—"A natural sucker," he would say, almost enjoying the feeling of humiliation. The last thing he expected was to be present himself at any interesting event.

He looked at Mary's photograph and felt a tinge of guilt. An engaged man had no right to the thoughts he had had last night about the auburn haired girl. Hilde. And what was worse he had dreamt about her. "You dirty old dog," he said to himself. Mary was his girl. They were to be married on his demob. leave. He gazed into the grey and white eyes, which seemed so full of judgement and reproach. "I love you," he said. The photograph showed the top of her brown woollen jumper. A fur coat, a fur hat came into his mind, auburn hair across a forehead. It was irritating, like a tune you dislike but which keeps coming back.

Doring returned with a jug of hot water, which he poured into a bowl, one of three large pieces on a marble topped wash-table that stood against the wall. Then he brought over a white pill.

"You will be better in twenty minutes wiz it, sir."

"O.K. Thanks," Howard swallowed it gratefully. "Is breakfast over?"

"Oh, no, sir. You would like me to bring it up to you?"

"I think I'd better go down if it's still on." He still had the feeling that there would be a parade somewhere that he ought to attend.

Doring was a little disappointed. He could always take a piece of toast and a pat of butter if he brought a tray up, besides having the undoubted right to anything left over. He watched Howard force himself out of bed. Unshaven, with a body that might have been powerful but was beginning to go to seed and pyjamas that had shrunk, the officer was not a pretty sight. Doring bowed and left the room. Outside, Hammond, the batman, was looking round with his superintending air.

"Good morning, Jimmie," Doring said, with a frightened smile of respect.

"Morning Hansy, how's yourself?"

"Oh, it is all right."

"How's the new officer?"

"All right."

"You looked after him all right? He's satisfied?"

"Yes, Jimmie."

"O.K. Scram."

Hammond knocked at Howard's door and entered. The new officer was shaving. Hammond inspected his baggage, his pyjamas and shaving equipment, a process completed in a second. He was not impressed.

"Good morning, sir. Everything satisfactory?"

"Good morning." Howard looked at him in surprise, unused to such hotel-like attention. "Yes, fine."

"If there's anything you want, just let me know, sir. I'm Hammond. I'm giving you Doring to look after you, I think you'll find he's satisfactory. If not, let me know, sir. I don't let them slack, sir."

Talkative type, Howard reflected. He went on shaving.

"I understand you're new to Hamburg, sir. If there's anything I can help you in, just let me know. I've been here all the time."

"What about a decent mattress?" Howard asked. There was something patronising about the batman's attitude which he resented.

"Mattresses very short, sir. Very difficult to get."

"You can get me one."

"I can try, sir, I don't think it's likely."

Howard was furious, but he remembered something else.

"Do you know anything about the N.A.A.F.I. rations? I missed mine coming away."

"That was yesterday, sir. I generally get them. I don't know whether you can have this week's. I mean you weren't on the indent, you see."

Hammond watched the redness spread over the back of Howard's neck. He was merely fencing to see how much the officer would take and what was the best method of dealing with him. They came and they went and by now he had become an experienced judge of character. He had developed clearly defined attitudes to the members of the mess. Outwardly respectful to all, he took no notice of the women. Now and then one of them would ask him surreptitiously, but with a false air of confidence, if he would sell a bottle of Schlichte for them; he normally obliged. He had little to do with the civilian men; they looked after themselves and in any case spoke German, so that they could give Hammond points if they chose. As to the army officers, whom he regarded wisely as his main concern, he acted as a black market agent for the major when the latter required it, and he was respectfully efficient to Hemsleigh and Styles. They were the only soldiers in the whole outfit; but he did not entirely understand their refusal to touch the market, nor was it very convenient, for both had threatened him with the sack if they caught him operating; the incredible thing was that two men who really had been in the war could be so blind to what was going on. "There's the hell of a lot of talk about it," he had heard Styles say, "but I'm inclined to believe pretty few chaps really do it." They perpetually worried for the good name of the occupation. Bloody marvellous, Hammond thought. Charlie Morton, now, was altogether different, he liked him but he was never quite at ease; he had the feeling that the officer was a jump ahead all the time.

"I can probably fix it so's you get them, sir. I'll see what I can do, sir." He could almost watch the relief creep into Howard's neck.

"Good oh," the latter said. He was at once very friendly. "See what you can do, old boy."

"I take your laundry every Wednesday, sir, there's a woman up the road does it for a couple of fags a week, if that's all right with you."

"Good lord, yes."

"I don't know whether you're short of marks, sir——" He waited to see if there would be any reaction. There was not. Howard merely finished his shave and began to wipe the soap. A similar remark to Hemsleigh and he had at once been told to get out. "If you are, sir, I can always get you some. It saves trouble."

"I've got enough dough, I think," Howard replied. "There's never anything to spend it on, is there? I've got about a hundred still."

"Very good, sir," Hammond said, puzzled. "Well, sir, if you want anything——"

"I'll knock three times and ask for you, old boy. Righty-ho."

Hammond glanced at the bottle of Pernod on the table, recognised it as Miss Blandison's and left him to dress.

Howard was surprised to find himself one of the first down to breakfast. Miss Hackster, Mrs. Pratt, Miss Blandison and Mr. Maxton-Hill were the only mess members present. The other places were untouched. They all looked at him as though they were astonished to see him at all.

"Welcome!" said Mr. Maxton-Hill. "How nice to see you so fresh and early."

"I thought I'd be late," Howard said. "Er—good morning, everyone."

"Good morning." Miss Hackster sat at the head of the table. She spoke with bright condescension.

"Good morning," said Mrs. Pratt. "Did you sleep well?"

"Well, but not long enough." Howard sat down cheerfully next to her and a waiter at once put a plate of porridge in front of him. "I need more than four hours beauty sleep, I must say, and I've a head on me like a sack of hot potatoes."

"We give you our pity," said Mr. Maxton-Hill. He sounded uncomfortable, and Howard was suddenly aware of a tension in the atmosphere. Kay Blandison, who had not spoken to him, wore an expression of iron. Mary had once looked just like that when he had kept her waiting too long. There seemed to be a long pause in the conversation, as if his entrance had caused it. The porridge was almost uneatable, but he stared down at it grimly. It was clear that in the present company frat parties were not a subject for discussion.

"Pratt," said Miss Hackster, "I do believe I left my handkerchief in my bedroom. How very annoying." She moved her chair back a little, expectantly.

"Oh, Sybil, I'll run up for you, I've had all I want and you're not finished."

"No Pratt, really, I simply can't have——"

But the table had already been shaken by Mrs. Pratt getting up, spilling Howard's coffee as she did so.

"No, Sybil, you stay just where you are."

"One would offer oneself," said Mr. Maxton-Hill, "if a lady's bedroom were not verbotenes Land——"

"So many offers of assistance!" Miss Hackster smiled, delighted. "I remember once wanting to move my deck chair on the Lido and so many people wanted to do it for me that the Contessa said, 'Sybil, there must be something divine about your personality!'" The tension in the room was over. Mrs. Pratt came back holding the handkerchief and received a gracious smile of thanks; she sat down like a schoolgirl who has received a compliment in front of the class. Miss Hackster asked: "Mr. Randle, do you know Italy?"

"I'm afraid not."

"How sad. Mr. Maxton-Hill and myself are both confirmed Italy lovers, while Pratt is a Francophile. Another adherent would have really tilted the scales against her!"

"The most I've been abroad is a week at Ostend."

He had been given his chance, but it would not come again. Miss Hackster closed her eyes as if to ward off something unpleasant, then smiled graciously again, "What a pity; one misses so much if one never lives out of England; one develops such a much more intensely broad-minded outlook—even Pratt in her dreadful Brittany!" Mrs. Pratt uttered a mouse-like squeak of pleasure. "But here is Mr. Hopwood. Here is an ally for you, Mr. Randle. A true little Englander."

Mr. Hopwood came in and sat down next to Kay who gave him a beaming smile.

"And how's Hoppy this morning?"

"Not too dusty, Kay."

"Hoppy has been here for two months," said Mr. Maxton-Hill to Howard, in the prevailing mood, "and he still can't get over the fact that Hamburg must have been a bigger port than Hull."

"There they go, pooling my leg again," Mr. Hopwood said, winking at Howard.

Breakfast continued happily. Miss Hackster told Mrs. Pratt another story about something the Contessa had said to her. Mr. Hopwood asked Howard if he had slept well and the latter answered carefully with the two words: "Yes, thanks." This time no harm appeared to be done. Miss Blandison, however, continued rather pointedly to ignore him. Mr. Maxton-Hill said that no one who had not seen a Venetian sunset could be said to have lived. Busch came in to whisper to Miss Hackster that the car had arrived.

"Thank you, Busch."

It was a signal for a general pushing back of chairs. Miss Hackster and Mrs. Pratt both produced small scraps of paper in which they wrapped the toast that they had not touched, after spreading it thinly with margarine. Kay Blandison did exactly the same, but she waited until the other two were out of the room and was rather more generous with the margarine. In this way they added to the rations of their German staff at the office. Then she followed them.

"A cigarette while the ladies prepare themselves?" Mr. Maxton-Hill offered his packet.

"Oh, thanks." Howard took one. "I say, what do you suggest I do—I mean, I suppose I ought to come along with you?"

"By all means. In what capacity have you joined our illustrious division?"

"I haven't the faintest."

"Do you speak German?"

"Not a word."

"You are an economist, an historian?"

"Old boy, I couldn't know less. I'm a stooge."

"The authorities have clearly moved with their usual uncanny precision, eh, Hoppy?"

"Looks lark it," Mr. Hopwood chuckled. "But doan't be worried about it, Mr. Rundle. We'll be very happy to have you with us." He overflowed with good nature. It was as impossible not to like him as it was to be impressed by him. He was the sort of man who would always stand in for an inconvenient duty or be over careful to pay for a round of drinks, friendly and helpful to the lonely and neglected in his own

85

hour of need. "We're a very happy little mess," he went on. "All things considered."

"What sort of racket is it?" Howard asked. "If you've got to be an economist, I may as well pack and go back to my bloody unit."

"I will explain," said Mr. Maxton-Hill. There was nothing he liked to do more. He made conversation with enthusiasm, using long phrases with the amiable sarcasm of a preparatory school master (which he had once been). "We belong, proudly and loyally, to the Control Commission for Germany, British Element, a body separate from the august Army of the Rhine of which you have so far been a member. Sociology Division is a section of the Control Commission along with other departments such as, to take a few random examples, Monuments, Fine Arts and Archives or Posts, Telegraphs and Telephones or Highways and Highway Transport or Coal Control. We differ from these admirable departments in so far as our purpose is not so much operational as advisory. We consider such aspects of the occupation as our respected director, Mr. Johnson Trant, considers would benefit from a Sociology Division report and we make that report. We also differ in that we are responsible only to headquarters; merely local Military Government detachments are to us as chicken feed. Since this is the only Sociology Division office in the whole zone you may well ask why we are in Hamburg and not at headquarters. I need hardly say there is an answer. Other branches were planned, nay, are still planned, but as yet this is the only one; the result of that is that our director must spend most of his time in the mysterious towns of Bad Oeynhausen, Bünde and Herford, where the greatest decisions and most solemn decrees are enacted."

"I see." Howard was still not clear exactly what the office did, but he was highly impressed by the speech.

"I will now sketch lightly the personnel side. Certain people were selected in London as being suitably qualified for aspects of the work. Mr. Johnson Trant is an eminent zoologist, a clear indication that he was the man to lead

86

sociological investigation, since he would bring a mind fresh and unprejudiced by previous work or experience in the subject. One must admit that there is a very fair analogy between a zoo and our beloved zone, to say nothing of its occupiers; one presumes that this was the principle on which he was sent."

At this Mr. Hopwood, who had heard the speech often before, rose, stretched himself and walked out. Mr. Maxton-Hill lowered his voice. "To proceed; dear Hoppy, whom all love, is a bluff stocky little Yorkshireman who was a failure as a textile engineer in his own country and was, therefore, sent out to advise Germans on how to succeed in theirs; he is now the Sociology Division's expert in the subject. Our doyenne, Miss Hackster, is a charming and cultured woman, against whom one can say nothing; dear Pratt, her assistant, is a sweet person against whom one would hate to say anything; but what sociological qualification either has neither I nor any other can tell you. One could go on and take my own case, but fortunately we are summoned."

Mr. Maxton-Hill rose. Howard followed him out, puzzled. He wanted to ask where Charlie Morton and the others were. In the hall the ladies were busy putting on their khaki or blue greatcoats. Suddenly Hemsleigh and Styles arrived downstairs, chorussed an unenthusiastic "Good morning," to which there was hardly an answer, and went out through the front door. Howard saw them jump into a shabby but powerful looking American sports coupé and drive off. Two Volkswagens, the small austere beetle-like peoples' car, were also waiting, together with the Mercedes Benz in which Howard had arrived the previous evening. The breakfast party climbed into the Volkswagens, murmuring politenesses to one another and observing a strict rule of procedure. Miss Hackster sat in the front seat of the first, accompanied by Mrs. Pratt and Mr. Maxton-Hill in the rear; Kay Blandison in the front seat of the second and behind her Mr. Hopwood and Howard. Both cars had German drivers, who had greeted the party with respectful salutes and an air of warm affection. Miss

Hackster's car drove off and the second was about to follow when Hammond came rushing down the steps.

"You can have these for your free ration, sir." He handed a round tin of cigarettes through the car's window to Howard.

"Well, thank you very much."

"That's all right, sir."

They were off. Mr. Hopwood and Miss Blandison decided that it was a raw day. Howard was conscious that she was still ignoring him and he wondered if after all he had been unwise to antagonise her by going to the party. However, he was pleased by Hammond's action over the cigarettes; the batman clearly recognised that he was not a man to stand any nonsense.

He pressed his face to the window and looked out on to the street scene. A party of workmen were pulling down a tree, an old man looked inside a rubbish bin, three or four little girls walked along hand in hand, singing a German song in squeaky unison. They passed through what had once been a busy shopping street; though unbombed it was almost as depressing as an area that had been destroyed. Postage stamps and small useless stationery articles were the only goods for sale; the bread and meat and newspapers had gone hours before. The Volkswagen joined the stream of military cars crossing the Lombard Bridge. There was something tantalising about the skyline round the inner lake. From the bridge it looked so calm and prosperous. The former offices of the Hamburg-Amerika line, the Dresdner Bank, the Woolworths looked no different across the water than they had before nineteen-thirty-nine. They passed the smart whiteness of Shell House, the office of the Town Major, and then up the Esplanade, where at number six two sentries and a corporal indicated Military Government headquarters. At the top on the right was the Esplanade Hotel, which now served as an extension building for more Military Government offices. A semi-circle of army cars stood parked in front, the only sign that inside there were no waiters serving breakfast, no chambermaids, pageboys or smooth receptionists.

The Volkswagen had to pause for the traffic light at the top of the Esplanade and then to wait for three tram cars, locked together to form a train, which turned slowly down the street, overflowing with a silent mass of passengers. The Volkswagen hurried across the crossroads and up past the Renaissance-style, nineteenth century post office. On their right was the Dammtor railway station, miserable with dirt and smashed windows, busy with thousands of travellers like a cheese being eaten out by maggots. The Volkswagen turned left across the tramlines that ran down the centre of the street, went through an alley, turned into a smaller street on the other side and pulled up in front of a house where the first car was already standing. A small, neatly painted board read: "Sociology Division Control Commission for Germany (British Element)."

"Eh, well, lad, here we are," Mr. Hopwood said. "Nicely tooked away from anyone else, as you see."

"When will the major arrive?" Howard asked. Kay Blandison had already swept ahead of them into the building, still dramatically annoyed. "I mean, what the hell am I to do? Is there some easy job, old boy?"

"Talking of jobs, no," Mr. Hopwood replied. "Teake my own case. Ahm concerned with textiles. That means ah've got to know me trade. Otherwise these cheeky German fellows roon rings round you. Ah think you'll have to join Hemsleigh and Styles on the liaison side. Best thing is to get fixed oop with a desk before the director returns and then noabody will say nowt. Good morning, Leo." He nodded to the bent old man who sat in the porter's cabin inside the front porch of the house. The old man stood up and bowed, trembling with agitation. They passed on. "Ah expect Leo will try to be a nuisance to you, so ah advise you to be firm with him from start. He'll try and sell you summat and he'll want to have your cigarette ends and so on. You'll have to stipulate to him that he can only have your ashtray at lunchtime and at end of day. Ootherwise he'll coom in pestering every time he thinks you've strook a match."

"I met a chap in textiles last night," Howard said. "Otto somebody. Complaining about it being difficult to get started."

"Eh, they never stop complaining. They think we're a welfare service coom special t'put them back on easy street."

"What happens on the ground floor?" Howard asked, for Mr. Hopwood was already leading him upstairs. The sound of several typewriters came through a half open door.

"Group surveys section. That's roon by Miss Hackster. She and Mrs. Pratt have their office at the back and the front two rooms are for the files and the German staff. Fifteen girls. Ah advise you not to go in if you can help it. What with no soap and the consequent application of cheap scent the atmosphere's a bit peculiar."

"Thanks for the tip," Howard grinned. He glanced at a door on which was a notice: British Personnel Only.

"That's our W.C." They turned upstairs again from the small landing and reached the first floor. "There's the director's office, Major Cardington and general administration, Mr. Maxton-Hill, and myself, the one with the glass-fronted door at end. Ah'll take you oop to Hemsleigh and Styles, though."

"Thank you very much."

"It's nothing, ahm only too glad to help, lad."

They went up to the second floor, where Mr. Hopwood continued, "Here's Mr. Hamilton, heavy industries, Miss Ford, light industries, Mr. Schrœder, statistics, Miss Blandison, agriculture and Captain Morton, religion."

"Religion?"

"Aye, and here's where I'll leave you." Mr. Hopwood knocked on a door, to which was a pinned a notice: "General Liaison—Captain Hemsleigh, M.C., Captain Styles, M.C." and he rather nervously opened it and intruded his head.

"Lads, ah've brought you Mr. Rundle. Perhaps you can give him summat to do."

"Good God, Hoppy, don't be ridiculous," said a voice.

Mr. Hopwood opened the door wide and stood aside for Howard to go in, which the latter did rather hesitantly; it did not sound as though he were being welcomed with any great warmth. He found himself in a small over-heated room with a large window. The two captains sat opposite each other at wooden tables, each equipped with in and out trays, blotters, pens, ink and a pile of English newspapers. Howard took in their rows of medals, long hair and suede shoes and he was at once conscious of an unusually deep feeling of inferiority. However, their expressions were friendly.

"We can't possibly give you anything to do," Hemsleigh said, in his very deep voice. "But do sit down and be comfortable."

There was a visitor's chair in between the two tables.

"Have a cigarette," said Styles.

"Well, thanks, old boy. But I've just got my free issue."

"I've got hundreds, honestly."

Howard took one from the gold cigarette case that Styles offered. The cigarette was of the more expensive, thicker than normal kind.

"Where do you get these from?"

"A little shop in Shepherd's Market. They're awfully good to me. They send me a thousand a month."

"Oh," Howard murmured, as he calculated what the cost of this luxurious arrangement must be. He added, using all his capacity for saying the wrong thing. "I suppose you make a small fortune out of it?"

"Good God, no!" Styles exclaimed. He had flushed pink with anger. "Certainly not."

"Sorry, old boy, no offence——"

"I take every kind of offence. I'm afraid I regard everyone who deals on the black market as a cheap bloody crook and if that includes you, Randle, I'm sorry. I think I'm speaking for Mike Hemsleigh as well."

"You certainly are, John."

"But, look here——" Howard protested.

"If there's one thing that's ruining the whole British name it's this shady revolting battening on some other poor devil's wretchedness. The Americans, the Russians and everyone else may be ten times worse and very probably are, but we shouldn't do it. That's my opinion. Isn't it yours, Mike?"

"Every inch, John."

Howard was by now red in the face, thinking bitterly that here it was again, the curse of misunderstanding which dogged him always and kept him down.

"Well, I've never sold a bloody thing for your information," he exclaimed, enjoying his crudeness. "So there's no need to carry on like that."

"My dear chap I'm most frightfully sorry," said Styles, unperturbed, but very much more amiable. "But it was you that inferred that I did, so I really think it was quite reasonable that I should infer that you did—what do you say, Mike?"

"Oh, I agree," said Hemsleigh. "It was all right, really, I think, but one's terribly sorry if you took it the wrong way."

Howard laughed.

"No offence taken where none meant, old boy."

There was a slight pause during which Hemsleigh and Styles tried to weigh him up. Howard looked out of the window pleased with the apologies he had received.

"Didn't I see you at the party last night?" Hemsleigh asked.

"Yes, I was there." He was about to add, "Didn't you see me carried out, old boy?" but he was not sure whether it would be well received.

"Rather dismal, didn't you think?"

"Well, I wouldn't have said dismal, exactly."

"I always find it depressing to look at all the girls in their party frocks. Don't you think there's something rather pathetic about it? I mean that they're all remnants, what's been saved from the deluge, and there'll never be any more new ones—not while they're young, anyhow."

"They didn't sound very miserable to me."

"Exactly. They do put up a pretty wonderful performance, don't they? Rather like the women who wash the front door-step when they're living in the basement of a ruined house."

"Are you actually posted to us?" Styles asked.

"Yes, I don't know why and nor did the major I met last night."

"Oh, lord!" Hemsleigh laughed. "Hugo Cardington wouldn't know. He's only supposed to run the office administration and deal with things like postings, I mean it's not reasonable to think that he'd know, is it? His clerk'll know, though. We might ask him."

"I can't think what I could possibly do," Howard said. "But I'd like to stay, I don't want to go back to my unit."

"Really? John Styles and I were only saying yesterday that we would, weren't we, John?"

"Yes, Mike. Damn good idea, I think."

"I tell you what, John, that was very interesting about your cigarettes; I mean the way you flared and he flared up, you thought he was black and he thought you were black. I expect roughly that incident will be repeated a hundred times today in Hamburg. The point is neither you nor he were black. Which proves our point again that the real proportion doing it must be minute!"

"Sound arguing, Mike. What do you think, Randle?"

"Well, I heard it going on in the mess last night——" Howard grinned.

"Yes, but of course Charlie's just a crook, I mean he's a very good chap, but he's a natural scrounger and you expect him to do it, not that he ought to. It's when Hugo Cardington does it or when Miss Hackster, say, gets Hammond to sell a bottle of her N.A.A.F.I. wine allowance, that is, when people whom you expect to be normally honest, who at home are normally honest, I mean just normal—when those sort of people do it that the thing really stinks."

"That's if you call Miss Hackster normal, John."

"For this point only."

"She's exactly the sort of person I'd expect to do a lot of miserable cheating under the counter with the local butcher so that she swindles all the housewives waiting outside in the queue, to go off home and eat a fat steak, and then eagerly sign some appeal to send rationed food to starving displaced

93

persons and consider herself broad-minded, left wing and humanitarian."

"Oh, exactly. By the way, Randle, what's your name?"

"Howard."

"I hope you'll loathe Miss Hackster as much as we do, Howard."

Howard was always prepared to loathe anybody, and he chuckled; he was rather dazed by the flow of words that the two captains poured out. All the same he was glad that they considered him a friend in the matter of the black market, about which they felt so deeply. For the moment conversation had ceased, Styles passed across a three days old copy of the *Daily Express* and they all read the newspapers. Howard did so without taking in a word. For once he was not regretting that he was not in on the racket. Styles and Hemsleigh were enthusiastic earnest young men, clearly of a high social status, and it occurred to Howard that to be friendly with them might be the best investment of all. It was by knowing people that you got a decent job in civil life; certainly not by hard work or merit. "Oh, yes, Randle," he could hear one of them saying in a few months' time, "damn good chap, knew him in Hamburg, he wasn't on the black market, I think we could use him." When this little dream was finished, Howard began to feel bewildered again. He still had no job here and neither Styles nor Hemsleigh seemed to be moving to introduce him to the major's clerk who was supposed to know everything. The atmosphere of concentration continued. Finally Howard coughed.

"Where do you think I'll find this clerk?" he said hesitantly. Styles looked up.

"My dear chap, I wouldn't hurry about that."

"I was thinking the major might have arrived by now——"

"I shouldn't worry about Hugo."

Howard was not entirely reassured, but he did not like to assert himself and leave the room. He sighed, crossed his legs and looked over the top of the *Daily Express* and out of the window at a notice on the building opposite. It read:

"Drückerei." Suddenly he could hear Charlie Morton's and Kay Blandison's voices mixed up in a nearby room. There was a knock on the door and the suave grinning young man who had let them in at the party the night before entered.

"Good morning, sir, good morning, sir."

"Morning, Scholle," Hemsleigh said.

Herr Scholle, who was dressed this morning in a green hunting suit, selected two sheaves of paper from a pile that he was carrying and put one on each table. He said, "Please, sir," bowed and left.

"Here you are," Styles said, handing his copy to Howard. "One sample of the work of the firm. It ought to be marked 'Handle without care.' Twenty closely typed pages on the development and use of the tractor on Schleswig-Holstein farms under National Socialism. That's from our Miss Blandison's department."

"Good Lord!" Howard looked at it with horror. "Do you have to know this sort of thing?"

"My dear chap, of course not. Nor does our Miss Blandison, although that may be slander. Actually Mike and I are about the hardest workers around here—that's except for Johnson Trant, the boss, and Bonzo Hamilton; they're both geniuses and work like mad, nobody knows what at, but they're the real brains of the outfit, I mean, for all one knows, they may be doing some active good. Don't you agree, Mike?"

"Pretty fair, John."

"The other people, you see, Howard—I'm referring to the civilians—they all put up a colossal show of working long hours, writing memos, cataloguing this and that and all sorts of nonsense, but they're all resting on German labour. Now Mike and I do our own job, which is (a) liaison personal—running off to some Mil Gov office when Bonzo or Johnson wants us to and soft-soaping somebody and (b) the main thing which is keeping the office in touch with what's on in England. We read the newspapers and mark out all the bits which the different departments ought to read, send them downstairs and somebody types them out into a coherent report. Actually

95

the job was our own invention, because there didn't seem much liaising to do. Pretty good idea, don't you think?"

Howard nodded. Their brief spasm of newspaper reading was now over. They were looking at him attentively. Since something was expected of him, he asked, "What's the German staff like, then?"

"They're like the Germans everywhere else," said Hemsleigh, smoothing his dark moustache. "Fantastically conceited, fantastically engrossed in self pity, fantastically class conscious, oh, God, what a bunch! There are variations of course. Some are pleasant to talk to and look at, some are dear old souls like old Fräulein Brosch——"

"And some are reptilian like Herr Scholle. He's a nasty, lecherous little black marketeer, one of the worst. We caught him once in front of the Waterloo cinema, dressed up in down and out clothes for some obscure purpose, and when he saw us, my God, didn't he disappear——"

"He was at the party last night, surely?" Howard said.

"At it? He practically runs those things."

"But even though they are so fantastic," Hemsleigh went on, "you've got to treat them as normal people. After all they might even be normal people if they'd had half a chance. I hate the business of treating them as natives. There was a wonderful man in the Atlantic the other day who'd just come back from Nuremburg and he was saying how he had the feeling when he crossed from the American to the British zone how much better behaved and altogether nicer 'our' Germans were. That sort of thing's ruinous. On the other hand, there's nothing so fascinating as watching Germans, I think, don't you? John and I have got our tables like this so that we can look down into the alley."

"Couldn't be more fascinating," Styles said. "You watch them come through and pay business calls on those offices, wearing super slick city suits, little trilbys and padded shoulders and you wonder what point there is in business in a ruin, or how they can possibly try and carry on in the old way. It's baffling. And what's in their minds?"

96

Howard shook his head. Both the captains seemed to be very worked up.

"Although, really, Mike, it's best at a concert. Götterdämmerung above all. When you see them pacing up and down in the interval, never speaking, looking ahead, eighty per cent. of them women and half the men minus limbs or eyes. Are they just thinking about their rations and the black market or are they remembering? So short a time ago the place was filled with glamorous uniforms, the women had their men——"

"And what do they think of us? That's the other basic question, John. What do they think of the self-satisfied, cigarette smoking little group of Englishmen and women who stand on the steps leading to their box, watching them all? Do they really think we take their food or is it just a line? If they really thought that, why are almost all of them so eager to help you, so polite and generous to you if you go to their homes? One can't really dismiss it as a sort of deep and subtle trick."

"I'm sure myself they hate us bitterly," Styles said.

"But only the so-called upper classes, although it's they who pretend to be more friendly. They think we've let them down."

"But I don't suppose they're able to believe we'll let them down, really, in the end. Germans can't read obvious signs."

"My God, how true that is."

"But anyhow they're absolutely fascinating to watch."

"Fascinating," Hemsleigh said. He looked rather sharply at Howard, for the latter wore a dazed expression. "Don't you agree?" he asked him.

"Oh, yes!" Howard replied. "You know I really think I ought to see about my job."

"But of course, my dear chap. Though Hugo wouldn't mind if you took a week's holiday first. He'll probably suggest it."

"Well, it would suit me." Howard chuckled with astonishment. "The place sounds like a home from home. How the hell do you get away with it?"

"You mean how does Hugo get away with it? John Styles and I work like the devil. So do most departments. So does most of the Control Commission. But Hugo gets away with it, Charlie Morton gets away with it, you can get away with it if you want to because, my dear chap, we're living in a totalitarian régime and that means there must be corners which aren't cleaned out where people can play around. People don't seem to realise that bureaucracy is the path to freedom. The poets are in the ministries, Howard; it's the so-called individualist, the stockbroker, the business man, the lawyer, who's afraid to grow his hair too long because of what people will say."

Howard nodded, uncertain whether he was meant to laugh or merely to agree. He fingered his tin of cigarettes nervously.

"Anyhow," Hemsleigh continued, "it's a damned good thing to have another army officer in this building who's not on the black——"

Howard looked complacent. Styles picked up his telephone and said, "I'll just get on to Hugo for you, that's if he's arrived."

"Of course it's extraordinarily hard to keep out of it," Hemsleigh went on. "It was only the day before yesterday I changed a cheque for some marks with a German friend of mine—she's got a relative in England so I send him the cheque —it was for seventy-five pounds, I think—and she wanted to give me a hundred pounds' worth of marks! It was all I could do to persuade her that I just wanted the proper rate of exchange."

"Amazing," Howard said, swallowing, taken aback by the casual way seventy-five pounds had been mentioned. He watched Styles at the telephone with some misgiving. He had noted before that people who could write large cheques without worrying were apt to enjoy rather greater freedom than others. The door behind him opened and to his concern Styles put the receiver down at once. Elizabeth Ford had come in. The captains smiled at her politely. Of the four women at the mess she was the youngest and most attractive.

"Morning, Elizabeth."

"Morning, John, morning, Mike, want something to read?" She was carrying a pile of papers similar to Herr Scholle's. "This one's taken us four months. It's Dr. Schellinghorn's baby and he's tremendously excited about it. Ruhrgebiet survey number six: elemental occupations. Thrilling!" She handed one to each and smiled at Howard. "How did you enjoy the party?"

"Dismal," said Hemsleigh. "All Charlie's parties are. There's such an atmosphere of conscious fratting, which I can't stand."

"Yes," Elizabeth said, "that's exactly how I feel." She paused at the door, looking pleased. "By the way there's something most amusing happening downstairs. Johnson's rung up from Bad Oeynhausen to say they're getting Friedeberg out from London and Bonzo's livid, he told Johnson he'd resign and he's now in the middle of ringing up about four brigadiers. I couldn't be more amused. See you later."

"God, they're all alike," said Styles, as she closed the door. "The antipathy these refugees have for each other far outweighs their hatred of the Nazis. No wonder the Germans can't stand them."

"But one can't help feeling sorry for them." Hemsleigh placed his new set of papers on top of Herr Scholle's, initialled them both and put them in his out-tray. "It's all very well to look critically from our own solid background. Bonzo's all right now, of course, he's an official, legal Englishman, he doesn't give a damn, but the others—are you going, old chap?"

Howard had stood up in desperation. He grinned sheepishly. "A call to nature, old boy."

"Use the one on this landing, then, there's a good chap. It's marked 'for German staff' and John and I always use it on principle. One really must protest against racial discrimination in lavatories."

In the passage outside Howard came face to face with Kay Blandison, who astonished him by lowering her eyes and gliding past him, whispering as she did so, "Feeling better?" He was still pondering this change of front as he went downstairs, when Charlie Morton caught him up.

"Howard, I've been looking for you everywhere! Did you get back all right last night? The old crow's feet are looking a bit marked."

"I got back."

"Running out on me like that, I didn't know what to think."

"Running out on you, my foot! You left me stranded——"

"Where are you going now—off to get stranded again?"

"I'm hoping to see the major and find out what my job is."

They were outside the door on the first floor landing, marked: "Major H. Cardington." Charlie Morton linked his arm firmly with Howard's.

"I'll fix that for you. Come on in." He rapped on the door with his free arm, opened it and pushed Howard in. The major was sitting at his desk, concentrating on a large sheet of paper. "Hugo," Charlie Morton said. "Hugo!"

"Oh, hullo, Charlie, leave me alone, there's a dear."

"Hugo, Randle here wants to know what his job is."

The major looked up, full of apology.

"I'm sorry, I didn't see you come in, I—I was busy fixing up my children's party. Magda's bothering me about it," he explained to Charlie. "Well, Randle, you see it's not really my pigeon to give you a job. Couldn't you wait a few days until Johnson Trant turns up again?"

"Hugo, you're missing your chance!" Charlie said, before Howard could answer. "This is a heavenly gift for you—he can be your P.A.! Deputy administrative officer! Think of the work you'll save——"

"It's not half a bad idea, Charlie," the major said thoughtfully. "But why all this concern for me?"

"Don't go getting ideas, Hugo. I'm not thinking of you, I'm trying to fix up my buddy. He's a dynamo for work."

"Well, Johnson will have to agree——"

"It's sold!" Charlie slapped Howard's back triumphantly,

and hurried him out of the room before the major could say any more. "God, I'm brilliant."

"I hope it's all right," Howard said. He was rather resenting his companion's high powered methods, which gave him no opportunity of offering his own opinions; all the more as he had none, but could only let himself be swayed as usual by whatever stronger personality was around. "When he's quite finished messing me about!" he thought. All he could do in protest was to look sullen. But Charlie was quite unconscious of that. They stood still for a moment in the passage, while he dry-shaved his chin with his hand and considered the next move in Howard's career. Suddenly a door opened and Mr. Hamilton came out.

"Wotcher, Bonzo," Charlie said.

"You know what they haf tried to do?" Mr. Hamilton exclaimed in a voice filled with disgust. "They were going to send Friedeberg! I've just been on to London and stopped it. Who do they think I am?" He disappeared into another door. Charlie tugged at Howard's arm.

"Right, we'll go and see Clayton, Hugo's clerk. He'll be working for you now."

They passed Major Cardington's room and entered the next office, interrupting two German typists and a British corporal. All three were at work. Charlie Morton introduced Howard. The girls, who had the fluffy prettiness favoured by the major, giggled, and the corporal stood up and shook hands. He was a quiet spectacled young man. "Hope I'll get something signed on time now sir," he said.

"Where can Mr. Randle have an office, Clayton?"

"I could throw Professor Heindorn out from next door, sir. Meantime he could go into Mr. Trant's secretary's room. It's empty."

"Fine. Where's Scholle?"

"In the building somewhere, sir. Shall I get him?"

"It doesn't matter, I just wanted to show him to Mr. Randle."

"When he comes back I'll send him along, sir. That's

if you're going to your office now, sir? I'll just show you it."

"O.K. corporal, I'll show Mr. Randle."

Charlie led the way back along the passage and through another door, marked: 'Mr. Johnson Trant, Enquiries, Secretariat.' This opened into an office severely furnished with filing cabinets and two typist's tables, one of which he immediately whirled into the centre of the room and, placing a chair behind it, he invited Howard to sit down.

"There you are, my boy. All set."

"I'm very grateful," Howard said, with heavy sarcasm.

"Now listen, Howard, this has been a very cute move. If there's one thing been lacking about this institution, it's been the scarcity of duty-free labels. Like a hawk that corporal guards them! And now—after a suitable interval of a couple of days—you do! Am I smart or just clever?"

Howard understood and he was shocked. Duty-free labels were the best possible cover for sending things back to England, dodging customs examination and other embarrassing probes. They were allowed so that soldiers could occasionally send small gifts of limited value without having to pay duty on them and they were meant to be strictly rationed. Charlie Morton's intentions were quite clear. If Howard were in charge instead of an honest corporal, the field was open. He tried to formulate an acid reply. The spirit of Styles and Hemsleigh was still strong in him. Under no circumstances was he going to play this game. Charlie had mistaken his man.

However there was a knock at the door and Herr Scholle came in.

"Good morning, Captain Morton. Z' corporal would be glad if Herr Randle would sign these papers."

"All right," Howard said.

"Scholle," Charlie said, putting his hand on the German's shoulder, "you met Mr. Randle last night, didn't you? A great guy this Scholle, Howard. Cherish him and he will cherish you. Isn't that right, Scholle?"

Herr Scholle smiled and bowed. He placed some type-written returns in front of Howard and murmured, "Is there anything else, sir?"

When he had gone, closing the door softly, Charlie shook with merriment.

"Did you see the hungry eyes as he looked at your tin of fags? You shouldn't be so cruel and obvious, Howard. He'll give you two-fifty for that lot, soon as wink."

"He will not," Howard said hotly. "My God, I wouldn't think of it."

"You'd be wise. Just feed him ten a time. Well, I must be getting back to my desk. I've got a couple of tame professors fretting for me to sign things. What say I call for you just before lunch and we have a quick one at the Atlantic?"

The door slammed behind him and Howard could hear his footsteps hurrying upstairs. He stared down at the papers in front of him, telling himself that he was indignant. What damned impudence to assume he would do that sort of thing —Styles and Hemsleigh had assessed his character far more exactly. "I may be a sucker, but at least I'm honest," he told himself grimly. There was the prestige of a British officer to consider moreover. No, he wasn't going to do any black marketing. Besides, what would Mary say? She was very correct in that sort of thing.

Irritated, Howard began to tear open his cigarette tin. A moment later, as he smoked, he reflected that there was of course the point that if he did save money out here, it would make things all the easier for Mary.

After all, it was a little different if you could write out cheques for seventy-five pounds. Naturally you wouldn't be tempted if you could do that.

He took out his fountain pen from the inside pocket of his battledress blouse and signed Corporal Clayton's returns. They were concerned with vaccination and the strength of the mess for ration indents; it was old ground, on which he felt at home.

Another point struck him. Supposing he went to have a

drink with Charlie Morton. If the latter obtained his marks so easily, the drinks would cost him next to nothing while Howard's round would be measured in real shillings. That was ridiculous. On the other hand Hemsleigh and Styles—but suddenly he was angry; damn it, they had no right to interfere. He came to a decision, and felt better. If Herr Scholle did not come in again, well and good; if he did, he might let him have five cigarettes.

"But not one more!" Howard said to himself.

He stared defiantly as a knock came at the door and Herr Scholle entered; and three-quarters of an hour later, standing beside Charlie in the crowded grill-room bar of the Atlantic Hotel, he told himself that the fifteen cigarettes he had sold for seventy-five marks did not lie on his conscience at all. After all, the poor fellow had been grateful. Howard looked at the price list that was hung up behind the counter with less anxiety than he had ever looked at a price list. Whisky one mark, gin one mark, sherry two marks, champagne cocktail six marks . . . he grinned as he read the notice beneath the list: "The Duty Officer has orders to close the Bar as soon as signs of intoxication become apparent." It was not at all surprising.

PART III

PART III

CHAPTER 1

I

IT was three days before Howard received a letter from Mary, re-addressed from his battery. He read it in the ante-room, where they were having coffee after lunch, to the accompaniment of the sound of Miss Hackster talking about socialism. Complacent and deep voiced, she spoke as a woman converted to a new and scandalous creed who was not ashamed to talk about it.

Everything was still much the same at the office, Mary said, recording her day to day affairs in rounded, precise handwriting. At home father had been in one of his moods. The dog was out roving again and heaven alone knew where he went, for when he came back scratching at the door he was always covered with filth. Mother was feeling better, but of course still in bed most of the day. Some men were removing the warden's shelter at the end of the road and when they came the first day, father had said they were probably going to make it watertight, now that it was out of use.

"I believe in nationalisation of the means of production," Miss Hackster said.

Howard sipped at his Serbian brandy. The letter from home was not having its usual effect on him, the irritation of having to be where he was, the homesickness for the cinema queue or the tennis club.

"Sybil, I'm afraid you're talking to a real old fashioned reactionary Tory!" Mr. Maxton-Hill gushed. "I must confess to a liking for the old order——"

"Slums and servants, big dividends and low wages!"

"One is ashamed to listen, Sybil, but there were other redeeming features, after all, old and gracious things——"

"I suppose you supported Franco?"

"I certainly did."

"The Vatican, starving peasantry, grandees!"

"Oh, but Sybil, don't you think there's something attractive about a grandee? To have one's own railway station——"

Mary had been to a symphony concert at the Albert Hall with her friend Susan. The journey home, an hour and twenty minutes, had been hardly worth it. There had been a long queue at Aldgate waiting for the bus and it was bitterly cold. However it had taught her one lesson. No matter how bad people said the east suburban service was from Liverpool Street Station, it was better to go by train. Anyhow the People's Palace in the Mile End Road gave concerts that were just as good and they were having them at Walthamstow and Leyton, too, so where was the sense in trailing over to the other side of London? Prices, she continued, changing the subject, were worse than ever. She had seen some couponless material which would do for covering cushions and she knew for a fact it had only been one and eleven three before the war and now it was six and fivepence. There was something wrong somewhere. It was about time the police started on the black market, those that weren't in it themselves. Tom and Edith next door were nice enough people to meet in their way although she wouldn't choose them, but the fact was Tom had had two eggs for his breakfast every day since before the war. Everything they touched turned to money, cash of course, no cheques, and it made a mockery of people like father, living hand to mouth almost on his civil service pension.

"'Z' cars are waiting," Busch said.

"Oh, thank you, Busch," Miss Hackster looked round. "Is everyone ready?"

Howard folded the letter without completing it or reading the regular message of love with which she always ended. The letter with its air of righteous complaint had come just at the moment when he was being nagged by feelings of guilt. It was ridiculous, for the cause was merely the cigarettes which he had sold to Herr Scholle. But why be concerned about it? Thousands of troops had been buying their NAAFI ration and canteen requirements by selling a few cigarettes a week ever since the war had ended. The astonishing thing was that he had been reluctant so long. He knew the reason. It was simply that the officers in his last mess had not done it and his battery commander had threatened disciplinary action. Both factors had kept Howard straight, one from his instinct to swim with the tide and the other from fear. Throughout his life his actions had been influenced by other people, never by private principle or determination. He had always been dominated and he had always been resentful about it. So he had been able to buy the marks because it seemed that many people in the Kasselallee mess did so openly, and it was absurd to go against the tide of Charlie Morton; but he was uncomfortable in case Hemsleigh and Styles should find out—and immediately be contemptuous of him—and there was still the slight fear about disciplinary action. On the few occasions when he had done wrong, he had always been found out and penalised, where others equally guilty had gone scot free. He never forgot the results of stealing a shilling from his mother's dressing table, cheating at Latin in the Lower Fifth exam, or the time the girl had screamed when he had harmlessly misbehaved; spanking, caning, public humiliation; that was the way it had always worked. It had been far easier to obey the rules, even though unwillingly. And now he had sold the cigarettes and would not be at all surprised to find himself brought before the military commander of Hamburg.

The two Volkswagens were crowded with their usual occupants. He sat in the back, worrying. He knew quite well how violent would be Mary's disapproval of what he had done. She was a wonderful girl; although God knew how the marriage would work, if it ever came off. She knew him as a Royal Artillery lieutenant. When she saw him without the benefit of his uniform he wondered if she would still be so determinedly affectionate.

Kay Blandison smiled at him.

"Howard, you do look down in the dumps. Bad news in your letter?"

"No, nothing."

"Anyway you did have a letter. Is she well? I always feel so sorry for anyone living in England nowadays."

"She's quite all right, thanks."

He sounded rude and Kay turned pink, telling herself that this was only a façade behind which he concealed a sharp passion for her. All men were like that, the silly creatures. She gave him an arch glance and turned her head away. He had looked so comic that first morning with his hangover and what with Miss Hackster clearly disliking him at once, as she had also disliked Kay, it was as much as she could do to keep up her annoyance. She had spent a good deal of time studying him in the last three days. Kay thought about men in two ways; arrogantly, building fictitious little episodes which eventually seemed to have occurred, and desperately, when she remembered that she was thirty-one and still a virgin; if it didn't happen soon, it would never happen. So she could convince herself that Howard was aching to put his arms round her and at the same time consider, panic stricken, that he was perhaps her last chance; he was not the first last chance that she had known. His coming to the mess had been a godsend. Charlie Morton and Hoppy were both married, Styles and Hemsleigh were out of the question, Bonzo and Peter Schroeder were both Germans, Hugo was lost to fratting and Johnson Trant, when he appeared, was on too high a plane for her; in any case she had found out that he was married. Howard Randle, who was merely engaged, remained; and apart from his eligibility, he attracted her. She liked his going-to-seed figure and weak resentful expression. He needed someone to look after him and you could see at a glance that the girl in the photograph by his bedside was as hard as nails.

Peter Schroeder, squeezed between Howard and Mr. Hopwood, exclaimed, "My God, did you see that slogan?"

"Where?"

"Chalked up on the wall—'Survivors of this ration period join the Communist Party!' What insufferable cheek. We're spoon-feeding these damned people to let them get away with things like that. It makes us a laughing stock."

"I think it's rather witty," Kay said.

"I think it's scandalous."

Kay walked beside Howard up to the office steps.

"What do you think of Peter?" she whispered.

"I'm afraid I can't stand the old school tie," Howard said. "These people who speak with a plum in their throats and think they're doing you an honour when they pass you the salt."

"Didn't you know he was German?" Kay giggled. "And Elizabeth as well?"

"Good lord, are they?"

"Sh! He'll hear. And they're Jews."

"They're bloody marvels, that's all I know," said Howard.

They nodded to Leo, the old man at the door, who bowed low to both of them. On the stairs a middle-aged German stood aside respectfully.

"Guten Tag, Mees Blantison, guten Tag, Herr Leutnant."

"Guten Tag, Herr Doktor," Kay smiled.

" 'Tag," Howard nodded, looking as imperious as he could.

"Bonzo says that man would be worth five thousand a year in England," she whispered.

"I couldn't care less."

"Just like a man!" she said. "Howard, you're looking thoroughly miserable; how about going out to the Country Club tonight?"

"I thought Charlie had something on——"

"Oh, they're all out swanning up to Lübeck—visiting D.P.s, that was their story—it's no good counting on them!" She had stepped purposefully between him and the door of his office. He was showing no enthusiasm at all for her suggestion, but he had no idea how to avoid it. She continued brightly, "A drink and a dance will do you good." She had the air of a determined hostess at a children's party.

"How can we get there?"

"Howard, you've been here three days and you're in the admin office! Never mind, I'll see to it. We'll go directly after dinner. Or why not have dinner there, it's not difficult to get a table if you're early and I'll stop working at six."

"Oh, all right."

Kay seized his left hand and gave it an affectionate little squeeze; then she hurried away. He noticed that she had large leg muscles, like a ballet dancer's. So had Mary.

Howard went into his office, puzzled and not as annoyed as he pretended to be. He found being sought after a most unusual sensation. He entered the room whistling under his breath. He had not yet been to the much talked of Country Club and it was quite a good idea to go. His last two evenings had been spent in solitude in the mess. The pace of the first night had not been kept up. People were busy with their own affairs and there had been no more parties. On the other hand the new standard of comfort and service by which he was surrounded had seemed to grow better and better. Hammond had found him a soft mattress, he had breakfast in bed twice, a gin before and a brandy after lunch and dinner. His work at the office was ludicrously easy, a matter of signing letters and returns which Corporal Clayton prepared; he had also had two visits to pay to Military Government offices in connection with the German staff; one to the food office to try and put some of the staff on a higher ration scale, a request which had been immediately turned down, and the other to the forestry office to gain permission for the staff to assist with wood-cutting parties in the forests outside Hamburg on the basis of keeping some of the wood for themselves as fuel, which had also been refused. "I'd like to know what wood they'd have given us if they'd won," the official said and Howard explained that he quite agreed with him, old boy, but he was merely doing his job; and they went together to have the excellent coffee and cakes provided in the tastefully decorated officers' room at the Y.M.C.A.

Howard sat down at his desk and pulled out Mary's letter again. She continued with complaints about the people living in the new pre-fabs that had been put up where a V.1 had demolished some houses in the road. She had seen 'Henry V,' but found it not so interesting as 'Cæsar and Cleopatra.' Now came the peroration. "Every night I am thinking of you, my darling Howard, hoping you are comfortable and happy. Every day is a day nearer your coming home for good and when I remember that I forget all my complaints. I long for the moment when your arms are round me again and I can kiss you to my heart's content and give you all that you desire."

A week ago, in the spartan discomfort of his battery, he would have obtained his usual pleasant thrill from the letter. Now he was unmoved, even chilled a little by it. Howard frowned as he folded it up and put it back in his pocket. There was a knock on the door and Leo, the porter, came in. At a distance of a few yards he was a comic little figure, like one of Snow-white's seven dwarfs, but close up his grey, shrivelled skin, covered with warts, and the smell of decay and his blood-shot sunken eyes were not comic at all.

"What do you want?" Howard snapped.

"Entschul'gen——Herr——darf——" The words came mumbling out of the decayed old mouth, mixed with spit. Leo was one of the few Germans in the Sociology Division whose English was limited. ". . . If you will be so goot. . ."

Howard understood what he wanted.

"Why the hell didn't you come during lunch?" he said roughly. The poverty and misery of the old man frightened him. He felt himself stiffen as Leo shambled over to the desk, holding his little tin open in one hand. He put a finger in front of his nose to ward off the smell that came with him and watched the claw-like free hand feeling for the dog ends in his ash tray and putting them into the tin. Leo turned towards him.

"Danke schön, Herr . . . danke . . ."

"Don't you come here again when I'm working, do you understand?"

Instead of going Leo closed his tin and drew out a musty looking old book from his coat pocket. Uttering little grunts and wheezes, each one of which made Howard sick to hear, he shifted round and stood beside his chair.

"Ein Buch, Herr . . . for zom zigarettes . . . ein Buch! . . ."

His warm, wet breath settled on Howard's ear.

"Kön' Sie alles lesen, Herr, was Sie wollen, nicht . . ."

"No, no, for God's sake——"

It was a dirty, out of date German encyclopædia which the old man had found in the cellar. He tried to sell it to everyone. Howard felt paralysed. He spoke roughly but it was not in him to deal roughly with the porter, who was so helpless and undefended, and he was afraid to give him any cigarettes in case he should produce something else.

"Ein Buch——" Leo repeated, but he got no further. Herr Scholle had entered the office, followed by a boy. He hurried to the desk, seized Leo by the scruff of his neck and shouted in his ear furiously, " 'Raus!"

Leo gave a grunt of pain and clutching his book and his tin he waddled quickly to the door like a crab. Herr Scholle thumped him on the back and aimed a kick at him that missed.

"So!" Herr Scholle smiled, wiping his hands as the door closed. "He will not bother you again, I think."

"Thank you," said Howard, who was relieved but shocked by the heartlessness that had been shown.

" 'Raus!" Herr Scholle repeated, imitating himself and chuckling with complacency. "Such language the old fool understands!" The boy who had come in with him chuckled as well. He was about sixteen, fair haired, thin and normally sullen looking. Herr Scholle frowned at him. "Mr. Randle, this is Stefan, the new office boy."

The boy stood to attention, clicked his heels and bowed low.

"When you press the bell, he will come."

"What's happened to you?" Howard asked. "Become a director?"

"Oh! So much to do!" Herr Scholle replied. "I am now required to translate and all for two-sixty marks a month, it is absurd." He turned to the boy. "All right, get out."

Stefan clicked his heels, bowed low again and then went out, tossing his hair.

"He has come from over the green border from the Russian

zone," Herr Scholle said. "What a type, he is quite low class and uneducated. One cannot sit in the room with him. You know, Mr. Randle, that is one of the hardest points about our position, the way we must mix with Germans not of our class. I do not like it. You have a cigarette for me?"

"Oh, sure," Howard said, bringing out his packet. "Any time."

"Zank you." Herr Scholle bent forward respectfully to hold the lighter for him. "Have you perhaps also a few more to sell?"

"No."

"Perhaps in another day."

"Maybe." He could feel Mary's letter burning in his pocket. It was crazy, this moral control she held over him.

"You have enjoyed the little party of Captain Morton's ze other night?" It was clear that Herr Scholle had come in for a chat. "It was good, no?"

"Very good." Howard wondered for a moment if he were making an impertinent reference to his passing out. But, though dressed like a film star on holiday, Herr Scholle was all respect and attention.

"You have not been long in Germany, I think, Mr. Randle? And never before the war? It is nice to meet such a good class of Germans I think. It is hard to meet the right type unless such meetings are arranged, and if one does not meet the right type, it is so easy to carry away such wrong impressions of Germany. So many people whom the English are meeting are such common people. If you like to meet a nice type of German ladies, Mr. Randle, I shall always be honoured to help you. You understand? I make myself a sort of liaison officer between English officers and ze best type of German. It is a work for peace, no?"

"It's one way of putting it," Howard said. "Rather a polite way, really." But the offer had reminded him again of the girl with auburn hair. Sitting in the mess on the two previous evenings, listening to Miss Hackster, Mr. Maxton-Hill and Mrs. Pratt, he had constantly told himself that he was a fool not to go round to the flat. The invitation had been clear enough and he knew the address. There was no rule against it, no illegality as with the cigarettes; but there was Mary. He felt himself a prisoner against her influence.

"Or if perhaps you are interested in German youth?" Herr Scholle said tentatively. "It is important also to make friends with the right type of German boy, to lead him into the path of democracy that he has, alas, never been taught. If you wish, Mr. Randle, I could also introduce——"

"Not for me, thank you."

Herr Scholle looked puzzled, although his perpetual nervous grin remained; there seemed to be nothing he could do to please. He might try other suggestions, but perhaps discretion was the best policy for the moment. It was disappointing. He bowed.

"Then if there is nothing——"

"Are there any English newspapers about?"

"I will send Stefan to look round the building."

Howard was left alone again. Not many weeks now and demobilisation was going to sweep him back to Mary, Mr. Waters, the office, insurance, the rush hour, the black Homburg and umbrella. In his moments of deepest depression he forgot his resentfulness of everyone else and despised himself. Even pimps like Herr Scholle showed some kind of initiative. Their movements were not little bursts of frightened activity; they weren't worried all the time what someone, somewhere, would say.

He went to the window and stared gloomily into the dirty inner courtyard. The backsides of other buildings were all around. Behind every window people were working at some business or other. Even the blasted Germans had solved things better than he had. He felt wretched. Nothing could be worse for the Germans, after all; everything that could happen to them had; it was a circumstance by no means devoid of comfort. They had not the private worries of a British army lieutenant. He felt for a cigarette mechanically and reflected that after his demobilisation he would probably not be able to afford to smoke. If only England were a total

ruin, a vast Hamburg, how much easier it would be. No need
to worry then; one could just aimlessly exist. But even so the
usual bastards would do all right.

He returned to his desk, feeling heavy and out of condition.
He had had too much lunch—that was another sensation he
wouldn't be able to afford—but in any case he knew that he
was running to seed. The army had stifled and buried whatever energy and initiative he had ever had.

There was a knock at the door and the sullen looking new
office boy entered, carrying a two days' old *Daily Express*. He
made his usual low bow as he handed it to Howard, who
stared at him haughtily.

11

They drove in sharp moonlight to the Country Club; past
the Dammtor station, the Bismarck memorial, the Reeperbahn
and ruins, followed by more ruins; then the first sight,
more impressive in the twilight than at any time, of
the battered dockyards across the Elbe, as the car drove
along the Elbchaussee. The dirty pathetic remnants of a
once prosperous suburb were on either side, old fashioned
houses and now and then a riverside café which had been
taken over by a naval or military unit. This had been the
best district in Hamburg. The houses became modern and
expensive looking, set in large gardens, managing to retain
some of the gloss and exclusiveness that they had once enjoyed.
There were trees, servants and quietness, a regimental headquarters, a few soldiers walking along with their girls or by
themselves. Howard said almost nothing, breathing the strong
smell of Lilies of the Valley which Kay Blandison had brought
with her into the car. She was not concerned about his
silence as she spent the time talking in German to the driver.
Her moderate fluency in the language was her one accom-
plishment and she never missed an opportunity to use it.
The driver was a heavy thick-set man who had been a major
in the German army and he told her a long story of how his
regiment had dealt with a Himmler man who had been sent

to spy on them when they were in Oslo. The ex-major spoke very good Norwegian—he had been there for three and a half years—and he had been disappointed that the end had come in the way it did. He had not known Quisling, politics had never interested him, he was only concerned to spread cultural relations. The Himmler man had been a most unsympathetic type, quite uncultured, but of course, as Miss Blandison well knew, it had been necessary to tread warily with such creatures. "Natürlich"—"Of course," she replied. They turned from the Elbchaussee into a side road. As soon as the present unsettled conditions improved, the driver went on, he had half a mind to go back there for good.

A floodlit entrance gate showed that they had arrived. The car drove up a narrow straight cobbled road until it was stopped by a British soldier who noted its number and handed the driver a slip of paper. They continued into the courtyard. The house itself, which had been the property of a tobacco millionaire, was half floodlit. It was like a white sugar model of a modern factory. Howard looked up at it in amazement.

"I hate it, don't you?" said Kay, as she stepped out. She added in German to the ex-major, who was standing at attention, " Pick us up at ten."

"Jawohl."

"Come on then, Howard."

The interior of the house was no less remarkable, with its tall entrance hall, oval dining room, the long, low lounge and its Berchtesgaden fireplace and window. The former library, in which there were still some books on the higher shelves, now served for dancing.

"Just like a little liner, isn't it?" Kay said. "Oh, good, it's the D.P's band tonight, they're much better than the others."

They spoke to an army sergeant who was acting as the *maître d'hotel*. With some reluctance he promised them a table if they came in ten minutes. Kay gave him her most ravishing smile and then pulled Howard towards the lounge.

"We'll find ourselves a seat and have a drink, Howard."

"What's it to be?" He was rather pleased to find something to say.

Kay made a face and considered.

"I think—I think—a champagne cocktail."

"Well, maybe you're right." He beckoned a pretty German waitress, who came over smiling and ordered, "One champagne cocktail and one large sidecar." He giggled.

"What's the matter, Howard?"

"The joke is me ordering a champagne cocktail."

Kay Blandison was not entirely pleased. She suspected that Howard included her as part of the joke. He was rather common, really. She stared angrily at the two Wrens who had come in escorted by young Guards officers. Anyone would think they owned the place! Plums in their throats, such accents were quite artificial and anyway, she thought, I look quite as natural here as they do. It was amazing, the opinion these Navy girls had of themselves. "Oodles, simply oodles of sand and blue sky——" one of them was squeaking. Kay could just imagine her out of her present dark blue uniform with its unnaturally white shirt in a flouncy lace affair at, no doubt, a hunt ball; surrounded by the same sort of over polite young men in blues. That would be her England— unlike the depressing little semi-detached house at Stamford Hill to which Kay went on her leaves. "The most awfully nice little Pole——" one of the Guards officers was saying. I certainly wouldn't be interested in a stupid boy like that, Kay told herself; and she accepted a cigarette that Howard offered her without a word of thanks.

Two angry looking army officers sat down next to them, shutting the offending party out of view. "I tell you it's a bloody scandal! I've told the director, I slipped the broadest hint I could to that ridiculous UNRRA man who came floating round last Tuesday, but it's no use, they couldn't care less about it. I've half a mind to blow the gaff to one of the correspondents."

The champagne cocktail and the sidecar arrived. Kay felt better.

"Roaming round the countryside, I told him, dozens of the bloody Blue division! Just suppose the Russians get to hear of it! And I'm told they've got pictures of Franco stuck up all over their huts and they burnt Republican insignia——"

"Well, here's to us," Kay said.

A quarter of an hour later she was repeating the phrase over a glass of Hock. The small restaurant was crowded. It was odd to think, she had already said, that Goering himself had been one of the tobacco millionaire's guests, had eaten some of his probably gargantuan meals in this very room. "You want to ask the doorman about him, he's been here all the time, you know. He says Goering was very nice and considerate. But they had some S.S. here who weren't so good." Howard ate and drank and listened to her. Kay went on with the Nuremberg trial. "We get such funny reactions coming into Sociology Div. The Germans' main objection to it seems to be that there's always the report on the day's proceedings after Radio Hamburg's night news; they say things are bad enough as they are without having to listen to that. And then we had a report on some Hitler Youths' reactions and they all said it was a frame-up, of course, but they didn't feel bitter about it, they said it was one of the rights of a victor. Siegerrecht, isn't it a lovely word—oh, of course I forgot, you don't speak German, Howard."

"Not me." He shook his head with the usual complacent grin that accompanied his confessions. The cocktail and the wine had induced a happy glow into his inside. He revelled in the buzz of conversation in the room and he let her prattle on without paying too much attention to her, except to wonder how much of a nuisance she would be at the end of the evening. Although she reminded him so much of Mary, that was one department in which there was no resemblance. Mary disapproved of sex.

"I know it's wicked of me, but in some ways I just can't help admiring Goering," she went on. The dab of powder had disappeared from her nose, which was now shining, and Howard also noticed a strange solitary dark whisker in the

120

middle of her right cheek; surely she knew that it was not ornamental.

"You like fat men?" he said.

"Oh, you!" Kay answered roguishly, delighted. "Howard, how dare you!" She pretended to be confused, sipped her Hock, looking at him over the glass, and whispered, "I'm not telling you what sort of men I like, so there. Not yet, anyway."

The food itself, some thin soup, a dried egg mushroom omelette and ice cream, was not exciting. It was a typical officers' club meal, described as wickedly luxurious by visitors returning to England. But the luxury was provided only by the wine on every table, the large cocktails and the liqueurs, which were a tenth of their price in London and could be enjoyed by people for whom they had always been and would always be out of the question at home. For Howard and for Kay, as for half the people in the room, it was like a long held private dream almost come true. Both of them before the war, the insurance clerk and the secretary, had looked through the glossy pages of *The Tatler* with envy and resentment. They had had the same feelings as they passed the Ritz or the Savoy on their way to a Lyons, as they looked from the gallery or the pit at the people in the theatre stalls, or from the top of a bus on to a passing Rolls Royce or Packard. A pint of bitter and a cup of cocoa, queueing in the rain, shining elbows, rush hours, the gang at the tennis club and night classes were not in the same world as champagne at Davos, bathing at Eden Roc or Palm Beach, débutantes, First Nights, chauffeurs, waiters and butlers; both Howard and Kay had wanted the latter almost as much as they resented the former; and now most of these once far away sensations were theirs. They had the chauffeurs, the waiters, the butlers, the champagne, the feeling of privilege. What they had not was property. As soon as he was demobilised or she lost her job, it would all be over and the struggle to keep their heads above water at home, which had been hard enough before the war and was apparently harder now, would begin all over again.

"Two large apricot brandies," Howard ordered.

"I am sorry, sir, but there is no more apricot brandy."

"Oh, hell, well, then——"

"Any Benedictine?" Kay enquired.

"Yes, madam."

"Two large Benedictines," Howard said.

The bill was forty-eight marks and used up almost all that was left of the money he had obtained from Herr Scholle for the fifteen cigarettes. The reminder served to dampen his feelings for a moment. It seemed that unlike Charlie Morton he could not be happily dishonest. He was convinced that there was a knowing look in the German waiter's eye and he felt self-conscious. Perhaps it was true that the other people in the room would pay their bills with money similarly obtained; but he was not convinced of it. There was a unit celebration in one corner, so it was quite reasonable that the party should be doing themselves proud without caring much what they spent. The Guards officers and the Wrens were at another table and they of course would have plenty of money of their own. The little Brigadier two yards away who was with a Control Commission girl, younger and prettier than Kay, could meet his bill out of his army pay; it seemed to Howard that he gave him a sharp enquiring look.

The tunes which the Displaced Persons' band played were all out of date. "Don't Fence Me In" was their newest number and it came out about every twenty minutes. The band was very proud of it, and every time it was played Kay, who was dancing tirelessly with Howard, would turn and smile at the conductor.

"They'd make a fortune in London, wouldn't they?"

"I suppose so."

"English dance bands are dreadful, I always think." As she spoke, she was convincing herself that she was accustomed to the smartest London night life, to the 400, the Milroy, the Bagatelle; and it wasn't really true that the only bands that she had danced to were at the seaside on her pre-war annual holiday, at war-time troops' canteens and at the dances that were run by the tennis club; that she had never even been to a road-house, except in the daylight. "Which is your favourite?"

"Victor Sylvester," said Howard.

"Oh, yes, but this sort of band is just right for a night club, don't you think?" She had a disconcerting habit of raising her head so that her nose almost hit his mouth; Howard kept wanting to draw away from her, but her grasp was firm and close. "Although personally I hate bottle parties." She added truthfully, "I never go to them."

"Not having bought fifty second-hand cars in the Battle of Britain and sold them after victory day, nor do I."

"Oh, how cynical you are. Are you always such a cynic, Howard dear?"

"All over," Howard said. "I tell you what, let's sit down and have another drink."

"Oh, no, Howard, dear, please let's go on dancing!" she begged, increasing the pressure of her arms. "Please!"

He gave in, for there was no one at hand like Charlie Morton to rescue him. He wished he knew of a polite means of thawing her. His legs were feeling tired and he began to regret the initial weakness of agreeing to come out with her. And, of course, he ought not to have sold those cigarettes to Herr Scholle. The guilty memory kept troubling him. Really, it was no wonder that he had always been a failure. He hadn't the guts to use his opportunities properly, just as he was quite unable to deal with Kay, just as he had remained a lieutenant, always letting himself be a convenience for other people.

"Howard, dear, you're looking miserable again." But before he could reply she noticed that Miss Hackster and Peter Schroeder were on the floor. It was most annoying. The Country Club dancing space was very limited and privacy was impossible now, just when, she knew, he was beginning to fall. She said, "Oh, look who's come, Peter and Sybil, of all people."

The other couple from the Sociology Division were dancing in a very much more restrained fashion, at least three or four inches apart, an expression of careful rapture on their faces. Behind her set smile, however, Miss Hackster had not recovered from a blow delivered at dinner in the mess. Mr.

E   123

Maxton-Hill had been invited to a small party at the Vierjahreszeiten Hotel and not only did he invite Mrs. Pratt, but the latter had rebelliously accepted; and moreover, ridiculous creature, she had blushed. Miss Hackster decided grimly that her assistant's life would be a misery tomorrow. But that was not all. Hemsleigh, Styles and Charlie Morton had heard the whole interchange and there followed a conversation she did not fully understand, in which she had a vague and uncomfortable suspicion that they were making fun of her. They seemed to be making dimly veiled allusions to the relationship between Pratt and Mr. Maxton-Hill. "Feeling rompworthy tonight, Adela?" Charlie Morton had said, and the two victims of the teasing looked not annoyed but foolishly bashful; and there had been *sotto voce* comments from Hemsleigh and Styles about the importance of mess procedure, which they were always discussing with mock solemnity in Miss Hackster's presence; a joke about her constant emphasis on her seniority, a joke that they were weaning Pratt away from her. All this was only suspicion; she could not be sure. And then the crowning annoyance when Charlie Morton tripped her into saying that "Anthony and Cleopatra" had been written by Bernard Shaw; for if there was one thing on which she prided herself it was her general culture. She had taken refuge in silence, looking forward to the day when the army officers would all be demobilised and only Control Commission civilians would be left.

"Ver' crowded," Peter Schroeder was saying. "By jove, theah's Kay and that new chap."

"They must have had dinner here," Miss Hackster said. "They didn't sign out. Poor Busch was wondering what to do." She was not displeased at being seen out with a man: Pratt would now hear about it twice over. And she liked Peter Schroeder. Of course he was a German and his imitation of the aristocratic Englishman was perhaps a little pathetic; but he took Miss Hackster at her own valuation, which showed that he could discriminate; and there was little doubt that he had come from a very good German family. "Hullo,

Blandison!" she smiled, as they passed close to the other couple. She had not made up her mind about Howard; he seemed rather a nonentity. Miss Blandison herself was quite satisfactory, so long as she was kept in her place and did not air her language. In Miss Hackster's opinion a knowledge of German was not a cultural asset like French or Italian.

Kay swung Howard away with some quick chassé steps.

"I suppose poor Pratty is sitting by herself. It's a shame the way Sybil treats her, don't you think? Or perhaps you haven't noticed yet. Let's see if we can see her." They paused by the band, where it was possible to look both into the lounge and into the hall. The place was crowded and noisy, but, to her relief, there was no sign of Mrs. Pratt. "They must have come alone. Let's sit down, Howard, shall we?"

"O.K., Kay," Howard said. He had been waiting for a chance to make the joke. She squeezed his hand in her appreciation.

They found two seats on a sofa in the hall and Howard ordered two more large Benedictines. He was so relieved to be sitting down that his feeling of guiltiness had receded. They lit cigarettes and sat back comfortably. Agitated conversations were going on all around. A South African captain with an Afrikaans accent kept jerking his elbow into Kay's knee as he talked to an English major about the American zone, which he had just visited. On Howard's right someone was saying, "Five shots of penicillin and you're perfectly all right!"

"All right, man, and then I got to Stuttgart—that was a bloody fine city, man, I'm telling you, before they rubbed it out—there's a damn great hotel there, the Graf Zeppelin, they use it for a transit place, and what's on the door, man, above the main entrance?"

"I don't know," the major said, sipping his brandy.

"The Hundredth Infantry Division!"

"Well, that's all right——"

"But what does it say in a damn great banner poster you can see for miles, man, just beneath it?" the South African exclaimed. "The Regiment of the Century! God, man! I ask you! I'm only a bloody colonial, but, God, man! God, man! The Regiment of the—don't let me go on! Don't let me go on!"

"Oh, dear, this man!" Kay whispered. "My knee!" A most annoying possibility had just occurred to her. The presence of Miss Hackster and Peter Schroeder meant that the four of them would have to share the same car going back to the mess, and the whole evening would be ruined. "Here are the drinks, Howard—can you get your money? It's such a squeeze —let me pay——"

"No, it's all right."

"Of course, it has an enormous effect on morality," a voice went on. "I believe the padres are simply furious. You see, some chaps keep coming back for more——"

"Well, bippety bop," Kay said, with her most intimate look. She decided to go ahead with the conversation she had intended for the journey back. "Tell me, Howard, dear, would Mary be jealous if she knew you were here with me?"

"Oh, no, certainly not."

"She sounds a very nice girl."

"How did you know her name?"

"It was on the photograph."

"Frankfurt!" the South African exclaimed, jabbing harder than ever. "Don't remind me. I send my driver to an O.R.'s billet—enlisted men, they call them—I ask you—and it's eleven o'clock. He knocks up the sergeant, who's in bed with a Fräulein; the sergeant doesn't even stir, he tells him where to sleep and as he goes out, he says, 'Switch de lide off, bud' —man, I ask you!"

"Tell me where you met her. You don't mind telling me, Howard, dear, do you? Only when you're parted, it's some- times such a comfort to talk; that's my experience."

"If you tell me about yours——"

"Oh, mine!" Kay blushed. "This man's elbow, Howard, really is too much——" She regained her composure. "I'd rather not tell you about mine. You see, he was a bomber pilot." She felt breathless; but the lie had gone down very well.

"I'm awfully sorry. You mean, he's——"

"He died. Please, Howard, I'm all right about it—really."

"That's the way it is sometimes, I suppose," Howard said philosophically.

"That's the way it is," she repeated, looking at the carpet. She squeezed his hand again and they sipped their Benedictines in silence.

"Francesca I think she was called, but she was this chap Ronnie's girl, you see—she said she'd had an Italian child, a German child, a Polish child and now she wanted——"

"And you mustn't say petrol," the South African went on, exasperated. "You must say 'Geass.' 'Have you gartny geass?' But, man, they never bloody well have any!"

Howard did not tell her where he had met Mary. There was nothing to be concealed about it, but he felt that she was wanting to know too much. Of course, if the poor girl had lost her bomber pilot, it was no wonder she was dying of repression; but it was no good her expecting him to help her out. It was all very well to enjoy yourself. That was another thing. Mary was his girl, he must remember that.

"Let's dance again, Howard!"

"Oh, all right."

He followed her without enthusiasm. Kay was conscious that something somewhere had gone wrong, just when the atmosphere had been full of emotion. She felt almost desperate. Of course it had been impossible with that awful man making so much noise. Probably Howard had been shy in front of other people. Miss Hackster and Peter Schroeder had left the floor and were looking on, chatting to each other sexlessly. No, there would be no escaping them.

The D.P.'s band played "Lili Marlene." The little Czech leader sang the words in English with a Cockney accent, and Kay crooned softly to Howard in German: "Unter der Laterne, vor dem grossen Tor, steht eine Laterne——" His determination to keep clear of her increased with every note. The strange thing was that the whole evening was reminding him of his meeting with Mary. She, too, had suddenly crooned in his ear while they were dancing, nothing like so emotionally as this, of course; but the similarity was there. "I think it's horrible to have the words in English, don't you?" Kay whispered. "They're so much better in German." And then a look of frustration came over her. The band was playing "The King" and everyone in the Country Club was standing to attention.

The journey back was worse than she had feared. Howard had to sit in front at Miss Hackster's insistence, for she was still reacting to Style's and Hemsleigh's remarks about mess procedure; and the other three squeezed together in the back, with Peter Schroeder gallantly balancing himself on an arm-rest and Miss Hackster talking about the record of the Conservative Party between the wars. Miss Hackster had been one of those who would have taken a strong line at Munich, they learnt. When they reached the mess, they found Elizabeth, Charlie Morton, Mr. Hamilton and Mr. Hopwood playing poker dice and it was suggested that they all joined in. Howard seemed agreeable.

"Let's have Busch bring us in some tea and sandwiches!" Kay suggested. If they were all to play poker dice, everything would be spoilt; and badly though things had gone, there was still some hope. "Don't play that horrid game, Howard, please don't! Come over here and talk."

Hammond stood at the door.

"Mr. Randle, sir, can I see you?"

Howard went out into the hall. The batman beckoned him out of sight of the ante-room.

"What the hell's this?"

"There was note came for you just after you went out. I thought you might like to have it."

"A note?" Hammond gave it to him and he looked without recognition at the writing of his name on the envelope. He split it open and read, 'I am having a very small party here tonight. It will be so nice if you are able to come. Otto is away again. Hilde N.' "Well, I'm damned," he said.

Hammond, who had read the note some hours before and sealed it again, looked at him enquiringly.

"Oh, blast," Howard said. He looked exasperated, and then he chuckled.

"What is it?" Kay had come out.

"Nothing, Kay—I—I think I'm going to bed." He checked himself just in time from saying that he had a headache, which would have meant aspirins and her overpowering medical attention. "Thank you for the evening."

She flushed pink, trying to control herself. In her uniform she was like an angry schoolgirl.

"But what——" she began, and then, "Good night, Howard, and thank you very much," she said. She turned on them and returned to the ante-room, slamming the door behind her.

"Anything I can do, sir?"

"Listen," Howard whispered. "In my room, old boy, you'll find a bottle of Pernod. Could you nip upstairs and bring it down without anyone seeing, while I get my coat on? I'll be outside on the entrance porch."

"Righty-ho." Hammond winked at him.

Howard went quietly into the cloakroom. A German girl was an entirely different matter, he told himself. It wasn't the same thing at all. Not a bit the same. Anyhow Kay had done very well out of him that evening. Besides he didn't have to account for his movements to her. Nor to Mary, if it came to that. He pulled on his greatcoat, feeling happy. It was one of the few occasions when he knew exactly what he wanted.

CHAPTER 2

SHE opened the door and seemed neither surprised nor particularly pleased to see him. She was wearing a simple black dress with a large white collar, and something better than Lilies of the Valley went with her.

"I'm sorry to be late. I only just got the note. Is this bottle any use?"

She took the Pernod and smiled. He had forgotten the smile.

"Always of use."

"I hope the party's not over?" he lied. There was nothing he hoped for more.

"Oh, no."

Nor was it—which was also disappointing—any kind of all-night orgy. He followed Hilde into the room, mentally undressing her as he went, and found what looked like the end of a prim, cultural little tea-party. A hard-faced youngish woman with straight hair brushed back sat round the little table with the little spectacled man he had met at the party and a man of her own age whose appearance was almost dazzling; he had very long fair hair, brushed neatly, a monocle, two duelling scars and several rings on his fingers. He wore an elegantly cut suit the colour of light chocolate, a white silk shirt and a dark tie with large knot. The sight of him made Howard at once feel like a tramp caught in the rain.

"Herr Rondle," Hilde said. "The Gräfin von Zellenbach, Graf von Zellenbach, Herr Dr. Neumann. Herr Rondle has brought this very nice bottle."

Howard found himself bowing over the hand of the woman with straight hair. A count and a countess; who the hell did they think they were? No need to look at him as if he were a serf strayed into a St. Petersburg salon, he thought resentfully. They were three Huns, three Krauts, three who could take a running jump at themselves. He wasn't as good as they were, he was better. But he wished Mary could know that at that moment he was meeting a count and a countess.

"How do you do?" she said. "You do not speak German?"

"I don't." No need to assume it, though, blast you. He turned to the Graf, who exclaimed, "Von Zellenbach! I am pleased to meet you, sir."

Howard's self-confidence oozed back, as they shook hands. "Sir" from a Graf; it was a nice sound. No Graf had ever called Mr. Waters at the office "sir." "I'd like that bastard to see this," he thought.

"Neumann."

"How do you do."

Dr. Neumann bowed, stood up and shrugged his shoulders.

"I think you should not ask one of us how we do," he said quickly. "The present situation does not allow of a reply suitable for the ears of an English officer!"

"Maybe things will improve," Howard offered. It did not sound convincing, but why should he feel apologetic about it? He watched Dr. Neumann's eyebrows flash up and down like a Venetian blind, heard him murmur something that sounded like "Huh!"

The Graf was doing some organising with the chairs and said, "Won't you sit down, sir?"

"And will you have a cup of tea?" Hilde enquired. She fetched a cup and saucer from one of the several cupboards in the room and they all sat down. Howard himself was perched rather uncomfortably on the front of his chair. Now he was feeling resentful again. "I haven't come for a bloody tea-party," he thought.

The tea was watery and had a slight taste which had no connection with tea. The silence in the room made him conscious that he had interrupted a conversation that had been suitable, no doubt, for Germans only.

"How about the curfew?" he asked. "The sirens have gone."

"We have fortunately all of us curfew passes," the Graf said. "If one knows the right person there is no difficulty, is there, Hilde?"

Hilde nodded and laughed.

"Lucky for you," Howard said. That meant they weren't staying all night, anyhow. The question was who was going to last out longer. "You have the hell of a good English accent."

"Oh, yes. I was educated at Oxford."

"You were?"

"Balliol." The Graf was very soft spoken and his words were purred out. "I had a most pleasant time there."

Howard was speechless; his own education had stopped dead as soon as someone had been found prepared to pay him a weekly wage.

"You're not an Oxford man?"

"No." Here was he, the victorious lieutenant, feeling jealous, feeling inferior. It was crazy.

"My wife has been in England a lot. Oddly enough we met there when she was on holiday and I was at the London embassy—of course, that was before Ribbentrop. You live in London, Mr. Randle?"

"Yes," Howard said sullenly, and wondered at the same time how the Graf managed to look so sunburnt and tanned, although they had only just come out of the winter.

"I am fery fond of London!" the Gräfin said. She looked at Howard with interest. "I stayed at the Ritz Hotel, it was nice. Alas, when shall we poor Germans see a Ritz Hotel again, Mr. Randle?"

"Ask me," he replied. For his part he hadn't seen one yet, except from the top of a bus.

"Poor Germany, poor Germany. After we have been through so much. But I think it will be allowed sooner or later, don't you? For some of us, if not for the ordinary people. It was so nice in England. I shall never forget. Goodwood, Ascot, Cowes! Oh, hey, hey! Where in London do you live, Mr. Randle?"

"East London. In a suburb."

"I do not know it, I think. Do you know it, Gottfried?"

"I'm afraid I don't," the Graf smiled apologetically. "You

132

see, I was in London for only about six months. I had a small flat in Grosvenor Square."

"But I think we shall try to go to Brazil. I have heard that perhaps Brazil will allow us to go there quite soon. Do you know, Mr. Randle?"

"I don't." He shook his head, exasperated.

Hilde brought the tea round again. It was received by all the guests, except Howard, with profuse thanks. She suggested that they might open the Pernod, and went away for glasses and a jug of water, while the Graf tackled the bottle with a little jewelled corkscrew which he carried with him. It had been given to him in India before the war by a Maharajah with whom he had been playing polo, he explained to Howard. Did he play polo? Howard did not—with rather curt emphasis. He was suspecting that the Graf and Gräfin were putting him in his place. Successfully.

He produced his cigarettes. The weekly NAAFI ration had come that morning and he was now well off again. The Graf and Gräfin grabbed one each with ill-concealed eagerness. Maybe they weren't so clever, after all. His eyes followed Hilde about the room.

Then with the Pernod and the cigarettes the atmosphere softened. Dr. Neumann condescended to join in the conversation, which turned to one of the stock subjects; how to improve the state of the British Zone.

"The fundamental issue is to break the apathy!" he declared. He spoke excitedly, making nervous little gestures with his hands. "It's the question of the whole ethic of German work. The NSDAP have over-worked the concept von Nietzsche—the work animal! This concept we must struggle and fight against! Somehow it must be persuaded to the Military Government that this concept is the real enemy."

"Some coal and some food would be more useful, I think," the Gräfin said.

"Nein! That is necessary, of course. The English must give us back our coal and our food, they must stop destroying our factories. Of course. But then the German worker must learn to work for to live, instead of to live for to work. In that way only can one achieve democracy. Abolish the Nietzschean concept."

"It is possible," the Graf nodded. "I am in agreement provided it would not mean an increase in proletarian intellectuals—they are our real national disease. But surely there is more hope in international understanding between the cultured classes in Western Europe?"

"But the only Germans who are allowed by the Allies to mix and work freely abroad are our atomic scientists and rocket specialists!"

"That is what I say!" Hilde broke in. "Where is the sense in treating us as if we were Poles or Russen?"

It was a nice pair of stockings she was wearing, Howard noticed. But he was beginning to feel irritated. The conversation was up in the air. They all seemed to have had the hell of a good time before the war, better than he'd ever had. Now they were complaining because the band wasn't playing for them all over again. Complaining! They should be grateful for living. And if his experience proved anything, in five years' time they'd be back at the Ritz Hotel on a short stay—on their way to Brazil—and if they woke up early enough they could peek out of the suite window and see him walking down Piccadilly. Probably in the middle of an ex-servicemen's hunger march. As for Hilde, perhaps he had been wrong; nothing at all new in that. Anyhow, the passing of the minutes and all this conversation were having a melting effect on the desire for her which the Country Club drinks had created; heartache was turning into heartburn and a touch of stomach acidity. He sipped his Pernod impatiently. Why invite him? Why a special note?

"Poor Germany, poor Germany!" the Gräfin said. "I think it is better for us to try to go abroad, don't you, Mr. Randle?"

"Of course it's just possible you may not find yourselves very popular," he grinned. For a moment he felt malicious. They had a nerve to be talking like this.

134

"Not popular? Oh, but why not? What have I ever done? I have many, many friends abroad!"

"You must understand that the Nazis were very unrepresentative of the German people, Mr. Randle," the Graf kindly explained. "They were a boorish clique, mainly of the lower middle classes."

"Lumpen!" Dr. Neumann spat.

"Your people don't seem to realise that many of the extremities, as it were, were carried out by foreigners, mainly east Europeans, you understand."

"Oh, I see," Howard said, his voice trembling with irony. "I didn't know the Gestapo was Polish, old boy."

"No, no, I would not have said Polish. They used Lithuanians and Czechs and so on. Of course, one can't deny that much of the administrative side must have been carried out by Germans. Himmler was a dreadful type. But even he, I think, was of Polish ancestry. Anyhow, a very little fellow."

"But why are such people given more food than the Germans?" the Gräfin wanted to know. She was outraged by the injustice of it all. "In all these camps they are looked after by the English, is it not, and go round making all sorts of crimes. And the poor Germans are not allowed to have arms to protect themselves from such ruffians."

"It's too bad," said Howard, giving up. He offered round his cigarette packet again.

The conversation became a discussion of the German writer Thomas Mann, whom all attacked bitterly. Dr. Neumann spoke with much admiration for ten minutes on a book called "Lotte in Weimar." But a good book did not excuse a German insulting his own people, when he had not shared their risks and suffering. They made several allusions to the revolt of the 20th July, with which it appeared that they were connected, and they glanced at Howard every time to see if he had noted it. The English guest, however, merely yawned. They bored him silly. They went on to attack refugees in general, with emphasis on those who were serving in the Control Commission: "die Halb und Halb"—"the half and halfs." When they spoke of the English it was with almost tolerant amusement, unless they were pretending to be exasperated by inefficiency, but the "Halb und Halb" had no quarter; they loathed them.

Howard was half-way into a sulky doze when they all got up to go, murmuring stately politenesses to Hilde. So the party was over. He stood up with them, feeling dishevelled and out of temper. The Graf and Dr. Neumann both assisted the Gräfin into an expensive-looking fur coat. They then dressed themselves in garments straight from musical comedy. The Graf had an elegant cloak draped round his shoulders and a Tyrolese hat. Dr. Neumann wore a dark green mackintosh that stretched from a high tightly-laced collar down to his ankles and on his head a cowboy sombrero. Howard's beret and greatcoat, whose buttons were unpolished, looked very dowdy in comparison.

The reason for his invitation was quite clear: he provided the cigarettes and the Pernod. Well, it was his own fault. Kay Blandison might look a fright in comparison with Hilde, but at least she was English. They followed each other into the hall, where the Graf asked him which way he was going.

"Kasselallee."

"I'm afraid we have to go in the opposite direction. It was awfully nice to meet you." The Oxford accent and the soft, easily spoken words sounded uncanny.

"Good-bye," the Gräfin said, shaking hands with him.

"Good evening," Dr. Neumann exclaimed confidently.

"Cheerio, then." The Graf permitted himself to be familiar. Howard was vaguely resentful about it.

He turned to Hilde.

"Good-bye. Thanks for the party."

"I am so sorry if it was perhaps dull for you, Herr Rondle."

He told himself that the pressure of her fingers on his hand meant nothing, he was quite unmoved by the auburn hair falling over her forehead in its careful negligence, by the quizzical look in her eyes, beneath which, he noticed, she was wearing some kind of green shading. It was rather attractive.

"Not a bit. I enjoyed it. Good-bye."

"Good-bye."

He went into the street with the others, where they all shook hands with each other again, bowed, clicked their heels —and Howard himself felt impelled to do a feeble imitation of it, thinking how they'd laugh if they could see him at home —and finally parted. He walked along, whistling softly. The impudence and complacency of these people was amazing. This girl Hilde seemed to think that he, a British army lieutenant, merely existed to protect her from policemen when she was out after curfew or to provide fags for her tea-party guests.

He nodded to the sentry outside the requisitioned house in the street. The sentry, a monstrously gloomy figure trying to hide himself in his greatcoat and scarf, murmured, "Good night, chum." Howard went on, frowning at the affront to his dignity; of course the man hadn't known he was an officer, but it was annoying that the mistake could be made even in the dark. He considered returning and making a remark to the man, not a reproach but something like, "Can you tell me the way to the Kasselallee?" or "Do you happen to know the time?" so that the soldier could appreciate who he was. He paused to light himself a cigarette and then strolled on. He thought suddenly that here he was, an unprotected, unarmed enemy officer, alone in the dark; how easy it would be for a couple of underground Germans to hustle him across the road and push him into the canal that ran alongside. The water that looked so pretty in the day time with its willow trees and bridges and boathouses now had a sinister appearance. The thought was enough to make him turn pale. The next moment he heard footsteps and felt terrified. It was just the sort of thing occupied peoples had done to German officers, who were probably armed to the teeth and goodness knows were more capable of looking after themselves than he was. His heart thumped and he hid the glow of his cigarette in the palm of his hand—but the footsteps belonged to two soldiers.

"The way she played that squeeze box, though," one of them was saying. "Smashing, it was."

Howard went on more confidently, and once more came to an abrupt stop.

He was thinking of the Graf and his luxurious past, when a remark that the German had made struck him with peculiar force. If you knew the right people you could get a curfew pass, he said; and Hilde had nodded—which meant that she had pulled a very fast one on Howard the other night when she forced him to take her home from the party. Then her brother Otto had been there and ruined the situation, which explained the mention of him in the note. Howard was staggered.

"Well, I'm damned!" he said aloud. And then he slapped his right thigh in amusement.

A moment later he turned round and went straight back along the street, filled with gay anticipation. This time he did not even notice the muffled sentry. He couldn't keep the grin off his face. He wasn't at all green, he had had his moments, but there hadn't been very many of them; and there hadn't been any at all since he had met Mary. Really, the control she exercised over him—it only went to show, of course, what a remarkable girl she was and how much he was in love with her. For three years and four months he hadn't strayed an inch, which had been in a way all the more praiseworthy because Mary received even his kisses with a kind of loving sacrificial air. And he could still hear the lash in her voice: "How dare you, Howard! If that's the sort of person you are——" Howard giggled. He felt pleasantly defiant and wicked.

She answered his ring. He was not sure whether she looked surprised or relieved.

"Herr Rondle? You have forgot something?"

"That's right."

"What then? I think there was nothing left."

"It was my curfew pass," Howard said brilliantly. "I'm frightened to go back without it. Some British military policemen might arrest me."

"Oh!" she exclaimed. Then she shook with laughter. "Oh! Schrecklich! Oh! Oh!"

Howard felt that he had made a success of his return, but he was disconcerted that she should regard the whole matter as comic.

At last she was relatively calm again.

"Then you must come and look for it?" she giggled.

"It's not a bad idea," Howard said, thinking: What an old bastard I am.

"You must make no noise."

They tip-toed into the flat. Howard noticed that no effort at tidying up had yet been made, and this was a reminder of Mary, who would be banging at cushions or running the tap for washing up almost before a guest reached the pavement. His mother had been the same.

Hilde went into the bedroom and came out carrying two small logs, which she put into the stove.

"Some black market wood!" she explained. "Very expensive!"

"I like the chimney going out of the window."

"Is it not dreadful? But I am lucky to have the stove. Before I had it, it was colt—oh, so colt here!"

"Well, the summer's coming now."

"I never think about the future. Tomorrow perhaps. But no longer. Please sit down."

"Would you like me to put these cups away?"

"No, no, the morning will do. Sit down with some Pernod and I will change my clozes."

Howard's sense of anticipation rose at her last remark. He took off his greatcoat once again and sat down purposefully on the small settee. It was nothing to feel guilty about, he told himself. Hell, if he'd spent his life in Bombay or Cairo like most of these fellows, there'd have been plenty of it before now. It was, after all, the accepted right of the soldier abroad. Hilde was merely Mademoiselle from Armentières. It was nothing to do with love or loyalty. Mary would have him for the rest of her life. Besides it was local misconduct that was humiliating. What a man did in another country was really beside the point. Howard poured himself out a little Pernod contentedly. Yes, by being the assistant adjutant of a training regiment for so long, he had missed a lot of fun. However, that was no reason to restrain himself now. He helped himself to water. Hilde's glass, he noted, was half full. So she must have been having a drink by herself after they had gone. Howard smiled. It was very different from Mary locking up the sherry.

Hilde came in.

"So. Now I feel better."

"Well!" Howard exclaimed. "That's lovely!"

She was wearing a satin gown which rustled as she walked. It was buttoned up severely round her neck and trailed elegantly along the ground.

"It is nice?"

"I'll say. Where did you get it?"

"Oh—Paris—two—three years ago." She sank into the settee beside him and he pulled out his packet of cigarettes. He was conscious that she was wearing a different and stronger perfume.

"You were a long time in Paris?"

"Six or seven months. In forty-three. My husband was there. You like Paris?"

He was going to say that he had never been there, but he stopped himself.

"All right."

"It is a lovely town."

He lit her cigarette and she leaned her head back, blowing smoke out vertically. She was relaxed and comfortable. She was in a different category altogether from anyone he had ever known. Her beauty was growing on him every moment, the hair, the small delicate nose and mouth, the line of her eyebrows, her graceful hands which she used like a dancer.

"Paris! Oh, such wonderful times we had there. It was all so chic, so spirited. A wonderful night life and yet so much culture, so many friends and parties, oh so many good

140

times and so much kindness. Sometimes I have to cry a little when I think of all that and now this——"

Howard was rather astonished.

"But wasn't it unpleasant with the French hating you and all that——"

"Hating? Oh, my husband and I had many French friends, such nice people, we did not think of politics. Then there was shopping, and parties with German officers, and the Ritz bar, it was a nice time—oh, a nice time——"

"Sounds it," Howard said. It was rather a shock to him to realise that Germans could remember Paris nostalgically, just as Englishmen or Americans did. You tended to think of them merely as humourless people grimly sacking a city they had overrun, plotting with collaborators, shooting hostages. It hardly made sense to imagine them shopping and having a good time, making love and dancing, remembering tunes, regarding the French people they met as benevolent hosts out to entertain the troops, utterly unconscious of what they had done, storing up memories. And all these glamorous things had been going on at a time when he was lucky to leave the training regiment's hutted camp once a week, lucky to have a depressing meal in a railway hotel with Mary if she had come up to visit him, lucky to have a few pints of bitter with the education and welfare officer. It was just another kind of injustice.

She was crooning softly, "J'ai ta main dans ma main, je joue avec les doigts——" There was no sadness about her, outwardly. She picked up Howard's hand and played with it for a second. She had long, scarlet fingernails. ("I loathe that habit," Mary had said, shuddering.) "Look!" she went on, dropping his hand. She raised a foot up in the air, so that the gown fell away up to the knee. "These shoes are also from Paris. Are they not amusing?" The shoe he saw was gaudily coloured with an immensely high wooden heel. Hilde giggled. "Such high heels—and the hats just the same—and young men with such long marcelled hair—oh! Paris! But it was also nice in Rome. Perhaps more elegant." Rome as well,

Howard thought; they'd known how to live, all right. But his mind was principally on the leg she had shown, and now withdrawn again, bare, smooth, slender, very lightly brown; he wondered hungrily what the rest of her was like. She smiled at him. "It's nice to feel that you are going back to such things—in London—I mean, that it's going on——"

He nodded. She was a perfect natural comedian. No doubt she thought of him with a flat in town, a little place in the country, a Rolls.

"Of course it isn't too easy in England," he said. Not for an insurance clerk, anyhow.

"Oh, perhaps not, but life is still life—here everything is finished—I don't know how I shall live. One is always tired, you know, with the food. But perhaps you will help us before next year. I think you do not know what it is like for us Germans."

"Well, do you know what it was like for the Poles?"

"For the Poles? But I do! We had many on our estate in Silesia. They were so nice! We were happy with them."

"Hell!" Howard laughed. He was past being exasperated. "I expect you were happy all right—but were they? They were slaves! They didn't ask to leave their country, you know."

Hilde shrugged her shoulders. She was a little annoyed.

"But I think so. They were only very little people, farm workers, you understand. I think they earned more money with us than at home."

"You amaze me," he grinned.

"It is true." She yawned prettily, with a little sigh. "Give me another cigarette—and some more Pernod."

He obeyed, thinking; she's never done any work at all, all her life. He half admired her for it. He lit her cigarette and then poured out the drinks.

"Well, down the hatch!"

"Down the 'atch—I do not understand. You must say Prost."

"Prost, then." They touched glasses.

"And we hear such terrible things," she went on. "I was

told that in Frankfurt women have been murdered and their flesh sold to the black market."

"You don't honestly mean to say you believe that?"

"I know even the name of the street—Taunusstrasse."

"And who's supposed to have done it? The Americans?"

"I think perhaps the American black men."

"I hope they got a good price."

"That is not nice." She was hurt. Howard looked at her fascinated that she could have treated such a story seriously. At the same time he felt sorry for her. She was like someone swept away in a catastrophe, who was still managing to sit on a raft with a few bits of her old furniture, trying to ignore the huge swirling waters of the flood around her.

"But it can't be true."

"No? But many strange things are happening in Germany. Here in Hamburg a few days ago a woman was found in a cellar, murdered, her wrists broken, her head had been—how would you say—knocked in and her tongue had been drawn out and transfixed with a—a stick. It was in the paper. Of course it was a Pole."

"Any more horror stories?" Howard shivered.

"Such things happen."

"All right, you've proved that. Prost."

"Prost!" she smiled. "What is your work in England? You are not a professional officer?"

"No, I'm—I'm in insurance." Now throw me out, he thought.

"Insurance—what is that?"

"Well, you pay some money, you see, every year, and then if you have an accident or you die——"

"Oh! Versicherungsgesellschaft! Then you must be very rich, I think. A friend of ours in Berlin owned such a business, he was very rich—such a beautiful house on the Wannsee— oh, such parties! We would sail in the yacht and swim and lie in the garden and brown ourselves. Oh! It is all over."

Howard felt relieved. He had no great desire to put up a show before her, but his normal instinct to publicise his defects were not operating. "I'm just a bloody clerk, my dear" was his usual line, which sometimes gained him a reputation for cheerful frankness, and sometimes merely annoyed the hearer. But Hilde took it so much for granted that he must be a man of means that he was reluctant to spoil the impression. Sitting next to her in the soft pink light, with the cigarettes and the Pernod and the perfume, he could almost believe it himself.

She was smiling.

"What's the joke?" he asked, with some concern. Whenever people laughed his first assumption was that he was the point.

"I was thinking of Berlin—of a time there once—it was a party in our flat. All must come dressed in old clozes, Napoleon, Katerina, Friedrich, you understand——"

"I get it. Fancy dress, we call it."

"We have put mattresses on the floor and it was forbidden to stand, one must go everywhere like a snake—and there was, oh, such a crowd! It was so funny!"

"You liked your fun and games, didn't you?" His own life had been constipated, he thought, marvelling. The things that went on were amazing. Tennis club dances, mess beer parties, evenings at the pictures with Mary faded into dull oblivion. For the Howard Randles life was a series of journeys on a season ticket, forwards and backwards on the suburban line; for others it was one excursion after another into different scenery and always in comfort.

"I have almost forgotten," Hilde said. "Otto has a message for you! When you have gone the other night he has said, 'I like that officer.' And Otto is so, when he likes a person, he must do something for him."

"Me?" Howard said. He sipped his Pernod in surprise.

"He said, 'Tell that officer if he come back, I know where I can get him fur coats for cigarettes.' So, I have told you." She blew out smoke slowly. "But I think you are not interested."

"Well, it's not the sort of thing——"

"Of course not. That I have told him. A few thousand

marks are worth little in Hamburg today." She laughed. "And for us it is no longer shameful to black-market. For you it is different. You are an officer, you have your business. It is what I said to Otto."

Howard had to have a large sip at his Pernod to steady himself. "A few thousand marks." He was overcome at the calm way she had mentioned it. There might be inflation going on among the Germans, but a mark was still sixpence at the Atlantic Hotel—and at the officers' shop, for which he still had all his coupons. However, she had assumed that the matter was of no concern to him and she went on talking gaily about the fancy dress party and how they had put all the lights out for an hour and passed round bowls of champagne.

"When was all this?" Howard asked. He was trying to forget the marks, telling himself that she was quite right, he was not interested. Those few cigarettes had been nothing, really. This was a bigger matter altogether, not to be touched with a barge pole.

"Oh, in the spring of forty-one. We have had a very nice flat looking on to the Tiergarten, you know, and really I have liked to live there better than anywhere! We had an old schloss in Silesia, but I did not like it. It was too old! And then there were not many peoples of our culture to speak with as in Berlin."

He shook his head understandingly, almost with sympathy. But all he could think of was the fur coats. Luckily it seemed there would be no return to the subject and it would be impossible for him to bring it up. He did not want it brought up. He wanted to forget about it.

"Such a party with old clozes we had two weeks ago also—but very small, of course."

"Here?' he said, astonished. "In Hamburg.?"

"Of course, why not? It was in the room of a friend. I was a peasant of Holland with a great hat. It was amusing. Such things take our minds off our circumstances."

"I'll bet they do. Was Charlie—was Captain Morton or any of the people——"

"Oh, no! The English come to some things but not to all. There are two social lifes in Hamburg. One with the English, the other without. So it must be. But if we should have another such party and you would like to come—perhaps, it will be all right—you would like that?"

"I think I would." The possibility of achieving a social distinction ahead of Charlie Morton, to say nothing of Hemsleigh and Styles, was most exciting. It clouded over his guilty thoughts about the fur coats. This was a girl who had lived a life of luxury, who mixed with counts and countesses and yet regarded him as an equal. Up to a point he had thought it was merely due to his nationality and the result of the war, he was an English officer, a member of a privileged caste. But now it was more than this, he was receiving individual respect denied to other English officers. Howard's self esteem rose. Insurance clerk, his foot; that was six years ago. This was his level now. He said, "Yes, it sounds a damn good idea. Good fun."

"You too like fun?"

"You bet I do!"

"So many Englishmen are so serious, I think."

"Not this one." He sounded very complacent and he winked at her; Hilde smiled and with a sudden gesture pulled him closer to her on the settee. The movement made him realise that he was now slightly the worse for drink. Slightly the better it should be, he reflected wittily. Howard Randle could take it. He knew how to live. He was astonished to find that she was looking sad. She bent her head sideways and leant against him so that his chin was buried in her loose wavy hair. She began to talk in a low voice.

"It is so nice here and so warm—all these memories have come back—I want to cry——"

"That's all right." Howard felt very protective. He managed to put down his glass on the table without disturbing her and then slipped his arm around her.

"I do not know if it is right to try to be happy."

"Oh, of course it is!"

146

"I think of my man who is missing. Those dreadful Nazis—it is all so terrible to think what has happened—if only the revolt had succeeded——"

"Revolt?"

"July twentieth, the generals' revolt, when my man was arrested."

"Oh, yes."

"I have not even a photography of him. They must all be left for the Russen—all—everything!"

"Where did all this stuff come from?" he asked. He had never seen so much furniture in a small room, and it was all solid and comfortable.

"I have brought it from my flat at the beginning of last year. Many people did the same when they felt the Russen were coming. All have fled to Hamburg or to the south to be with the English or Americans. But sometimes I wish that I had stayed and died. I will die next year—for when our money is gone—what then can happen to us—everything is finished. Even now I am often hungry for hours. You cannot understand. I must not speak in this way. It is dull for you. But there are things I cannot forget, when the Russen came to our village—and I must hide in the woods and see the burning and the terror—oh, such things we have not deserved——"

He began to kiss her and she held on to him tightly. He thought gently, what harm had she ever done but to have a good time. Of course it wasn't reasonable to expect her to understand the Russians. But it took a broadminded person like himself to realise that, he reflected. She was a pretty girl who had known great misfortune, he was an army officer away from home—that was the way to look at it. In the circumstances, to be civilised, what he was doing was his duty. His lips found her ear, its lobe, the neck beneath. Her head turned upwards and he kissed her chin, her cheeks, and her lips. Then she was kissing him and his mind ceased to think or have any kind of guilty reaction. Her sharp nails pressed painfully into his skin, and for a moment she was still.

"Are you married?"

"Not yet."

"You will be—an English girl—in London?"

"Oh yes."

"Of course." Her mood of depression was over. "How does she look—fair and beautiful?"

"Dark."

"And her name?"

"Mary."

"Mary. And yours? You have not told me. I cannot call you Herr Leutnant always."

"Howard."

"Howart. Mary and Howart. That is nice." She pushed him gently away and a suppressed yawn made her body quiver. She stretched out her arms, then dropped them and smiled. He looked disappointed. "I feel—oh—zufrieden! Nice. Howart, you would like a little dance moosic? There is still some from München, I think." She pointed over her shoulder to the corner of the room behind the settee. "Over there. Go and make the switch, Howart."

His head was throbbing when he stood up. He walked over to the little white radio with a rather forced steadiness. He felt as if he had been rebuffed, but he was not altogether sorry. His old humorous sense of inadequacy stirred. Maybe he was a fool. He switched it on and when the light behind the dial glowed turned the tuning knob round. Most of the stations were dead. Then he found the dance music.

"Not too much noise!"

"O.K." He tuned it down. It faded right away and he fiddled with the knob again. He said, "You never explained the curfew pass, you know. What was the idea?"

"Oh—that night I felt I must—I must have a man with me."

The music returned. He decided that the reception was good enough.

"You did?" he said, returning; and then he caught his breath. He hadn't heard her move, but she had unfastened the gown and slipped her arms out of the sleeves, and she

148

was there waiting for him, smiling. From the radio the voice of American Forces Network, Munich, Germany, was drawling, "——from Bad Nauheim—gosh, everyone's in Bad somewhere tonight—guess most every place in Germany's bad; well, here you are, Joe, the greatest of them all—Harry James!"

Somewhere in Munich, a few hundred miles to the south, a needle dipped and a gramophone record began to play.

CHAPTER 3

I

"Fancy you being down to breakfast!" Kay said. "I thought you'd joined the lazy ones for good. Are you feeling better? I thought of coming in to see you last night in case there was anything you wanted, but I decided not to."

Howard swallowed a spoonful of porridge.

"Oh, yes, I'm better," he said.

"There's nothing like a good night's sleep, is there? I put my ear to your door but I couldn't hear anything so I thought you must have tumbled straight into beddy-byes."

"That's what I did."

"I'm sorry if I made you drink too much, Howard. You see I've been here longer and so I'm more used to it, I suppose. I expect you'll be writing to your Mary to say you've met an awful type of girl who leads you astray. You dare."

"Blandison, I am thoroughly ashamed of you," Miss Hackster smiled whimsically from the head of the table. "Not only did you not sign out but you left the water running in the bathroom, so that it was only lukewarm."

"Oh, Sybil, I swear I didn't."

"I enquired particularly from Hammond and it could only have been you. I didn't want to mention it last night."

Howard went on with his porridge, relieved that no further attention was being paid to his night's sleep. There was an uncomfortable silence round the table. Kay pretended to be calm and unconcerned, but her face was pink and inwardly she was furious. However, she was optimistic about Howard and she soon began to think about him again. Although he had been so tiresome about going to bed, she felt that last night had been a success. He was a little shy and silent, probably afraid of women—but if only Sybil and Peter had not turned up at the Country Club, any inhibitions would have been spirited away. She felt indignant about his Mary, who was doubtless some good-for-nothing girl he had met very little, who had trapped him into an engagement; she knew the sort, she could tell from the set of the lips in the photograph. Certainly there was no need for her to feel any conscience about helping Howard to have a good time, being friends with him. And if he did decide that he preferred her, well, it was only lucky that he had seen in time. Kay bit her lip. She was off on the usual fatal train of wish fulfilment, while the reality was that Sybil was in a temper and anxious to take it out on all the Control Commission civilians in the office. Except for Howard the Army was not present and therefore the jobs of everyone at breakfast had to be looked after. They could be sacked. They all ate their breakfast carefully, asking for the mustard and the salt in hushed voices. Really, there were times, Kay thought, when you got to the end of your tether, you positively could not stand it another minute. But, of course, to go back to England as somebody's secretary wasn't very inviting either. Oh, dear. And all because of Pratty going out with Maxie. She wondered if it were true after all that Sybil was a lesbian. She could hear them both arguing at two o'clock in the morning and from the extra powder she could see that there had been tears. This atmosphere would go on all day. Somehow, she thought, she must make Howard take her to the Atlantic for lunch. He was

150

looking rather tired, poor lamb. Has he got up for breakfast simply in order to see her? Facts were facts and here he was, after all; and the last two or three mornings he had stayed in his room like the others. She brightened. If it were so, Sybil could go to hell.

"I'm glad the sun is shining at last," she said. "It makes Hamburg so much less depressing, don't you think?"

She had spoken across the table to Mr. Maxton-Hill, who was, except for poor Mrs. Pratt, the least comfortable person in the room. He looked at Kay gratefully.

"One is always thankful for it, Kay—one of the few untaxed pleasures that remain."

Mrs. Pratt blushed and Miss Hackster's icy good natured expression remained set. In the circumstances it had not been a diplomatic phrase. He tried to turn it neatly. "Though talking of taxes," he went on hastily, "I do feel we ought to protest to London. Johnson will never do anything and Hugo isn't interested—besides it's not his pigeon, really. It's bad enough to have to pay half one's income away, but worse not even to receive the income!"

He made a little coughing sound which was meant to be a casual chuckle. Usually Miss Hackster could be drawn on this, and then they all had a hate conversation directed at higher authority, ending with the common determination to resign and go home—except for Peter Schroeder and Elizabeth Ford, whose naturalisation papers might be ruined by any show of independence. But none of them meant it seriously. Bed sitting-rooms, uneducated landladies, lonely cups of tea, the conversation of fellow prep school masters or of girls in the office who had never travelled farther than Hastings, of the diabetic lady downstairs or the food crank next door, the blowzy wife—all of them had a dismal secret picture of home. Though the Kasselallee had its disadvantages, discomfort was not one of them, and they knew it would pay them to stay as long as they could. It was easier to talk about England than return there.

He was not in luck. Miss Hackster said nothing. Really,

she was very like his headmaster's wife, that odious woman. Oh, if only things had continued as they were in the early thirties, when he was a happy, contented Berlitz teacher, with a room and a life of his own. It was agony to remember the low rents and cheap food, the clean brightly decorated brothel only five minutes away, his little library of Tauchnitz, Albatross and Obelisk. Since then everything had been a nightmare, the return home, the school, the war-time ministry. He finished his toast, sipped his tea which he took without milk, and lit himself a cigarette, noting with distaste the nicotine stain on his fingers. The Control Commission, the life here in the Kasselallee had been a gift from heaven for him, not a substitute for the old days, of course, but it enabled him to be unhappy in comfortable conditions. And he knew very well the value of the work he did once inside his office. It made him particularly vulnerable.

"Has anyone heard the latest news on Friedeberg?"

It was Elizabeth Ford, who sat next to Peter Schroeder at the bottom of the table.

"One heard that Bonzo was not too enthusiastic——" Mr. Maxton-Hill murmured unhappily.

"Oh, Bonzo was livid!"

"Why, is that someone new coming here?" Kay asked, wondering at once whether it was a man or a woman.

"I understood that Bonzo had stopped him," Howard said. Everyone looked at him in astonishment. For a newcomer to be adding a little gossip on a Control Commission subject immediately gave them all a sense of unity. They had no defined code, but were aware when it was broken. Their whole existence lay in their intimate knowledge of certain names in London and at headquarters in Germany, in discussing them with everlasting interest. If Howard could join the game so quickly, was he something more than a dull lieutenant who had come by mistake from a military unit— did he have Control Commission contacts? Howard was not aware of the change in the air. He added vaguely, "I overheard him telling Charlie——"

The interest he had aroused dispersed at once.

"I hope he has," Elizabeth said. "A dreadfully rude, pompous man."

"I think it's a great pity, if it's so," Miss Hackster said. "Friedeberg has an excellent brain. I admired him very much in London, though I know he was disliked by some people." She was referring to a happy period when she had worked in a Belgravia office, concerned with unimportant details of a secret war project. She smiled in a martyred way. "But then one has often noticed the tendency for someone with a good brain to be disliked. Isn't that your experience, Pratt?"

"Oh, yes, it is, Sybil." Mrs. Pratt could hardly say the words quickly enough.

"One respects him," Mr. Maxton-Hill said.

The toast and margarine parcel was being made up, the signal that departure for the office was imminent. Miss Hackster stood up and was caught in a shaft of sunlight.

"If only one were setting out to shop off the stalls in the Piazza," she sighed. "With gaiety everywhere instead of this drabness and bomb damage, with priests and peasants and little coloured Madonnas——"

She left, followed at once by Mrs. Pratt, and there was a sense of relief in the room, though no one commented on it. They did not trust each other enough.

"A boat on the Thames would suit me," Peter Schroeder said. "With a pretty gel in it of course." He was more painfully English than ever, rather complacent about his special position this morning. As Miss Hackster's Country Club escort he had nothing to fear, unless there was no justice. "A punt and a gramophone," he went on. "Just the job, I think."

"I'd like a boat on the Wannsee." Elizabeth yielded to an impulse to be German in order to annoy him. His overacting sometimes irritated her.

"And then sit in a café and eat cakes full of Schlagsahne!" Kay said.

"What's the matter with the Alster?" Mr. Hopwood said.

He had been very quiet this morning. Profoundly grateful for the happy chance of leaving his wife and achieving an undreamed of standard of living at the same time, he hated trouble of any kind in the mess. Now the atmosphere felt better and he began to hope that everything would be all right. "You can teake a boat out for a mark, you know. Good exercise. That's what ah'd do."

"Oh, no Hoppy, it's miserable to have to look at Hamburg!" Kay gathered her spare toast and margarine to make her morning parcel. "But then of course it would be the same nowadays with the Wannsee and there wouldn't be any luscious Schlagsahne."

"I didn't know you knew Berlin," Elizabeth said.

"Oh, yes, I was at the university for a time," Kay said carelessly. She did not like Elizabeth.

"Really, what did you study?"

"Literature and history—of course, I wasn't there very long——" It really had been a short course in commercial German, undertaken with the hope of getting a job with an Anglo-German trading firm. But something made her refuse to admit such a dull idea. Kay preferred to think of the bleak Foreigners' Institute in the Dorotheeanstrasse as if it had been a finishing school for débutantes.

"Literature from the Nazis must have been rather amusing."

Kay controlled herself with difficulty, and made no reply. She rolled up her parcel and stuffed it into her handbag, which hung on a long strap from her shoulder and accompanied her everywhere. Elizabeth, she reflected, was the only woman in Sociology Division who did not take a little food to the office for her staff. It was typical, quite typical.

"Have you been to the Garrison Theatre this week?" Elizabeth asked.

"Er—no, I haven't," Howard said. "I don't even know where it is." The question had been directed to him and interrupted the dream of guilty triumph in which he was indulging. Kay looked up sharply. This was a danger she had overlooked.

"It's just by the Hauptbahnhof. I wanted to know what it was like. Some of these variety shows are frightfully good."

"Yes, they are, aren't they?" Kay said. If Howard was to be forced into taking Elizabeth to the Garrison Theatre, it was not going to be with her help. "Howard, I've got an idea. It's so lovely out, why don't you and I walk to the office? It only takes a quarter of an hour."

"O.K." he agreed, rather to her surprise. Howard was feeling generous and even anxious to be kind. He had not been so pleased with himself for a long time; the whole episode had gone off remarkably well. Hurrying back to the mess two hours before, creeping upstairs, he had felt his deception of Kay on his conscience. He did not expect it to be undiscovered. He could hardly believe the quietness in the house. Her door was shut and, even better, his own was ajar, so that he made no noise at all. When Doring came in with the early morning tea he was shaving and his bed had been suitably ruffled. Only Hammond knew where he had been and he was quite confident of the batman's discretion. He had lied to Kay, he had slept with an extremely passionate German girl, he had been disloyal to Mary, and it seemed that nothing would come of it.

Outside it was bright and warm in the sun, though chilly out of it, and they went along bravely without their greatcoats. Kay was glad, for she knew that her own coat made her look rather dumpy and she did not want to spoil her figure in front of Howard. There was no getting away from it, he was more cheerful than usual this morning, he was even whistling softly, "I'm a Little on the Lonely Side," and she had to pant to keep up with him.

They had to walk carefully over a plank, where some young Germans, fair and bronzed and stripped to the waist, were digging a hole in the pavement, repairing drains. Kay had to speak to one of them who was in the way. "Entschuldigen Sie," she smiled at him. What muscles he had! "Guten Morgen!"

"Morgen, gna'e Frau!" he smiled back.

"It's amazing how friendly they are sometimes, isn't it?" she said, as they went on, although she was rather piqued that the handsome youth had said "Frau" to her. Why not "Fräulein"? But perhaps it was a mark of respect. "Of course it makes a difference if one speaks the language—You know, I'm sure it would be much better if we flatly made our zone a sort of colony and brought out one of the Royal family as Viceroy. You'd be surprised the number of Germans who suggest it."

They walked along two side streets, full of early twentieth century, yellow-stuccoed villas, some in ruins but most of them in a state of shabby preservation. It was possible to glimpse the huge rooms, the pillars and archways that made each house a miniature castle, the stained glass round the large winter gardens, the solid ugliness of it all.

"They used not to live on a thousand calories here!" Kay said. She thought vindictively of the enormous meals that had once been consumed inside the houses. "Just imagine the miles of sausage, the hundredweights of Sauerkraut and Schnitzels and whipped cream!" She giggled and linked her arm with Howard's. "Can't you just see them?"

"I expect some still do," Howard said.

"Well, they don't look like it!" Her humanitarian instincts were aroused. "You know, in spite of all they've done, when you look at their pinched faces, it's horrible to think we have enough and they haven't. The girls are always fainting at the office. About six weeks ago I brought back a pound of butter, some cheese and sugar and bacon from Copenhagen —very little—and took it to a woman in the Kasselallee who was a friend of a Danish lady I met. When she saw it, she whispered to me, 'You know what this means?' and burst into tears all over me! I felt so awful."

"What about the Dutch and the Poles?"

"Oh, Howard, you men!" She squeezed his arm. "You just can't be sentimental, can you? Always seeing the logic of everything! But of course you're quite right. I say, would you like to see the concentration camp trial that's going on?

156

We've all got passes for the press seats and I believe it will be very interesting today."

"I like your train of thought."

"Now you're teasing me, Howard! I don't mind."

"I'd quite like to see it, anyway."

"All right! I'll collect you at about a quarter to twelve." Kay felt triumphant. It would be child's play to go on to the Atlantic from the trial.

II

"Everything will come right," Charlie Morton crooned, as he entered Howard's office, "if yew'll only berlieve ther gypsee——"

"Hullo, up early, aren't you?" Howard said.

"Me? You are talking to Stakhanov Morton, my friend. Already, at mid-morning, my files are up to date. Choose which you like, Evangelical Lutheran, Evangelical Free Church Committees Union, the Free Evangelical Lutheran Faith, the Evangelical Lutheran Committee of Zion—I got my tabs on 'em all!"

Howard grinned, but he was uncomfortable. He did not feel the same friendliness and understanding for his visitor that he had at their first meeting. After all, he had an aristocratic German girl, while Charlie was carrying on with a vulgar red haired Displaced Person, and, except for one small incident, he had kept clear of the black market. Hemsleigh and Styles were really more his style.

"It's inspiring."

Charlie bent over the table and pointed a reproving finger at him.

"Three o'clock in the morning and not in his room!"

"What's that?" Howard was startled.

"Don't give me that surprised look. I just happened to be passing, that's all. Less than a week after arriving here! I felt so ashamed. Don't tell me you were next door."

"I don't tell you."

"But gallantly walking with her to the office, breathing in

the dew of the Spring morning! St!" He slapped Howard on the back approvingly. "I knew you were a bloody dark horse, old boy. Trust a man who's been on the road! I sniff 'em out."

"What can I do for you?"

"Like that he talks!" Charlie sat down, tilting the chair backwards. "To me that fixed everything. That's gratitude. That's life. Ho hum, another day! So he's busy. All right, to business. Have you got your pincers on the labels yet?"

"No." Howard shook his head uneasily. Here, at once, was a moral crisis, one in which there was no possible compromise. Either he was currupt or he was not corrupt.

"So slow he is! Get 'em quick, there's a pal. Time's marching on for me, you know. Demob at the end of next week—did you see my date had come through? Hugo stirred himself at last and got the boys moving at Eight Base Sub-Area."

"You lucky sod." Howard felt a stir of hope. If Charlie were going, it would be easier not to give in, to remain true to his own standards.

"Twelve days, my friend, and then—England, Home and Duty-free!"

"You've got a lot of stuff?"

"Quite a pile. Lenses, some jewellery, fountain pens— usual stuff. I need about fifteen labels to be comfortable."

"Won't the A.P.O. sniff something?"

"The postal boys? Not if I sent to different names and addresses. You've got to get yourself organised, you know." He stood up. "Well, there you are, old pal, tempus fugit, see? So if you'd kindly get cracking and wave the care of them there labels from the good and honest corporal, it'd be midy fine, pal, midy fine!"

Howard didn't like it. He felt as though he had just been asked to join in a burglary. It was also irritating that Charlie should assume his willingness. The easiest course was just to say nothing, to keep putting him off. On the other hand Charlie was not the sort of person who could be put off very easily.

"Why don't you ask Hugo?" he said.

"What? Well, I'll tell you. Because Hugo's not above taking a cut himself, but when it comes to other people, he's suddenly very, very honest! Moreover he delegates everything to the corporal, and the corporal's as obstinate as a mule. The whole thing's crazy, they've got hundreds of the things, unaccounted for, they don't have to worry. All these scruples in this place, it makes me laugh."

Howard was silent. Charlie stared at him with sudden concern.

"You wouldn't be going to tell me you're not giving——?"

"Well, I don't like it."

"Jesus!" Charlie ran his hands through his brilliantined hair and stared at him. He had dropped his clownish air. Howard turned pink. "But that was the point of your coming in here! You agreed to it."

"I didn't. You—you just assumed I did."

"That's rich! I help you get fixed up. The first bloody minute you're here you sell a tin of cigarettes to Scholle, God knows where you were last night and now you have the sauce to talk like the Fifth Form at St. Dominic's! It won't do, my friend. This matter of labels is just a little convenience. I can go somewhere else, I can get them if I take the trouble. Wake yourself up! Pull yourself to pieces!"

"Well, go elsewhere, then." The reference to the cigarettes made him angry. Scholle must have told him. "Anyhow it wasn't a tin, it was just a few."

"Just a few!" Charlie was pacing to and fro. "My God, that line annoys me! The hypocrisy of kidding yourself you're honest because you're only a little dishonest. It's not as if I were a big operator. But, by God, I'm not ashamed to let you know what I'm doing. This is a chance to make a bit and I'm taking it! I despise this business of selling a bottle of this or a few fags just to keep your expenses down and then pretending not be on the black. That's Hugo's ridiculous attitude, that's Kay Blandison, that's everybody——"

"It isn't everybody——"

"Oh, God, I suppose you've been talking to Mike Hemsleigh or John Styles. They're crazy. But I'll tell you something else. They've got money and I haven't. Nor have you. Not if you're just a jerk in a bloody insurance office. They can afford to strike attitudes. I can't. What sort of reward do you think you'll get for not having taken your chance when you could? I'll tell you. Damn all! You've been five or six years in the bloody army while all the bastards in civvy street have been coining it and now you want to pretend to show moral difficulties when your own bloody government's obviously giving you the chance to help yourself!"

"How do you mean?" Howard's anger had changed to misery. Whenever anyone shouted at him he had an overwhelming impulse to agree, to give in.

"Do you think the Field Cashiers don't know what's happening? The men nobody knows? Why do you suppose they let us go on using marks in the Clubs and the canteens? They know where they've come from. Why do you suppose they've been lenient to the troops at the customs? They know the loot's going through. The war's been over more than a week, you know. And they're not going to have a special currency for us here until August! That's when the wives and so on are coming out, when the army that's fought the war will be home and you just have regulars and young soldiers here! It's an official way of saying: 'Help yourself, boys.' If it isn't, I'm crazy or they're raving mad!"

Howard lit himself a cigarette. His heart was pounding. Charlie came to a stop in front of his table and bent down to stare at him.

"Wait a minute now," he grinned suddenly. "Have you been pulling my leg, you old bastard?"

Howard returned his grin. There was a battle going on within him. He wanted to be re-established in Charlie's estimation, but he also wanted to remain high in his own.

Charlie nodded, as if he had just understood something.

"You wouldn't be angling for a cut, would you?"

"I don't know what you've got."

"Well, I'm blowed!" Charlie whistled admiringly. "For

160

heaven's sake! Talk about dodgy——" He broke off, for there was a tap on the door and Kay Blandison came in. "Hullo, Kay! You're looking adorable."

"Be quiet, Charlie." She was in her coyest, most excited mood. "Are you ready, Howard? It's a quarter to."

"Yes, O.K." He pushed his chair back in relief and stood up. He never thought he would have been so glad to see her.

"Kay, I'm surprised at you!" Charlie said. "Arm in arm this morning, now dragging him out to lunch——"

"I'm doing no such thing, Charles Morton, so there. We're going to the trial."

"All those nice camp guards?"

She tried to freeze him with a look, and turned to Howard. "Come on, let's leave this nasty character."

"I'm on my way."

Charlie accompanied them to the stairway landing.

"I'll let you have a fountain pen," he said to Howard. "Does that make the difference?"

Howard chuckled in a meaning way.

"You think again."

"You bloody old rogue!" Charlie's voice followed him down the stairs, but the friendly note was still in it. "Don't you forget, I can unfix that phoney job of yours if I choose to!"

"That's your story," Howard called up to him. "So long."

They nodded to Leo and went down the steps into the alley. He was relieved for the moment, but still worried. He had bought peace in the argument at the price of Charlie thinking him a pure trickster. It would be difficult to keep up this bargaining front for long.

"We can walk quite easily," Kay said. "It's not much farther than Dammtor station—a little way up the Rotenbaumchaussee. Did you know Charlie was going at the end of next week? We'll have to have a demob party for him at the Country Club—and we can celebrate Bonzo's naturalisation at the same time. When are you leaving us, Howard?"

"It's about a month, but it would be just my luck to be deferred."

"I wouldn't be sorry."

"I would." He said it because it was the conventional thing to say, but the thought of going home did not thrill him at all. It was really all the worse now that he had made himself comfortable in the Army at last.

"I suppose when you've all gone they'll send out some dreadful old refugees to us—and then the wives will come, of course—that's where they're making a great mistake in my opinion. I know my sex, I'm afraid. It simply means there'll be cattiness and gossip, and snobbery and social distinctions —can't you just see a T.O.I's wife not speaking to a T.O.III's? Pity a poor girl like me! I expect we'll be accused of robbing husbands and heaven knows what. It's a shame when we all get on well as it is, don't you think? I mean, I believe a man and a girl can be just pals, don't you?"

They had passed the Esplanade Hotel on their right and the squat old war memorial on their left. They crossed under the railway bridge and came to the large square in front of the station. Five roads ran into it and there was a halting place for trams. On the far side there was a circus tent and a fair, which had not yet begun the day's work. Close to it, on a corner between two roads, there was a neat looking hutment, fenced in. This was a model of a pre-fabricated home put up for British troops to inspect and see what lay ahead of them when they were demobilised.

There was always a long queue on the island tram-stop, and it always looked the same, patiently waiting, apathetic, poker faced: tired little workmen in their peaked chauffeurs' caps, their skin lined and yellowish; girls in what was left over from their old wardrobes, feathers and colours that did not seem quite natural, as if purposefully feminine; young men in alpine hats and dyed converted uniforms; young men without arms or legs, with cheap crutches and hungry faces, their tragedies taken for granted, arousing no pity; sullen, weary middle-aged women; men in waisted suits and over-smart little trilbys, the opportunists, the smart ones; boys of fifteen and sixteen in their super-short black trousers, and white ankle socks, their arms round each others' backs; and round their feet and in the gutter a few dirty, happy urchins playing like sparrows.

"I always say it's much more interesting to walk," said Kay, whose arm was now once again linked in Howard's. "You can look into their faces, can't you? I mean, if you're in a car, you don't see anybody really. Did you notice that girl? What a look of hate she gave us! Or perhaps it was only at me—they don't like to see English girls, you know. It's not surprising, of course. Why, only this morning I had some figures to go through and, do you know, in Templehof in Berlin there's only one boy of eighteen to twenty-one for every ten girls of the same age!"

"He must have quite a time," Howard grinned.

"Oh, you!"

They had to wait for some cars to go by—the usual powerful German models with British uniforms of one colour or another inside—and then they crossed towards the Rotenbaumchaussee. Howard saw two direction notices, one of which said 'Swimming Baths' and the other 'War Crimes Trial.'

"Down there is the Botanical Gardens." Kay pointed to the road on their left. "That's where the Social Democrats have their big meetings. We all went to hear Schumacher the other day. He's supposed to be the coming man, you know. Oh, look, here's some communist propaganda on this wall —and on the pavement, too. Really, I don't think they ought to allow it on the pavement, it's so untidy." They paused to inspect some red stencilled representations of two clasped hands—this was meant to be the Social Democrats and the Communists merging into the Socialist Unity Party. The hands were scattered about everywhere for a few yards like outsize confetti. "Still, it shows it's not all apathy, doesn't it?" she added. She often spoke of the Germans as if she were a schoolmistress and they were her pupils.

Their next stop was in front of a newspaper stall. The few papers had all been sold early in the morning to a large queue

163

of people, who were prepared to wait for hours to read amateurishly presented news which they were convinced was propaganda and lies. Now the stall was deserted and there was no one behind the narrow wooden counter. Outside it there was a copy of the front page of the paper. There was a headline about the Nuremburg Trial, which had to be featured on the front page, by order. The second story was a long speech about economic recovery in closely printed thirty line paragraphs. Kay explained it all quickly to Howard. At the corner of the page there was the comic relief department, a little drawing of a girl sitting next to a fat man in evening dress. Kay pretended to find it amusing.

"The girl is saying 'Don't you feel the pangs of conscience when you consider that with the guns you made people were shot?' and he replies 'But, look here, I used to give a thousand marks a month to Winter Help!' "

"It's a scream," Howard said.

Next to the newspaper was a black and white poster: "Potato Supplies: The Central Office for Food and Agriculture, Fisheries and Forestry in consultation with the British Military Government announces——" Then there was a large board containing personal advertisements: the inevitable long list of search notices accompanied by the old German Army Field Post numbers—'Obergefr. Georg Hausmann, last seen at Sarajevo (Croatia)——'; amazingly sanguine items, considering the ruin of the country—'Young merchant, 26 years old, with many-sided knowledge and capacity for independence requires a position in a large merchant business or factory, eventually to take over or become a partner, Box number——' or 'Girl, if possible experienced nurse, not over 30, who can speak and write English and is perfect typist and stenographer, for gentleman suffering from paralysis, required to join family at once. Applications with salary required to Box Number——'

Kay became conscious of someone besides Howard standing next to her and regarding her with curiosity. He was a tall German who had not bothered to obey the order by which uniforms had to be dyed. Glancing sideways at him she had to repress a shudder. The lower part of his right nostril was missing and he had no left eye. His old field-grey tunic was smelling mustily in the spring sunshine. He ignored Howard. He smiled down at Kay, showing a gold tooth.

"Haben Sie vielleicht eine Zigarette?" He spoke with a deep lisp and a particle of his spit caught her on her cheek.

"Nein! Ich habe keine!" she said quickly.

"What's he want?" Howard enquired.

"Oh, he's asking for a cigarette. I've told him I haven't one."

The German stared at her for a moment, undismayed. Then he shrugged his shoulders and shuffled past them. Howard was relieved. He had been afraid there might be some kind of scene in which he would undoubtedly be shown up as a fraud.

"He had a damned cheek to speak to you." He felt it was necessary to re-establish himself. Kay, however, was not worrying at all. She was translating items from the Offers of Marriage column.

"Listen, Howard! 'Woman, forty-four years old, brown hair, good complexion, height 1.45, weight 58, with 15,000 marks, would like to meet gentleman with two-room apartment with view to marriage'—'Girl, twenty-five years old, non-Jewish, blonde, height 1.6, interested physical culture wishes to meet young gentleman with similar interests, room available Blankenese'—I bet she wears jackboots."

"It's as good as 'Health and Strength'."

"Oh, well, we'd better go on to the trial," Kay said. She had been reluctant to get there too early in case he was bored and wanted to leave. They strolled along again. Two German women passed them, gossiping to each other. One of them said, "I hear they've had no Schnaps in America for months——"

They passed a few empty shops and approached a tall building with two entrances outside which there were sentries. At the sight of Howard their bodies stiffened, their rifle butts clattered, they came to attention and sloped arms. Kay hurriedly unlinked her elbow from his. As Howard passed the first entrance which was not to be used, they gave him a smart butt salute. He saluted casually back. The performance was repeated at the second entrance, which was a turning under an archway leading to a small courtyard. Howard's self-esteem was now right back. He even felt superior to the Military Policeman who stood guarding the door into the court. They showed him their passes to the Press Gallery and went inside. Here a second Military Policeman crept to another door and pushed it silently open. This led into the courtroom itself.

It was a hall the size of a large gymnasium. Kay and Howard found seats easily, for only two British correspondents were present, together with some German journalists, a Frenchwoman, a small party of Danes and, Kay noticed with annoyance, Hemsleigh and Styles. Wherever she took Howard it seemed they must find someone else from the mess. Her companion however was only concerned with the two rows of camp guards who were on trial. His interest in coming had been tepid, but now that he was here he stared at them fascinated. They sat in a long box-like structure which ran along the left hand wall, white faced with prison pallor, with numbers on their chests, as if they were footballers, dull, normal-looking men and women, bored but not depressed, their hair brushed and carefully parted or done according to habit. But the sight of them even in their captivity, with the row of red-capped Military Policemen and women standing placidly behind them, was chilling. Howard had to jerk his gaze away from them to look at the rest of the courtroom.

The President, an army brigadier, with the Judge Advocate General, a civilian lawyer grotesquely wearing the wig of an English court on his right, and two majors and a naval officer sat in a similar box along the right hand wall, directly opposite the prisoners and the line of German defence counsel, in their black gowns, who sat beneath the dock. The prosecutors' table was in front of the Press Gallery and here, with his back towards Howard, a tall middle-aged British officer was on his feet, interrogating a witness. The witness box was

166

at the far end of the court, flanked by a desk at which three uniformed interpreters were sitting. As soon as anyone spoke, his words were translated into German or into English, so that there was an air of deliberation about the proceedings. A little bald-headed man was in the box.

"And so you are telling us that you saw Klotz, Ekhoff and Johannsen in the camp and on the parade ground on the day that the party of Russians arrived?"

The witness listened to the German translation and then nodded his head.

"Jawohl!"

"Yes," the interpreter said.

"And you can see them among the accused?"

As soon as the interpreter had translated, an official ordered brusquely, "Zwei—auf! Vier—auf! Neun—auf!" and numbers two, four and nine of the prisoners stood up, looking expressionless.

"Those men are Klotz, Ekhoff and Johannsen?"

The dialogue went on strangely as if between the prosecutor and the interpreter, with the German interjections slowing it up.

"Did Klotz beat you?"

"Many times."

"What did he beat you with?"

"A whip."

"Did he always carry a whip?"

"He always carried a whip when I saw him."

"Nice guy," Howard whispered, but Kay paid no attention to him; she was leaning forward, listening intently, like a film fan. Howard looked over the rest of the court. In front of the judges, shorthand notes were being taken by soldier clerks. At the back of the witness box there was a gallery for distinguished visitors. It was empty. Finally there were two upper galleries facing each other, one for British troops above the prisoners and the other for the German public above the judges. The German spectators watched the proceedings with intense concentration. Some were law students. There were many women. Unlike the German lawyers, who seemed oddly prosperous, as if their lives were being carried on precisely as before the war, it would have been easy for any of them to replace the prisoners and look much the same. Not that they were obviously sadistic; but nor were the prisoners. They had the same sallow appearance, the tidiness, the expressionless, dead faces which were nevertheless ready to break into sarcastic smiles—at anyone's expense, not necessarily the British. It was almost as fascinating to look up at them, to glance from face to face, as at the prisoners themselves. This was the German people, forty or fifty representatives of the enigmatic millions outside. When one of them suddenly looked in his direction and caught his eye, he turned hastily away, embarrassed; but just as quickly he was staring up again in astonishment. The face had been Hilde Nahler's.

He was sure of it. Sure also that he had seen a gleam of recognition, of surprise. But there was no sign of her now. The face was not there. Where she had been—he could swear it—there was now a spectacled young man. The gallery was crowded, a place would be filled in a second. Somehow in that moment when he looked away she had ducked out of sight. The sound of a door closing somewhere convinced him. It must have been her. But why the drab clothes, the grey coat and hat, like the other spectators? It was unnatural. It couldn't be that his imagination was playing him tricks. Why think of her at that moment? Howard looked down, closing his eyes tightly. He felt uneasy. He looked up again. Even if it had not been Hilde, the girl he had noticed was no longer there; and that girl had had auburn hair.

"This ought to be very interesting!" Kay whispered. "Kaminski's going into the box. He's very important. The others were jealous of him because he used to sleep with the Kommandant's wife and he's been getting his own back by telling everything. A man in War Crimes told me."

In his private confusion Howard had not noticed that the witness had left the box and that one of the accused, a dark

168

gipsy-like young man was being sworn in by the chief interpreter in front of the President.

"He's one of the worst," she went on, shuddering. "Horrible things!" Her eyes were bright, as if she were really enjoying herself.

"He looks capable of anything."

"Fancy being under him!"

"Anything——" Looking at Kaminski, who now strolled to the witness box, Howard forgot about the auburn-haired girl in the horror of all the stories which had become part of the background of his generation, the stinking, frightening names of Belsen, Dachau and the rest. He moistened his lips with his tongue. "Christ."

"I'd like to deal with them," Kay whispered. "That's what they want. The same done to them." She put her finger hurriedly to her lips, for one of the majors beside the President was looking in her direction.

The laborious question-and-answer procedure went on. A second interpreter was now working and the first sat back with his eyes half closed. Kay gave Howard an intimate little smile and settled down again to listen. The smile did not disappear entirely and her hands were clasped tightly on her lap, as if from excitement. He looked up at the gallery, but all the Germans were staring down at Kaminski. He couldn't see an auburn-haired girl. Now he was not so certain about it. He shrugged his shoulders imperceptibly and watched the prosecuting officer, as he rummaged about the papers on his table, speaking at the same time.

"I put it to you that it's rather—rather strange that this loathsome event should have occurred, not merely in the camp in which you lived, but in the block of that camp in which you slept?"

"I cannot explain that."

"You have heard the story from—from Klotz and from Meyer and from Bredfeldt, all of them substantially agreeing in the details—of how the bodies were driven slowly across the parade ground the following morning in the full view of the camp inmates who were forced to sing at the same time?"

"Yes, I have heard them."

"But you do not remember?"

"I do not remember."

"You heard your Kommandant say that you were always present at that early morning parade?"

"Yes."

"Now are you trying to say that your Kommandant and Klotz and Meyer and Bredfeldt are all lying?"

"No doubt they are telling the truth as well as they remember."

Some of the prisoners remained immobile, including Kaminski himself, others looked up and grinned, and a half suppressed snicker spread through the galleries.

"I suggest that you do the same. We'll consider the night you do remember. This night of October second, when the mixed party of Dutch and Frenchmen arrived. You were with Helmcke, the adjutant?"

"Yes."

"How long had you been with him?"

"An hour or two."

"What were you talking about during this time?"

"I don't remember."

"You were a junior member of the camp staff and you had an interview with the adjutant lasting at least an hour, surely not a usual experience for one in your position, and you forget what it was about?"

"Well, it was private."

"It was to do with Frau Pätzel? All right, never mind what this private matter was about. You were present when Helmcke was informed of the new prisoners' arrival?"

"Yes."

"What did he say? What orders did he give?"

"He said there was no room in the camp for them and that they should not have been sent."

"Presumably he also gave some orders? Did he say what was to be done with them?"

"Yes, but I can't remember exactly."

"Did he order that they were to be hanged?"

"He said something like, 'They must be done away with—it's not fair on the others.' "

"You took that as your instructions to hang them?"

"Yes."

"Did you personally think that was a very sensible way of solving an overcrowding problem?"

"I was not paid to think."

"Anyway, at approximately nine o'clock you personally hanged them in Block D?"

"Yes."

"How did you do it?"

"Well, there was a small room as far as I remember with a beam across it. We fixed up a rope." Kaminski stared placidly at the ceiling as the interpreter translated. He seemed to be quite unconscious of the tension in the courtroom. Howard could hear Kay's quick, deep breathing. The half smile was still set on her lips.

"Who is 'we'?"

"Some of the ordinary prisoners helped."

"Oh, the prisoners had to make your gallows? All right. How was the actual killing done?"

"We put a chair under the rope and they stood on it in turn. We pulled the chair away."

"Where was Helmcke while this was going on?"

"He came and watched the first twenty. Then he went away."

"How many were executed?"

"Between fifty and sixty."

"And when this—this task was completed did you report to Helmcke?"

"I went to do so, but he had gone to the Kommandant's room, and he usually stayed there all night."

"But for Helmcke you would not have carried out these murders?"

"It was not my job to give such orders. I would have favoured a more humanitarian treatment."

"Such as you gave the witness Czerwionka, who is crippled for life?"

"With Czerwionka there was a consideration of punishment."

Suddenly the calm, nightmare story was interrupted. There were consultations between the President and the prosecutor, signs between officials. The Military Policemen on the doors braced themselves. Kaminski stepped back and walked meekly to the prisoners' box, where he found his seat like someone late at a concert. The President announced that the Court would assemble again at two o'clock. In obedience to the warning notices which were posted up, everyone rose, including the prisoners and the Germans in the public gallery, as the President retired through a door behind his box, followed by the bewigged Judge Advocate General, the majors and the naval officer. The prisoners (some of them chatting happily), were shepherded out by their red-capped escorts through a similar door. The prosecutor was tidying up his papers. One of the defence counsel was telling what appeared to be a funny story. They gathered round him in their black gowns like a group of public-school masters on Speech Day. The galleries emptied, including the Distinguished Strangers', where an Admiral accompanied by two pretty Wrens had been watching for the last ten minutes. A Military Policeman removed the half-drunk glass of water from the prosecutor's table. It was lunch time.

Outside the sun was still shining.

"What did you think of it?" Kay asked.

"Better than an 'H' film," Howard said with a shiver. "Christ."

They came out into the courtyard, blinking, into the middle of the small crowd of German spectators. He looked everywhere, but there was no sign of any auburn hair. But he was now sure that he had been mistaken. It had been some obscure trick of the mind. Hilde had had enough troubles of her own without wanting to come and listen to this.

Hemsleigh and Styles joined them.

"Hullo, Kay, hullo, Howard. Want a lift to the Atlantic?"

Howard was about to refuse with thanks, but Kay said rapidly, "Oh, John, that's ever so sweet of you, really it is, because we haven't got a car here and it's much later than I thought; but we weren't really going to the Atlantic, were we, Howard? Or would you like to?"

"I haven't got any money," he grinned.

"Oh, don't be silly! I'll pay."

"I'll lend you some," Hemsleigh said. "I can let you have a hundred."

"Well, really, I don't like to——"

"Look, there's nothing to it, I want to go to the Field Cashier, afterwards, anyway. We can call there."

Howard received the two fifty-mark notes, helplessly, and they all moved towards the street. Once again there was the clatter of the sentries' butt salutes, which the three officers returned, while Kay looked complacent. It was not often that she had the pleasure of being out with three men; and John and Mike had never been very friendly. The car was parked on the other side of the street. It was battered, powerful, American.

Hemsleigh and Howard climbed into the back, where they sat cramped between petrol jerry-cans. Styles and Kay were in front.

"Enjoy the show?" Hemsleigh asked.

"It's quite a hit. What a lot of bastards! It's hardly believable."

"Who do you mean—the spectators?"

"The spectators?" The words came out with a gasp, for the car had jerked forwards at remarkable speed.

"Yes, of course. John and I only go to watch the spectators. Most interesting! Everybody looking jealously at the unfortunate prisoners. Never seen so much envy in my life."

"Don't listen, Howard!" Kay turned round, roguishly. "Mike and John always try to pull your leg! They never say what they mean."

"My dear Kay, surely you realise it's the truth."

"I can't see there's much to be envied if you know you're going to be hanged," Howard said.

"Hanging! It's a cheap price for all the fun they've had; that's why they're so calm about it. Think of their position! They were actually ordered and paid by the State to let loose every repression they had. These boys could commit any crime they liked without even thinking about punishment. Every little sensual whim could be satisfied. The whole fabric which governs everybody else didn't apply to them at all! How do you know what some of us would have done, if we'd had such a chance? Opportunity's a fine thing. Why, of course, those camp guards are the envy of everyone who looks at them. The trouble is we just can't imagine a life without moral or civil laws hedging us in. But that's what they had! And the only paltry condition was obedience. They were the most privileged people in the world. Don't you agree with me, John?"

"Oh, absolutely, Mike."

"You ought both to be ashamed of yourselves! Oh! Goodness, I thought you were going to hit that policeman."

"No, he's a frightfully nice little chap. Always waves me on."

"Which was the adjutant?" Howard asked. "The one that got tired after watching twenty. He seemed a nice type."

Kay answered him at once. "Oh, Helmcke? That's the one they never caught. He used to sleep with Pätzel, the Kommandant, who was number one, of course, the one with silver hair. Helmcke and Kaminski had that camp in their pocket."

"You see?" Hemsleigh said. "She's revelling in it. How can anyone go back to the *News of the World* after all this? Why do you suppose every country has to have penalties for murder and sex crimes, if it's not a deterrent to people who want to do them? You've only got to look at our people or Americans working the black market. They know they can get away with it, there's no danger—so they do it! It's as simple as that."

"But not everybody does it——" Howard protested.

"No, but a lot of people do it who wouldn't, if they thought penalties were attached that would really catch them."

"It's like picking your nose in the bathroom," Styles said. "No one can see you do it."

"John! I think that's perfectly disgusting!" Kay exclaimed.

They parked the car in front of the lake, which was glittering. Although all the buildings were shabby, including the Atlantic itself, it hardly seemed credible that half this city was rubble. Under a blue sky everything looked better, faces were more content. The usual children, running round on bare feet, were at the steps of the hotel waiting for cigarette ends. A little boy made water in the gutter on the other side of the road.

"It's really a Latin scene, isn't it?" Hemsleigh said. "It's pleasanter really than that dull old Teutonic cleanliness. Of course, as usual, our home-based humanitarians have got it all wrong. It's precisely the children that you don't have to feel sorry for. They're having the time of their lives."

They went into the hotel, and the party split up. Hemsleigh and Styles went into the grill-room bar on the left.

"That black moustache!" Kay said. "It always makes me want to laugh. Let's go to the Long Bar, Howard. There's a drink you simply must have called a 'Kapitän-Leutnant.' The U-Boat officers used to have it there during the war."

A Russian officer, a serious, middle-aged man, came down the stairs by the reception desk with his Russian servant, who was staggering cheerfully under an assortment of cases. An ENSA party was clustered round the desk, giving theatrical unreality to their khaki uniforms. The Russian looked at them curiously and went on out through the doors. Kay decided that the blonde hair of the girls was dyed, then took Howard's arm and conducted him firmly out of the vestibule down a long corridor, which led to the bar. She continued to talk, but he was only half listening. There was a devilish refrain pounding on his mind. "No danger," it ran, "no penalties, no risk! No danger! No penalties, no risk——" He tried arguing with himself. People like Charlie Morton could go

175

down a sewer and come up smelling of violets, when people like himself would merely smell of the sewer. It wouldn't work, he'd never done that sort of thing, he was afraid—and that was the root of it all, fear and fear alone. And it was all wrong. "They know they can get away with it," Hemsleigh had said, "there's no danger——" No danger, no need for fear.

III

It was inevitable, Kay thought furiously, that Charlie Morton should be in the bar. It was always the same. Everything was spoilt for her. If it wasn't her mother at home in Stamford Hill, it was someone from the mess here. Just when she wanted Howard for herself.

"Why, it's the old Kay herself! And escort! The man snakes won't talk to."

"You're talking, aren't you?" Howard said wittily.

"Hell, he's in that sly old mood again!" Charlie was in excellent spirits, and he was not in the least perturbed by Kay's cold stare; a happy extrovert, he was not even aware of it. He had seen them from the far end of the noisy, overcrowded room and hurried through the mass of R.A.F. pilots, kilted Army officers, uniformed women. He was not alone. Coming elegantly up in his rear was Panting, who had rescued Howard at the frat party. He carried himself as before, his sleekly brushed head bent forward, his fingers twined together in front of his chest, lovingly guarding a glass. "You know my buddy Conrad, don't you, Kay?"

"I don't think I've had the pleasure."

"Kay Blandison—Conrad Panting. Is that the wrong bloody way round? I get worried, I'm so uncouth."

"Enchanté." Panting bowed.

"Howard, my son, you want to know Conrad. He has the best contacts in Hamburg! He's colossal, aren't you, Conrad?"

"One tries to arrange one's affairs," Panting murmured. "Up to a point one succeeds. Oh, dear!" One of his hands fluttered to his throat with a steadying motion. He smiled gaily. "I'm charmingly drunk, don't you think? Not like all these other ghastly people."

"That's right, Conrad, you take it easy like a good boy."

"I'm not a good boy and you know it. I'm extremely naughty," Panting told Kay, in a confidential whisper. "I have a fin-de-siècle craving for wickedness, especially when it's slightly abnormal." He recognised Howard and became quite animated. "But, my dear, it's you! What a lump you were! It was like carrying an elephant." He touched him caressingly on the stomach. "You simply must do something about your weight. Another time I might not be there to suffer for you—and there might not even be a beautiful German girl to smooth your forehead. What was her name?"

"I haven't a clue." Howard flushed. He had felt impelled to lie.

"Wasn't it Hilde somebody——" Catching Kay's eye he stopped short. "I'm probably quite wrong. I was thoroughly drunk. I even went home wearing a woman's hat! Wasn't it dreadful?"

Kay agreed with him, but thought that he himself was even more dreadful. However, it was one of Panting's keenest pleasures to feel that he was being despised.

"I've just been talking to the most dreary correspondent, haven't I, Charlie?" he went on. "He says it's scandalous to see so much drink as they have here! Jealousy, of course. He'll be passing out in a minute, odious fellow. I said to him we had far more in our mess and there had been three deaths, hushed up. He could hardly wait to get out his notebook!"

"It doesn't seem sensible to me to tell a journalist an untruth," Kay said.

"But, my dear, he's certain to distort it!" Panting was most amused. His free hand fluttered over his hair. "Why be truthful to a man who sends back stories of luxurious feeding when he's surrounded by a million under-nourished people, or who calls a slightly discontented queue in front of a baker's shop a good riot? Besides, I could have told him much worse things, couldn't I? I just kept it to good, solid old drink, something he understands. Oh, dear! Gnädiges Fräulein, I can see by your eyes that you disapprove of me!"

"A cat can look at a queen," Charlie laughed, thumping him heartily on the back. "Be your age, Conrad, old son."

"Charlie, I simply don't know why I allow you to be one of my friends. I suppose I shall just have to buy the drinks, as usual. I'm just another kind of public convenience, as far as I can see."

While he was away Charlie told Howard, "He's nuts, but he's smart. He's got a NAAFI manager that eats out of his hand. Get you anything you want. He operates in a big way."

"I think he's odious!" Kay said.

"Would he be interested in fur coats?" Howard felt a rush of blood to his forehead. He was amazed at himself for asking the question.

Charlie whistled.

"Christ, have you found a pile? I thought they'd all gone months ago. What are they—Luftwaffe?"

"I couldn't say exactly."

"Conrad'll be interested all right. Come to that, so am I. Are you serious, you old bastard—oh, excuse me, Kay! My manners."

Howard noticed a small brigadier standing a yard away, accompanied by an obsequious Guards subaltern. They could easily have heard. He went cold at the thought, and grinned sickly.

"No, not really."

"Raising my hopes," Charlie said, disgusted. "Or are you putting out one of your subtle feelers again? He's the worst of all of us, you know, Kay. One of the quiet ones. Don't you trust him."

"I trust him completely!" Kay smiled at Howard.

Panting returned with four champagne cocktails.

"My terrible correspondent is now tighter than ever——" he began, but Charlie interrupted him at once.

"Look, Conrad, there's a new client for you here—my chum

178

Howard. Fur coats. He's a devil, I warn you. Does the old hard-to-get, don't you, Howard?"

"Well, that is interesting!" Panting stared at Howard fondly.

The brigadier and the subaltern, each with a small glass of sherry, which they were sipping in moody, polite silence, were still close by. Howard tried to control his feeling of panic.

"No, really, he's talking drivel, old boy." He chuckled feebly. "I—I'm not in the game at all, worse luck. Er— cheers." With horror he saw that the brigadier was approaching them. Thank God, anyway, that he himself had done nothing. All the same he began to perspire. The brigadier touched Charlie on the shoulder and said something in a low voice.

"Just outside and round to the left," Charlie replied, directing him towards the bar entrance. The brigadier smiled, nodded and waddled away with his subaltern. Howard closed his eyes, limp with relief.

"Brass hats are always asking me that question," Charlie said. "They see in a flash I'm a man who knows."

"What fun it must be to have a little Guards boy for a pet," Panting sighed. "Which reminds me, I'm about to have a great social triumph. Gertie von Schwollenburg is introducing me to a real princess. I'm most thrilled, because I've never met royal blood in the flesh, to coin a phrase. I once saw the Windsors on the Carlton terrace at Cannes, but that's as far as I've got. We shall have tea together with Gertie, who has the most delicious buttered scones. Poor dear, she has to starve for three days afterwards. And incidentally, what stories she's told me about Berlin! The parties! The most shameless things—and as for what went on in the country, well, it seems a good time was had by all. Of course Gertie was a friend of Goebbels, but even so one never really thought of them as having a good time in that way, did one? I mean they may be dans-la-merde now, but my God what a bean-feast they've had! One really feels most jealous."

"It seems you were on the wrong side!" Kay snapped.

"But certainly not now, my dear!" Panting smiled. "Still, you mustn't mind me. I'm always saying the most awful things. I mean, I quite expect you were the sort of person who was parachuted behind the lines?"

"I was the sort who worked and did my duty!"

"Let's have another one," Charlie suggested.

Kay shook her head.

"No, really, thank you, Charlie. Howard and I ought to be having lunch, didn't we, Howard? I've got tons of work to do at the office." A moment later she was hurrying Howard out of the bar, murmuring scathing remarks about Panting. "There you are, you see, Howard, that's just the sort of person Charlie meets. All this fratting, I think it's horrible. And all that black marketing! Goodness knows, I'm not a prude, but there are limits, aren't there? I mean, I don't mind just a little. Of course Charlie barks more than he bites. I'm very fond of him really, although he is such a tease. What was that about a German girl smoothing your forehead? I hope it wasn't true!"

"Of course not."

"I'd give you such a piece of my mind if I thought it was!" She squeezed his hand. "We'll have to eat in the grill room, don't you think? I'd sooner look at Mike and John than those two."

The grill room was a series of rooms joined together, the outer ones overlooking the Alster. They were given an inferior table by the white-tied little head waiter. Hemsleigh and Styles, of course, had one of the best, far away from them. But Howard found the sight of them a relief. His mind was full of one subject: fur coats. It was plain enough that Charlie and his friend had taken him seriously. They took it as a matter of course. The point was, if he could bring off a deal, it would keep him for the rest of the time he was in Germany without touching his pay; and that would be a help towards his future with Mary. After all, Charlie's argument had been quite right; the civilians in England had had a soft enough time, it was madness not to take an opportunity like this.

The ex-soldiers would be at the back of every queue for houses and jobs. He thought of his interview with Mr. Waters again; and of his office colleagues who had had promotion after promotion, simply by staying at home. Look after number one; it was the only sensible thing to do; everybody did it.

Except people like Hemsleigh and Styles. They sat at their table, silhouetted against the window, talking as usual. They represented the old law-abiding values, still strong enough in Howard to make him feel guilty about himself. He did not desire their contempt. Besides, would Mary want to profit in that kind of way? Her remarks about the neighbours in her last letter made it seem unlikely. On the other hand Mary need not know. She had never enquired into his Army finances and they could easily be covered with technicalities, if necessary.

"Oh, dear, it's omelette again!" Kay was looking with disgust at the menu. "It's almost as bad as the Country Club. Don't let's have anything to drink, Howard, dear, because I simply must work this afternoon. Just have a liqueur afterwards."

"Suits me," Howard said. He was still far from used to the lavish spending he had seen. However cheap the prices, money could still disappear quite quickly.

The charge for lunch was six marks and the final bill—after Kay had gossiped inter-departmental politics and scandal for half an hour—was a mere twenty but it was ten shillings in honest money, more than half his day's pay. There had been advantages to the austere life of the battery, in spite of the boredom. Howard sighed.

They were joined by Hemsleigh and Styles on the way out and Kay again had the pleasure of an escort of three. In an excess of generosity she dropped her half-smoked cigarette on the pavement, so that the children could scramble for it. Howard drew in several more puffs, feeling rather ashamed, and copied her. The two captains were smoking cigars.

They drove away from the hotel at the same confident speed as they had approached it, under the railway and past the Lombard Bridge on their right, and then alongside the smaller lake. The Field Cashier's office was in a bank on the Jungfernstieg, the wide promenade at the far end of the lake. Howard's moral problem had reached a crisis as he followed the captains out of the car, with Kay smiling after him demurely. He owed Hemsleigh a hundred marks, which meant two pounds ten. But it would obviously be necessary to cash more than that, for the transaction would be done in their presence. It didn't take many champagne cocktails at six marks each to see the back of two pounds odd. But it was really painful to send good money down the drain when it was so easy to get the marks for nothing. Hadn't Charlie said that Kay Blandison and the rest all did it just a little? Just sufficient in fact to cover their expenses? On the other hand there was this undeniable attraction of being accepted by the two captains as someone of their own kind.

The two captains each drew four hundred marks. Howard wrote out his cheque in his Advance of Pay book slowly, first filling in the columns for the address of his bank, his personal number, his rank. But the decision had to be made. He decided on two hundred and forty. He wrote in the figures under 'Sterling Amount': six pounds. Six solid, unnecessary pounds.

The Army Pay Corps lieutenant behind the counter handed over the notes. Howard took them and passed two fifties to Hemsleigh.

"That squares us, old boy."

"Oh, thanks very much, Howard."

It was worth it, after all. They knew now that he was all right. It was proof. Here at the Field Cashier's was where he got his money. He was convinced that he could read approval in the backs of Hemsleigh's and Styles's necks. They thought him a good chap, a sound type. The knowledge was cheap at the price. There remained only Charlie Morton and the label question to disturb him.

He crossed the pavement with them, looking confidently at the passing Germans. For once he did not assume that their glances concealed sneers; they were far more likely to be feeling a decent respect for the best kind of British officer.

When they climbed into the car again and Kay said, "That was quick work!" Howard experienced a new sensation, suddenly, out of the blue. It was freedom. He had established himself. Therefore he could act as he pleased. He need no longer be influenced by Hemsleigh and Styles. He could be his own master. It was delightful. He hummed gaily, so that Kay turned round to give him an extra smile. He winked at her.

"Where did you get this car?" he asked Hemsleigh.

"Well, it's John's really. A man in his regiment who was being demobbed gave it to him. Awfully lucky, really. It's frightful to be here without a car, don't you think?"

"I do." Yes, he certainly did, now he thought of it.

Back in his office, he rang the bell at once. The boy came in and bowed.

"Stefan, ask Corporal Clayton to come in and see me."

"Jawohl!"

The corporal entered a moment later, looking rather surprised. He was rarely sent for. He kept himself to himself, read a book in his billet in the evenings, and longed to be sent home, where he would continue his studies in cost accountancy and forget all about this foolish military interlude.

"Yes, sir?"

"Corporal, about those duty free labels—you keep them, don't you?"

"Yes, sir. The major handed them to me."

"Right. I'll have them locked up in here in future. You've got a book accounting for them?"

"Yes, sir, but I don't know if the major——" the corporal checked himself, remembering his junior rank in time. It was part of his kingdom disappearing. He felt indignant.

"What's that?" Howard demanded.

"I'll bring them in, sir."

Howard whistled softly to himself, took out some papers

from his in-tray and signed them. The corporal returned with a cardboard box and a notebook.

"You'll find a list of everyone who's had them in here, sir. The major said they weren't to be handed out freely."

"Is there a copy of the receipt we gave for them?"

"Only a '108' somewhere, sir." The corporal looked at him and spoke very much on the defensive. "You see, we took them over from a regiment that was disbanded."

"Most inefficient," Howard grunted. "They ought to have been sent back. All right, corporal, thank you."

Corporal Clayton gathered up the signed papers and left, almost slamming the door. Howard chuckled. It was too easy. Why on earth had he been hesitating about it? If there were no outside check on it, Charlie could have two hundred labels for all he cared. He had asked for fifteen. Howard counted out twenty and put them in his pocket. Then he stood up and took the box and the corporal's notebook to a cupboard, in which he locked them.

He ran upstairs and knocked at the door of Charlie's office.

"Come in! Well—what do you know!"

"Quite a little nook you have here," Howard said. He looked round with appreciation. The room was furnished in great comfort. The desk at which Charlie was sitting was large, the chair cushioned. There was a thick carpet, a telephone, two typewriters, an oil painting of a country scene on the wall and even a sofa. He took the labels out of his pocket and put them on the desk. "There you are—little present from Uncle."

Charlie shook his hand.

"What a pal! I appreciate this. Saves me a lot of bother."

"Glad to do it, old boy." He sat down on the sofa. "There was something I wanted to ask you."

"Now don't spoil your gesture."

"Are those fur coats worth going for?"

"You bet they are!"

"The thing is I'll need cigarettes—I don't know how many—it occurred to me your friend might help, old boy."

184

Charlie leaned back on his chair and laughed.

"I thought you'd be up to something, you old devil! I could tell. Well I expect something can be arranged, given there's a good percentage. Christ, I knew you were a dark bloody horse."

"Opportunity's a fine thing, isn't it?" Howard grinned. "Someone was telling me only today." Hemsleigh's voice came dimly to his mind; he had forgotten what it was about. He took out his case and threw a cigarette across to Charlie, then lit one for himself and relaxed on the sofa, watching the blue and white smoke intermingle, enjoying his new pride, as Charlie agreed with him.

PART IV

CHAPTER 1

DURING the next few days, Howard found that once you saw your way clear, life was improved. A drink ration of two bottles of Schlichte, one bottle of German brandy and a bottle of whisky was distributed to each member of the mess. Howard was fortunately in the room when Mrs. Pratt received hers and as she could not afford it all, he undertook to take half her ration in addition to his own. He then sold the three bottles of Schlichte for eight hundred marks to Hammond, who sold them to three of the waiters for nine hundred. As the entire cost of the one and a half rations had been under a hundred marks, Howard felt it was a very satisfactory transaction. He took the brandy to Hilde's flat and kept the whisky in his bedroom. He could go to the Atlantic or the Country Club with the comfortable feeling that he had a month's pay in his pocket which could be spent without affecting his bank balance. It gave him more confidence all round. Almost within a few hours he developed a new friendliness, a greater consideration for other people. He found himself thinking regretfully of his battery; they had been a very pleasant lot, really; unsophisticated, that was their only trouble. Moreover he was no longer so impressed by people. He now regarded Hemsleigh and Styles with some amusement. They were charming, but ineffectual. He smiled warmly whenever he saw Kay, but it was the confident smile of one who knew how to keep clear. He wrote a long letter to Mary, which contained love and sympathy, and not a grouse, not a word of personal complaint. He lost his feeling of inferiority with Hilde. With a thousand marks in his pocket book, he too was one of the gentry. The second time they were together it was he who took the initiative. Her response was overwhelming. Afterwards, as they sat drinking his brandy, he felt not the expected depression, but elation. He thought that he could look at her for hours, tirelessly. Her smile, her soft murmuring

189

voice with its accent and her grammatical mistakes entranced him more and more.

"I think we are happy together, Howart?"

"I am. Are you?"

"Oh, I am very happy, but you cannot understand why. I am perhaps wicked."

"You?"

"Yes, I am serious, Howart. I am a wife, or possibly a widow. If he comes back, what will he say if he finds I have had love for an English officer? All the same it is fine. I like to love you, Howart. You love me also a little?"

He nodded.

"But not so very much, I think. Englishmen are cold. They are not romantic. That is why I say you cannot understand me. I think it is necessary always to have a little love. Oh, this brandy! I am drunk."

"You're lovely."

She smiled at him and began to croon in a low voice, looking at him through her glass:

"Ich bin von Kopf bis Fuss
Auf Liebe eingestellt,
Und dass ist meineWelt,
Sonst garnichts!"

"You could make a fortune doing that!" he said.

"You know it? Marlene Dietrich?"

"I don't know what it was all about but it sounded terrific." Hilde looked hurt.

"Terrific? You did not like it?"

"Terrific's a compliment!" he chuckled. "You're thinking of terrible."

"Oh! How stupid I am! You will think me very stupid, speaking so badly."

"I don't think you're stupid."

"What, then?"

"I think I love you."

"That is nice."

It was clear to him not only that he did love her, but that he did not love Mary. In fact, a little shudder of relief went through him as he reflected that they had nearly been married on his last leave. A close shave; and it had been his own suggestion, but luckily Mary's common sense had prevailed. "It's better to wait until you're out of the Army and know where you are, Howard." Not that he imagined all at once that his future lay with Hilde. The present was enough, and Mary was no part of that. He had remembered her for a second and now she was gone. He gave himself up to the intoxication of looking at Hilde, who liked his direct gaze and acted prettily, blowing out smoke rings, half closing her eyes, making sensual little movements like a cat, doing all the things that Kay tried so hard to do. Howard could not bear it. He stood up and went over to her. He kissed her repeatedly, smoothed her, hugged her. Hilde laughed and panted. It was just what she wanted, but in a minute, like an over-petted animal, she suddenly became unresponsive.

"That is enough, Otto may come tonight and we must not be like this."

He let her go, reluctantly.

"Surely he won't come now?" He glanced at his watch. It was eleven o'clock.

"It is possible."

"Do you want me to go?" As he spoke they heard the sound of the former air raid siren, which was used to warn the population of the approach of the curfew time; three short alternating notes at eleven, two blasts at a quarter past and one long blast at half past, when the curfew was on. It had been put back an hour for the approaching summer.

"It is awful that they make that noise! You know what we call it? The voice of Military Government! Oh, life is terrible!" She looked depressed. "But no, of course, do not go. Otto will like to see you. But he would not like to think that we have love together. That we are friends he is glad. Otto has always said that the Germans and the English should be friends."

"Of course," Howard agreed. "And by the way that reminds me. You weren't looking at the trial the other day, were you? I could have sworn that I saw you."

"The trial?"

"Yes, you know, the concentration camp trial."

"Oh!" she exclaimed. "Must you always be talking about those dreadful places? Do you know what it must mean to us even to hear that wort? Please do not say it ever, ever again! Of course I would not be there. I do not understand how anyone can go!"

"I'm sorry, my dear," he said, confused. "I didn't think it was you, of course, I knew it couldn't be."

Her skin was silver white, her eyes dark and angry. He thought that she had never looked more beautiful.

"I think you hate us all. It is terrible for us."

"Of course I don't hate you."

"The Germans, the Germans, always the Germans."

"You're quite wrong, Hilde, honestly."

"Honestly?"

"Cross my heart."

"Cross—? I don't understand. But I forgive. Now—one more nice kiss and then no more." She pulled him close again and kissed his lips for a full minute. He felt her tongue, and his agitated hands worked up and down her back. He was flushed, his heart pounded, a vein stood out throbbing on the side of his forehead, he was overcome by a sense of power. The kiss ended. She turned her cheek to his mouth and whispered.

"No more."

"Let's go back . . ."

"No, I said,—Otto may come." She caught her breath as he began to kiss her again. Then she bit hard at a little fold of skin under his left ear. He grunted with pain.

"Christ, be careful."

She giggled.

"You are a bad boy. Now put on your coat."

He returned sulkily to his brandy, while she patted herself

back to composure. He had a sip of it, poured out some more and then put on his service dress tunic, which was lying on the back of the settee.

"So," Hilde went on. "That is better. Is it also the same in England that a brother is careful of what his sister does, but does himself as he likes?"

"I wouldn't know. I was an only child."

"Typical Englishman! So silent always. Howart, I think I have much love for you." She raised a warning finger, for he was getting up to go to her again. "I think here is Otto."

The steps outside continued upstairs. They went on chatting, which meant that he listened while she talked. It seemed to him that not only was she physically more attractive but she was also more intelligent than any girl he had ever known. She talked about the theatre, of the Berlin actors and actresses who had come to Hamburg, many of whom she knew personally; about literature, and she splashed her conversation with quotations, some in English, some in French. Howard was used to this kind of conversation, for Mary was an enthusiastic supporter of the Old Vic and Sadlers Wells in London and liked everyone to know it, but she had never reached Hilde's level. He marvelled to think that an hour before she had been lying on her bed, thoroughly enjoying herself and him. And now she was talking about Bernard Shaw, curled up on her chair like a kitten, with her legs tucked underneath her, both hands holding her brandy glass as though it were heavy for her and the auburn hair which had first fascinated him falling lazily across her forehead.

"As I see it, Howart, he is continental rather than international, and it is because of this that the Germans have appreciate him more than the English. There is always Shaw in Germany. Even now at the Kammerspiele they are giving 'Frau Warrens Gewerbe'; but I am told that often there is not Shaw even in London. For us that is not understandable."

Howard nodded. It was not a matter on which he had any deeply felt conviction. He relaxed in the chair that had once belonged to a Tiergarten flat in Berlin and reflected with amusement that Hilde went with brandy just as well as Mary, poor dear, with a cup of cocoa. It was a small world, all right, if you didn't see much of it. But now he had learnt that you had only to lift this or that curtain and you could perceive the most exciting possibilities waiting for you. It was all a matter, really, of understanding your own worth. Most people he had known at home, for example, would have been lost in this situation; and here was he only not coping with it, but its master. This most attractive, well bred, well educated girl was his mistress. She made no bones about wanting him. It was amusing, if not disconcerting, to remember his previous triumphs, the hurried incidents of a car-park, a tennis club, an Army dance, which had made up his manly score. He simply hadn't known what could be done; he had gone through life in blinkers. He thought with sympathy of the thousands of fellow travellers on the dreadful East London journey to and from the City, who never stirred outside their rut. Well, it was fortunate, on the whole. Someone had to go through with it, it might as well be them. But it was no longer going to be Howard Randle.

The future, which had been a nightmare, now became a daydream. England was full of people who lived pleasant, interesting lives. Now that he had found himself, he was bound to be one of them. Anyhow there was no question of his returning to the domination of the mediocre Mr. Waters at the office. His way would be very different, something like that of Mr. Butlin, for example, with his holiday camp idea. Or who else? Selfridge, perhaps—that was it, start a shop, but do it with a new approach, new ideas. Or think of the man who had started greyhound racing. Why, there was no limit to the things you could do, provided only that you had the vision, the confidence. And this business of taking a profit out of the German black market, what was it really but legitimate opportunism? Wasn't that the foundation of every successful man? You needed to step outside things every now and then, and take a good calm look at what was going on.

Butlin, Ford, Selfridge, Woolworth, Randle. The world took you at your own valuation.

"Ah! Mr. Rondle! How are you, sir? How are you?"

Otto had arrived, startling him out of his serene thoughts. He had opened the door without warning, uttered a sigh of exhaustion and seen Howard. At once he beamed angelically and hurried over with his hand outstretched.

"Oh, er—hullo," Howard said, wincing at the handshake.

"Mr. Rondle, I am so glad to see you again! Yes, yes!" He turned to Hilde and kissed her forehead. "Oh! Travellings all the day. Na, schrecklich!" He wriggled out of his enormous mackintosh and then proceeded to empty its pockets. There were two small loaves, a pound of butter and a tin of milk. "A few calories, no?" he winked at Howard. Hilde took them all into the bedroom and locked them away. When she returned Otto opened a haversack with the air of a conjurer and disclosed a dozen pieces of coal. He chuckled, "And some heatings!"

"Oh, you should not do such things!" Hilde scolded him. "It is so dangerous."

"No, no! It is safe!" Otto laughed, as the coal was also stowed away. "That is, sir, if you do not denounce me to the Military Government!"

But for the "sir" Howard might have felt a little irritated at the assumption of his neutrality. "After all," he thought, "I am an occupation officer, not a D.P." However, the "sir" made it all right. It was one gentleman closing his eyes for another. He grinned.

"Have some brandy."

"Brandy! Oh, sir, that is a nice sight. Yes!"

Once again Howard found himself liking her brother. It was hardly surprising if Germans were gloomy, and for someone to be so unperturbed by circumstances was refreshing. Otto seemed to be perpetually bubbling over with good spirits. Unlike the other people whom Howard had met with Hilde he had an enviable capacity for taking life as it came, Berlin parties in the piping days, black market and curfew-dodging now. It was impossible not to be attracted by a man who insisted on being so cheerful.

Otto ate a thick doorstep sandwich, which Hilde brought him, and then they settled down for a chat over the brandy. Outside, like the English "All Clear" after an air raid, the final siren moaned into the night. Otto gave them an amusing account of train travelling, from the point of view of the passengers on the buffers, while Hilde uttered little moans of disgust. Then the conversation turned to politics, in which, Hilde said immediately, she was not interested; it was not right to discuss them in front of a lady. Howard noted that as soon as Otto had come in, Hilde had become very much more careful in her behaviour, almost like the conventional Hausfrau. Otto brushed her objections aside. She did not seem to mind. Howard reflected that the Germans trained their women well.

"I am a Social Democrat," Otto said. "It is the nearest of our Parties to your Labour Party. As an officer you naturally support your Labour Party, which is your government. In the same way as a former officer I support that party which is nearest to my government, which is the Military government. So is it democratic. Oh! But how many of these Dummkopfs —of the Germans—there are who do not understand this way of democracy. I am sometimes hopeless for them. But believe me, Mr. Rondle, we will learn—the Germans will learn democracy! Yes! I am confident."

Howard had not quite followed this reasoning, but he nodded amiably.

"Yes, I expect things will settle down," he said.

"Of course! But first, I am convinced, we must become an English colony like Australia. I have thought of this matter very deeply, and I can tell you, Mr. Rondle, there are many of us, good Germans, who wish for this."

"Australia's not a colony, old boy."

"You must first understand the present German situation," Otto continued, ignoring him politely. "The Russian and French zones are lost for the moment. But in making these

196

zones permanent parts of their countries, the Russen and the French make a great, great mistake. In twenty years Germans will be in both governments, for they are better cultured, isn't it, and must rise. The American zone under all these Polish and Czech Jews must be ruined. There might perhaps be a small Anschluss with Austria. So. There remains the British zone. You are our hope, Mr. Rondle! Are we not blood brossers? Shakespeare, Shaw, Oscar Wilde are part of our own culture! The link of Hannover with your Kings is unbroken— although it is true the people there were shocked by the terror-bombing. Mr. Rondle, I say to you, if a vote is taken among all the peoples, ninety pro cent will say 'Yes!' Of course there are already parties for this aim. The 'Nieder-saechsische' people and so on; but I have no time for such. Splinter parties are all wrong—have we not been told by your leading officers? No. This vote must be taken through the Social Democrats, through Schumacher, in alliance with the Labour Party in London, so that it can be done democratically and correctly!"

Otto had worked himself up with enthusiasm. He smiled at Howard expectantly. The latter coughed; he felt rather at a loss.

"I suppose something of that sort may happen," he murmured. The fellow meant well enough, but it was amazing that they should be so oblivious of what the world thought of them.

Otto seized his glass.

"Let us drink to it, sir!"

"O.K. Cheerio."

"Cheerio!" Otto leant forward in earnest and continued. "And the next step is for all German liberals to lead Western Europe into a liberal bloc . . ."

"Oh! Politik, Politik, Politik!" Hilde exclaimed, her hands stopping up her ears. "It is too much! I will be mad. In my opinion there is only one division in this world: men and women."

"She is right!" cried Otto laughing. He patted her shoulder and turned to Howard again. "All men are brossers! Isn't it?"

197

"Absolutely," Howard said, and they drank another toast, touching their glasses. Otto began to rhapsodise over the new sentiment. How could people make war on each other, he demanded, when all were so nearly similar? Why, he had once met a dozen Polish officers, prisoners, and really they had been quite good types. But then the leading people of Poland, Germany, England, Hungary, perhaps even France, were all much the same, were they not? It was pure stupidity that made men fight each other. When you came down to it, you had to blame everybody or nobody. But, of course, he had always had internationalist feelings.

"I must be going." Howard stood up. He had begun to feel very sleepy.

Otto went with him through the door and out into the hall. Hilde, rather to his surprise, remained behind, after saying, "Good night, Mr. Rondle." So she was not calling him "Howart" in front of Otto. It was amusing. Howard went out on to the doorstep.

"Another time you must stay longer, sir. We must have a good long talk." He glanced at the door of the flat behind him and spoke confidentially. "I do not know if my sister has said about some fur coats—I can help if you have an interest."

"She did mention it a day or so ago. Actually I said I wasn't."

"You understand, sir, I wished only to be of use . . . ."

"But I did mention it to a friend of mine and he was interested."

Howard felt that this sounded lame and unconvincing, and he flushed; Otto, however, nodded.

"Then you would like to have some?"

"It depends how many cigarettes are wanted."

"Oh, not so many! Perhaps three hundred, four hundred—it is a service for you, Mr. Rondle. If your friend can find a use for ten or eleven coats, that is all that matters. I am not a Jew! It will be necessary to drive twelve kilometres out of Hamburg . . . ."

Otto explained rapidly. If Howard could produce a car,

which he must drive himself, they would go together. The coats, and other articles, were held in a small depot for the unused stores of the 42nd S.S. Panzer Korps, which except for arms and ammunition had for some reason escaped the close attentions of the English. The German in charge of the depot was a friend of Otto's and there would be no difficulty at all. They shook hands warmly at the end of it all and Howard walked briskly away down the street. He passed the sentry in front of the Army billet and said, "Good night!"

"Good night, sir!" The sentry drew himself up cheerfully as he answered.

CHAPTER 2

I

"WELL!" said Panting. "How delightful! Coats indeed. Fancy there being more of them. My dear, it's very thoughtful of you to come to me. Moreover it's so nice to feel that in spite of Charlie going, I shall still have a contact in Sociology Div."

"Five hundred will do it," Howard said. He had come to Panting's office, where the latter was engaged in controlling a small German industry, the day after his conversation with Otto.

"If they're good, it's very cheap."

"I think they'll be good. The man who's taking me knows what's what."

"Don't tell me it's your famous Herr Scholle."

Howard shook his head, grinning. How easy everything was, he thought; if only you went the right way about it.

Panting looked at him quizzically, then leant forward with

his elbows on the desk, the tips of his fingers touching. The female coyness disappeared for a moment. "As to terms. Firstly, if the whole thing's a flop—either you don't get them, or they're bits of old rabbit skin or what have you—I'm content merely to receive back the cigarettes within ten days. Secondly, have you any customers in line?"

"Not yet, old boy." Howard was a little taken aback at the new business-like tone of the conversation.

"Then, provided always the coats are what we imagine, I can fix that and collect. You do the deliveries. We split fifty-fifty."

"Don't swindle yourself."

"Listen," Panting said, with patience. "I'm being generous. A few dreary coats don't mean anything to me, my dear boy. You provide the trouble and the articles. I provide the cigarettes and the benefits of my—how shall I put it?— organisation. Fifty-fifty. Take it or leave it, and now is the time to say no."

"All right, you win."

"Have a car outside the Reichshof at two o'clock and I'll bring them out to you. Twenty-five twenties. There was no brand specified?"

"No."

"I'll do a mixture, then. Senior Service, Gold Flake. Perhaps a few Camels."

"Mighty fine."

"I'd ask you to come and have a drink at the Atlantic, but I'm meeting a particular friend. Would you like a half pint of 4711? I'll fix that for you. Well, give my love to Charlie. Look at my in-tray! Anyone would think they paid me to work."

Business was over. The mincing voice had returned and Panting saw him affectionately to the door.

"I can't think what Charlie wants to be demobbed for, can you? I mean one can't live in England nowadays, can one? Still, when he's gone, Howard, you can take over the drink I let him have. That's friendship, not business. I suppose you'll be taking over everything from him. Take my advice and keep clear of that red-haired D.P. bitch of his. A profit soaker if ever there was one. But of course you have Hilde—Hilde——"

"Nahler."

"Oh, yes." He smiled after Howard as the latter went out through a room full of busy-looking secretaries, then returned to his desk to continue running his industry, a job he performed with great efficiency. He had every incentive. He had secret gentlemen's agreements with half a dozen firms, waiting for the future, when normal commercial life was resumed. None of them would be able to refuse him. He knew too much.

Howard walked across the Lombard Bridge, whistling "Lili Marlene." Everything had now been arranged. Charlie had agreed to loan his car, a two seater Ford—which would be his for good in a few days' time—and all that remained was the job itself. Panting's terms were on the stiff side, but his taken-for-granted, business approach to it had cancelled the last traces of reluctance. Howard chuckled aloud, and two demobilised Wehrmacht men with grey skeleton faces turned to stare after him.

Howard was especially pleased about his future ownership of Charlie's car. He had found it irksome to have to travel to and from the office as a passenger in one of the Volkswagens, which were controlled by Miss Hackster, while the other Army officers transported themselves. It was a sign that he was part of her mediocre kingdom, like Mr. Hopwood or Mr. Maxton-Hill. Charlie's car would make a firm division, and, not the least benefit, he might find it easier to keep away from Kay, without offending her.

He looked benevolently at the crowd passing him. Yes, they must have had a hard winter. The spring sunshine made it difficult to keep your feelings of justice about them as tight as ever. A man mending a hole in the road was a man mending a hole in the road, a pretty girl was a pretty girl. There, but for the Grace of God . . . You had to be broadminded about these things.

The depot was half an hour's drive from the Altona station in Hamburg, where he had arranged to pick up Otto. Although it was a warm evening, the latter insisted on wearing his large mackintosh. "The way we Germans must live today, it is good to be prepared for all bad weather." A Communist meeting was being held in some nearby hall and loud-speakers relayed a speech to apathetic passers-by: "As a former holder of the Knight's Cross I shared this shame and desolation. Where stood German Youth? I was lost in a sea of doubt, of mistrust. I listened to so-called politicians with their so-called cures. I heard the voices of the old men. All the voices in Germany are the voices of old men. So it seemed." It was a young man, wallowing in hysterical self-pity. "Then I heard the voice of the Communist Party. Again I listened with scepticism. So great had been my disillusion. Suddenly I felt arrested. This voice, this new voice—it was speaking to me! As I drank in the inspiring message, my body and my spirit took on new life. Faith and purpose returned. German Youth! I call on you to take this path! As a former holder of the Knight's Cross . . ."

"Such impertinence!" Otto cried, as he stepped into the car. "Why is it allowed? That I cannot understand, Mr. Rondle."

"What was it all about?"

"A Communist swine claiming to have held the Knight's Cross! And I, a democrat, a man of July 20th, must listen. Ach!"

"Well, that's freedom of speech," Howard explained. The car—a 1938 Ford coupé—was easy to handle and he felt a pleasant sense of proprietorship over it as he drove along, leaving the Communist loudspeaker behind. "You've got to let the other fellow have his say."

Otto laughed.

"You are right! Oh, so much we Germans have to learn. Twelve years of silence are not quickly forgotten. But it is hard for men of July 20th to stand by, you understand."

They were passing through a half-mile patch of ruins. It had been a working class residential district and there were several burnt out blocks of flats. Otto sighed, looking abruptly sad. "It seems to us that so much time is lost on words. We have yet to learn your patience and toleration."

"It'll come, old boy." Howard enjoyed this master-pupil relationship.

"It is good to be in a car."

"Not bad, is she?"

"Before the war I had a great Mercedes sports car. It flew on the roads like an airplane."

Howard was not concerned. You only envied other people's pasts if you yourself had no future.

"What happened to it?"

"It was destroyed in a terror attack."

"Bad luck."

"I wish I had been able to keep it."

"I bet you do." Howard was sympathetic. They had left the destroyed area and were entering a district of small modern red-brick houses. They seemed neat and solid. It crossed his mind that you could see the same kind of house everywhere on the outskirts of London; as also, no doubt, of New York and Paris. He hoped the people were happy in them. Of course each one would now be overcrowded. How odd it was, he reflected, that a hundred people might be living in a dozen small houses, and yet it was possible to pass by without seeing a sign of a human. He swerved the car to avoid a jagged hole in the middle of the road. He said, "I suppose it'll be about twenty years before they can do something about these roads. The autobahns are bad enough, the way the cement's cracked down the middle."

"Of course——" Otto was still thinking about his Mercedes. "If I still had had it, the Americans would have taken it. But if I had been able to hide it, then it would have been very good. You know what I would do?"

"No idea, old boy."

"I would go with an English officer or a Canadian to

Holland and sell it for five thousand gulden. We have each a half and we come back with some real money. You know, our poor German marks can buy nossing. But a pound, a dollar! You can have everything in Germany then. So is it."

"You mean you'd change the gulden?" The car rattled as they went straight over a hole. Howard had been so intent on Otto's words that his concentration on driving had faltered.

"Of course. It would be a quarter of a million marks. There is a café on the Reeperbahn where I would have such a sum in five minutes. I could buy all the loaves of bread I want!"

"What an amazing chap you are!"

"You think so? Why?" He looked pleased.

"Well, the way you and Hilde have lived—and now you know all about that sort of thing—it's amazing."

"With Hilde it is different. She is always thinking that one morning she will wake up and all will be as before. All the day she tries to pretend. For a man, of course, it is easier to understand what is happening. I am glad you are her friend, Mr. Rondle. I think somehow since you have known her she has been more happy. You have also noticed?"

"I couldn't say I had." He managed to glance sideways, as if to the side of the road. Otto was looking at him, their eyes met for a fraction of a second. There was nothing out of the ordinary in his expression. It was enquiring and friendly as usual. Howard flushed and, as he stared ahead, he increased the car's speed.

"My sister is a beautiful girl, don't you think?"

"Very."

"It is sad for her. She does not know what has happened to her husband; but I think he will not come back. That is why I am glad you are her friend. After a time a woman needs these things. Else she is lost, she has no place."

Apparently it was a hint that he knew what was happening and had no objection. Howard was almost annoyed with himself at feeling so pleased.

"How far now?"

"Another kilometre only, sir." Otto took off his hat, a Tyrolese trilby, and fanned his face with it. They passed a camp of scrappy-looking huts on their left. He gestured towards them. "Homes for bombed Hamburgers. Ugh! Nasty smelling, I think."

"You don't sound very sympathetic, old boy."

"I do not like Hamburgers. They are dull, provincial." He leaned forward. "Now! Here we are."

They drove into the entrance yard of a small, rather shabby, yellow barracks. Two untidy Germans in fatigue dress stood at the gate and saluted the car with enthusiasm. Otto shouted at them and they pointed to a doorway. Howard drove towards it and Otto clambered out, hurrying round to the other side of the car to open the door for him. He then insisted on carrying the cardboard box which contained the cigarettes.

Inside the barracks there was a smell of soap and a canvas-matted, stone stairway. The building had the deserted air of a school in holiday time. It was odd to think that only a year before it had been overflowing with German soldiers, parading, training, grumbling, going on leave. A man was leaning over the second floor banisters, waiting for them.

"Ulrich!" Otto cried. He hastened up the last flight to seize the other's hand, which he was still shaking when Howard arrived, breathing heavily from the exercise. Ulrich was introduced to him as, "Mr. Jürgens, formerly Colonel of the Luftwaffe." Defeated and unfrocked or not, a colonel was a colonel, and Howard was slightly impressed. Herr Jürgens was tanned and athletic-looking with the beaming smile of a toothpaste advertisement. Howard managed to say, "I'm glad to meet you," in a suitably offhand way. Herr Jürgens bowed and shook hands as if this were a moment he had been waiting for for years. He said nothing, however, as he did not speak English. But his German was most fluent and he talked to Otto incessantly with Howard following behind. His function was apparently to be there, and no more. They went downstairs at once and across the former barrack square to a store hut, which Herr Jürgens unlocked. The hut was stacked from floor to roof with German army debris, flags, belts, brooms, cookers, mess tins, tables.

"All this," Otto explained, after a flow of German, "the English have counted."

There were six large packing cases in a corner at the far end of the hut. Herr Jürgens went towards them, picking up a crowbar on the way, and hacked at one of them energetically. Otto winked at Howard and made various comic gestures, which seemed to him pointless. The case was prized open. Herr Jürgens pulled out a coat and held it up proudly for display.

"And this," Otto laughed, "the English have not counted!"

"It looks damn good to me."

"The S.S. always had the best." He turned to listen to Herr Jürgens, who was saying something in a tone of irritation, and went on, "He is angry that the Luftwaffe never had such coats."

The coats were certainly magnificent. Outwardly of dark grey cloth, they were lined with thick squirrel fur.

"For the East Front!" Otto shivered. "Brr! It is better zat they are now for ladies I think."

When Herr Jürgens saw that they were considered satisfactory he pulled out eleven more. Howard was excited. This was business, all right—and how simple, how ridiculously simple it was.

They refused to allow him to help carry them over to the car, in which the coats were packed down tightly in the space behind the two seats. Then, Otto informed Howard, Herr Jürgens suggested that he should have the honour of giving them a glass of Schnaps in his room.

"That's fine by me, old boy." Howard would have agreed to anything, although he was anxious to return and report the success of the visit to Panting. They went upstairs again and were conducted to a room that was comfortable but bare. There was a desk, a carpet, a bed and three not very easy armchairs. There were photographs of stags and deer on the walls. Herr Jürgens stowed the cigarettes away in a cupboard, then took out a bottle of German gin, three glasses and a large photograph album. The drinks were poured, Howard said "Prost!", which the two repeated benevolently, implying that he was very clever to have remembered the German word. Herr Jürgens drained his own glass with one manly gulp and then opened the album. It was clear that he had always kept his camera handy when travelling. There were dozens of pictures of him hunting, fishing, ski-ing, always healthy and tanned and equipped with the toothpaste smile. "He is a very great sportsman," Otto explained softly. There were further pictures of him standing beside various handsome motor cars. Finally, the hit of the book, there were his war-time adventures. This section consisted mainly of photographs of British merchant ships before and after being bombed by Herr Jürgens. The latter explained his technique with each to Otto, who passed it on: "For this one Mr. Jürgens has flown low, then up up and down down like this to drop the bomb, a 250 kilo—and in the next one you can see this boat half in the water, only nine minutes later—and there I think are the heads of some English seamen swimming, isn't it?" There were some interesting snaps of an American ship hurrying to neutral Portuguese waters a few hours before the American declaration of war on Germany, while Herr Jürgens hovered hopefully above in his bomber, waiting to hear that he could go in and win. "But here she is safe and there is still no war, he must turn back."

"Jolly bad luck, old boy," Howard said. He was telling himself that but for the fur coats he would have been giving his host a piece of his mind. But business was business and irony would have to do instead. However, the album was then put away, with Otto expressing thanks for the treat they had had, and Herr Jürgens insisted that they had a little more Schnaps. He put a question to Howard, through Otto.

"Mr. Jürgens wishes you to hear his views on the organisation of football in the British zone."

"With pleasure."

"There would have been no national socialism in Germany,

he says, if the people had all football or tennis or golf to pursue in their free time."

"Tell him he's got something there."

Herr Jürgens then spoke for several minutes. Otto nodded as he made each point and finally turned to Howard. "Mr. Jürgens thinks that the English must make small football unions everywhere. Then you have the possibility arising out of their coming together of the new birth of a German football union, to which the present zonal boundaries must set no limits. There are enough politically clean sportsmen to make sure these unions will be democratic. Moreover, the English may be satisfied that this new orientation will exclude any national socialist or militarist bias, and that the goal will be health and the upbringing of German youth on a democratic basis. Mr. Jürgens wishes your advice, sir, to whom should he writes these ideas?"

"I'll find out and let him know."

Howard was proud of this answer, which was very successful, and as they went down to the car again Otto had to translate several phrases of the ex-Luftwaffe-colonel's gratitude. The coats lay snugly in the back. Howard looked at them fondly as he climbed in. He switched on the engine and the headlights.

"What a lucky man to have such a job!" Otto sighed. The car moved off and Herr Jürgens was left behind in the dusk, waving happily. "He is a friend of one of the Hamburg senators."

"That's the way to get on." Howard trod on the accelerator. "Look here," he continued, "you've had nothing out of this deal. Won't you take one or two of the coats?"

"No, sir, no!" Otto said. "It is nossing. You see, it is terrible for us that we cannot do for a friend as we should. A German cannot say 'Come to my house and have a drink' for he has no house and he has no drink. But he can perhaps make a little service. Besides you have already given to me many cigarettes."

"Well, it's damn good of you." There had been a hundred left over from Panting's cigarettes. He had given Otto fifty and kept the rest for himself.

"If I find a car we can take to Holland, then we shall share our gain!"

"Good enough!" Howard laughed. "And I'll send you half my salary when I become Prime Minister."

"Okay! Okay!"

"Seriously, the only thing I'm worried about is that I can't take you and Hilde to the Atlantic and have a party there." Hundreds of Kay Blandisons were privileged customers, but a girl of Hilde's class and breeding was barred. It was ridiculous. He felt angry about it.

"It is enough for us to have your friendship, Mr. Rondle."

"I can take you back to the flat or do you want to be dropped off, old boy?"

They were in Hamburg again, with the ruins on either side of the road. Howard thought of Hilde with pleasant excitement. When they reached the flat, however, he was disappointed. She had gone to the theatre. He drove by himself back to the mess, where dinner was in progress. He called Hammond and told him to go and stand by the car. Since the wine deal the batman had become his respectful ally. Then he rang up Panting, who arranged to meet him at the Sociology Division's garage in an hour.

He drove there slowly and parked in the secluded mews, a hundred yards from the office. He chain-smoked a few cigarettes. To the pleasure of the prospect of financial gain was added that of risk. This was no way to be found, for example, by the Provost Marshal. The slightness of this possibility made its existence all the more enjoyable. He had always felt that deep within him there was a streak of adventure. He chuckled silently.

He jumped as a small figure suddenly appeared by the side of the car. It was the usual under-nourished little boy, with the look in his eyes of a pet animal at meal-times.

"Zigarett, pleace? Zigarett?"

"Oh!" Howard relaxed and frowned. "No, no—geh' weg, geh' weg."

The boy's eyes were peering into the car.

"Geh' weg! Get to hell out!" Howard's voice was strained. The boy withdrew a few inches. Then he felt compassion. "All right, you little bastard, here."

He took out the ashtray container and emptied the half-dozen ends into the boy's hands, as a car entered the mews. It drew up behind the Ford, stopped and its headlamps turned out. It was a small civilian business van. As soon as the boy saw it, he disappeared.

"Are you there, Howard?"

"Yes, old boy." He smiled broadly.

Panting and a stout German in a camel hair overcoat got out of either side of the van.

"Well, well, my dear boy, fancy seeing you here!" Panting came up to the Ford and looked in. "I've brought a gentleman with whom I have had profitable associations before. Herr Buchenwald or Belsen or something, I forget which. If he likes the goods, we load everything into his van and you'll have no tedious distributing to do."

"Fine," said Howard. He got out. "They're packed behind the seats—not too creased, I hope. Shall I haul one out?"

"No, I'll do that, Howard. My friend has rather a retiring nature. When strangers look at him he feels self conscious. If it's all right with you, my dear, just leave us here to see what we can see with a torch and you go and stand by the entrance of the mews, so that if any of those tiresome German policemen come patrolling along, you can call out to us what nice weather it is or something in English. My friend has an even greater horror of meeting German policemen, he's just a mass of complexes. O.K.?"

"O.K." Howard said. He lit a cigarette and strolled away. The street, half of which was burnt out, was quiet. The little boy must be around, but there was no sign of him. Behind there were a few vague sounds from Panting and the German, and an occasional glimmer of light. On the wall of the building under which he stood there were some printed posters. "Tanzschule" was the heading of one, "Ilse Wernher Singt" of another, and scrawled in chalk beside them: 'Freie neues

Deutschland in der grossen Völkerfamilie.' Howard looked at them without interest. Once he heard some steps and gazed in alarm at the other side of the street, but it was only a Tommy walking along with a Fräulein. A man's voice began to sing, accompanied by a concertina. It was a sad, haunting song, 'Wir sind die Mursoldaten.' It came from a room somewhere above him. The singer sounded forlorn and hopeless, an attitude which fitted the surroundings, and then suddenly gained strength at the end, as if triumphantly. "Fancy wanting to sing here," Howard thought. He took out another cigarette and lit it with the stump of the old one, which he threw away. At once there was a scamper close to his feet. The little boy giggled, and ran off.

"Howard, where are you—ah!" Panting joined him. "Well, my dear, everything's fine. He's quite pleased, we've loaded and he's just going to back out."

As he spoke the van's engine started.

"What has he paid?" Howard asked.

"I'll tell you in half a second."

The German backed his van down the mews and passed them. His snap-brimmed trilby was drawn down over his forehead and Howard could not glimpse his face.

"Now I have a little suggestion," Panting said. "A nice drink at the Atlantic?"

"Yes, but how much——"

"Howard, such greed! As a matter of fact, he's given me quite a nice Leica, and since I can't give you half a Leica, we'll have to agree to terms. Will five thousand marks suit you? It's a generous offer. One can't rely on getting ten thousand for a Leica nowadays. There's almost a deflation setting in."

"It'll suit me," Howard said.

He could hardly believe that he had spoken so calmly. It was the equivalent of over a hundred pounds, four or five hundred dollars. And he had made it in one evening. He could feel his heart thumping.

They went back to the Ford. Panting took a bag from his

pocket and counted out a hundred fifty-mark notes. Then they drove away down the Esplanade and across the Lombard Bridge to the Atlantic, where they ordered a bottle of champagne.

CHAPTER 3

I

Now he was living. He moved through the hours in a constant mood of exhilaration. He had needed a start, that was all. Then, if you had brains, it was easy. They said nothing succeeded like success, and it was true. All the same you had to have your wits about you to seize opportunities. That was his particular talent, for which, until now, there had been no scope. An example was his brilliant coup in the lavatory of the Country Club. Kay had organised a party to celebrate Charlie's demobilisation and Bonzo Hamilton's British naturalisation. Howard found a new and delightful pleasure in standing expensive rounds of drinks, for which he did not have to count the cost. Moreover he was popular. Instead of being on the sulky outskirts of the conversation he was always in the centre. 'Howard' was the most used Christian name. Then, in the lavatory, he had met a slightly drunk young officer, who happened to be looking at the contents of his wallet. Howard noticed that there were two English pound notes and asked him at once, in a confidential whisper, if he would like to sell them. Pound notes were supposed to be left behind in England. The young officer winked at him.

"What offers?" he queried.

"Thousand per cent. Give you eight hundred in fiftys."

"O.K.! But, listen, my dear friend, my old pal, don't tell my mother."

"Depend on me, old boy," said Howard. He handed over the marks on the spot and received the pounds.

He returned to the party, which was holding a discussion on the post-war condition of England. Dinner was over and they were having coffee and liqueurs.

"Charlie, it's simply mean of you not to sign on," Kay cried. "Think of all the horrible queues and rush hours and restrictions you're going back to."

"Don't you worry about me, my love. I'll be having a nice safe mild and bitter while you're being stabbed in the back."

"By a werewolf, I suppose. I don't think."

"No, by the wives when they come out."

"Beast! I'm glad you're going, so there. Howard, darling, Charlie's being mean to me, as usual."

"England's all right, except for the high cost of loving," Charlie said. "I've got it all lined up. I'm going into furnishing, see. Anything you've got to have dockets and priorities for. Lino, stair carpets."

"Where will you get your supplies?" Hemsleigh asked.

"It's bloody simple, if you know how. You go to all the big stores and see the floor manager for your particular line, slip him two or three quid, say you'll be glad to know when he's got some goods coming in. He'll be on the buzzer in no time. Then you buy at retail price and take it along to your own place. You can afford their price because the customers won't find any stuff in the big stores and so they have to come along and pay yours. The big store bosses are O.K. because all they know is their goods are sold at the normal price. You see? So everybody's happy."

"Except for the customer."

"So what? He's dodged his income tax."

"My God, if that's what we're like at home," said Styles, "it's pretty damn funny that we're out here to get the Germans straight."

"Of course it is!" Charlie said. "We're a dying doctor trying to cure a dead man. You boys give me a pain. Face facts! Look at old Howard. He won't starve in civvy street, don't you worry."

"That's an absolutely typical remark," Hemsleigh said. "You fellows that go black marketing about are all the same. You're always hinting that everyone else is doing it, so as to justify yourselves."

"I resent it," Howard grinned.

"Why, you're the worst of the lot of us, you old bastard," Charlie said. "But I admire you. So quiet and smooth, it's wonderful."

"No, I wouldn't think of going back," Major Cardington was saying at the other end of the table. "When I look at England, I thank God I'm a regular. It's murder to try and get a flat in London, you know. My wife almost had a breakdown."

"You can't get anything livable in under eight guineas a week," Elizabeth agreed. "It's too absurd."

"It must certainly be very difficult for a stranger," said Miss Hackster. It was a reproof. She was prepared to be kind and understanding to Elizabeth or any other refugee. But they had no right to be critical about affairs in England; that was a privilege reserved for natives, Miss Hackster considered, although she had lived in Italy for most of her adult life and was never tired of saying that, really, she thought as an Italian.

Howard listened without paying attention. Whatever the words the mess conversation always sounded the same. His mind was concentrated on the two pound notes he had gained. The clever thing to do was to hand them to Otto, who would be able to buy all the food he wanted for himself and Hilde. The eventual reward should be considerable. A man who

214

could see no farther than his nose would sell them at a profit to someone with spare marks who was going back to England; but not he. He looked round the table complacently.

"When are we going to haf a clear policy?" Mr. Hamilton asked. "How can Whitehall expect us to govern if we haf no clear directive?"

"Because that is the English tradition," Miss Hackster said, irritated by 'we.' "Don't you agree, Pratt?"

"Oh, I do, Sybil."

"Howard, a penny for them," Kay said, with her most whimsical smile.

"I was thinking of a beautiful girl, Kay."

"Mary?"

"I didn't say so." He was pleased by the immediate self-satisfaction in her eyes. It was a shame that she was so unattractive.

The pound notes were a greater success with Otto than he had dreamed. Hilde's brother waltzed round the room, uttering German cries of pleasure. He seemed quite overcome by Howard's friendliness. Hilde kept repeating, "It is not necessary, Howart, it is not necessary." She used his Christian name in front of Otto now. Howard smiled at them both affectionately. One made him money, the other made him love. They were quite a combination.

Otto then began a habit of disappearing discreetly for an hour, so that Howard could be alone with her; and he had a suggestion, to which Howard eagerly agreed.

"Mr. Rondle, if you have many marks, shall we not go shoppings together in Hamburg? It is better when a German goes into a shop. The prices are then not so high. And there are many things I think you will like to take with you to England."

"That would suit me fine, old boy."

Two days later Charlie Morton left to be demobilised. The night before he left, there was another party at the flat of the red haired Displaced Person. Hemsleigh and Styles, Mr. Maxton-Hill and Elizabeth were there besides Howard and

215

the host, who had spent much of the previous week dispatching half a dozen packing cases to England through the Military Forwarding Officer. Morose and shy on the previous occasion, Howard was now the life and soul of the party. He danced all the time and his infectious laugh was always breaking out. Hilde came with Dr. Neumann and as he watched her talking vivaciously, Howard felt himself quicken with delight. He looked at the other Occupation representatives with something like condescension. Within two or three weeks he had fixed himself up better than any of them. It was no surprise when Charlie said to him, "Old pal, this is the only serious thing I'm saying tonight—when you come out, get me on the blower and we'll talk about doing some business together." Howard assured him that he would. The future looked rosy when people started to want you to work with them. His own demobilisation was only a few weeks off, but he was no longer worried about it. Leaving Hilde would be the only tough part.

Charlie's departure benefited him in two ways. Firstly he took over his car for his own use, which made it very much easier to go shopping with Otto. Secondly he moved into Charlie's bedroom on the floor beneath his own. It was not only a better room, although all the saleable objects in it had been sent to England by the late occupant, but it had also the advantage of increasing the distance between Howard and Kay. The latter was desperate. She had suspected that there was a German girl and Elizabeth had given her one or two catty hints; but she had retained hope, for although they had not gone together again to the Country Club he had always smiled at her and she had imagined—but when she saw his things going downstairs, she knew that once again it was the end. She had tears alone in her own room. She sat down on a chair and stared at her hands. They were good hands—everyone said she had nice hands. She was restless and afraid. She got up and moved about the room, hating her life. She stopped in front of the mirror and peered at herself, full face, three quarter face. She held up a mirror so that she could see her profile. Yes, yes, she was desirable.

Grimly she convinced herself. She was still young, if she kept her chin pointing a little upwards so that light did not pronounce the tell-tale shadows. Men admired her figure, the man with the Air Force moustache in the train last year had told her so. She had been a fool not to let him go on. It was her own fault, she had been too frigid and he had lost interest. She thought he had got out at Rugby, but later she saw him again in another compartment, talking to a blonde. Their eyes met as she passed down the corridor and she had given him a look to freeze a river. She saw them go down the platform together when they reached London. He was carrying the blonde's suitcase. Well, it was her own fault, she had frightened him away. But where had she gone wrong with Howard?

Kay gazed helplessly at the mirror. However, it was not her habit to remain depressed for long. Almost unconsciously her mind began to reconsider the other men in the mess. Hoppy had been looking sad lately. Perhaps he was hurt because she had neglected him. She felt a ghost of hope returning, went to her bag and picked out her compact, and began to powder her nose.

Howard made it a fixed rule with Corporal Clayton that everything that required signing should be passed into him before lunch. At two o'clock in the afternoon he picked up Otto in the car and they went shopping. Street names became familiar to him: Dammtorstrasse, Kirchenallee, Glockengiesserwall. They would drive slowly along until Otto halted him.

"Here, I think we get something!"

There were few shops left in Hamburg and the majority of these dealt in collectors' postage stamps, which had become a small independent currency of their own, or art. There were thousands of artists in the city and their paintings, most of which were poor landscapes, were on sale everywhere. The buyers were Germans who preferred to put their money into any kind of commodity in the search for a little security. Troops could not afford the landscapes; they went in for reproductions in colour of photographs of themselves, done

217

in oil, pencil or water colour. Otto would go after old maps and similar oddities which had a market value in England and with which there was no difficulty about customs; he was surprisingly well informed about such things. The only other shops sold knick-knacks of one kind or another, sets of china, jewellery, suitcases. Quite a remarkable collection began to be assembled in Howard's new bedroom and every day he clearly advanced in Hammond's respect. The batman often came in for a chat while he shaved.

"Honestly, Mr. Randle, sir, I admire you," he remarked. "Tell the truth, when you first come, I didn't think you had it in you. But I never seen anyone get so much so quick!"

"It's just getting organised, my boy," Howard told him with a grin. "Think, then act, that's my motto."

Hilde insisted on him going with her to a German theatre. They had seen "Intimitäten," which was a translation of Noel Coward's "Private Lives." Fortunately, Howard had seen the play in London, otherwise it would have been incomprehensible; all the same the experience was worth while. The theatre was a converted technical school lecture hall. The audience was middle class, the men with high collars and the women with what Howard told Hilde were "bits of tired rabbit." Everyone kept their overcoats on, since there was no heating. The South of France scenery was excellent, the players rather too middle-aged and their make-up too obvious—but that was because the stage came right up to the front row of the stalls. The abundant Martinis and cigarettes caused mirth. "Everyone will wish to be an actor, I think," Hilde whispered. There were sighs of admiration at the sight of the evening dress. Instead of "Someday I'll Find You," they sang "J'attendrai" and "Night and Day." The rough and tumble scene on the sofa in Act II went down very well, but apart from this the audience seemed to be a little at sea. Hilde began to translate a note on the back of the programme to Howard. "Why should we thank the theatre?" it ran. "For joy in the beauty of words, their sound, their sense. Joy in the beauty of the human voice . . ." Fortunately she was stopped by the gong that was struck behind the curtain before the lights went down. Howard thought it was charming of her to take it so seriously. Afterwards they had coffee and rolls and butter with Otto at her flat; it was part of the fruit of the two pounds.

"Everything will soon be better," Hilde said. "Frau Meinecke has told me so this morning. There is a conjunction which indicates great good fortune for Germany in a year. That is little time to wait."

"Astrologie!" Otto laughed. "That increases so much in Hamburg, it is a scandal, Mr. Rondle."

"Did she not foretell the calory cut?" Hilde said angrily.

"I will foretell things if you will pay me also fifty marks for half-an-hour!"

"Howart, tell him not to speak, not to say one more word, I shall lose my—my what is it . . ."

"Temper," he chuckled. They often bickered, like a brother and sister in a nursery, and he enjoyed watching them.

"I shall lose my temper!"

Howard's marks soon ran out and he had the idea of selling Panting some duty-free labels. This was also a brilliant success.

"My dear, they're so convenient for sending cameras home. Camera boxes, I mean, naturally. The lenses, of course, go in one's pocket."

He paid Howard in German gin, which could fetch up to three hundred marks a bottle. Herr Scholle, who had lacked extra-office employment since Charlie's departure, was eager to be an agent at the price of a few cigarettes. Howard suggested that he did some shopping for him. Herr Scholle's speciality was "Tausch," which meant barter. There were several shops where Germans could leave articles, with a ticket attached to them which stated what was wanted in exchange. There were similar advertisements in all the newspapers and information posts: "Gentleman's overcoat, herring-bone model, size 50, raincoat, size 48-52, lady's town bag of best material, wash towel, Mont Blanc pen, all new—

for People's Receiver radio, direct or alternating current, and feather bed"; "38 Classical books, including 'Faust'—for accordeon 120"; "Youth's suit, first class (for 17-18 years), shirt, two collars and tie—for lady's bicycle with good tyres." Through Herr Scholle some of the bulkier items which Otto had bought with Howard were changed for something more portable, such as Leica films. Howard began to use some of his duty-free labels to send small parcels home. They had to go to Mary, but he warned her that his things would start arriving and need not be unpacked. She was not inquisitive.

Mary's letters, which came regularly every third day, seemed to have been written from another world. It puzzled him to reflect that not so long ago the sight of her writing on the envelope had cheered him for a day. Her constant theme was the inadequacy of the east London transport system and how wonderful it was going to be when the extension of the underground railway was opened. Howard had always been interested, the black-coated workers' queues, the rush hours affected him personally. But now it was simply impossible for him to see himself as an insurance clerk. That kind of future was not for a man of his shrewdness and opportunism. "I really have decided that the best thing is to catch a 96 and stay in it until you get home," Mary wrote. It puzzled him to know how he would react to her when he saw her. Love seemed out of the question. He was unstirred when he read those self conscious end-pieces, put in, it seemed, from a sense of duty, because a man expected to read that sort of thing: "And, Howard, darling, you are always in my dreams. Isn't it exciting that in two months we shall be married and with a home of our own, just the two of us, alone? I can hardly believe it." Howard could hardly believe it, either. But the whole thing was cut and dried, even the home. Mary's father's best friend was a small property owner and they were to have the lower floor of a semi-detached house. However, all this was at the back of his mind. There was time enough to see to all that when he returned. He wrote kindly but unpassionate replies to her letters.

He also discovered that he did not love Hilde. Her sensuality astounded and excited him; at first, unable to get her out of his mind, he had assumed that this was the love he had never really felt for Mary. But he had come to know that he had her under control. He enjoyed her, she was a new, slightly thrilling habit. It wasn't love. In fact he was uncertain whether the fascination was not already wearing a little. This occurred to him on the evening he drove Elizabeth Ford out to the Hamburg Golf Club. They were to meet Hemsleigh and Styles, who had been playing a round, and go on to a party at a mess in Blankenese.

"I hope this isn't going to be one of these late orgies," Elizabeth said.

"Not for me, anyhow," Howard answered. He had told Hilde to expect him at eleven.

"It will probably be an awful bore. I'm beginning to wish I hadn't accepted."

Howard nodded without interest; they were driving down the Elbchaussee, past the road that led off to the Country Club. Elizabeth's bored, casual tone did not fool him. She had been careful enough to force the invitation from Hemsleigh at lunch-time.

The Golf Club and the course were set in pinewoods. Players could borrow a bag of clubs which belonged to one of the former German members. Like the Atlantic Hotel, the staff remained but the customers had changed. Germans were no longer allowed. It was a well-fitted, luxurious establishment, which had escaped any kind of war damage; nor was there an active sign of military occupation. Everything looked as if it were a quiet, normal day a few years before, when all that mattered was getting your handicap down, discussing the stock market or the vulgarity of a Party boss's wife. The locker-rooms, the bar, the mid-week emptiness; it was all just right. But the large, modernistic lounge with the garish railway-poster murals, depicting liners on the Elbe and sporting scenes, men and women playing golf or tennis in pre-war fashions, was somehow ghostly. There were lists of the prize-winners of the various club trophies. English words like "cup," "scratch," "bogey" and a few English names were scattered amongst the German. Time, according to the lists, had stopped in 1939.

"German naval officers used to play here so that they would know what to talk about to the English," Elizabeth said.

Howard was looking about him admiringly.

"Nice little set-up they had here, eh? D'you know I'd give a few quid to go back ten years and see them all in here, the fat so-and-sos." He chuckled. "They had their eye on the ball in those days, didn't they?"

"My father was a member here. They made him leave."

Her voice was strained. Howard cursed himself. He had made a black there, all right. Of course, he had forgotten that she was a German. These refugees made life very complicated: you had to be careful when you opened your mouth.

"I'm awfully sorry."

"It's all right," she smiled. "Honestly. Don't think about it. Let's go and have a drink on the terrace. Perhaps we'll see them coming in."

The waiter who came out to them apologised that there was no champagne. He recommended the Club Martinis.

"Bring a couple of large ones," Howard said.

"Don't you ever drink singles?" Elizabeth asked.

"Not that I can remember." He glanced at her, met her eyes and looked away. He was feeling oddly surprised. She had been in the mess all the time since he had arrived and he had never noticed her particularly; yet she was not unattractive. For a start she was younger, slimmer and better looking than Kay. She wore no make-up, so that the first impression she gave in her blue Control Commission uniform was rather school-maamish; but this seemed to be a contrived effect. Lipstick and eyeshadow would be as natural on her small, pale features as they were clearly unsuitable for Kay. Her fingernails ought to have been scarlet, not prim and white.

"When you first came, I thought you were a quiet type."

"And now?" he asked, delighted.

222

"Well, you almost put poor old Charlie in the shade, didn't you?"

"I'll tell you what I think."

"Go on and tell."

"I think that sometimes in the mess you want to let your hair down and yell."

Elizabeth laughed. "Oh, God! Do I make it that plain?"

"No, it's a good act, all right."

"I wish I could be like Peter Schroeder. He's really convinced himself that he's fond of Sybil."

She glanced at him as if wondering whether she had said too much. The waiter brought their Martinis. Howard raised his glass and sat back comfortably. The view from the terrace was attractive; a flat, lawn-like expanse of grass and then blue sky with fleecy white clouds on top of the pinewoods.

"Cheers." He sipped. "You know, talking of Peter Schroeder, both your accents are simply unbelievable. I mean, you'd never be able to tell . . ."

"If you didn't know."

"Quite. Honestly I didn't believe it when I heard."

"Who told you? Kay?"

The question sounded casual, but he could sense anger hidden behind it. He said: "If you once lived round here and your father was a member of this club, for example, don't you have an odd feeling at being here. . ."

"We get used to odd feelings." She wasn't laughing now, and he noticed how tightly her fingers were gripping her glass. "Sometimes they're very nice—such as when I found the S.S. man's wife at Oldenburg who had bought our carpets and other things at an auction."

"Your parents . . ."

"They're quite safe in London, thank you; Peter's went to the gas chamber, they weren't so lucky. Oh, God, I'm being a bore. You know we're both Jewish, I suppose Kay mentioned that as well? And that we're waiting to be naturalised and that we're still Germans? We're always being reminded that we may not stay on British rations if we don't behave, you know.

And heaven knows the Germans don't want us. Die Halb und Halb, they call us, the half and half, neither one or the other —and not wanted by either."

"Yes, I think I've heard that," he said, embarrassed.

She drank her Martini down and sat breathing quickly for a moment. Then she smiled.

"I was a bore to go through all that. But sometimes if one finds a sympathetic ear it all pours out at once. I'm awfully sorry, but it's all gone now."

"Say it all again if you want to."

"Do you think John and Mike are playing round again? They are the limit, they were supposed to be waiting for us when we came. Still—the idea of this party is a bore, isn't it—some red-faced Colonel being terribly matey and the same chatter about everything, I really wonder if it wouldn't be a better idea. . . Oh, no, forget it."

"What?" he insisted.

"Well, I just thought for a second we might give them the slip and go off to the Country Club by ourselves."

"It's the hell of a good idea."

"John and Mike won't notice, they'll be too busy discussing the truth about the German People." She was light-hearted again. "Which is the boring subject to end all boring subjects."

He was wondering if the whole performance had not been an act, and she had really intended to go with him to the Country Club all the time. On their way out he glanced at himself in a mirror complacently.

Half an hour later, as the light was fading, they sat at another little table at the Country Club, on the terrace looking down at what had been the tobacco millionaire's garden, with champagne cocktails between them. By then he realised that she was throwing herself at him hard. It was done much more subtly and enjoyably than by Kay Blandison, but she couldn't fool him. However he found nothing wrong in the situation. She was intelligent, not too talkative and her pale coolness was a relief in a way; Hilde was so exotic. They dined and danced, and drank some more. She certainly grew prettier as the evening wore on. It occurred to him that it might be a good idea to stand Hilde up, just for once. There was never any harm in asserting oneself.

II

It seemed that he could not go wrong. The next day Hilde was tearful and sulky, but within five minutes she was in his arms.

"You have forgotten me, Howart, I was here waiting, waiting—oh!"

"It won't happen again, darling, honestly. Ich liebe Dich." He pressed his lips against hers. She was stiff and unyielding. "Dich," he whispered. Something like a sob escaped from her, and then she gave way. He thought: "I'm good."

"You has been with another girl, I know, I know."

"Ich liebe Dich." That was all you had to say, though repetition might be necessary. But he had discovered something else; there had been a sharp little pleasure in causing her anxiety and then relieving it. He pulled her close again, kissing her until she gasped for breath. He was deliriously happy. He had her on toast, he chuckled to himself.

But he was rather put out when she told him that Otto had gone away for a week on one of his keeping-in-touch business trips.

"We'd fixed up to go shopping tomorrow. He might have let me know."

"He was waiting here last night, but you did not come. He must go at once when he gets the transportation."

Howard frowned. It was reasonable, of course; Otto was naturally more interested in keeping track of his textile business than helping him to spend his marks. All the same he felt that a little more consideration might have been given to him. Hilde sensed that he was not pleased.

"I think you are sorry Otto is gone and I am still here,"

she said. "It would be nicer for you if he were here and I not."

She was hurt and he was accordingly mollified. There were, after all, advantages to Otto's absence; although the latter had been most discreet in staying out of the way when Hilde and he wished to be alone together, it was impossible not to feel that he might reappear at any moment.

It was a good week. They drove out to Travemünde, a former seaside resort beyond Lübeck, and lazed on the empty beach with the wine and sandwiches he had brought from the mess. They went to the travelling circus that had arrived in Hamburg by the Dammtor station and to the fair that accompanied it. They went to the cinema to see the English film "Love Story," which made German audiences weep. Howard took with him a typewritten pass, which stated: "The bearer has permission to be present at performances of films or plays intended for German personnel only, in the interests of this Division (signed H. Randle, Lieut., R.A., for Controller, Sociology Division)."

The Controller himself created a stir in the mess by arriving for a two-day stay. Howard and Hemsleigh and Styles were not affected, but the remainder of the staff from Major Cardington down to Mrs. Pratt became at once extravagantly fond of their duties. Mr. Johnson Trant was a tall, vague man with a high sense of integrity, which he assumed existed in everyone else, and a first-class academic brain. He was accompanied by two very correct majors, who said little but "Thanks very much" and remained anonymous for the duration of the stay. All conversation at meals—breakfast was well attended for the two days—was concerned with the German problem. Words like "Democracy," "SPD," "KPD," "Adenauer," "Fusion," phrases such as "No sense of humour," "Can't possibly argue," "Hope for Youth" occurred with regularity. Miss Hackster, who prided herself that she was always a success with high officers, coyly supported the Russians and the Communists whenever possible and said several times, "Of course, Mr. Trant, I'm terribly Left!" At the office the German staff was equally excited. They bowed before Mr. Johnson Trant, who blinked back uneasily, as before an eastern despot. But Howard soon found that this was nothing like the visit of a colonel or a brigadier in the Army; there was no snap check of the duty-free labels. No sooner was it mentioned that he was about to be demobilised and that his function was to assist with the administration than a glaze of disinterest came over Mr. Johnson Trant's eyes. Howard saw no reason not to take Herr Scholle out shopping.

Scholle was a smart young man, both in appearance and in nature; but he had not Otto's grasp of affairs, nor was he so amusing a companion. Howard realised that he did not belong to the same class as Hilde and her brother. He was one of those superior clerks who had managed to avoid joining the Party, so that he was free to take a job under Military Government. Germans who collaborated with the British were not all shy about it. His greatest achievement was a dozen pairs of silk stockings. He asked Howard what size he required and the latter replied, automatically, "Nine," which was Mary's size, and then added, "No, make it a couple of nines and the rest eights." Eight was Hilde's size and, in any case, Mary would be just as delighted with two pairs. Herr Scholle's commercial method was to announce arrogantly that he was the representative of a high English official and that unless the seller complied with what was wanted, it would be just too bad for him. In the same way, when they were held up by a procession of Trade Union workers who were on their way to join a large meeting in the Botanical Gardens, Herr Scholle had leant across and pressed his finger on the hooter, ignoring Howard's protests, and as the procession parted to give them room to drive through, he shouted out in German, "Can't you see this is an English officer's car?" Although Otto appeared very often to share Herr Scholle's general contempt for Germans, he would not have done that. He was much more sensitive to what was done and not done by an English gentleman, Howard realised; and the latter's attitude to Herr Scholle became more brusque. As far as business was concerned the pleasantest event of the week occurred by chance in the Atlantic Bar. Howard was sipping a champagne cocktail by himself—he had called in on his way back to the mess for lunch—when a Control Commission official who stood next to him discovered that he had come out without any money. Howard at once offered to change some marks in return for a cheque on the man's English bank, and in this way recovered the six pounds he had changed at the Field Cashier's. The waste of that sum had been worrying him a little. At the same time he had the pleasure of generosity, by giving the man fifty instead of forty marks to the pound. It was a good thing to be kind to people who didn't know how to look after themselves.

He became impatient for Otto's return. He had several thousand idle marks, most of them from the sale of Panting's gin. Living at the top rate, only a small proportion of the money could be spent at the Atlantic, where he was becoming known as a client who tipped well with cigarettes. His entry into the grill room was like that of a well-known customer at any fashionable restaurant. The white-tied head waiter bustled up to greet him and he had a table at once, whether or not there was a queue. Howard behaved as though he had been used to this sort of thing all his life. He was not worried about it coming to an end when he was demobilised because his self confidence was now so great that he did not believe it would come to an end. He liked to be open-handed. He gave drinks to strangers. He entertained Elizabeth. He developed a taste for a special Sauterne which was not on the wine list. He entertained Kay and Mr. Hopwood—he saw them come in and insisted on them joining him. He was so pleased with himself that he was not in the least taken aback the next day when Hemsleigh and Styles refused to lunch with him. He nodded pleasantly and went to join Panting and a couple of the latter's friends at the Long Bar. One was a very smooth, deep voiced young Guards lieutenant and the other a bleary red-faced major. It was like a meeting of big business men.

The Guards officer had made his start by having half a ton of coffee sent to Brussels two months after the end of the war. The major had been interested in car-running. He bought cars from Germans and drove them to Paris, to be sold second-hand. He had done very well, it seemed, but things had become much more difficult since politicians and zonal boundaries had taken the place of the rough army rule. He had managed to get a couple of Mercedes back to England through Rotterdam, but they had begun to watch the ports rather too carefully. It was a pity, the major thought, because in England nowadays the most extraordinary types seemed to have money and be quite willing to spend it.

"The place is ruined," the lieutenant agreed. "As soon as I get home I shall be off like a flash to Paris. For one thing it's the only place you can get a decent flat easily."

"How will you live there?" Howard asked.

"Oh, I shall flog sterling," the lieutenant said. "It's a sweet racket."

When the major asserted that he normally used a running capital of a hundred thousand marks, Howard realised that he still had some way to go. Among other things the major, for example, had bought himself a boarding house in Brighton. It would be a pity, Howard thought, if he had to leave Hamburg without bringing off a deal of that nature. He was certainly not less capable than they were.

"Though I'd take a job if there was a chance of getting near a diplomatic bag," the lieutenant said.

The four gazed at the crowd surrounding them in the bar with friendly contempt.

CHAPTER 4

Mary wrote to say that sometimes it was all she could do not to hand in her notice at the office and content herself with some local position. Father was in favour of it, but then, of course, the money was useful; and she and Howard were going to need all of that that they could get, the disgraceful way prices were going. If the Germans had anything worse to put up with than the City rush hours, then they had something to worry about. She had been to a Mozart concert by the B.B.C. Symphony Orchestra at the People's Palace. Tom and Edith next door had the builders in. It was scandalous because they had no war damage at all and of course it was all under the counter, people seemed to have no shame at all.

Howard found the letter amusing. She was still under the impression that he would return to the grind at the insurance office. She had a pleasant surprise coming. He had ideas already. A man at the Country Club had told him one. It was just a case of taking the trouble to go to the depots where they were selling off Government war stores. Then you sold at an inflated profit through newspaper small ads. Howard chuckled to think of it.

Meanwhile Otto was still away and he spent all his spare time with Hilde, pleasantly enough. She seemed to become more infatuated by him than ever. An instance was the afternoon they drove into the country, provided with an unauthorised pass which stated that Howard was permitted to carry civilian passengers in connection with his duties for the Sociology Division. They turned off the Kiel road and went through several little villages which were colourful and seemed unchanged by the general conditions. The horses and cattle looked thin and listless, but it was possible to buy asparagus if you knew where to go. Hilde, of course, knew. The weather was fine and the ground dry enough for them to lie on it for a couple of hours. The only person they saw was a slowly moving old peasant with a picture-book curling moustache, who touched his cap to them. "Such a very nice old man," Hilde whispered. "I think the country people are not so spoilt as the town people, where a clerk will carry himself as if he were an officer." Howard nodded and kissed her, which he did every five minutes, while she went on rambling in her soft voice about the Silesian house, Paris and Rome. Once she said, "If I were not German, Howart, if all these terrible things had not been, would you then wish to marry me?"

"Yes," Howard had said.

"That makes me very happy."

"Would you have wished it, too?"

"Oh, of course!" she exclaimed and he noticed that her eyes were moist. It pleased him absurdly; he could feel his heart thumping.

"That makes me happy, too."

"For that I give you reward," she whispered. "What shall it be?"

"You know," he said, smiling. He sounded much calmer than he felt. His right arm supported her head, his left searched unsteadily for the zip fastener at the side of her frock and he pressed his lips into her cheek.

"No, not now!" she giggled. "Tonight, we have a nice time, Howart. But now I give you another reward. I tell you a secret and perhaps—stop now, Howart."

"All right." He controlled himself reluctantly. "What's the secret? I hope there's money in it."

"Of course. It is Dr. Neumann, he has a nice Ford motor car, so new and chic—1939—much, much nicer than your car, Howart. . ."

"So what?"

"It is hidden."

"How do you mean?"

"He has not declared it. All cars must be declared for the English and all the nice ones have of course been taken. But now he thinks, it will be a long time before the Germans can have cars again and he has anxiety that he has not declared—if the English find it, he must stop being a publisher and go to prison and so, and so, all those things—therefore, he says, he has decided to sell it."

"How much?"

"A thousand cigarettes, perhaps some whisky. . . ."

"Well, it's no good to me, really. After all, I'm going home soon, I couldn't take it with me. Besides we have to have special labels and so on for cars, we can't just pick one up and drive it about, you know."

"Oh, yes, but I have thought, you have already a Ford, the label can do for both, isn't it? The right numbers can easily be painted. But of course it is perhaps not of interest for you."

"It isn't really. It would have been if I'd heard about it a couple of months ago."

"But you will tell no one?"

"Of course I won't."

"I think it is time we go back to Hamburg." She seemed disappointed and Howard was annoyed with himself. If you were fond of someone and tried to do him a favour, it was naturally irritating for it to be refused. He pulled her close again.

He drove her back to her flat and then went on by himself to the mess to pick up some sandwiches. It had become a habit for him to have most of his meals with her and Hammond allowed him to take liberal rations. They ate them together to the radio accompaniment of the American Forces Network.

An hour after curfew Otto arrived. He was tired and red-eyed, but in his usual excellent spirits. He kissed Hilde and shook hands with Howard.

"Such a journey. I must dodge and dodge from street to street to avoid these little boy Schupos that are patrolling everywhere, all so important, with their chests out—so! Hilde, I have butter and I have cheese, alas no Kohle." He exclaimed with delight when he was invited to finish Howard's rations. The latter could hardly wait to plan some more shopping expeditions.

"I've still got some marks to fling around, old boy," he said, as soon as Otto was sitting back, looking refreshed.

"O.K.!" Otto laughed. "We will find some more things, isn't it? I have heard of a small shop in Oldenburg. We go there if you wish."

"Fine. As soon as you like."

"Dr. Neumann wishes now to sell his car." Hilde said. "I have said it to Howart, but he goes so soon back to England it is of no interest for him."

Otto found this very amusing. He slapped his legs with merriment.

"I think he is afraid it shall journey the way of my poor Mercedes! He is a wise man to hold it no more. We Germans must realise that such things are gone for a long, long time. First we must learn to live as a democracy, and then perhaps we will have our Mercedes again, mit Genehmigung der Militärregierung, naturally! With your permission, Mr. Rondle, that is!" He bent forward eagerly. Howard was offering him a cigarette. "Oh, thank you! Thank you! You know, all the time I have been away, I have been dreaming of your cigarettes."

"I was saying to Hilde, it's a pity I didn't hear about the car before. But I'm being demobilised so soon, it's not worth while. After all, the car I've got is quite good."

"Dr. Neumann's car is 1939 and like new!" Hilde said to Otto. She was as enthusiastic as a salesman. "So shining and so everything!"

Otto winked at Howard. "I think my sister is getting fifeteen pro cent of the sale, isn't it!"

"I hate you, I hate you!" she exclaimed. Otto laughed and Howard was amused. She had absolutely no sense of humour, he reflected. Her outbursts of temper were charming. You could understand how it was that people often said you had to treat the Germans like children.

The subject was changed to a long account from Otto of his trip. He told a story well and he was particularly good on the subject of travel discomforts. Howard thought to himself that this philosophical approach would be a lesson to Mary at home with her perpetual complaints. Otto went on to say how sad it was that everywhere he had gone the popularity of the English was diminishing. He was talking about this and quoting the opinions of an old friend of his whom he had met in Essen, a man who had always held very liberal opinions and had shared Otto's private views about the Party, when he paused.

Both Howard and Hilde looked at him questioningly. Otto had the air of a man struck with amazement. He began to mumble to himself in German, then to smile and look excited.

"Du lieber Gott!" Hilde said. "Bist Du denn verrückt? Howart, I think my poor brosser is quite mad."

"I have a great idea!" Otto laughed. "A great, great idea! Mr. Rondle, you remember I have once said to you, if I but had my Mercedes, I vould find an Englishman to take him to Hollant and make a great sum of money?"

"No—oh, yes, I do—you mean, getting gulden."

"Yes, yes! But now we can do it, if you shall wish. We shall take the car of Dr. Neumann!"

"It sounds a bit bloody risky to me, old boy. I'm not one of these boys that dodge through frontiers, you know."

"Oh, it is nothing. Every day it is done."

"It sounds a bit dangerous to me," Howard said uncomfortably. He was conscious that his reaction did not show him in an heroic light. But Otto's enthusiasm was already fading.

"You are right," he agreed. "There is the Englishman speaking, always so cool. You think at once all round, while we Germans, when we have an idea, we must do everything at once."

Howard smoked rapidly, a sign that he was inwardly disturbed. He recalled his conversation in the Atlantic a few days previously with Panting and his two friends. The major had talked quite calmly about taking cars to Paris and to Holland as well. He had even shipped them through Rotterdam to England. This idea was much less complicated than that, and there would be money in it that made all his previous deals chicken-feed.

Hilde said: "The husband of Sophie Kastner went to Hollant with a car with an English sea officer, I think, and has come back with many, oh many gulden."

"That may have been in the early days," Howard said. "Things will be more organised now, for certain."

"You are right, sir," Otto nodded. "It is sad, but you are right."

"Of course, if it can be done without any risk . . ." Howard stopped short.

"It would be a fine chance, also for the diamants," Otto murmured to Hilde, who at once looked angry.

She said: "No, no! I have already told you, I shall keep them."

"But why, but why?" he asked, with an air of great resignation. "With gulden we can eat for a year, for two years!"

"Please do not speak any more of it!"

Otto's reply was angry and in German. Howard settled back in his chair, feeling a little relieved. If they had one of their quarrels—he had no idea what it was about—perhaps the whole thing would be forgotten. He did not want to be tempted. He could remember Otto saying, on their way to Herr Jürgens and his fur coats, "It would be a quarter of a million marks." That was Panting's standard, the Guards lieutenant's, the major's. It meant several hundred pounds, the whole answer to the problem of settling down in England. Successful people were merely those who took their opportunities. Nor was it dishonest. Hilde had said the man was anxious to be rid of the car. But there'd be hell to play if the car were stopped at the frontier. He didn't like risks. He sat in his chair trying to forget the whole thing, while Hilde and Otto argued with each other, incomprehensibly. But she broke it off on a sudden and turned to him.

"Howart, it is dreadful of us to talk in German like this. We have a silly argument. You are not going to Hollant, therefore it is all the more silly. It is about my diamants.

235

They are given to me by my farder when I am eighteen years old, they have been hundred years in our family and Otto says we shall sell them to this man in Hollant, and I will not, I will not! Am I not right?"

"Mr. Rondle, these diamants are worth as much as a motor car. For what use are such things in our Germany today? If we sell them for gulden we are rich in the only way that matters here, we can buy on the black market all things to eat. We have still some marks, yes, but they are without value, and tomorrow they will be less."

"And tomorrow the diamants will be more also," Hilde said.

"I do not think so. For today the old gentlemen in Amsterdam are liking to start their business as much as they can. Tomorrow the business is already started. But we shall not go, it is idiotisch to talk, talk, talk of it."

"I do not talk. You are talking."

"They're worth a lot, then?" Howard asked.

"They are nothing!" Hilde said.

"Show them to Mr. Rondle!" Otto laughed. "Nothing! I get five thousand gulden like this for them!" He snapped his fingers. "In zree minutes!"

"You are not interested to see them, Howart?"

"Well, jewels don't mean anything to me, you know, but I'd quite like to have a look." He said it calmly, trying to control the excitement that had risen in him. Five thousand gulden was money, the real stuff that could be changed into pounds or dollars. There was a bottle of brandy on the table and he topped up all their glasses carefully. Hilde had gone into the bedroom and they could hear her unlocking a drawer. Otto winked at him.

"The ladies are ever sentimental, isn't it?"

Hilde returned, carrying a small black satin box, in which there were fifteen small stones, each separate and imbedded in its own cavity. They had a greyish tint and they sparkled beautifully.

"They are Brazilian," she said. "They were in a band for my neck, which I did not like so much, and I have had them

236

took out for to make a band for my arm. But we have had the war and so and so . . ."

"They look pretty good to me," Howard said. He gazed at them with respect. He thought of the four guinea necklace he had bought Mary last Christmas: at the time it had seemed to him an extravagant waste of money. It was fantastic that these were worth a small fortune. But they certainly looked the real thing. He told himself that he would have been sceptical if they had been trying to sell them to him, so that it was safe to believe in their value.

"And with me they stay!" Hilde said, with a chilling glance at Otto. The latter shrugged his shoulders. She closed the box and returned with it to the bedroom.

Howard grinned, "That seems to settle it, old boy."

"It is sad," Otto said. "One cannot find ten thousand gulden every day!"

"You said five just now!"

"Five for the diamants, five for the car." Otto looked at the bedroom door and lowered his voice. He whispered, "You have a little interest?"

"Well, a little," Howard answered uneasily. "But as I told you, I'm not taking any bloody silly risks . . ."

"I find out all what must be done!" Otto winked at him and raised his voice as Hilde came in from the bedroom. "Come, Hilde, yo ho and a bottle of Rhum—is that not right, sir?" When he laughed he looked cherubic and young, fifteen years younger than when he was serious. "You know I would very much like to learn some English folk songs, such as this 'Long Way to Tipperary,' isn't it? How does it go, Mr. Rondle?"

"Have another brandy instead, old boy," Howard advised him, affectionately.

They met to go shopping on the two following afternoons. Neither expedition was as profitable as usual. They tried several streets in the neighbourhood of the Altona station, but there was nothing of value to be bought. It was depressing and it made the idea of Dr. Neumann's car all the more attractive to Howard. They went into a large café on the Reeperbahn and discussed it over two glasses of weak beer. Otto had found out some details of the trip to Holland.

"All we must do is to paint the car wiz exactly the marks which are on your own car. Mr. Rondle. Then I am hidden in the baggage. We cross the frontier at one or two o'clock . . ."

"Yes, and I'm arrested at five past."

"It is not so, they are not so curious at this time. There are of course two posts, English and Hollandish . . ."

"Dutch, old boy."

"Dootch, yes. But there are times when the English post has Polish soldiers. It is possible for me to find out when. Polish soldiers do not ask a British officer anything at all. Nor the Dutch. Give him a cigarette, he shall see nothing. Oh, yes, and I am in Polish uniform."

"What?" said Howard, startled. "How do you manage that?"

Otto winked. "That is not so difficult. One must buy on the black. There are many deserters, isn't it? Of course it is very expensive—but for us, it is worth."

"How are you going to get back as a Pole, if there are Poles at the frontier post?"

"Because, sir, then it will be again English soldiers, who are not interested in a Pole who returns to Germany. Of course they would stop a Pole who leaves Germany. But a Pole who comes back cannot be making a crime, isn't it?"

"It sounds all very fine," Howard said doubtfully. "Anyhow, if we've sold the car, how do we get back at all?"

"That is simple. We have a lift from Canadian lorries."

"And that's how it was done with the Naval officer?"

"So it was done."

"And how do we know when the Poles are on guard?"

"I find out," Otto said confidently.

"Are you in the underground or something?" Howard chuckled. But Otto did not take such a remark lightly. He was hurt.

238

"Mr. Rondle, sir, I am a man of 20th July, a democrat——"
He broke off. He was staring over Howard's shoulder towards
the door of the café and there was suddenly fear in his eyes.
Three or four British military policemen led by a sergeant-
major had entered. There was a general buzz of commotion,
and a word went all round: "Razzia!" About two hundred
people were sitting in the café. They looked poker-faced and
resigned as one of the red-caps stationed himself in front of
the main entrance and a second went across to the exit by
the kitchen. The fat, white-aproned manager went up to the
sergeant-major as if he were the most welcome guest he had
ever seen.

"What's on?" Howard enquired. He was quite at ease.
They had nothing on him.

"It is a raid," Otto said. "Mr. Rondle, you must say I am
your driver. Otherwise I must go and explain and explain—
it is terrible." He sounded casual, but there were beads of
sweat on his forehead. A dozen helmeted German policemen
now came into the café. They stood there looking important,
but did nothing. The sergeant-major and his assistant began
moving from table to table, looking at papers. He seemed
mainly interested in women and now and then he ordered
one to go and join the German policemen. They did so with
docility. One woman attempted to argue, but the sergeant-
major interrupted her by banging on the floor with his stick.
The woman almost ran.

As they approached Howard's table, the latter signalled to
the assistant, who came over at once and saluted.

"What's this?" Howard asked.

"Oh, it's just a V.D. check-up, sir. Place is getting a
reputation. They'll be putting it out of bounds, I expect."

"Well, look here, this is my driver. That's all right, I
suppose?"

"Oh, yes, sir. You can go if you like, sir, we'll be here
twenty minutes."

The incident intoxicated Howard. He walked out through
a lane which the German policemen made for him. Outside

a small crowd had gathered round the doorway. Three lorries with some more policemen stood against the pavement. The policemen saluted him. He acknowledged them casually. Otto ran towards the Ford and flung open the door for him.

"Look here," Howard said, as they drove away, "if you're quite certain about this Holland business, and if you can make all the arrangements . . ."

"O.K.!" Otto exclaimed.

"How about getting the car—how much does this Dr. what's-his-name want?"

"I think Hilde will arrange with him we pay when we come back. Perhaps two-three hundred cigarettes now as a—as a . . ."

"Deposit? All right, that's easy. I can get him plenty of Steinhäger, too."

"Prima!" Otto said. "And for twenty cigarettes I get a painter who says nothing."

Howard dropped him as usual by the Altona station. As they pulled up, he said suddenly, "Look here, if and when we do get there, do you know where to go?"

"Of course," Otto replied. "I have been stationed for two years in Hollant and I have a good friend of me there. We go straight to him. He is a man who buys very quick."

"How do you know he's still there?"

"He is there."

"Are you quite sure he'll still deal with you? I mean it may have been all right when you were occupying them . . ."

"No, no, he is a man of great international feeling. He knows that I, too, am a liberal." Otto winked sideways. "It will be all right, Mr. Rondle!"

"I hope so!" Howard grinned. Otto got out, pulling down the brim of his trilby as usual, as if in an effort to make himself look mysterious. "I'll see you at Hilde's." He added with admiration as Otto disappeared in the crowd, "You black marketing rascal, you!" and laughed aloud. Then he drove back to the office and looked through the papers that Corporal Clayton had put in his in-tray.

CHAPTER 5

OTTO was as good as his word. Five days later he told Howard that the painter had been secured and that he was in process of negotiating for his uniform. He required two bottles of Steinhäger gin to support his bargaining.

Howard gave him three. It pleased him to appear over-generous. At the same time he was developing a new quality. At first his sudden prosperity had created self confidence and good nature, but too many champagne cocktails and liqueurs soon made him look more bloated. Now he was being overtaken by greed. He could think of nothing else but the five hundred pounds he was to make in a couple of days. That and the money he was now saving, since he had to spend none of his pay, plus the value of the 'commodities' he had bought, would all add up to a good start in civilian life. Greed also affected him by making him expect a service whenever he gave something away. Otto and Hilde repaid him amply. But in the mess he began not to offer cigarettes or stand drinks, unless there was a motive for doing so. His popularity, founded on the high spirited mood which the fur coat transaction had created, now declined. He was already finished for Hemsleigh and Styles, who at last realised that he was busy on the black market. Kay Blandison did not feel the same stir of interest when he came in. Elizabeth, surprised and piqued that she had been dropped after their evening together, avoided him; and so did Peter Schroeder, who always had a sensitive feel for a social wind. Howard was unconscious of all this. As far as he was concerned Hammond and the waiters were serving him better than anyone, and that was all that mattered.

He became impatient to get on with the trip and his only anxiety was that his demobilisation date might come through too early. He decided that it would be the last of his profit-making deals. After all, they were technically illegal, although he did not regard them as dishonest; but a wise man knew when to stop. He would return to England six or seven hundred pounds better off. It was a good enough prospect. Howard whistled happily to himself at the thought of it, sitting in the mess or working through his papers at the office, where Herr Scholle was extremely sulky; for Howard had ceased to do business with him or to keep him in cigarettes, without a word of explanation.

Things were going well, however. First Hilde allowed Otto to persuade her to sell her diamonds. And then Dr. Neumann, the owner of the car, had been most helpful. It had been decided that Howard should not be brought into the sale and it was left to Hilde. She reported that the doctor was agreeable to receiving five hundred gulden when they came back. It was not much for a car in good condition, but as Howard said, "We really don't need to give him anything; after all, I could easily report him for having hidden it." The car was located in the garden of Dr. Neumann's house in Volksdorf, a rural-looking suburb, which was about a twenty minutes' drive from the Kasselallee. It was a saloon, coloured a brilliant light blue, which the painter whom Otto had found was turning into a dull, military khaki green. Howard and Otto drove out every day to see how he was getting on. They met the owner only once and he invited them in for a glass of Schnaps, which was in fact part of the 'deposit' that Howard had provided. The car was not discussed, except for a meaning remark by the little doctor about the value of foreign exchange on the black market; otherwise the conversation was entirely taken up with his complaints about the iniquity of a man in his position being forced to have refugees living in all but two rooms of his house. He told Howard that it was very sad to Germans of liberal thought, who believed in the idea of a West European tradition, that the English were losing their popularity.

As soon as the khaki green was dry, the painter copied all the signs and figures on Howard's car. He was a middle aged, jovial man with the consumptive look which was becoming common among the workers. He spat as he talked his

Hamburg German and almost bowed to the ground every time he saw Howard. The car was finished in a week and the painter disappeared, highly satisfied with forty cigarettes and a bar of soap. They took it on a trial run round Volksdorf. The engine was in a good condition. Next there was a most important detail to be seen to. This was the form number '85' which had to be pasted on the windscreens of German cars requisitioned by Military Government. Without it a car was not allowed on the road. It was therefore necessary that the form '85' which was on Howard's own car should be transferable to Dr. Neumann's. This was easy, since both were Fords and the painter had copied the number. They steamed the label off carefully and used some sticky paper which Howard had found at the office to fix it temporarily to the other car. They were now ready for the first real test. Howard drove the car to the nearest British petrol point and was given petrol and oil without any difficulty. Moreover the soldier on duty checked the label. He returned to Volksdorf feeling triumphant. He had no longer any doubt about being able to cross the frontier.

The next day Otto reported that he had obtained his uniform. In the evening he dressed up at the flat. It was a battledress with 'Poland' on the shoulder badge and a Divisional formation sign on the sleeves. There was no doubt about it, he looked a perfect, though somewhat untidy Polish soldier. Both Hilde and Otto shook with laughter and Howard kept repeating, for five minutes, "It's amazing, it looks marvellous!" Then Otto changed back again and they had an enjoyable party together, with Steinhäger and Howard's evening rations.

Commercially it was an uninteresting period. His only coup was to buy a 'British Warm' officer's coat at the Hamburg Officers' Shop with marks and sell it to Mr. Hopwood in return for an English cheque for five pounds. It was not much but it was better than nothing, and helped to calm him while he waited. However, within a week an evening came when he arrived at the flat as usual and Otto was there to greet him: "Mr. Rondle, I think tomorrow is a good night for us."

The next morning Howard applied for forty-eight hours' leave from Major Cardington. The latter was still busy, as he had been for weeks, on his plans for a party for hungry German children.

"My dear fellow, of course," he said. "Where do you think of going?"

"I want to visit my regiment."

"Not a bad idea. That's fine, off you go, my dear chap."

Howard wrote out a pass for himself to go to Holland, pressed on it the Sociology Division stamp and signed it himself. Every detail had been planned to a nicety. He had lunch at the Atlantic, quietly, speaking to no one, and then he drove back to the office garage to leave his car, after removing the official work ticket and the form '85' which was now stuck on only by four half-inch pieces of paper and therefore easily transferable. He told one of the Volkswagen drivers to take him back to the mess and arranged that he should be picked up after tea. He wrote a short letter to Mary, who had been complaining that she did not hear from him, and then slept on his bed for the rest of the afternoon. At tea time he asked Hammond to make him up a large tin of sandwiches, enough to last two people for a couple of meals. The batman winked at him. He had a pornographic imagination.

"They don't half want it, don't they, sir?"

"This is strictly business," Howard said.

"Right, sir, I believe you. But don't go agreeing to sign on, like I did."

"You made a mistake there," Howard chuckled. He was in a friendly mood. "Do you realise you soon won't be able to spend marks in the NAAFI? That'll fix you."

"I tell you," Hammond nodded, "this occupation won't be no fun in a year's time, I know. Have you ever noticed it, sir, how if ever you get a good spot in the army, the high-ups always manage to spoil it for you in the end? Once they start on that lark, you might as well be home in England."

The Volkswagen dropped him a hundred yards from Dr. Neumann's house. The driver asked if he wanted to be picked up later. Howard shook his head and then stood on the pavement, waiting until the beetle-like little car was out of sight. He carried a small haversack, in which were the sandwiches and his washing gear, and an army blanket.

It was a pretty road with a few medium sized houses on one side and a wood on the other. Otto, in his Polish uniform, stepped out of the wood, beaming. He saluted Howard with a flourish.

"Please, I wish a lift to Warschau!"

"You'll do," Howard said. "They'd go for you in Scotland in a big way."

"So?"

"So. You've got the diamonds all right?"

Otto tapped his battledress blouse and winked. "It was with great reluctance that they are finally given!"

"I can believe that."

The car was ready for them, but as usual no one was about. Howard stuck on the form '85' and they got in. Twenty minutes later they passed the Hamburg main railway station and they turned away from the city centre towards the road to Bremen. Otto stretched himself comfortably.

"It is a long time since I travel so well, Mr. Rondle."

Howard said: "Well, I must say, I admire the way people like you are so philosophical about things. Though I suppose we would have been much the same if you'd beaten us."

"All peoples are the same. One day the world will realise it. Then there will be no more war."

For a quarter of an hour they passed through acres of Hamburg ruins, crossed the bridges into Harburg, and finally they reached the autobahn. Howard felt a rising elation within himself. After all, this was quite an adventure. He reflected that if he had only found out his capacity during the war, he would probably have dropped behind the lines somewhere as an agent. He chuckled at the plentiful notices warning British drivers not to carry civilians.

Otto's particular pleasure was to see German lorries pulled up at the side of the road, while troops and German policemen inspected the papers of their apathetic passengers. He seemed to think it was a very good joke, and almost as good when they passed two old women who were hauling a heavily laden cart and he shouted out at them, gesturing that they should move in closer to the side of the road. It occurred to Howard that though Germans might feel sorry for themselves, they had singularly little sympathy for each other. On the other hand it made Otto a very convincing Pole.

A few kilometres along the autobahn military policemen were directing all transport except staff cars on to a side road. The Ford was taken for a staff car and waved respectfully on. Howard laughed aloud. Everything, including the car's engine, was going very well.

On either side the great dull north German plain stretched out for miles. Occasional bridges over or under the autobahn were the only relief. Only one lane of the road was in use for the other was a store for old tanks, vehicles and every kind of warlike store, becoming rustier every day. After an hour Otto suggested suddenly that Howard should stop for a moment. He drew in to the side. They were alongside a big store of petrol jerry-cans. Otto looked up and down the road and then jumped out.

"I think we have some of these."

"What for? They're empty."

"They will be a nice covering for me on top of the blanket, when we cross the frontier."

"It's a damn good idea."

Otto loaded a dozen of the cans into the back of the car and they started up again. After another hour they reached the depressing, twisted remains of Bremen, where huge letters over a sports field, announcing 'General Ike Stadium,' and the sardonic roadside notices 'Drive carefully—Death Is So Permanent,' indicated that this territory was occupied by the

United States. The sight of American troops made Otto remember the negroes he had seen in Munich and Frankfurt and he spoke reproachfully of what he considered an insult to the German people.

"Well, you asked for it," Howard said. "Once you start making wars you've got to bear in mind that you may lose them."

Otto forgot his depression and smiled gaily.

"You are right! It is our so-called Fuehrer I should be blaming. Now shall I not drive, Mr. Rondle, through Vechta and Lingen and until Reine and then I think I must go under the jerry-cans."

They changed places outside Bremen. The evening was beginning to set in and Howard felt tired. He dozed for an hour, while Otto kept the Ford going steadily. They went through an area of Canadian occupation and then they came to the Poles, the only troops who seemed reasonably contented. The few Germans about looked as dull and dispirited as the countryside. This was the main route from Kiel and Hamburg to Antwerp or Amsterdam and army signs with the road's code number guided them all the way. The Ford was only one of hundreds of freshly painted cars with khaki uniformed passengers that went on it every day. No one gave it a glance except soldiers out for the evening, who were trying to thumb a lift. Germans did not bother. Their only hope was one of the slow-moving lorry trains which could often be jumped on as they went along.

By the time they reached Reine it was nearly eleven o'clock and the streets were dark and deserted. As soon as they had passed through the town Otto pulled the car into the side of the road. He said that they were only twenty minutes from the frontier and he thought it was a little early. They had a sandwich and a drink from a flask of brandy which Howard had brought. Then they lit cigarettes. Howard watched his companion's eyes gradually close into sleep and envied him. For the last hour he had felt his nerves increasingly on edge and it had been an effort to match Otto's calm.

He was not anxious about the frontier; but he wanted to get it over. However, he was astonished to find that he was next conscious of Otto shaking his shoulder.

"It is half-past one, Mr. Rondle. I think we now go. Through Gronau and then—Hollant."

"Right you are, pal." Howard sat up and wiped his eyes. "Hell, it's damned cold."

Otto was busy taking the jerry-cans out of the back. When they were all outside he wrapped himself loosely in the blanket and lay on the floor behind the two front seats. Howard pulled the blanket over his head. Next he picked up the jerry-cans one by one and placed them carefully on top of him. He took some time over it, in order to get the most casual effect. Now and then he asked Otto how he was feeling and the latter uttered muffled sounds of satisfaction. Howard reflected that civilian travel in post-war Germany was good training for little escapades like this. When he had finished, he buttoned up his own greatcoat, sat in the driving seat and lit himself a cigarette. This was the moment for the hidden military policemen to emerge and arrest them. But all was quiet. On either side the over-cultivated fields receded into the gloom. Howard chuckled and pressed the self-starter.

The road was cobbled and for Otto's sake he went at a medium pace. The latter seemed quite comfortable, however. Howard whistled softly a tune called 'Laura.' Five hundred pounds; then no more; then England and a future, full of initiative and ideas. "Just the job," he said to himself. He drove through Gronau, feverish with excitement. Five minutes later the Ford's headlights shone on the warning notice that the frontier was ahead; and also on a British soldier who was signalling for a lift.

Howard pulled up. It occurred to him that it was a good proof that you had nothing to hide if you were giving someone a lift.

"Hop in."

"Just up to the post, sir." A young soldier's fresh red face

248

appeared in the window. Howard saw that there was another one behind him and his throat grew dry.

"There's hardly room in the back—"

"That's all right, I can pile in, sir." The soldier opened the back door of the car, climbed in and straddled the jerry-cans, while his companion got in beside Howard. The latter was suddenly perspiring.

"You doing the frontier guard tonight?"

"Yes, sir. It's just another five hundred yards. Dull job, sir."

Howard remembered Otto's forecast that Poles would be on duty. That was why they had come on this particular night. It meant that at last things were going wrong. Now on a sudden he felt a great desire to forget the five hundred pounds, to turn the car round and get back to Hamburg. But it was too late. His foot remained on the accelerator and there was a swinging torch in the middle of the road ahead.

He pulled the Ford in slowly as the sentry with the torch motioned him. The two soldiers opened the doors and jumped out, saluting and thanking him. The torch shone into his face. Howard tried to look unconcerned. He was frightened and his hand shook as he felt for his wallet. The sentry shone the torch into the back and played it lingeringly over the jerry-cans. The post bar across the road remained down.

Howard found his wallet and took out his identity card, work-ticket and leave pass. The sentry looked at them care-fully, and then shone his torch on the form '85' on the windscreen.

"Right, will you just come in and sign your name, sir?"

He got out clumsily. There were two or three soldiers standing round, and inside the post half a dozen more, some asleep, the others sitting at a table. So this was what Otto had said would be a cursory examination. Howard bent down to scrawl his name as illegibly as possible on a list which a Corporal showed him, and next to it the number of the car. This did not worry him, for if there should be an enquiry later as to why that car had not returned through one of the frontier posts into the British zone, there was a Ford with exactly the same number in the Sociology Division's garage. What was worrying him was his conviction that the sentry was at that moment discovering Otto. But he dared not look round until the corporal was satisfied.

"Right ho, thank you, sir," the corporal said.

Howard turned. Nothing seemed to have happened. The sentry was still by the car. He went back and climbed in.

"What have you got in the back, sir?" the sentry asked.

"Some empty jerry-cans and my kit." He made a great effort. "Of course I wouldn't say there isn't a bottle of whisky."

"O.K., sir, carry on." The road bar was raised.

Howard switched on. The Ford moved. They were through the first post. His heart pounded, but he restrained himself from speaking. The Dutch post and another sentry with a waving torch were already in sight. The night's darkness was beginning to lessen and there was the cold tang of another day in the air.

He stopped the car again and two or three Dutch soldiers loomed round. He showed his identity card.

"O.K. No civilians?" The torch flashed round the car.

"No civilians," Howard grinned. He could feel the sweat now making his neck clammy.

"O.K., O.K.!" The second road bar went up and the car went slowly through. They were in Holland. Squat, neat, comfortable houses were on either side of the road.

He drove on for five minutes, hardly believing that it could be possible. An intoxicating feeling of triumph began to take possession of him. Gradually his instinct for caution faded. He brought the car to a halt and said, "All right, old boy, you can get up!" He shook with laughter as the jerry-cans moved and Otto's blanketed figure emerged.

"I think I am almost a dead man, Mr. Rondle!"

"You're a bloody marvel, old boy. You'd better have a swig." He handed over his brandy flask.

Otto took it gratefully. He seemed very little ruffled by his experience. After he had had some brandy, he said, "I think perhaps we must drive on for a few kilometres until we are in the country, and then I would like to walk up and down."

"O.K." They were in what looked like the suburb of a town. The whole atmosphere was different from the other side of the border. There was friendliness and security in the air. Well-kept gardens could just be discerned reaching down to the pavement on either side of the road. The dust and mustiness which was everywhere in Germany, in rooms, clothes, towns and villages, had disappeared. Here everything was as neat and fresh as if a vacuum cleaner had been passed over the whole place. Howard started the Ford again and they drove on under a white railway bridge and then through a deserted shopping street.

"This is Enschede," Otto said. "I have known it very well in 43."

"What happened about those Poles who were supposed to be on guard at the frontier?"

"There I have made a great mistake, Mr. Rondle."

"You'd better be sure they aren't there when you go back, or they'll start talking Polish at you, and then where will you be?"

Otto laughed. "Then I shall have much trouble, I think!"

They were through Enschede and travelling along a wide straight road. A signpost read: 'Arnhem, Utrecht, Rotterdam.' Otto was looking out sentimentally. Soon they were in the country again.

"The Dootch are a quiet, goot people. I found it very sad that we must occupy them, Mr. Rondle. Of course they have not our culture, but I have liked many of them. Here we will stop if you please, and then I think it is better if I drive, for the way will now be complicated."

Howard pulled in again and Otto got out. He walked up and down quickly, flinging his arms about and taking deep breaths. Then Howard opened his tin of rations and they ate a sandwich each, before moving off again, this time with Otto at the wheel. The strange clear light of Holland was now dawning quickly. Otto turned the car off the main road, so that they left behind the Rhine Army and Canadian Maple

Leaf signs and were in the real country, on a straight narrow cobbled road, with farmland on either side. Now and then they passed an early worker, going placidly on his way. Howard looked without interest at the potato fields, orchards, cornfields and the occasional, still sleeping village, neat, clean and solid with its easily visible interior scenes. He began to doze and fell asleep. When he woke again, they were in the square of a small town and the car was at rest. Howard sat up, rubbing his eyes.

"Hell, I didn't know I'd gone off—what's the time? How long have we been here?"

"It is twenty minutes after seven. I too have slept. We have been here one hour. It is four or five kilometres from here that we do business."

Howard brightened.

"Bloody good show—when do we get moving?"

"In perhaps an hour. My friend likes to sleep, you know. But you will like some coffee and eggs, I think? I have been to the café in front of us. It is opened and they will give it to us for twenty English cigarettes."

Howard winked at him.

"I suppose they think you're a Pole."

"I have spoken in very bad German. You would like some coffee?"

"Lead me to it. My throat's like a bag of sawdust."

A solitary waiter welcomed them into the café. He seemed already to be on familiar terms with Otto and he gave Howard a respectful nod. As he sat down Howard told himself that a nod from a Dutchman was really worth half a dozen bows from the defeated Germans. Their table stood against the plate glass window that looked out on to the square. The café itself was looking gloomy. It was a long narrow room stretching back from the street, with a counter at the far end, next to a most complicated looking radiogram, which was fitted with bells, pulleys and cogwheels. The waiter disappeared through a door behind the counter and next a woman's voice was heard; then her head suddenly appeared to inspect them for a second before withdrawing again. Howard and Otto lit cigarettes and looked contentedly out on to the square. Every few minutes they caught each other's eye and chuckled about the way they had come through the frontier. When the coffee and fried eggs arrived, they were in an excellent mood, and Howard had seldom enjoyed food more. At the end of it the cigarettes were handed over to the waiter in a happy little ceremony. Then Otto spoke some halting German, after which he turned to Howard and said: "Sir, I will now take a small wash." He nodded, and Otto went off with the waiter to disappear with him behind the counter. Howard played with the beer mats on the table. They were marked 'V. Vollenhoven's Bier.' He noticed a small billiard table in the corner of the café. Really, it was a pleasant, cosy little place, he reflected. He began to gaze analytically at the people who were now passing by on the pavement outside. They were plain, sound-looking people, without the neurotic sulkiness that distinguished the average passer-by in Germany. It was pleasant also to see the line of neat, gaily coloured shops on one side of the square, and the windows above them all with green or red shutters, and the modern semi-detached houses opposite them, so well and solidly designed, with their wide rectangular windows, narrow bricks and big roofs, and the pretty front gardens that ran directly on to the square. It was all charming, civilised, unhurried. A man went by with a cart, loaded with flowers, then a party of scouts, then two or three small children, who were suffering from rickets. There were not many cars and no buses, and a small knot of people gathered at one corner of the square, where the main road entered, hoping to thumb a lift. The khaki Ford, with all its Rhine army and Control Commission signs, alone on the white painted parking space in the centre of the square, looked very grand. It seemed almost a pity to sell it. But only almost, Howard smiled, thinking happily of the money to come. He had sat there by himself for ten minutes when Otto returned, fresh and glowing, his fair hair neatly brushed back.

"Now I am a new man, Mr. Rondle!"

"You look it, old boy."

"You would like a wash, sir? He will give you hot water. Do you know it is one year since I have had hot water for shaving?"

"Well, I suppose a shave would do me good. Though I'd like to get that bit of goods outside moving. The sun's shining, you know, and people can see things."

"I will get your bag." Otto smiled, standing to attention beside him, and then walked smartly out towards the car. "He's over-doing the act a bit," Howard thought, with a trace of anxiety. He hoped that Otto would not let his confidence run away with him. It only wanted a policeman to ask for his papers. But he returned with the haversack and stood to attention again as he handed it to Howard, together with the Form '85.'

"I have taken it off, to make sure we do not forget it later."

Howard coughed, a little irritated. Really, Otto was beginning to take too much upon himself. After all, he was a British officer and he could manage things as capably as was necessary, without having every move thought of for him.

"That is, if you agree, sir—or shall I take it back?"

"No, no, leave it." Howard took the form and put it into his pocket, mollified. He left Otto with a few cigarettes and followed the waiter to the back of the café. They went behind the counter and through into a small passage, at the end of which was the kitchen door and a small stairway. The woman who had inspected them earlier came out of the kitchen and smiled at Howard. She was fat and motherly. The waiter went back to the café.

"I am speaking a little English. You have like your eggs?"

"Wonderful."

"I am cooking water for you."

"It's very kind of you."

"It is nothing. You are British or American?"

"British."

"I am once in London, when I am a little girl. The Tower

254

Bridge!" For some reason she giggled. Her double chin shook. "Up and down! Up and down!"

"That's right, the Tower Bridge," Howard smiled, anxious to be friendly.

"Go upstairs please and through the door on the left. I will come with water."

"Oh, yes, thank you." Once again they exchanged bright smiles and Howard passed her, with difficulty, and climbed the stairs, which were narrow and steep.

"If you put your trousers and shoes outside the door, I will press and clean them," she called after him.

"That's very kind of you, I haven't much time, though——"

"It will be a moment only."

"Well, thanks."

Howard found himself in a small, musty smelling bedroom, with a large double bed, a wash-stand with a jug and basin, and a skylight for a window. He sat on the bed and pulled off his shoes, one by one. It made him feel better. He emptied his trouser pockets, then undressed so that he stood in his shirt and pants. There was a knock at the door, which opened sufficiently for a kettle of water to be passed through. Howard picked up his trousers and shoes and handed them out in return.

"Thank you very much."

"It is nothing. I will be very soon."

He took the kettle to the basin and within a couple of minutes his face was covered with lather. The sun came through the skylight, making a bright yellow strip on the bed, and through it also came a few sounds from outside, including one which made Howard hold his brush steady in the air for a moment, before he grinned at himself and went on. He used a new blade in his razor and it felt good against his skin. After he had dried his face he went over to the door and looked outside, but the woman had not yet brought up his things. He returned to the wash-stand, poured out a little more water into a glass and cleaned his teeth. He made a second trip of inspection and this time the empty floor outside and the shut door of the kitchen below made him feel impatient. A quarter of an hour had gone, and the sooner Otto and he got rid of the car and the diamonds, the better he would be pleased. However, he might as well have a proper wash; and he was soon soaping himself with unusual energy. He crooned, 'I'm a Little on the Lonely Side.' But when he had dried himself, and put on his shirt and tie again, and brushed his hair, and there were still neither shoes nor trousers outside the door, he began to feel angry. He sat down on the bed, frowning, and lit a cigarette. Obviously he couldn't go down to the kitchen in his pants. He could shout —but they might not hear, or not understand, in any case he would make a fool of himself. So he went on sitting there, blowing out smoke rings and watching them mingle with the dust in the strip of sunlight. He had been there for five minutes, when he felt uneasy. On a sudden a thought had occurred to him which was so disturbing that it made him take his cigarette out of his mouth with a jerky movement and then stare at the linoleum-covered floor, his eyes wide open and unblinking. It was a sensation like that of a traveller who thinks he knows his road, when all at once he realises that he took a wrong turning twenty miles back; no landmark or anything definite suggests it, it is an abrupt feeling of going wrong. In this way Howard wondered if he were being tricked, if the sound he had heard while shaving had after all been the Ford driving away. No sooner had he thought it than he had a deep conviction that it was true; and immediately he tried to persuade himself that it was not. Perfect nonsense—Otto at this moment was impatiently smoking his last cigarette at the table, the car was still in the square where they had left it, the woman had probably been called to do some job, perhaps to see a tradesman.

"Bloody fool," he told himself, and another silent five minutes went by. He lit a second cigarette and smoked it rapidly. When he had stumped it out, desperation at last made him go to the door and shout down the stairs. "Hallo! Hallo!"

The kitchen door opened at once and the woman appeared. "So you are ready?" she asked.

"Yes." He gasped inwardly, flushing at this proof of his idiocy. Naturally she had expected him to shout. She must have been wondering what on earth he was doing. He retreated from the door as she came up the stairs. The shoes and trousers were handed in, balanced on her podgy arms. Howard stepped forward to take them, hiding himself modestly behind the door. He thanked her warmly and the woman protested with great friendliness that it was nothing at all. Howard dressed himself as quickly as he could, and hurried down the stairs and along the passage into the café. He was a yard past the counter when he stopped, and turned pale. The café was empty, except for the waiter, and he could see through the tall window on to the square that there was no car in the parking place.

Without any hope he walked to the door and went outside, where the waiter had by now arranged a few tables, on each of which there was a bowl of gaillardias. The square was quiet and sunny. Yellow and orange awnings now covered most of the shop windows and each narrow brick of every building showed out clearly in the light of the day. People were still waiting at the corner for a lift. A jeep full of Canadians drove by, kicking up dust. On one side of the café was a grocer's shop, whose stock was principally United States army tins of Meat & Vegetable. On the other there was a hairdresser. Howard stared helplessly from one advertisement to another. 'ATA schuurt schoon zonder te krassen—een Persil product.' 'Kapper—antiseptische bediening—Dames—Heeren.' There was a bicycle shop on the corner, with some tyre-less machines on view, and next to it a direction post, which said: 'Amersfoort.' The fat woman was part of the trick, of course. She had his trousers and shoes, while Otto got away. How simple, how innocent—they had fooled him at their leisure. He looked again round the square, while the humiliating thoughts came tumbling after each other into his mind. He turned to the waiter, who had been watching him casually.

"When did he go?"

The waiter shrugged his shoulders and said, in Dutch, that he did not understand.

"When did he go?" Howard repeated, raising his voice. The waiter pointed over his shoulder towards the kitchen, and went off towards it. After a moment the fat woman came out. She was still smiling. He asked her for information in a calmer tone. He was already telling himself that maybe Otto had merely gone to do the deal and would be back in due course.

"I will ask the waiter," she beamed. While she was gone, he sat down again at the table and discovered that he had only half a dozen cigarettes left.

"He had gone since perhaps five and twenty minutes," she informed him on her return, as if it were a piece of goods news. "He does not know in what direction. Perhaps to Amersfoort? It is something wrong?"

"Oh, nothing, he's just stolen my car, that's all," Howard said grimly.

The fat woman reacted at once. Her smile disappeared and her eyes narrowed. She said, "Stolen—then you must tell it to a policeman at once. I shall telephone for you—"

"No, no," he exclaimed, in panic, and saw at the same moment the hint of satisfaction in her eyes. He knew that she was in it, and the waiter, who now stood leaning against the counter, staring at him. They hadn't a care. They knew he wasn't telling any policeman.

"Perhaps he will come back," the fat woman said. "Wait here for an hour. Two hours."

Howard did not reply. He remembered how deftly Otto had ensured that he had the Form '85', so that there would be no questions in Hamburg. The whole affair had been worked out brilliantly, except by himself. And what had been Hilde's part, he wondered, sickly. It was the most stabbing thought of all. He stood up with all the dignity he could muster and nodded to the fat woman, trying to seem at his ease. He put on his greatcoat and picked up his beret and his haversack.

Neither the fat woman nor the waiter moved. They watched him placidly and he went out into the square.

He went quickly towards the main road, determined on one thing; somehow he must get back to Hamburg as soon as possible. He was hot and sweating after fifty yards and he had been walking along the straight, tree-lined, cobbled road for two hours before a Canadian lorry stopped and picked him up. The driver was a cheerful little fellow and within the first five minutes he told his exhausted and miserable passenger that he had just made twenty thousand francs on the Brussels black market. The following morning, twenty hours later, Howard reached Hamburg in the back of a jeep, sandwiched between four hearty subalterns who picked him up in Oldenburg. They dropped him in the Dammtorstrasse and he went at once to the Sociology Division's garage.

CHAPTER 6

His car was still there. He nodded to two of the German drivers of the Volkswagens, who had just arrived for the day's work. It was not yet time to go and fetch Miss Hackster and the others. They stared at him and when he caught sight of himself in the car mirror he understood why. His face was grey and unshaven, his hair awry. He looked and felt like a criminal about to be arrested after a chase. His hand was shaking when he switched the motor on. He was scared.

He drove at once to Hilde's flat, taking a parallel road behind the Kasselallee, so that they should not see him by any chance. He was expecting anything: two empty rooms, a German from upstairs saying, "Nahler? I don't know the name." But the name had been on the door. They couldn't say that. He sweated as thoughts tumbled headlong across his mind, mixed up as in a fever.

But she was there. Slim as a boy, green eye shadow, auburn hair, it was all there; she was real. The sight of her made him feel just a little better. To his surprise she was up and dressed, wearing a plain grey suit.

"Howart?" She stared at him just as the Volkswagen drivers had. "Was—what is the matter? Where is Otto?"

"As if you didn't know," he said bitterly. He pushed past her into the sitting room. It looked exactly the same. Maybe he was wrong, he prayed that he was wrong.

"As if I did not——" she was repeating. She followed him in, astonished.

He turned round.

"What did you know about this trip?"

"What did I know——"

"For Christ's sake stop repeating what I say."

Then she seemed to understand the condition he was in. She looked at him anxiously and sat down, facing him.

"What has happened?" she asked. "Where is Otto? Howart, tell me."

To Howard the room was swaying round her. She sounded genuine. It occurred to him that perhaps after all she didn't know. He seized on the hope once more. He said: "I last saw him in some damned Dutch town."

"In a town?" There was a faint relaxation of her attitude. "In Hollant?"

"It was at a café, near the place we were going to sell the car and the diamonds. I had a shave and a wash and when I went back he——"

"What are you speaking of, Howart? I think you are pulling my legs? Why were you in Hollant? How can Otto have been there?"

"Christ, you knew we were going to Holland!"

"But of course not, Howart." She was calm and soothing, unmoved when he took a step towards her as if to strike her.

His eyes were bloodshot. "You cannot be feeling well," she said. "Howart, lie down. You are having a bad dream, I think. I must go away for an hour to get my bread, and then I must work with Dr. Neumann as you know——"

He was trembling.

"We discussed the whole thing here—you were angry about him taking your diamonds—it was you who suggested Dr. Neumann's car——"

Hilde laughed.

"I think you are very, very ill! Diamonds, cars—Dr. Neumann has no car! How can I talk of it?"

He sat down, wiping his forehead. The events of the past few hours crowded in on him, piercing, screeching, tearing. It was then that he became conscious of her grey suit. He had seen it before, somewhere. His brain cleared, a single image suddenly appeared. The girl in the gallery at the concentration camp trial. It was this suit. Her suit.

He said, amazed: "So you were at the trial."

"Trial?" She wasn't ready for it and she coloured. She lost her composure. "Howart, I simply do not know what you are talking about. I think you are unwell."

"Stop playing this game," he said. "What sort of bloody fool do you think I am?"

"You must have a drink."

He began to talk quietly as if he were reflecting aloud for his own benefit. Facts were settling into places by themselves. He was like a man who has been climbing upwards through a cloud and now comes to clear daylight again; but below and behind him the clouds are still there, inexorable and dark. For the moment he was not even angry.

"You were at the trial. You said you weren't. You arranged the car, the trip with him, you knew all about it. Now you say you didn't. You're lying and you know that I know you're lying. He was never here when you had guests. He never went to parties. The only person he met was Dr. Neumann, who's in with you on the car. He travelled at night. He said he'd been a member of the Party. But he wouldn't have to

261

leave the country for that. Why didn't you want me to see you at the trial?"

Now she had lost her calm. She opened the cupboard where the drink was kept and took out a quarter full bottle of brandy. The bottle shook in her grasp. She poured it out unsteadily, trying to control herself. She took the glass to him with a ghost of a smile. He ignored it, he looked up into her eyes with the gaze of a child. He tried a long shot.

"There was a connection between him and the trial?"

"You must drink this." Her voice was all wrong. He knew that he had hit on the truth.

"That's fine," he said. "That's absolutely fine." Then his fear came back and he felt sick with it. He began to sweat again. He said: "He was the adjutant. They never got him." Kay Blandison had said that when they were driving away from the trial. There were other things she had said which he would have been well advised to listen to. That had been his instinct, too, but he'd let himself be persuaded—he cursed himself bitterly. He said: "Christ, and I've been sitting with him, a swine like that. And you made me sleep with you with this up your sleeve. You bitch—you——"

Above all he was feeling humiliation. She had had him just where she wanted him. Of course, it had had to be him. It had to happen to Howard Randle, not to the other bastards who had done what he had done and more, Charlie, Panting, the Guards lieutenant, they got away with it, but not he. Not he. Anger and fear coursed through him, while she stood there in front of him, a half smile on her lips, her hands working nervously on the brandy glass.

"How can he get away in Holland?" he said dully. "He won't stand a chance. I could easily find that café again." Now once more he sounded, as if he were talking to himself. "That'll be part of a chain, of course, the sort of thing we did. And your Dr. Neumann, they can pick him up in a second."

"You will make a report?" Hilde said.

"Of course." It was inevitable.

She sat down again, facing him. She was set and white and her expression had an hysterical arrogance about it.

"I think you will do nothing. If you make a report on Otto, you must make a report on yourself."

"If you think you can keep me quiet——"

"Otto is now away, he is gone. You will only make troubles for yourself."

"Yes, and for you as well."

"For me, yes. It will not matter. I have done nothing."

"You've sheltered a criminal."

"That must be first proved. I think only you has seen him here." She might have been discussing the weather.

The enormity of what he had done began to dawn on him. He had walked into the simplest of traps with his eyes open, simply out of greed. He looked at her with horror, as if she were some kind of exhibit. It was hard to imagine that he had felt passion for her. Now she stirred only repulsion in him. There was a fiend beneath the beauty.

"I'll have to report it," he said, and a chill went through him. "I'll be court martialled."

"It is not necessary, it is foolish." A change came over her face, softening it. She looked as though she might cry. She whispered: "I am much unhappy, Howart."

"You're unhappy. That's rich." To his amazement he realised that she was trying to attract him once more. She moved from her chair and knelt down beside him, kittenish and pathetic. He hated her as he had hated nobody in his life. He said with contempt: "I suppose he was your lover, too. You said he was your brother, which I take it means he wasn't your brother."

When she looked up at him, tossing her hair, he was fascinated to see that her eyes were moist. She put both her hands round his right wrist and lifted it against her cheek. He pulled it away roughly and hurt her. She answered by flinging herself on him, kissing him, trying to get her arms round his neck. He struggled against her and finally had to pull her hair hard.

"You are terrible!" she moaned. "But you are wrong, he was not my lover. He was a friend, an old friend, and we have said brother because otherwise you might think that. But what I have said about loving you, Howart, was true, all true——"

"You wanted someone to help him get out and you picked on me at that party," he said. "You saw in a flash I was the ideal silly bastard and you were right."

"At first we tried to deceive you, but later—later I have felt love, Howart—I am speaking the trut'. Now I am glad he is gone, I do not like the bad things he has done. Now we can be alone, Howart. There will be no one else."

He stared down at her. She was on her knees again, imploring, using everything she had in her eyes. She seemed to be feeling no guilt at all. She thought it was natural that they should carry right on from where they left off. He said: "I'd sooner sleep with a cobra."

"I do not understand——"

He stood up. "No, maybe you don't, but I do. At last. The next time I see you, my sweet bitch, we'll be in a Court. I'll willingly get myself court-martialled to see you finished even if I go to prison myself."

As he went towards the door, she tried to pull him back and he shook her off. He thought, "If I stay here I'll kill her." He paused and for a moment an odd sensation tingled through his fingers. He looked at her smooth white neck, which was turning strangely into a blue colour. She was on her feet now and her mood had changed to anger. He clenched and unclenched his fists. His fingers wanted to get round her neck and he himself felt powerless to stop them. Then he heard her cold, infuriated voice.

"Go and make report. It is you who will suffer."

His dizziness faded. He stepped towards her, raised his right hand and caught her a stinging slap on her cheek. She gasped, but she did not move. She was too astounded. Howard turned and went out, slamming the door. He hurried down to the street and climbed into the car.

"I would have murdered her," he said to himself, in wonder,

as he switched on and let in the clutch. He half expected her to shout at him from the window, but everything was still. A tall boy in very short black trousers walked by on the pavement, giving him a sullen look. The sentry in front of the military billet farther down the road was pacing up and down, bored and hungry. The sight of him pulled Howard together. He sat up and tried to look calm as he drove by. "I suppose I'm bloody well ruined." It was curious to be able to have a thought like that and mean it. At the corner of the Kasselallee he pushed in the brake and stopped the car. Two hundred yards away the Volkswagens were loading up. There they all came, down the steps, Miss Hackster, Mr. Maxton-Hill, Kay Blandison and the others, going off to work, to spin their little plots and intrigues, to kid themselves they were important, that they weren't failures. And he, the worst failure of the lot, had found them pathetic. Anyhow they'd have a tasty morsel to gossip about soon. The Volkswagens started off. Hemsleigh and Styles' car and the major's Mercedes remained in front of the mess. Howard decided that their owners would still be in their bedrooms, and he drove gently down the street.

Hammond, who was always available when there was little likelihood of service being required, welcomed him.

"Been on a bender, sir? Have you had breakfast?"

"Is there any hot water, old boy?" Howard asked, thinking how strange it was that he could talk logically at such a moment. "What I'd like is a bath. And some breakfast, I suppose, yes—upstairs."

"Water's piping 'ot, or was an hour ago. You go on up, I'll see to it, Mr. Randle. Trip successful?"

"It was quite a trip."

The batman shook his head admiringly and Howard went upstairs. Luckily he had to meet no one and when he shut his bedroom door behind him he sighed with relief. For the past hour he had forgotten his weariness, but now it came over him suddenly. He walked slowly across the room and sat on his bed. It was an effort to bend down and unlace his shoes.

When he had kicked them off he sat with his face buried in his hands, his elbows on his knees. He felt as though he wanted to sob; but he had forgotten how to do it. His foremost sensation was one of immense loneliness. There was no way of undoing his folly, no one he could turn to. He was finished. He would have a bath and a shave, and then tidy himself up in boots, gaiters and belt. They would put him under close arrest for a start. Then the court martial, followed by cashiering. They might send him to prison or, since he would have lost his commission, even to a military detention barracks. The thought terrified him. When he had been the assistant adjutant at the training regiment, it had become a matter of course to deal with men sentenced, and though he always made happy, sadistic little remarks about them to the regimental sergeant major, he had always felt an unspoken sympathy for the victim. Sweat broke out again on his forehead. He thought, "I couldn't stand it! It would kill me."

The entrance of Doring with some hot water steadied him.

"Good morning, sir, I bring in one second some tea."

"Thanks."

"Ze water runs in ze bath."

"Good."

The German poured the water into the wash basin and padded his way softly out. For him Howard was still as he had been two days before, on top of his world. And for Hammond as well. They wouldn't be running to get him his breakfast and his bath, if they knew. He stretched himself and took off his battle dress blouse. He went over to the basin in his stockinged feet and peered at himself in the shaving mirror. The quantities of champagne and liqueurs that he had been drinking for the past few weeks had left their mark. His face was pale, blotchy and unhealthy. He looked terrible. Outside, Hemsleigh and Styles passed on their way downstairs. He could hear Hemsleigh's voice, saying passionately, "It's so fantastic, all we need do is to give up a hundred calories a day each——" Shaving made him feel better until he remembered the story that in a detention barracks you had to shave in thirty seconds with a razor one of the guards brought round. The bath however revived him again. The comfort of the warm water playing round his body soothed him mentally. A hope occurred to him that if he went to the War Crimes people and gave them his information, they would fix it so that he was allowed to go free. In that case he would have to go with them to Holland and try to find the café where they had been. Of course Otto might have already fled the country and be on his way to South America or somewhere; on the other hand the fat woman and the waiter, when they saw that they were cornered, might give him away. There might be a gun battle, a chase—and Howard, distinguishing himself gallantly, would wipe his record clean; it might even be suspected that he had done it all on purpose, to trap the man. Perhaps he could say that, anyway? But time was passing quickly. He must hurry, or everything would be too late. He got out of the bath and as he did so his terror returned. He dried himself unhappily. He knew too well that things wouldn't work out well, they always went against him. He had been a fool to imagine that this life-long habit had suddenly changed.

He pulled on his dressing gown and returned to the bedroom. It seemed unusually cosy and secure. It was fantastic that this was perhaps his last free hour. It was no good thinking that the War Crimes people would fix anything for him. For others, perhaps; but not for him. He ought really to tell Hugo Cardington first, that was the correct procedure, and he had probably not gone to the office yet. He went over to the window and looked out. The Mercedes was still there.

"Oh, Christ!" he said, helplessly. Every day the papers talked about arrests and trials and sentences, and you read about them gaily as if they occurred in another world, along with gas chambers, mass deportations, tortures. You never considered it happening to yourself.

Meanwhile Otto was on his way. That was the inescapable fact. Howard sat down on a chair and bent forward, with desperation on his face. Every second of delay made his crime worse. It was only by reporting at once that he would have a chance of convincing them that he hadn't known. Even then it was only a matter of degree. Whichever way they looked at it, he had smuggled him over and at best his motive had been the black market. It was not a pretty situation.

A paralysed feeling took hold of him, so he went on sitting there in misery, clenching and unclenching his fists. The worst of it all was the overwhelming humiliation. He was a failure at everything, and a fool into the bargain. He began to work up resentment and anger, but his position was too bad for that. The possibility of the detention barracks reared up again in his mind, the perfect kit lay-out, the running everywhere, the pack drill, the company of private soldiers. He dreaded all of it.

There was a knock on the door, which made him start, and Doring entered. He was carrying a slip of paper which Howard recognised as the laundry bill. He approached him noiselessly with his moronic, obsequious smile.

"The wash." He flourished the bill in front of Howard's face, triumphantly.

"All right, put it down somewhere."

"Eight marks fifety."

"Give me my trousers, then." He watched him go over to the bed, on which his battle dress was lying. He felt a slight wonder that the German had evidently seen nothing strange about him. "Are you sure everything's back?"

"All is back, sir." Doring returned with the trousers.

Howard felt in one of the pockets and drew out a squashed cigarette packet and an assorted pile of money. He took out two cigarettes from the packet and handed them to Doring, together with a ten mark note.

"O.K."

"Zank you, sir. I bring some breakfast."

After the door had shut behind him, Howard remained slumped in his chair. He glanced at the packages in the corner which contained the 'commodities' he had bought with Otto and Herr Scholle. Some had already gone. These he had been proposing to send by the Military Forwarding Officer. He wondered if there was a quick way of getting rid of them. There would be no means now of taking them home and there was no sense in keeping black market evidence around. But he did not move in his chair. He thought bitterly once again, "Why me? Why did it have to be me?" People were probably smuggling Germans out on purpose every day. And then, but for Kay Blandison taking him to the trial that day, he would never have guessed who Otto was. The joke of it was that he wouldn't have agreed to smuggle a good German, let alone one of the camp swine. People talked about justice, mercy, the love of God. "I bloody well don't think!" he thought savagely, his lips moving with the words. But a minute later he was praying, "If there is a God, help me, for God's sake help me!" Fear, humiliation, self-pity followed each other and returned. He glanced once at the back of the frame of Mary's photograph. It was almost funny to imagine the shock she would have. How she would suffer! His features took on life for a moment at the thought. The long outraged letter he would receive—if he were allowed to have letters. On the other hand she might be self-righteous and forgiving, she was horribly good at it and the prospect of that till the end of his days was almost worse than the immediate crisis. He was fond of her at heart, but he had always half resented his feeling that she was too good for him. Her love usually seemed an act of charity, as if she had chosen a man to accompany through life and she wasn't going to shirk the least duty. He looked away from the frame, his state of mind more confused and miserable than ever. Outside the Mercedes car started. That was Hugo Cardington on his way to the office. "Now I'll have to go there," Howard thought, without stirring in his chair.

Doring came in with his breakfast.

"You are tire-ert, you must sleep more," he remarked, with a solicitous glance at him. He put the tray on a small table and brought it over to the chair. This was normally the moment when Howard said, "Take that bloody rissole away, Doring, I'll just have toast." He had come to rely on it and he stood there waiting.

"What do you want?"

"It is breakfast, sir. Right for you?"

Howard looked down at it. The sight of food was nauseating.

"I don't want it."

"No, sir?" Doring could hardly believe him. He whisked up the tray and was out of the room before Howard could change his mind. He hurried to a large airing cupboard at the end of the landing and ate it all up in the darkness.

Howard stood up and began to dress. While he was brushing his hair, there was another knock at the door, and again, terrified, he expected anything. But it was Hammond, who had brought him two letters. He slit open the first and read: "Dear Chum, Be a pal and get on to Hammond about some laundry I left with him, will you? He has a list and is a b. liar if he denies it. I got back without paying a cent except on liqueurs. But the man next to me had the drill. He had his arm tied up in a plaster of Paris cast. It was fractured, he said. The stuff he had in that fracture when we got in the train at Dover was astonishing. It's a sweet idea. You try it, pal. Give my luv to Kay, a kiss to A. Pratt and a smack on the bottom to the Hackster woman. Cheers. Be seeing yer. Charlie."

"That's Mr. Morton, sir, isn't it?"

"Yes," Howard nodded. "He wants some washing."

"Trusting, isn't he?" Hammond was indignant. "I put it in the post yesterday. Leastways I meant to."

"I'll write and tell him you're hurt."

"How's he getting on in civvy street?"

"He doesn't say, but he sounds cheerful."

"Well, is there anything you want, sir? Buy anything good while you were away?"

"No, not really. What's been going on here?"

"Nothing, really, except they've got this children's party this afternoon. We're decorating the mess for it. Twenty kids coming. You won't get a chocolate ration this week, by the way. Rich, ain't it? Feeding the poor little Germans. I'd like to see how much chocolate they'd have given our kids. Of course you can't blame the children, I suppose."

Hammond retired. His conversation had helped Howard to feel a little calmer. He put the second letter, which was from Mary, into his hip pocket, finished his hair and pulled on his tunic; for he was wearing his service dress. He would have put on his Sam Browne belt as well, but it had not been polished since his posting to Hamburg. He hummed a couple of bars of 'Don't Fence Me In' almost jauntily. The idea of being arrested had after all a certain glamour. This sudden devil-may-care attitude ceased at once, however, as soon as he went through the bedroom door. Now he was on his way to Major Cardington. Within twenty minutes the horrible machinery would be in motion. Once again sweat lined his forehead. He paused for a moment, remembering that he had done nothing to remove the few black market goods that were packed in his bedroom. They would be found, of course, and he would be questioned as to how he had obtained the typewriter, the set of china, the gramophone records. But he was not capable of any action; only of thinking helplessly. He went on downstairs and noticed in the cloakroom two new suitcases and a yellow mackintosh lying on top of them. Busch, the waiter, was ready to hand him his beret and he asked him whose they were.

"They are of Mr. Friedeberg, sir."

"New civvy type just come," Hammond added from the doorway that led downstairs to the kitchen. "He's up at the office now."

Howard nodded and went through the front door, down the steps and into his car. The engine started and the car moved off down the Kasselallee, round to the right and towards the Alster lake. He drove with an unreal feeling, as if his hands on the steering wheel or the gear lever were guided by something other than himself. He had to tell Hugo what had happened. Otto had to be caught. But when he reached the Sociology Division he went straight to his own office, sat down at his table and stared fixedly at the square of clean white blotting paper that lay on it. Once again he was paralysed. He could hear the ticking of his wrist watch. The door opened and Corporal Clayton came in, carrying a pile of papers for the in-tray.

"Oh, I'm sorry, sir, I didn't know you were back. The major said would you go and see him at once when you came in."

The corporal glanced at him, unaware that he had said anything momentous. He thought the lieutenant looked rather pale.

"When did he say that?"

"Five minutes ago, just after he came. Are you feeling all right, sir?"

"Yes, I'm O.K. Thank you."

The corporal left, quite unconcerned as to how Howard felt. His enquiry had been automatic, a routine politeness. When he saw the door shut, Howard sagged, his face fell forward on his hands, and his whole body shook. They had caught him. There was no more time. Dry sobs caused an aching in his throat. He felt bitter hatred towards Hilde and Otto, and bitterest of all towards himself. What a fool—what a fool! He prayed, in a husky whisper, "Oh, God, save me, do something for me, oh, God, oh, Christ!" There were steps outside and he pulled himself together, with a chilled shiver. The steps passed. He stood up, breathing heavily, bracing himself as well as he could and started his gallows walk; through his own door and across the landing.

"Come in!" Major Cardington said. "Hullo—I've got something for you."

Howard swallowed painfully. It was possible that Hugo did not know the precise details, had merely been ordered to arrest him. A voice on the telephone from the Area Security Office had perhaps said, "You have an officer called Randle? We want to see him." His hand shook as he took the slip of paper that the major handed to him. It was a note from the local Army H.Q. informing the administrative officer of

Sociology Division of the date of Lt. H. Randle's demobilisation.

"Lucky you got back. I've fixed a medical for you tomorrow morning. Successful trip?"

"Yes."

"Good show. Look here, Howard, you've got a pretty good NAAFI contact, haven't you? I've this flaming children's party this afternoon, and what we want is some soft drinks, and nuts, and that sort of thing. D'you think you could nip down and get hold of something? Our supplies are a bit ropey."

The meaning of the words, of the print on the paper in front of him, slowly became clear. He thought, "Hell, I'm going to get away with it." Nothing had proved that, of course. It was a sudden feeling. He made the decision as he stood there, with Hugo Cardington looking up at him expectantly, that he was going to confess to nothing. Hilde and Otto had been right, and Otto had already escaped. Even now he was probably on a boat leaving Rotterdam. In four days—the paper said—he himself would be on his way to England, out of the Army, away—free. He said, with an effort: "Yes, I'll try."

"Good show," Major Cardington said. "Guess what, that damned Hackster woman wouldn't give up her chocolate. Lot of drip about Yugo-Slavia's starving children and I don't know what."

Howard returned to his own office, chuckling softly. It was almost a hysterical reaction. From the moment he had guessed Otto's identity, it had not occurred to him that he would not be found out. But now that he realised it was possible Otto might get away undetected, his sense of duty and of resignation vanished, replaced by a bounding optimism. He had always believed what he wanted to believe; never more strongly than now. He lifted the pile of papers out of his in-tray and began to go through them rapidly. When he had finished he sat back with a sigh, and remembered Mary's letter. He took it out of his pocket and slit open the envelope. The

273

closely written two sides looked as neat and unemotional as ever.

He was surprised to find himself enjoying it. Mary and her bosom friend, Susan, had queued for half an hour outside the stage door at the New Theatre and had been rewarded by a personal glimpse of Laurence Olivier. The buses were worse than ever and a girl conductor she had had the day before had been most rude. Howard could say what he liked, but she held that being a clippie was not a suitable job for a woman. The builders were still in next door for Tom and Edith, needless to say, and it was an absolute scandal, when other people's essential war repairs were waiting. Father's shoulder had come on again, she was sure it was the food. He had lost his temper over the dried egg they had had for breakfast and the same evening they read in the papers that the Germans weren't starving at all, and if this were the case, why should we divert wheat to them? Had he a definite date yet? She was longing to see him again and kissed his photograph every night. Howard felt warmth and affection stealing over him.

There was a knock at the door and he looked up with a trace of his recent fear. It was Kay, smiling and affectionate. She closed the door carefully behind her and hurried over to him.

"Oh, Howard, so you are back, after all, I swore I saw your car, listen, I've got Friedeberg outside." She whispered rapidly, close to his ear. "Bonzo says he's not to be left alone —there's such a row on with Johnson Trant, personally I think it's silly, but these refugees are all the same, aren't they —and Howard, dear, I did want to go down with Hoppy to the trial, because they're having the sentences this morning, so would you be an angel and take him to the Atlantic or somewhere?"

He said: "The sentences? You mean the camp trial?"

"Yes, they say all except three will be hanged."

"And the adjutant—what about the adjutant?"

"What adjutant?" she said, surprised. "Howard, aren't

274

you feeling well? You look so pale! Oh—the camp adjutant. I expect they sentence him in his absence. Yes, I bet those beasts aren't feeling so nice this morning."

"Yes, all right, wheel him in." He had control of himself again, though inwardly he was cursing himself. "I've got to go somewhere for Hugo for his kids' party or something——"

"And there's a row on about that," Kay said. "He wants his German woman, Magda somebody, to come and Peter and Elizabeth have complained about a German coming to the mess, and Sybil's agreed with them. Of course I can see their point—Howard, I must rush, thank you ever, ever so much——"

She went to the door, opened it and beckoned to someone outside. "Here's Mr. Friedeberg, Howard. Mr. Friedeberg, this is Lieutenant Randle, who's going to look after you. I'm going off to hear some death sentences. Isn't it gruesome of me?"

"Perhaps that is the word," Mr. Friedeberg said. He was a thin man with greying hair and a high forehead, and clearly he had never worn a uniform in his life until two days before. He bowed slightly as Kay left and then shook hands with Howard. His accent was German, and he spoke a correct, clipped English. "How do you do?"

"How do you do, I'm just an office stooge round here. Not a sociologist or anything, I mean. Kay suggested we went to the Atlantic and had a drink. That's the officers' club, of course."

"I have no money," Mr. Friedeberg complained. "Otherwise, I would like——"

"You mean you haven't any marks yet?"

"No, none."

"You have a cheque book?" Howard asked, his spirits rising. "I mean, an English cheque book? You have? Well, look here, Mr. Friedeberg, I can let you have some marks, I'm being demobbed in a couple of days and it'll save me the trouble of turning them in officially. I tell you what, the real rate's forty, but I'll let you have fifty to the pound. What'll you have, a fiver, a tenner?"

"Forgive me if I misinterpret you," Mr. Friedeberg said. "But I was given to understand in London that fifty would be rather a poor figure for such a transaction."

Howard stared at him and then laughed.

"You win!" he said admiringly. "Well, now, I'll sell you eight hundred at eighty, that's double your money."

"I suggest a thousand."

"Damn it!" Howard chuckled. "All right, all right." Ten pounds sterling was ten pounds sterling and besides, the whole thing made him feel better. Hell, everyone was in it . . .

PART V

OUTSIDE, August sunshine, London dust, hay fever. Inside, the long first-floor room with its green table lamps, typewriters and filing cupboards looked as gloomy as in November. But the solidity of the Oxenbridge Assurance Company (subscribed capital 2½ million, capital paid up 1 million) made up for the absence of air conditioning and tubular furniture; there was the pension scheme and there was also the chance of slow, but steady advancement—although there had been some spectacular rises during the two World Wars. The young men in the department could glance wistfully or determinedly from their desks at the frosted-glass door which led off from the first-floor room. Inside was a thousand-a-year man; who must die sometime. With security, of course, went discipline, its inevitable companion. If you wanted to get married, for example, you had to ask the departmental manager. It was a nominal procedure and always carried out in the friendliest way, but the compulsion was there. The departmental managers at the Oxenbridge had great influence. Those who were militarily inclined had always found a surprising number of keen young amateur soldiers in their departments; and in the same way golfing managers developed golfers, cricketers cricketers, literary men found easy material for debating societies. Although Howard knew that the Oxenbridge was not the only concern in which this phenomenon occurred, it still annoyed him. He had invited Mr. Waters to his wedding as the honoured guest, he played tennis because Mr. Waters was known to be keen and a regular Wimbledon visitor, and he carried a rather dull morning newspaper to the office, because Mr. Waters also carried it; but he did these things with an inward, surly reluctance. "It makes me sick," he said frequently to Mary. "The way they suck up to him, you'd never believe it."

279

It was a minute past six and Howard was just finishing. They frowned upon clock-watching at the Oxenbridge, and if you were to have any hope of becoming one of the thousand-a-year men, six o'clock had to be ignored as if it were a point in time quite without interest, except for typists, office boys or the more elderly clerks who had decided to give up the struggle. But it was astonishing how between one and five minutes past chairs were pushed back, and grunts and sighs indicated that the day's work was over. Bingham, his neighbour, who had been a sergeant in the R.A.F., said: "I say, Howard, did you see that smashing Packard outside at lunchtime?"

Howard nodded. "Just about right for me," he said.

"See the tart inside? She was about right for me."

"You'd better win a pool this winter. It's your only hope. They're not for suckers like us."

"Sometimes I don't think you're happy in your work," Bingham said. "You shouldn't have gone and got married, you know. Stay free and single like me." The mark of a burn stretched from his right cheek down to his chin. "Yes, I could do with that Packard, too," he went on gaily.

"Well, save half your salary in this place for the next fifty years and you can buy the back tyre."

"Look out, here's the old man."

"Mr. Randle!"

"Yes, Mr. Waters?"

"Is that Haley-Cohen schedule ready yet?"

"Yes, Mr. Waters, I have it right here." Howard gathered together three typewritten sheets of paper, fastened them with a paper clip and got up hastily from his desk. Mr. Waters was waiting by his door. He was a grey-haired man with thick horn-rimmed spectacles, thin features and sarcastic lips. People said: "He's all right when you get to know him," which meant: when you were no longer afraid of him. He was not yet all right for Howard, who walked quickly towards him, trying to look brisk and efficient. He said: "I've checked it right through and I rang Mr. Cohen on the point about the bedsprings. He confirmed his original estimate, so I've left it as it was."

"H'm," said Mr. Waters, who always said this when he could think of nothing more explicitly critical. He glanced at Howard over the top of his spectacles, and saw a flushed, stout young man in a tightly fitting, grey striped 'demobilisation' suit. Howard was not one of his favourites, Mr. Waters was always suspicious of ex-officers and was fond of saying that they couldn't expect the carpet to be laid out for them. "Did you read that appendix on fidelity guarantees I sent round?"

"Oh, yes, Mr. Waters." Howard flushed more deeply. It was a lie and he knew that Mr. Waters knew it was a lie. "As a matter of fact I've—I've put it in my case to take home. I thought I'd read it through quietly, after—" he added astutely, "a couple of sets of tennis."

Mr. Waters' expression softened.

"Not a bad evening for it, is it?"

"Very good," Howard said. "Plenty of bite in the turf just now."

"Yes, so there is with us." Mr. Waters became suddenly mellow, confidential. "My small daughter's coming on remarkably, you know. I'm getting her properly coached, Randle, that's the answer, that's where the Americans have us. We're never thorough. You've got to stand behind a child for hour after hour and shout 'Flex!' every time the ball comes to her, make her knees straighten automatically, instinctively. Yes, I think the little girl's got a great future, if she keeps working at it. Alice Marble, Helen Wills, Betz, any of them—what's the secret? Work."

"I agree with you, Mr. Waters," Howard said, and thought: "You silly old sod." The manager dismissed him with a nod more friendly than usual and he returned to his table, pleased with himself but angrily conscious that he had been crawling as hard as anyone.

"Invited to tea?" Bingham asked.

"Not bloody likely, old boy. He hates my guts."

Howard cleared up his table, collected his trilby and light raincoat and left the office. He was in the middle of one of his frequent moods of discontent. He looked with hate at a chauffeur who stood by a large car, waiting at the entrance of the Oxenbridge building. It belonged to some lucky bastard, no doubt, whose father had left him a couple of hundred thousand; and probably the chauffeur earned more than Howard, who was so hard up nowadays, what with the rent for the ground floor of a semi-detached house, and the frightening flood of other expenses, that he always knew how much money he had with him down to the nearest threepence; and this evening he had eleven and threepence. Then he glanced with equal hate at the patient figures waiting in the bus queue ahead, the mockery of the black Homburgs and umbrellas, the demob suits, whose patterns one often recognised, the girls pretending to be attractive. He thought, "What an ugly set of bitches," and joined the end of the queue, angry at the ill-luck that made him a clerk among clerks, a fellow of nonentities. The girl next to him, who was pretty, considered him a miserable devil and stared away myopically across the street. Howard felt in his pocket for his cigarette case and remembered that he had had his self-imposed ration for the day. That brought Mary to mind, for she had been trying to make him give up the habit altogether; which meant that he would do so, sooner or later. Mary loved him and he loved her, but she never gave him a minute's peace. That fantastically expensive honeymoon at Torquay, which had absorbed almost all his black market profits, seemed now to have been spent by two different people. He came back to the present sharply, as the bus at last approached and was seen by the queue to be full up already; it did not even stop, the passengers looked out smugly. Howard thought, "And if it goes on like this, we won't even afford the tennis club next year." But if they had a baby it would be out of the question anyway; and Mary wanted a baby. Behind him now the queue was ten deep. He had just noticed this when he realised that someone was calling his name.

"Howard! Howard!"

A car had drawn in close to the queue and its driver was waving excitedly. Howard saw with astonishment that it was Charlie Morton. At once a new conflict of emotions started. For a second he pretended not to know him, while he decided on his attitude. Then he waved back.

"I thought it was you, old boy!" Charlie shouted. "Move over, can't you?"

"Well, I'll lose my place——"

"Blast your place. I'll take you where you want to go."

By now half the queue were staring at Howard, who pushed his way, red-faced, to the car and got in beside Charlie. The latter shook hands with him heartily.

"You old so-and-so! Sly, slinking old Howard! Not a word! Not a note! How long have you been out?"

"Oh, months. Well, I've been busy——"

"All right, all right! I know my bloody place. Come on, let's go and have a drink." The car was already moving rapidly in the traffic. "I know a pub where they give you all the whisky you want. Wouldn't believe it, would you?"

Everything that Charlie was wearing was both new and expensive. Howard was conscious of it all, the suit, the shoes, the tie, the shirt, and he was sick with envy. The general effect was something like a model in Charing Cross Road, he told himself; but it was no consolation. Here was success, here was money. And there was the car itself, a thirty horsepower American job, secondhand and pre-war, of course, but worth a small fortune in the present market. How the hell could it be done?

Charlie concentrated on his driving and there was no need to talk. Howard fell into a train of thought which had gripped him for weeks after he had been demobilised. "I'd have done that sort of thing but for the trip to Holland. But because of Otto I'd better keep myself quiet." Otherwise he'd have been smart, taken risks, made money. Like a woman who thinks that men would fall for her if she would only give them encouragement, he told himself that in going back to the

Oxenbridge, to the secure, poorly paid job that was open to him by law, he had been obeying a considered decision; had he chosen, the car and all the rest of the set-up could have been his. Moreover, as soon as Mary had realised that he had doubts, she had been adamant that he should return to the Oxenbridge. Secretly he had been relieved. And soon he had almost forgotten Hamburg, Otto, Hilde and the crime he had committed. He had made about a hundred pounds selling his black market purchases and cashing the cheques he had received for marks; it wasn't enough to haunt him; and as for Otto's escape, what did it really matter? From the moment that he was confident Otto would not be captured and that therefore he himself was out of danger, Howard had philosophised happily: "Judge not that ye be not judged." But now the sight of Charlie had brought it all back.

"You went to Tournay?" Charlie said. "Did they accept your marks? I fiddled them beautifully. Quite a nice little officers' club there. Didn't you like your contrast between the last meal there—chicken, champagne, strawberries—and the first meal in good old England—meat, beans and a cup of stinking char?"

Howard chuckled. "Back to reality," he said. "Yes, it was just the same."

"But don't forget you had your postcard from Monty. Don't be ungrateful." Charlie pulled the car sharply into the curb and stopped in front of a narrow fronted public house. "Here we are."

He slapped Howard affectionately on the back and they went into the saloon bar. The barmaid said, "Evening, Mr. Morton," and a man in a bowler hat, who was reading the evening paper, looked up and nodded to them. Howard thought at once that he looked like a detective.

"Two doubles, Elsie," Charlie said, and then turned to him. "Well, tell me all about yourself, you old soak."

"Not much to tell. I'm married." He noticed with horror that Charlie only received two shillings change from a ten shilling note. "Soda, please."

"So he's married." Charlie squirted some soda into his glass and passed it to him. "I bet she doesn't know what a shameless old fratter you were. Cheers."

"Cheers." The whisky gave him some courage. He smiled uneasily, "You look pretty well. What's been happening to you?"

"Well, I've been getting myself organised, you know. Plenty of good rackets around. I got into fancy paper goods, carnival stuff. There's a fortune in any shortage, don't you find? What's your racket, old boy? You know, believe it or not, I've often said to myself, 'I wonder what that scoundrel Howard's doing? I bet he's looking after himself.' I've often laughed about those duty-free labels."

Howard glanced in alarm at the man in the bowler hat, who looked as if he were listening to every word.

"I'm stringing along," he said, flushing. He was not going to confess to Charlie that he had become an insurance clerk again.

"I bet you are, you sly old dog."

Howard was saved from more detailed queries by the entrance of two of Charlie's business friends. They were older but otherwise similar in their appearance. Howard realised that he had not the money to buy a round of drinks and tried to refuse the second double whisky that was passed to him. Money was clearly no problem to the other three, although they talked of nothing else. "He said 'Five hundred, that's the limit', I said 'Guineas', he said 'Done,' " an anecdote concluded amid laughter in which Howard tried weakly to join. He had had his day for talking big. A wallet was produced to pay for another round and he saw the roll of notes, black and white fivers. He began to look for a means of escape. They weren't interested in him. By now Charlie must have summed him up. One of his friends suddenly asked Howard if he were short of clothing coupons.

"You bet I am," Howard said, hoping that this would seem an explanation of his comparatively drab appearance.

"I can let you have a hundred if you want them. Only two bob each."

Charlie roared with laughter. "You won't get away with that. Howard's as wide as they make 'em. Don't try and do business with him, I'm warning you."

"Well, thanks very much, but I'm not really interested," Howard said.

"What did I tell you? You'll be giving them free before he's finished. What's your racket, Howard, old boy? You didn't tell me."

Howard gulped. An old, discarded plan came into his mind.

"Government stores," he said. "Buying, selling. You know." It was not a thorough description, but they were quite satisfied. They all said that Government stores were fine and they all knew someone who had made a packet out of them. Howard noticed that the second round of double whiskies was nearly at an end. He had to get away. He said desperately, looking in surprise at the clock behind the counter, "My God, is that the time? Charlie, I'm awfully sorry, I simply must go like hell——"

"It's twenty fast, always is," the barmaid said.

"I've still got to go."

They tried to persuade him not to go, and one of them ordered a third round, which postponed the crisis; but he remained quite firm. "It's most important," he said, and winked cunningly. "Just a little transaction, you know." Then they gave way.

"Anyway, I'll drop you there," Charlie said, accompanying him towards the swing door.

"No, no, really, old boy, I'm quite close," he insisted.

"Well, where can I get hold of you? We must have a real get-together. Any news of Kay Blandison or Hemsleigh and so on? They say the place is finished now. Dull and dreary, and your pay is your money. I suppose the Atlantic bar is like a tomb."

"I haven't heard from anyone."

"Well, it's grand to look at you again. What was your number?"

"It's in the book," Howard lied. "Look up Randle, H."

"O.K., that's a date! It's a pity you've got to push like this, though. You'd like those pals of mine, Christ, they've taught me a thing or two about rackets. It's an amazing life, isn't it? Just a jungle. I keep going, somehow. Tell you what, bring your wife up and we'll have a night out in town."

"Bloody good idea," Howard said. "Cheerio, then. Au revoir."

He left the swing doors and Charlie behind him and hurried along the pavement. Fortunately he was only two minutes from Holborn Underground station, so he wouldn't be more than forty minutes late for Mary, who would believe that Mr. Waters had kept him. Thank God, anyway, his eleven and threepence was still intact. He hoped fervently that Charlie Morton would not catch sight of him again. He told himself that he no longer felt any envy of his money. Obviously it had been earned in a near black market way; you had only to look at the friends to see that. It was fantastic to realise that he himself had been like them in Hamburg. "Yes," he thought with pride, "I can be like it if I want to." But he did not want to. There was a devil inside him, but it was under control. He saw a policeman looking into a closed shop. He turned round and glanced at Howard. The latter stared at him squarely, and went on. Wasn't it, after all, a luxury to be able to do that with an easy conscience? Of course it was. They could keep their clothing coupons, their silk ties, their secondhand cars bought at inflated prices. He whispered aloud: "At least I'm bloody well honest!"

With this temporary satisfaction he reached the station. He bought an evening paper, joined the queue at the ticket office and went on his way home to Mary.